TAKEN WITH A
GRAIN OF SALT

AARON
GALVIN

Aames & Abernathy Publishing

Taken With A Grain of Salt

Salt Series: Book Two

Copyright © 2014 by Aaron Galvin

Revised March 2016

Published by Aames & Abernathy Publishing, Chino Hills, CA

Edited by Annetta Ribken. You can find her at **wordwebbing.com**

Copy Edits by Jennifer Wingard. **theindependentpen.com**

Cover Design by M.S. Corley, **mscorley.com**

Book Design and Layout by Valerie Bellamy, **dog-earbookdesign.com**

Small waves photo © Mibseo | Dreamstime Stock Photos &

Stock Free Images

ISBN-10: 1503051242

ISBN-13: 978-1503051249

Printed in the United States of America

this one's for Dad.

✗

to Quynn
Hope you enjoy
the reads! ☺

to Guyen
Hope you enjoy
the prints.

"COME AWAY, O HUMAN CHILD!

To the waters and the wild

With a faery, hand in hand,

For the world's more full of weeping than you can understand."

– W.B. Yeats, excerpt from *The Stolen Child*

CHIDI

I WEEL FIND YOU, CHIDI. AND KEEL ZE ONES YOU run weeth.

Chidi stirred awake. Bright lights bathed the inside of the SUV. She smelled gasoline. Heard the quiet thrum of a pump, a constant clicking as fuel clunked through rubber piping into the vehicle's gas tank.

Chidi wiped the blurriness from her eyes.

Zymon's Selkie guardian, Wotjek, slouched outside her window, his hand at the pump. Despite his casual stance, his vigilant gaze was locked on the darkened road and interstate ramps not a quarter mile away.

Chidi sat up.

The balding man she once considered mousey stared back at her in the rearview mirror. Now, she thought of him as a rat.

"It seems I was wrong about you," said Zymon Gorski. "I had not thought a beautiful girl would risk sleeping in the company of strangers. Lucky for you I am no slaver."

Chidi ignored his taunt. "Where are we?"

"Does it matter? You are free now, girl. Relax. Sleep soundly like your friend."

Chidi had not noticed Racer also slept. His head against the window, he snored contentedly, oblivious they had stopped at all.

She glanced over her shoulder to the back seat where the two kidnapped teens remained unconscious. "Wh—" She swallowed to quench the dryness in her throat. "Where is Allambee? Why have we stopped?"

"Is that worry I hear in your voice? Yes, I think so. But then only a fellow slave would recognize it as such. Tell me, do you even now fear your master will find you?"

Chidi would not deny it.

Zymon chuckled. "Fear is not a bad thing. It has kept me safe these many years on the Hard. To cast it aside is to forget the one truth all slaves know..." His gaze flickered to her again. "Anyone can be taken."

Chidi fought off a shudder. "Where is Allambee?" she asked again, firmer.

Zymon lazily jerked his head in the gas mart's direction. The brightly lit interior highlighted racks of junk food at the threshold to tempt any customers. Through the window, Chidi saw him— a boy on the eve of reaching his teen years, perusing the aisles in an environment as alien to him as this new freedom felt to her.

She reached for the door handle.

"Do you see what I do, girl?"

Chidi hesitated.

"Fearless," Zymon whispered of Allambee, almost in awe. "The simple thought we might leave him behind has never occurred to his innocent mind."

Chidi's fingers left the door handle.

"What must that be like?" Zymon said. "To think the best of people...trust implicitly?"

"I don't know." Chidi nudged Racer.

His eyes fluttered open then closed to sleep again.

"Nor I," said Zymon. "Its bait comes in many forms, but in the end, trust is a trap. And so I trust no one—"

Chidi watched Zymon's gaze drift to his guardian still at the pump.

"None but Wotjek." Zymon opened his door, glanced back at her. "But perhaps we must all learn to trust again…yes?"

He chuckled at the irony of his own question, then stepped out of the vehicle.

Chidi dug her elbow into Racer's rib cage, needling him awake.

"Ow!" Racer sat up. "What're you doing, Chi—hey…where are we?"

"I don't know," she whispered. "Still in Indiana, I think. You were supposed to stay awake!"

Racer rubbed his eyes. "I tried, Chidi. Really, I did." He looked out the windows, surveyed the area. "Where's Allambee?"

Chidi kept her focus on Zymon as he rounded the back of the SUV to speak with Wotjek in their Polish tongue. She hated not understanding the words they spoke to one another, though her knowledge of other languages aided in guesswork. *Maybe if I listen long enough I can learn—*

"Chidi," Racer said.

"What?"

"Where is Allambee?"

Chidi snapped back to their situation. "Inside. We need to get him back out here."

"Okay." Racer shrugged. "Let's get him."

Chidi noticed Wotjek watching her as he cleared his stringy

hair out of his face. *He has cold eyes.* She decided. *Henry eyes.* She glanced at the empty road and interstate again. The slave fear Zymon spoke of wrapped its frigid fingers around her heart and squeezed, ever so gently.

"No," she said. "One of us needs to stay here."

"Why?" Racer asked.

Zymon chuckled outside the SUV, then walked toward the gas mart.

There was a rattle and clank as Wotjek pulled the gas pump free of the tank and replaced it on the island station. A second later, he resumed his spot in the driver's seat—quiet and smooth as shadow. She and he locked eyes in the rearview mirror.

I weel find you, Chidi...

Chidi fumbled at the handle. The door wouldn't open.

"Chidi," said Racer. "What's wrong? Where are you going?"

"I-I need to pee."

The doors unlocked with a unanimous *click.*

"Don't go far," Wotjek said, his voice low and accented by his native tongue. His command did not carry the harshness Henry's often did, but it didn't lack gravity either.

You are with me now. Chidi understood. *For better or worse.*

She hurried out.

"Chidi..."

"Stay here," she said to Racer, noticing Wotjek yet watched her. "I'll be right back."

Racer sunk back into his seat. By the look of him, she guessed he still did not understand why she asked him to remain. He may not be nearly so innocent as Allambee, but Chidi knew then she had signed on to care for two pups. Racer would fight alongside her if need be, but passion meant little against a Selkie like Wotjek. Their fight with him at the Shedd Aquarium had been evidence of that.

Chidi scurried through the open ramparts in the gas pump island and toward the mart. The doors jingled in welcome as she opened them.

A gruff attendant behind the counter narrowed his eyes at her as she walked in. No sooner had his gaze left her than it went to Allambee.

Two black kids enter a gas station after hours with no one around. She predicted his thought process. *Both dressed in hooded sweatshirts.*

The attendant sucked his teeth and his right hand slipped beneath the counter. He did not bring it back up. "Can I help you with something?" he asked her.

"Restroom?"

"We only got the one. There's a fella in there right now."

A white fella. Chidi inferred by his tone. "I can wait."

The attendant nodded in affirmation she absolutely would. He scratched at his bushy beard with his free hand. "Mind if I ask where y'all from?"

"Chicago," Chidi said.

The shake of his head was slight, but there.

"Chidi!" Allambee hurried to her side, carrying a bag of pretzels, a couple candy bars, and bottled water. "Zymon said we should eat. He told me to pick out some food for you. I found dese."

He gave her the bag of pretzels and grinned.

Fearless. Chidi smiled back. *And innocent.*

"You two friends, I take it? Homies?"

Chidi glanced up at the attendant, anger she often fought down while under Henry's yoke stirring within her. "Yes."

"Well, he's been in here a good long while. 'Bout time to make a decision, don't you think?"

Allambee slouched. "I-I didn't know what to choose—"

"He's not from here," said Chidi.

"Don't think I ever heard truer words spoke," replied the attendant. "So where's he from if it ain't Chicago?"

"Kenya," she said.

The attendant snorted. "Course he is. Bet you are too, huh?"

"No. I come from somewhere else." Chidi gave Allambee the pretzels. She strutted toward the counter, eyebrow raised. "Should I tell you where?"

The attendant stood up at her approach and still he kept his hand on something beneath the counter. Chidi assumed a gun.

"Pardon me."

Chidi turned to see the poor excuse for a bathroom door left open. The lights inside revealed molded tile and graffiti attendants had long since abandoned scrubbing.

Zymon left its doorway to approach the counter. He carried a wooden rod with keys attached to the end. "Is there a problem?"

"No problem, mister." The attendant leered at Chidi. "This girl was about to tell me where she and this here boy come from."

"Is that so?" asked Zymon.

"So she says. And I was about to tell her I don't care. Long as they both get back there right qui—"

Air whooshed past Chidi's face as Zymon whipped the wooden rod up and cracked the man in the head with it.

Groaning, the attendant leaned against the countertop to steady himself.

"A most impolite thing to say." Zymon proceeded calmly around the counter. "Especially to one whom I owe my life."

Zymon slapped the rod across the inside of the attendant's elbow.

Chidi swore his ligaments snapped, to judge the sound.

The attendant's face smacked the countertop as he fell. Zymon clocked him in the head with another swift blow. The attendant slumped into the case of cigarettes. His chest rose and fell, but he did not get back up.

Zymon brushed what little hair he had left back into place then hung the wooden rod back on the wall's place nail. He looked to Chidi and Allambee. "I trust you're nearly ready?"

"Wh-why would you do that?" Chidi asked.

"What exactly did I do? What you wanted to?" Zymon pointed to the attendant. "A most despicable creature. I've tolerated a fair share of them in my lifetime. More than I care to say. It has taken me these many years to learn I never had to. That if no one stands up to them, these…vermin…multiply. You must learn this lesson also." He said to Chidi. "You who have so much to offer and don't yet realize."

"How's that?" Chidi asked.

"You have a gift for linguistics, but you also know too much fear." Zymon nodded in the attendant's direction. "I'll put your language skills to good use. The fear you must quell on your own."

Zymon opened the cash register.

"What are you doing?" Allambee asked.

Zymon stuffed the bills in his pockets. "What is necessary. We needed fuel. Now we have that and money to spare." He glanced at the security camera fixed in the corner above him. "Take anything you want from this place now. If you are not in the SUV when I finish ridding the evidence, we leave without you."

Zymon took the wooden rod off the hook. He climbed atop the counter and smashed the camera with it, then inspected the wiring that ran through the adjacent wall. Muttering to himself, Zymon jumped down from the ledge and went to pry open a supply door around the corner.

Chidi turned back to warn Allambee. "We need to—"

He stood inside the entrance, his gaze fixed on something outside, not parked beneath the gas station's metal canopy.

What's that sound? Chidi took a step toward the door. Then she recognized it. *A siren...*

The anger the attendant had warmed inside her went cold, doused by the sight of flashing blue and red lights bound for the station.

Leave. Her conscience urged. *Now.*

"Allambee..." she squeaked.

"What is that rack—" Zymon stopped mid-sentence. His eyes widened and he dove behind the counter.

What is he searching for? Chidi's fear rooted her to the floor. Forced her to watch the events unfold.

The driver's side door of their SUV opened. Wotjek scrambled out, stumbled through the small openings between the pumps and across the fuel tank island, determined to beat the approaching death knell.

And then Chidi saw Racer, the boy who hadn't yet realized what the older Selkie did, his expression confused at why Wotjek would abandon him in such a hurry.

"Racer!" Chidi screamed too late.

The police car never slowed as it veered into the lot. The driver's door opened. A body fell out, tumbling and turning across the pavement like a spindle with no thread to unravel.

The police car careened into the back of the SUV. It jolted the parked vehicle forward and tipped into the tanks. The clamor of metal striking metal shut out the screaming siren, but only just.

Chidi threw her arms up to shield her from an explosion that never came.

The pumps shuddered under the attack against them. One fell into the concrete aisle.

The SUV lay flipped on its side. A glittering spider web had taken over the windshield, marked with smatterings of blood. And at the base, tucked between the glass and dashboard, the hooded, tannish hide of a California Sea Lion and its owner's blond hair.

Racer... Chidi thanked the Ancients she saw only the back of his head. Looking into his blue eyes, once filled with hopeful freedom, and seeing them turned lifeless would wreck her. *I'm going to find a way to buy me some fakes,* she remembered him saying at the Shedd. *And once I get them, I'm gone. None of you will ever see me again!* Chidi closed her eyes, her cheeks warmed by tears.

"Wotjek," Zymon whispered.

Please. Chidi shook. *Not again...please, don't let this happen again.*

Her prayer went unanswered.

A figure stumbled out of the darkness like a demon cast from hell and drawn toward the light. Thin lines, freshly cut from the gravel he had landed upon, bled out and streaked across his wizened face. He scarcely seemed to notice as he staggered toward the destroyed SUV, the pale gleam of his black dagger catching the light as it swayed with each step he took.

"Chee-dee…" Henry Boucher called in a singsong voice. "Where eez my Chidi…"

CHIDI

CHIDI PAWED AT ALLAMBEE'S HOODIE. SHE PULLED him back from the door, brought him down beside her. She crouched near the aisle and peeked through a pair of spinning towers—one holding sunglasses, the other flavored suckers.

"Come out, Chidi!" Henry snarled. He strode toward the wrecked SUV and opened the trunk.

The legs from one of the Dryback teens flopped onto the asphalt.

Henry gave them little attention. He knelt to survey the inside, sneered at not finding what he desired. Then he turned to the gas mart.

Chidi shrunk away, certain he had seen her.

"Do not worry," Zymon said calmly, even as he used the counter for a shield. "Wotjek will protect us."

Will he? Chidi risked a peek.

The Leper she once feared looked a lone sentinel, all that stood between those inside and Henry. Wotjek deftly tied his hair back, arched his back like a cat might stretch, then settled in a battle stance.

Henry stopped near the wrecked gas station island, propped his foot on the fallen pump. He seemed unfazed to Chidi's mind. *Why should he be? They both wear the same Leper coat.*

The two men appeared of a similar age and size. When it came to blows, Chidi guessed the outcome relied on which Selkie had the most fight in them. She knew which that would be, despite Zymon Gorski's continued faith in his guardian.

"I only want ze girl!" Henry shouted. "Give 'er over and I weel let you leeve."

Wotjek did not reply. He did, however, glance over his shoulder at the gas mart.

Move, Chidi. You have to move! Her conscience hustled her along. Wotjek might die for Zymon Gorski, but she harbored little doubt he held the same regard for her life.

"Allambee," she whispered. "We have to go."

"Where?"

Chidi scanned the area. The mart had only three short aisles.

Across the way, Zymon hunched low between the counter and bathroom. A short hall continued past him.

Didn't he go back there to turn off the security camera?

"Will you give 'er over?" Henry asked.

Chidi scurried down the aisle of chips and corn nuts toward the western wall. She headed for the furthest row south, where the corners met, to the wall lined with coolers and soft drinks.

"Or must I keel you first?"

Squatting, Chidi now clearly saw up the row to where Zymon had earlier disappeared.

The path ended in a wall.

No. Chidi sunk to the floor.

"What is it?" Allambee asked amid the sounds of scuffling outside.

Chidi skulked up the row to look out. She saw Henry snarl, swipe at his calmer opponent.

Wotjek turned in her direction. His left cheek bared open, oozing red. He evaded a second attack, catching Henry's wrist and turning it back.

Henry's reef blade clattered to the ground.

Chidi's spirit soared. *Kill him, Wotjek! Do it!*

Wotjek forced his opponent to a knee, then head-butted Henry in an attempt to finish him. The blow enlivened Henry. With a feral scream, he lunged at Wotjek. Bit the other man's cheek.

Wotjek cried out, losing his hold as he flailed at Henry's face.

No! Chidi thought as Henry palmed Wotjek's face with one hand and wrenched his head back. *Get away. Move, Wotjek.*

Henry pushed his opponent against an ice cooler, pinning him. *Go, Chidi!*

"No!" Zymon called out. "Not my Wotjek."

Chidi shook her head, knowing the end had come. With no way out but the front door, it would only be a matter of time. Soon enough, Henry would finish the one Selkie capable of protecting them. Chidi knew even she and Zymon fighting alongside one another would not stop Henry's rage. A dark desire lived inside him, one gifting strengths no sane folk could fathom.

"Yes!" Zymon said. "Fight, my friend. Fight."

Chidi glanced up. Wotjek had fended Henry back. The two wrestled for control over the other, each hurling punches at the other.

"Chidi…" Allambee tapped her, pointed at the cooler door she leaned against. "What is back there?"

Chidi pushed off the glass and peered inside.

Gallons of milk lined the racks of the cooler behind her. The next held icy chips with stacked quarts and pints of ice cream.

Behind it all, empty space between the end of the racks and a wall lined with painted milk crates stacked atop one another.

Chidi flung the door open. Yanked the milk off the racks, not caring that several burst open when they landed on the floor and soaked her suit. Her fingers clawed between the wire slats as she attempted to free them and create a space to crawl through.

The racks held strong, screwed in tight to support the weight of the items they once carried.

Chidi fell to her butt and kicked at the middle rack, imagining Henry's face when each struck home. She didn't stop until the rack clattered off the concrete floor on the opposite side.

"Wh-what are you doing?" Zymon asked.

Chidi ignored him. "Go, Allambee." She pushed him toward the vacant space. "Crawl through!"

Allambee went headfirst, ducking low to not strike his head on the rack still wired above.

Chidi glanced outside. Both Lepers had bloodied the other, but Henry stood tall with more fight left to give. *He won't stop until Wotjek's dead.* She knew. The hunger for violence had its hooks in him now. It would not relinquish its claim until it supped on death.

Chidi winced as Henry again lashed out at Wotjek, his fists connecting. Her body recalled what his blows felt like. Chidi looked away and found Zymon hunched, tears streaming down his cheeks.

"*Come on!*" she hissed.

Her voice seemed to call him back to reality. Zymon blinked, and she witnessed him make the decision to abandon his companion, the will to live overtaking any ties to the fallen Selkie outside.

Zymon hesitated only a moment, a glance to see if Henry might see. Then he crawled across the aisle to join Chidi.

Chidi scurried over the racks. Her Silkie suit kept her body warm while the cooler's cold nipped at her ears and nose. Chidi snorted the chill from her nostrils, pushing herself onward.

Allambee had remained near to help her through the opposite side.

"Look out," she said. "Move. Find an exit!"

Allambee scampered away as Chidi squirmed through the tight fit. She put her hands on the ground, now slick with spilt milk across concrete. Her hands slipping, she used them like feet to walk her upper body out of the cooler. She tipped out the other side, pulled her legs through, and rolled away to allow Zymon a means of escape.

Chidi hustled to stand. She surveyed the dim area; nothing but a small hand-truck and the boxes and old plastic crates she had already seen.

Allambee grunted near the wall.

A door! Chidi's spirits rose for a split second, then crumbled. *Why can't he get it open?*

She hurried to his side, pushed her weight against a door that refused to budge.

Allambee sighed. Shook his head.

"No…" Chidi said.

"What is it?" Zymon asked, his head and shoulder already sticking out of the cooler wall. "Is there a door?"

"Yes," said Allambee. "It will not open."

"No…" Chidi said, hitting the door with her shoulder. "No!"

She rammed it again.

The loose chains that locked the door rattled on the opposite side.

"No!"

"Help her, boy!" Zymon said as he pulled his legs through the cooler.

Allambee hit the door with Chidi on the next turn.

Again, the chains rattled, and again the door held firm.

Chidi grit her teeth. *Open!*

"Chidi..." Allambee's voice quivered.

She looked through the open cooler door.

Wotjek lay on the ground with Henry on his chest, pounding away at the Selkie foolish enough to face him.

"It's locked?" Zymon asked.

"Yes," said Chidi. "Help us."

She made to ram the door again.

"No," said Zymon. "We do not have enough force. Not enough weight as we are now..."

"What do you mean as we are—"

His meaning clicked in Chidi's mind. She looked down at the slippery floor.

"Wet and slick," said Zymon. "Almost like ice, yes?"

Chidi donned her crème-colored hood, the one patterned with what resembled flowing white sashes encircling her extremities. She pictured her Salted form—a Ribbon Seal—and ordered the changes sweep across her body.

She felt her upper and lower body bulge like a water balloon filled almost to its bursting point. The growth overtook her thighs and shins. Her ankles went lax, her toes extending into long flippers. Whiskers sprouted from her cheeks and her face morphed into a dog-like muzzle. Her ears sucked into her head, leaving two holes the size of quarters. Though currently blind, Chidi knew her eyes changed from their normal brownish hue to the seal's charcoal black.

Chidi opened her eyes, the transformation complete.

The slippery floor welcomed her, begged her seal brain to slide and play as nature always intended the animal to do.

"Yes!" Zymon said.

Chidi used her left flipper to pull her along the surface, felt her body glide over the thin layer of milk. She flinched at the touch of human hands across her back.

"Calm yourself," said Zymon as he positioned her at the back of the cooler. "Now, push off this to strike the door. Hurry!"

The seal brain didn't understand what its human counterpart meant to do. Chidi leveraged her weight down on her flippers, then pushed off. She careened across the floor toward the door and tucked her head at the last, slamming into the one thing barring her escape.

The door rattled along with her brain.

Clean air filled her nostrils for a moment.

The door shut again.

Chidi shook off her dizziness.

The blow had weakened the old chains enough for Allambee to open the door a few inches. His shoulder prevented his escape and he pulled himself back inside.

"Almost!" Zymon said. "Please, hurry!"

Chidi made for the cooler and another attempt. She positioned herself faster this time, barely allowing her weight to settle before pushing off.

Again she hit the door, jostled it a few inches further.

Allambee fit his head almost all the way through. He came back inside grinning. "Once more!"

Chidi nodded her seal head. She wriggled back, settled in for one final try. *Please work. Please…*

She pushed off with all the strength her hind flippers had left. Again she tucked her head.

The door budged easily. The scent of air remained and Chidi knew she had accomplished her task. *Yes!*

Allambee squeezed through the opening.

Glass crashed behind her.

Chidi whipped around.

The noise had come from Henry throwing Wotjek's body through the gas mart doors. He stood in the shattered remains, his face wild and red.

Zymon scurried past her.

Wait! She directed her thoughts toward him. Then she remembered having thrown her earrings away. Carelessly tossed aside her only means of communication with others. All because Zymon had told her and Racer doing so *truly* freed them of their former yokes.

No!

Zymon grunted, half outside already. His lower, pudgy half all that kept him from escaping the stockroom.

No! Chidi lunged and bit at him. *You have to free me!*

Zymon squeezed through. He turned back, reached for the seal's mouth to free Chidi from her Salt form. "Come, let me—"

"*Chidi!*"

Zymon stopped short. His eyes drifted past her, back to the mart from whence the voice came.

"I weel 'ave you, Chidi." Henry yelled.

Chidi barked at Zymon to call his attention. *Help me!*

Zymon looked at her, his face awash with terror. "I-I'm sorry..."

Then he vanished.

KELLEN

THE STEEL FLOOR PULSED BENEATH KELLEN.

Driving. Kellen rightly surmised of the iron beast he found himself in. *But to where?*

God only knew.

Kellen certainly didn't. His throat was raw from the obscenities and threats he had shouted after Oscar Collins shoved him inside the bus hold. He had given up screaming threats for his release long ago. Or was it only a short while past?

How long I have been in here now? Twenty minutes? An hour? Maybe two?

Kellen couldn't speak to that either. The absolute dark made it hard to tell much of anything aside from the bus's movement and the stench. Worse than the musty locker rooms at his high school, he swore Oscar kept a dead thing in this hold before him.

At least they took it out.

He picked at the dried flecks stuck to his biceps and hair on his arms. When Oscar first pushed him inside, Kellen thought the floor coated in water to make him slide. Water left no flakes upon drying though. It also didn't feel as sticky as what coated his extremities now. Only later, when he needed to pee, did he assume the former wetness might be urine. Perhaps the last occupant lost control of their bladder.

Not about to pee on myself.

Or so Kellen once told himself.

Now, it felt like he might break that promise.

The pulsing cage around him did nothing to help the matter. His bladder reminded him how bad he needed to go every time Kellen's thoughts drifted to the rattling.

Kellen distracted himself by picking at the flecks and imagined pounding Oscar Collins's face in upon his release. *I'll bet the midget would even help me.* Kellen brushed at the smaller bits that refused to pry free. The more time passed, the more curious he grew at what the dried pieces were. He risked a smell.

Nothing. Not even a hint of odor.

It's blood. A voice inside him said. *Someone else's blood...*

The thought made Kellen brush harder. His skin warmed at the rubbing, palms scratched against the dryness, irritated. *Someone's blood is drying on my arm.* Kellen slammed his elbow against the metal wall. "Let me out!"

He spun. Pounded it with his fists, determined to beat through the wall.

"I said let me out!"

The skin on Kellen's knuckles broke open anew.

"You can't keep me in here!"

Rather than the cool of metal, now his fists found the wall slick-coated.

My blood. Some part of his conscience said. *Is this what happened to the last person in here?*

The thought took away the pain in his knuckles. Kellen struck the wall with more than hatred. "Open the door! I need out of here!"

Fear drove him to strike harder, again and again.

Exhaustion made him quit.

Kellen slumped away. Lay on his back. His fists oozed stickiness down the back of his hands and into his palms.

"Aaaah." The groan came from the back corner of the hold.

Kellen sat up. The first thing he had done after seeing the door slammed shut was to explore the cell. Inch-by-inch, he had palmed around the rectangular hold until he stumbled over the body in the back.

He thought the man dead initially, perhaps from where the stench originated. Years of lifeguarding made him test the man's pulse. He found it weak, but there. Kellen had wasted no time in searching the man's pockets for any weapon or tool he might use to pry open the door. He found nothing.

"Oh, my head," the man said with a Southern drawl.

Kellen said nothing. He listened to the iron shackles clatter as the man moved.

"No," the man said, his fetters clanking louder. "No! *No!*"

Over and again the man pounded his shackles against the floor, shouting obscenities in a voice that made Kellen realize how pitiful his own claims must have sounded not a few minutes ago.

"Is anyone out there?" the man asked. "Anyone in here?"

Do I let him know he's not alone?

"Caspar! Either of you in here?"

Caspar. Kellen remembered the name. The deputy marshal who freed him of his cell at the Lavere County Jail had been named Caspar. The same marshal who held a gun to Kellen's head and kicked him into the battle between men and seals. Now that man was dead. All Kellen's fault too, according to the girl, Marisa Bourgeois, who had been Caspar's captive.

What will this guy do if he finds out his friend died because of me?

"I won't go down without a fight!" the man shouted. "You hear me, you sorry Selkie slavers! You'll not take me like you did my wife!"

Slavers? Kellen's mind raced.

"Ah, my head."

Kellen pictured the stranger rubbing his temples, based on the clamor of shackles.

"Not like my wife...not like Susie..." the man whispered, his voice breaking. "Oh, Susie..."

The shackles scratched and clattered, jostling. Unlike before, they sounded closer now.

He's moving! Kellen scooched away from the wall.

The metal paneling rebounded as he moved.

"Who's there?" the man asked, his tone firm. Demanding.

Don't say—

"Speak up."

Kellen listened to his cellmate moving, drawing closer.

"From the echo in here," said the man. "It don't sound like you have far to go. Can't avoid me for long."

Kellen remained still and quiet.

"You don't talk, the more I think you and I aren't gonna be friends, partner. Speak up. Won't give you another chance if'n you make me find you in all this dark. I'll throttle you first and find out who you were after."

Kellen didn't doubt the man's sincerity. He did wonder whether he would win if it came to blows. He'd been in his fair share of fistfights over the years. One couldn't talk smack and not expect an opponent to step up every now and again. This matter seemed different. Kellen had always been able to pick and choose his fights before. At least against those close to his age. The fights with his father were another matter altogether. Kellen never knew when Martin Winstel would stumble in to wake him, eager for a bout.

No son of mine would back down from a fight. Kellen could almost hear his father's slurs. *You really my boy, or you just some bastard son of that whore that left me?*

Kellen reached for the familiar anger he had learned to store away, allowing the blood on his knuckles to feed it. *I'm not shackled like he is. I can move faster.*

The ceiling warned against it, refusing to let him stand hunched over, let alone mount an effective attack against an unknown adversary.

"All right," said Kellen, his fists ready to strike. "You're not alone."

The man paused. "Who are you?"

Screw that. "Tell me your name fir—"

"I'm U.S. Marshal David Bryant," said the man. "Your name. *Now.*"

"I don't think so."

"You sound scared, boy."

"I'm no boy," said Kellen.

"Well, you don't sound like a man yet either. How old are you?"

"Old enough." Kellen's cheeks flared. "And you say I'm not a man? This from the guy who I just heard crying about his wife?"

Bryant humphed. "Least you got some fight in you. Stubborn too.

You might be of use after all. Guess you're not shackled, huh? Can't be. You move too quiet. They don't find you dangerous enough? That why they didn't put the shackles on you?"

"Who's they?"

Kellen tensed when Bryant didn't reply. His ears perked in wait for the sound of Bryant tearing across the floor to throttle him.

"You a runner, kid?" Bryant asked, finally. "You been Salted?"

"Huh?"

"Tell me what you know about Selkies," Bryant said.

Kellen thought back on all he'd witnessed at the jail: the long silvery seal with fangs that tore the throat out of Officer Campbell, a former swim teammate of Kellen's. How the same seal had transformed into a man after. Then another seal, one bigger than even a walrus, that slopped toward a desk and destroyed it like a child scattering a house of play logs.

Were they Selkies?

"Guess that's a no," Bryant remarked on Kellen's silence. "So how'd they do it? They use some hot girl to drop a little something in your drink at a party, then *boom*. You wound up here?"

Lie. Or else he'll keep asking.

"Yeah…" said Kellen.

"Right," Bryant sighed. "Don't feel bad. You're not the first one, kid. Got all these schools warning girls to keep watch over their drinks. Not a one of 'em ever thinks to warn the guys."

"That what happened to you?"

"No. They shot me with something. Tranq, I'd reckon. Knocked me out." Bryant sighed. "I'm like you though. I never been Salted either, despite what some Selkies might tell you. You ever heard of a guy called the Silkstealer, kid?"

"Nope," said Kellen. "Sounds like a fag, whoever he is."

Bryant chuckled. "Hardly. But if you ain't heard of the Silkstealer, then by God, you ain't been Salted."

"You keep saying that word...Salted," said Kellen. "What's it mean?"

"Depends on who you ask. Only know what I been told. None of it pretty. Guessing by where we're at—" Bryant rapped his shackles against the floor. "I bet we're both gonna find out firsthand soon enough. Well, now, pretty sure I've answered some of your questions. What's say you answer mine. Ready to tell me your name yet?"

Kellen settled in, his back against the wall again. "No."

"Right. Guess I'll have to make up one for you then. Answer me this though. You ever hear of a couple good ol' boys named Caspar?"

Kellen's heart caught in his chest. He still remembered the deputy's accusing eyes as he fell. Marisa Bourgeois forewarned Richard Caspar would die that night because of Kellen. It didn't matter that Kellen had not physically done the deed. *He saw me turn to run... only a second, but long enough to wind up dead.*

"No," said Kellen.

"Pinocchio."

Kellen's forehead wrinkled. "Huh?"

"That's what I'll call you," said Bryant. "The little boy who liked to tell lies."

"I didn't—"

Hands latched onto Kellen's ankles, jerked him toward the center of the cell. His head slammed against the wall at the quick movement. The fetters rattled as Bryant crawled up his body, the weight of the marshal bearing down to pin him.

Kellen imagined his father, the stink of alcohol breathing down on him. Growling, he tried to wrap his arms around Bryant's back to throw him.

The marshal foiled the attempt by digging his elbow into Kellen's bicep.

"Ah!" Kellen cried out at the pinch.

"Listen, *boy*," Bryant's voice came directly above him. "We're in a bad spot, you and me. Need each other if we 'spect to get outta this. I don't wanna hurt you, but I need answers so you're gonna tell me what I need to know. Where's the Caspars? You know who I'm talking about. Took long enough to think about their name, so don't you lie to me again."

"I don't—"

Bryant needled his elbow deeper.

"I-I only met one…" Kellen winced. "Rich…Richard…that's what the girl called him."

"Girl?" Bryant's voice turned angrier still. "What'd she look like?"

"She was b-black. Crazy. T-told Caspar to kill me before…h-he died."

"Richie…" Bryant released his hold on Kellen. "Dead?"

His heart racing, Kellen shoved Bryant off. He scrambled away until he reached a back corner. Flipped round to his stomach, put a knee to the floor, and his back foot against the wall like a sprinter prepped to lunge off a starting block. His bicep throbbed in rhythm with the pulsing walls. Kellen waited for even the slightest sound of rattling cuffs near him, his legs tingling with anticipation.

"How did it all go so wrong," said Bryant.

Kellen guessed the marshal had not moved from his former position, judging by the echo.

"Richie was my partner. Him and his daddy, Edmund." Bryant cleared his throat. "Tell me, did you see it happen? Who killed him?"

Don't tell him Richie died because of me. Don't tell him what the girl said. Kellen's conscience warned. "This other guy, Oscar…shot him. Said he and his group were like police chasing after the girl. That the Caspars tried to stop them."

"Oscar Collins," Bryant spat. "The Crayfish's son."

"The what?" Kellen asked.

"Was there a dwarf with this Oscar? One that talked with a Boston accent?"

How does he know? Kellen relaxed his position. "Yeah…he told me to run away."

"Come again?"

"After they killed your friend, they took this old marshal—"

"Edmund," said Bryant. "That's Richie's daddy. Did they kill him too?"

"No. Not that I saw anyway. Just your partner, Richie, and Sheriff Hullinger, and the other cops, Murphy and Cam-" The name of his former swim teammate caught in Kellen's throat. "Campbell. They're all dead."

"And the girl," said Bryant. "Tell me about Marisa Bourgeois."

"Still alive, last I knew. Oscar, the dwarf, and a couple others led them outside."

"Them…but not you? Why didn't they take you with them?"

Oscar wanted me to choose. Kellen's anger returned. *Stay behind and go to prison, or come with him and become a seal like I saw his people do.*

"You were a con, I take it." Bryant remarked on Kellen's silence.

"I—"

"Don't bother lyin'. You didn't come with my group, and you're not a Selkie. If you met Richie and Marisa that means you was in the cellblock. I remember sending the pair of them back before Dolan and his crew knocked me out."

Kellen wouldn't deny it.

"Listen," said Bryant. "I don't know what you were in for and, for now, I don't care. You and me have found ourselves in some pickle, Pinocchio."

"Stop calling me that. It's not my name."

"Wanna tell me your real one?"

Kellen didn't.

"Fine," said Bryant. "Then Pinocchio it stays until you do. You ever read that story?"

"No."

"Yeah, I didn't figure. You don't strike me for the reading type." Bryant said. "Well, let me tell you about this little boy who told lies. One day he stumbles across these couple guys who tell him all about this great spot they know. They call it Pleasure Island, the place all little punks can go to get away from their parents. Do whatever they like. Gamble, smoke, get drunk, you name it. Sounds like quite the trip, don't it?"

"Whatever. Sure," said Kellen.

"Right," Bryant continued. "So Pinocchio and his friend go to this island willingly enough. Have their fun awhile. Then, Pinocchio's buddy, he sprouts himself some ears and a tail."

"Huh?"

"Yep. See this island…it turns them boys into the jackasses they let themselves become."

"It turns them?" Kellen scoffed.

"Into jackasses." Bryant affirmed. "Makes slaves out of 'em. Irony is they chose to go."

"I didn't choose this."

"Sure you did. Me? I'm the one who didn't." Bryant rattled his shackles. "Why else would they lock me up and not you?"

"I *didn't* choose this," said Kellen, insistent.

"They drag you in here kicking and screaming? Toss you in 'cause it was easier than shackling you?"

Kellen said nothing.

"No," said Bryant. "There's always a choice, Pinnochio. I reckon you made yours when you saw 'em change. Thought it might be neat to have the same power for yourself, huh? Not that I'm faulting you for that, understand. First time I seen someone transform into a seal, I's ready to jump at the chance to do the same."

"Why didn't you?" Kellen asked.

"'Cause a them ones I found later that told me their stories. Where they'd come from and what they'd seen. Things they been through just to make it back to land. I saw the worry in 'em. Heard the fear in 'em voices when they told of those who'd come ashore to drag 'em back to that realm beneath the waves."

The dark closed on Kellen now. Suffocating. He couldn't tell if Bryant made up such stories to scare him, but the fervor with which he spoke made Kellen doubt it. *This life isn't what ya think it is.* Kellen recalled Lenny Dolan's words. *Things can always be worse.*

"What do we do?" Kellen asked, surprised at the fear in his own voice. "How do we get out of this?"

"Now you're thinking right, Pinocchio," said Bryant. "They screwed up putting the two of us in here together. I know the stories, and you ain't chained up. With any luck, Edmund is in another of these cells. Any idea how long I was knocked out?"

"I-I dunno. It's hard to tell anything in all this dark."

"Right. Well, they took us in Indiana. Might be we have enough time on our hands to plan before they reach the Salt."

"The Salt?" Kellen asked.

"Yep. And from what I hear, it ain't no Pleasure Island, Pinocchio," said Bryant. "It's a watery hell."

CHIDI

NO!

Chidi tried pushing her head through the jamb, her seal face scratched and torn at her inability to go further. She relented for a moment then pounded her skull against the door. *No! No! No!*

The door went no further.

Trapped.

She heard tapping behind her.

Henry stood on the opposite side of the freezer, grinning. The sound came from his dagger, freshly blooded, rapping against the glass. "Zere you are, *mon amour.* Will you come out like a good leetle girl—" He pressed the blade against the glass. "Or shall we dance?"

Chidi growled back.

Henry's grin broadened. "Always ze fire in you, my Chidi. Zat eez why I can never let you go." He opened the cooler door. Knelt to crawl through.

Don't let him in! Chidi waddled to the opposite side, the one entry for Henry. She bared her teeth, barked.

"Ah, ah, ah!" Henry said from inside the cooler. He swiped his blade at her.

Chidi ducked away. She feinted toward him.

Henry's blade whistled where her face would have been. He cursed at another miss.

A standoff. Chidi realized. *He can't come in any further without being vulnerable, and I can't revert to human without help.*

"Chidi…" he said quietly, "sooner or later—"

"*Chidi!*"

She glanced to the exit door. *Racer?*

Blood matted his hair and forehead. Remnants of glass embedded in his scalp caught the glint of the security light outside. Racer waved her over. "Chidi, come on. Hurry!"

She spun to waddle back.

"No!" Henry snarled behind her.

Chidi slid toward the door, careful not to strike it. *Free me!*

Her seal voice only barked.

Racer took hold of her upper lip, peeled it up then back.

The changes swept over her, her sealskin falling away like a discarded robe. It suctioned back, morphing into a hooded onesie, and her human form returned.

Racer released his hold on her hood.

Chidi pushed him outside the moment she had hands. "Run!"

She swung her leg over the chains barring the door and stood on her tiptoes, teetering to clear it.

A blade scratched concrete behind her. Chidi glanced back.

Henry had cleared the coolers. Now, he climbed to his feet. "No!" he shouted. "Stay!"

Never. Her foot touched pavement on the opposite side. Chidi fell for the ground, whipped her leg up to clear out of the mart. She used her momentum to roll heels over head and then to her feet.

The door shot out three inches, but still the chains held. Henry's blade sliced through the air, searching for purchase. It found none. He squeezed his head out to look.

Chidi threw herself against the door, smashing Henry's face in the jamb. "Die!" she screamed. "Why won't you die?"

Racer choked her back by her hood. "Come on, Chidi!"

She shoved against the door a final time and wheeled to run alongside Racer. Both made for a cornfield not twenty yards away.

The wall of stalks loomed large as she leapt over the small ditch separating the plots of land. She landed on the other side and plunged into the corn. Racer grunted behind her as the leaves tore at their faces and hands like sandpaper. Chidi scarcely felt them, her fear of Henry driving her onward.

"Chidi." Racer called.

Don't stop. Deeper and deeper Chidi ran. *Don't ever stop.*

"Chidi!"

Remember what he did to Sasha. Chidi sped up.

"*Chidi!*"

Chidi spun. "Racer, what—"

She saw him sucking air and stumbling, twenty yards behind her. Coughing from his asthma, or woozy from his head wound, she didn't know. Chidi turned away, looked up the row where the dark promised to conceal her if only she continued on.

Leave him. Her conscience urged.

"Chi—" He coughed.

She swung back.

Racer reached a trembling hand in her direction. "Chidi...please. Hel-help."

"*Chidi!*" Henry's voice echoed over the field. "I weel find you, Chidi."

She ran back, yanked Racer to his feet. Threw his arm around her neck and helped him limp deeper into the field.

The stalks a few rows over rustled.

Chidi tensed at the sight of a shadow moving through the corn. She unslung Racer. Clenched her fists as the corn tassels jostled side-to-side.

"Chidi!" Allambee lurched across the cornrow to hug her.

She wrapped her arms about him. "Wh-what happened? Where did you—"

"I made him leave." Zymon stepped into the row.

Chidi bristled at the mere sound of his voice. She pushed Allambee behind her. "You left me."

Zymon nodded. "And mean to again. But first, I would have you listen, girl."

"*Chidi!*" Henry's voice howled across the night sky.

"Listen that the boy might live," Zymon continued. "Do you hear what I do?"

Chidi did—the sounds of Henry battering the door open. The rusted chains clammering to their breaking point. Soon he would be free.

"Do you believe we can defeat him if we stand together?" Zymon asked.

"We ca—" Racer coughed. "We can. If we stood—"

"No," Chidi to Zymon. "We can't."

Zymon sighed. "I thought not."

"Please," said Allambee. "Let us go from this place. Let us hurry!"

Zymon ignored the request. "Look at them," he said to Chidi. "These pups behind you. Your master comes for you alone. Did he not say so earlier?"

Chidi's eyes welled. *No…don't…*

"And he will kill us to obtain you, as he did my Wotjek, yes?"

Chidi chewed her lip. Nodded.

"You know fear already." Zymon purred. "Have lived with it in that other world and survived this long."

She shifted her gaze to Allambee, saw him wince at the sounds of Henry thrashing their direction. *I won't leave him.*

"Will you keep these pups from such a fate…" said Zymon, "or add our souls to your conscience?"

Chidi glared at him. "You don't speak for them. You're afraid—"

"I am." Zymon admitted. "As are we all. Yet you are the only one who can save us now. Will you do that, Chidi? Will you save our lives?"

Chidi heard Henry's victory cry and the door bang against the gas mart, loosed of its chains.

"Chidi, no," said Racer. "We—" He coughed. "We can fight him."

And die. Chidi knew. *Just like Wotjek…and Sasha…and—*

She pushed down the teeming faces in her mind. Locked them away in that dark place she never meant to revisit. She turned from Allambee, not wishing to remember his innocent face if she acted too late.

"You will protect them?" she asked Zymon. "You swear it?"

Zymon nodded. "On my daughter's life."

"*Chidi!*" Henry roared. His voice sounded closer now. Entering the cornfield.

Chidi bolted in the opposite direction. "Henry, this way!"

"Chidi, no!" Racer shouted.

Run. Don't look back. She angled up a different row, sprinted alongside it.

"Where are you, Chidi?" Henry called.

Lead him away. Chidi's heart pulsed faster. "This way. This way!"

Other footfalls, heavier than her own and taking longer strides, joined hers. They closed in fast.

"I hear you, Chidi," Henry taunted.

I can't outrun him in the open. Her mind raced in wonder of what to do should the field come to an abrupt end.

The corn. She determined. *The corn must be my ally.*

She deviated from her current path and made for a diagonal course. Smaller and thinner than Henry, she maneuvered through the same rows that hampered him.

Henry cursed at her sudden move. He followed anyway, creating a wholly new path in his wake.

Further. Just a bit further. Her strength waned from pushing through the stalks. Chidi glanced behind her.

Where the marathon sapped her strength, Henry seemed to draw from it. He bulldozed through the stalks, each step drawing him closer to her. "I weel 'ave you, Chi—"

"Ah!" a new voice shouted.

Stalks snapped broken behind her.

Chidi stopped. She saw Henry wrestling with a tan-hooded figure amongst a bed of corn. The pair rolled as one, each clawing and snarling to gain the upper hand. Chidi stepped toward them. *Who...*

"Run, Chidi!" Racer shouted. "Run!"

Henry positioned his leg to stop them from rolling further. He scrambled atop his foe. Raised his dagger in the air.

No! Chidi ran at Henry and dove for his midsection. A gasp escaped his lips at the strike. She carried his body off Racer and tried to roll away.

Henry moved too quickly, catching her by the ankle.

She blindly kicked at his face.

He grabbed her other ankle, pulled her toward him, climbing her body until he straddled her. "Foolish, girl."

Chidi swung to punch him.

Henry easily dodged it and used her momentum against her. He rolled Chidi to her stomach, palmed her face and forced it to the ground, smashing it so far into the dirt Chidi felt suffocated.

"When will you learn?" he asked through gritted teeth.

"Chi…" Racer coughed nearby, his asthma crippling him. "Chidi…ru…run."

It's too late.

Henry pinned her wrists together and pushed them to earth above her head. His dagger pierced her Silkie suit, grazed her bare skin, and came out the other side. He buried the blade to the hilt, chaining Chidi to the ground. Henry leaned forward, brushed the bits of hair from her forehead.

Chidi squirmed.

Henry patted her cheek. "*Shh, mon amour.* Leesin'," he said. "Do you 'ear 'im? Hmm? Sucking for air…clinging to life." Henry bent to her ear, whispered. "Remember what I promised you?"

His weight left her.

Chidi craned her neck. Not wanting to see, knowing her owner did not go far.

Henry proved her correct, gone only far enough to lord over Racer's prone body.

The young catcher stirred. "Chi…di…" he coughed.

"She cannot 'elp you," Henry said, kneeling. "No one can but me."

No. Chidi tugged at her daggered confine.

Henry knew his work well. The dagger did not budge.

"Leave him be," Chidi said. "Please!"

Henry chuckled as Racer struggled to rise. He took hold of Racer's suit and pulled him to a sitting position. "You see? I alone can 'elp you."

"Chidi…" Racer's voice wavered. He looked in her direction.

Henry slapped him. "No…no…" he tsked. "You look at me, now. What eez eet I 'ave 'eard you say so often on our 'unt?"

"I-I don't k-know—"

"Oh." Henry pouted. "Don't know…or don't weesh to remember?"

Chidi attempted to lean the opposite direction, to use the momentum to fetch the blade free. *Come ooon!*

The blade refused to stir.

She saw fear held Racer's stare on Henry as her owner drew a second blade from his other boot. "No!" she cried. "Please. I'll go with you!"

"You weel," said Henry. "In time. But now I weesh to know why zis pup believes Lions are better zan Lepers?"

Racer choked. "I-I don't believe—"

"No? Zen why say eet so often? Hmm?" Henry let the tip of his blade trace under Racer's chin, up the opposite cheek, stopped its tip near the corner of the young catcher's eye. "Tell me now. Which Selkie eez better: Lions or Lepers?"

"Lep-Lepers," said Racer.

Henry's cheek quivered. "I don't believe you. Chidi, do you believe 'im?"

Chidi tried telling him she did. That she believed there had never been a truer statement.

Her voice would not allow it. Each time she opened her mouth to speak, she only croaked.

Henry took the blade away from Racer's face. Stood to his full height. "You see?" he asked, stepping behind Racer. "She does not believe you. Zat makes you a liar."

"Pl-please," Racer said. "I-I'm not ly—"

"I despise liars." Henry stroked Racer's golden hair, almost like he meant to part the strands to either side. "And, you see, I 'ave promised my Chidi one truth over and over."

Chidi shook her head. *Please, God. No...*

"To not act now would be to lie to 'er," Henry cooed. He grabbed a handful of Racer's hair, yanked the boy to his feet, and jerked his head back. "And I never lie to my Chidi."

With one swift move, Henry brought his blade to Racer's bare throat and drew it across.

Chidi transfixed her gaze on Racer's last moments, unable to look away. The widening of his blue eyes, the gurgle of his sliced windpipe, his body's final seizes even as Henry held him up.

She watched the life of another Selkie who dared run with her fade away and added Racer's name to the list of those now dead on account of her.

Racer sagged in Henry's arms, yet her owner held the boy in death's embrace. Only when the convulsions ceased did Henry loose his victim. He knelt beside the body, rolled the pup to his stomach, and plunged his dagger into the suit neckline.

Chidi retched. She tried to tune out the sounds of Henry stripping away the Selkie suit from its former owner. *Why?* She turned her head from the filth she spewed. *Why must it always end this way?*

Heavy footfalls clomped nearby. The dagger binding her plucked free.

"Open your eyes, Chidi," Henry commanded.

Do it. Her conscience begged. *Only more pain awaits if you do not.*

Chidi obeyed as Henry looked down on her, Racer's bloodied Sea Lion suit tucked under his opposite arm. He offered her his hand to help her stand. Chidi noticed it glistened darkly. Knew what stained his hands.

Behind him, Racer lay stripped naked. His eyes Henry left open, however, and Chidi struggled to imagine Racer lay awake, nestled in a bed of cornstalks, wanting nothing more than to admire the night sky.

Remember him as he was. Not like this. She closed her eyes and tried conjuring images of Racer at the Shedd, saving them from Wotjek. How her heart soared when he and Ellie released her from her bonds not a few hours previous. *Not like this.*

Firm, wet, fingers clinched her jaw. "Look at 'im," said Henry.

Chidi's eyes fluttered open and all her happy memories of Racer faded, replaced by this last sight of an innocent boy who Henry granted a final release from slavery. The same grant he would never give her.

Henry mercifully twisted Chidi's gaze away from Racer and forced her to look on him instead. "You see, Chidi? I told you I would find you." Henry stroked her cheek with his other hand. "I weel always find you."

"Why?" she asked without thinking. She shrunk, half expecting some sort of rebuke from him. A slap, or punch, at her daring to question him.

"Because you are mine," said Henry tenderly. "You are my Chidi."

GARRETT

"HELLO?" GARRETT ASKED THE LINGERING DARK-ness. The scent of chlorine clouded his nose. He suspected he knew this area well. Reaching around, he ran his fingers in the cool grooves of painted cinderblocks laid atop one another. He slid his hand up the wall face, unable to find its end. With nothing else to guide him, Garrett walked forward. Each step put gingerly forward as if it might be his last.

An invisible, icy finger grazed down Garrett's backside as he fumbled in the darkness. Its touch hastened him to keep moving.

There's nothing there…nothing at all.

The finger would not be dismissed so easily. Its former light touch now pushed him onward.

In minutes, his cinderblock guide changed into a smooth door. He glanced down at the thin tracing of light where its base stopped an inch from the tiled floor.

A cold breeze flowed from beneath it.

Gaaaaarrrrrreeeettttt…the breeze whispered. Or was it the dark-ness behind him?

Garrett ripped the door open. Heat smacked him in the face. Garrett welcomed it, rather than the cold black he came from. He stepped out the door and recognized where he was.

The pool...I'm at school.

The still water seemed a crystal-clear mirror, dyed hazy green by the underwater lights embedded in the sides of the pool.

A bench creaked in the student bleachers above him.

Garrett jumped back. The locker room door did not budge.

"H-hello?" his voice echoed throughout the empty room.

The darkness gave no reply.

Garrett tried the door again. *Who would lock me out? Why?*

He heard three padded steps behind him, then a splash.

Garrett whipped around.

The diving board bounced up and down so heavily it had left the rails. *THONK! THonk! thonk!* It went, until finally settling.

Garrett saw expanding ringlets in the water. Something had disturbed its stillness. He stepped forward, stopping with a few feet to spare before reaching the pool's edge.

Something swam at the bottom. Its tan half halted. The grey swayed side-to-side.

Garrett stepped closer. His bare toes gripped the edge of the pool and he winced at a slight prick from the tile. A trickle of blood dripped into the ledge and then the pool, staining the water.

No. He knelt and tried to scoop his defilement out with cupped hands.

"Wouldn't do that..." a raspy voice came from the middle of the pool.

Garrett glanced up.

A thick-bodied and bare-chested man bobbed in the water. He leered at Garrett with unflinching, greenish-gold eyes.

"Who are you?" Garrett backed away from the edge.

The man smirked. "Call me...Ishmael."

"What are you doing here?"

"I'm the one who came to call," Ishmael mocked Wilda's Southern voice. His face grew serious. "I'm here for you…to take you home."

Ishmael seemed to effortlessly glide toward Garrett, yet he did not use his arms to paddle and remained upright.

Garrett backed away as the stranger neared.

"Why do you flee?" Ishmael opened his palm to Garrett as he reached the pool's edge. "Don't you want to come home with me, Garrett?"

"Wh-where's home?"

"Oh, look at you! You're shivering." Ishmael said sympathetically. "You'll feel warmer if you jump in."

"No…" Garrett took another step back. "It will be colder in the water."

"Will it? Come with me," Ishmael insisted, motioning toward the middle of the pool. "I'll show you such things as you couldn't begin to dream about. You can bring anything you want. Take whatever you want."

"I-I don't know," Garrett stammered, backing away until he reached the locker room door. He turned from Ishmael and fumbled with the handle, praying for it to open.

"Bring anyone you want…" Ishmael said quietly.

Garrett heard a giggle. "Sydney?"

Like Ishmael, she seemed to bob effortlessly in the water. Her grey eyes beckoned him closer. "Garrett, come with us," said Sydney. "Come with me…and we'll play."

Garrett took an unconscious step forward. "I want to, but…I-I don't know…"

"He doesn't want to come with me," Sydney pouted to Ishmael. "I told you he didn't want me."

Sydney sobbed.

Ishmael wrapped his arm around her. "You shouldn't deny a lady what she wants, Garrett," he said coldly. "Don't you desire her? Don't you wish to be with her?"

"Y-yes, but—"

"Then come with us."

"No," said Garrett. "This isn't real. It can't be real. I'm dreaming. You're a dream."

"Am I?" Ishmael asked. His lips parted in a cruel smile, revealing pointed teeth. "Let's ask her…"

Ishmael brushed Sydney's hair aside and kissed her neck. He worked down to her shoulder, his eyes open and focused on Garrett. Ishmael stopped at Sydney's shoulder blade. He lifted his lips from her pale skin. Then he bit her.

Sydney's body went rigid. Her arms flailed as she clawed for Ishmael's face, screaming.

"No!" Garrett howled. He ran toward the pool, yet halted at the edge.

Ishmael shook his head back and forth, ravaging Sydney's shoulder. Her blood gushed, streaked the water crimson as she writhed and convulsed beneath his bite.

"Please stop!" Garrett begged. "I'll come with you! Just don't hurt her anymore!"

Ishmael released his hold. Sydney splashed into the water face first.

"You will come with me, Garrett Weaver," said Ishmael. "One way or another."

"Yes! I'll come with you! I'll go with you, only please let her go!"

"No. You had your chance. Now I want both of you…" Ishmael looked past Garrett, up into the stands.

Garrett turned.

Someone sat in the student bleachers; their feet propped on the navy guardrail, their face cloaked in shadow.

"Take him," Ishmael commanded.

The figure leaned forward into the light. Poked his head through the rails.

"Kellen?" Garrett said. "What are you doing—"

"Take him!" Ishmael snarled.

Kellen stood robotically, his face blank as he walked toward the stairwell, disappearing from view.

There was a faint slap, slap, slap followed by a swishing noise, like something dragging.

From around the corner, a seal with a black backside and a silvery, dark-spotted underbelly waddled onto the deck. The seal tilted its head quizzically at Garrett as if studying him.

Garrett heard a splash. He spun around.

Ishmael had vanished.

Sydney's lifeless body remained—floating face down in the middle of the pool. The water had turned unclear and choppy, splashing over the edge. The tip of a triangular fin broke from the water near her face, its sharp edge pronounced high above the surface. The fin circled her.

"Sydney!" Garrett cried out.

Come in, come in. Ishmael's voice echoed in Garrett's mind. *In where it's nice and warm.*

The fin bumped into Sydney, rolling her onto her back. Her eyes fluttered open. She coughed.

"Sydney!"

"Wha—Garrett…" Sydney moaned. "What happened?"

The fin passed in front of her.

Sydney's eyes widened. "Garrett! Help me!"

You will come with me, Garrett Weaver. Ishmael promised. *One way or another.*

The fin nudged Sydney, prompted her to scream again. "Help me!"

Garrett stared into the red water. His body shook. "I-I can't…"

You can, said Ishmael. *Come into the water.*

Garrett would not. "Please," he cried. "I can't…I can't…"

Very well. Take him, seadog.

A low growl came from behind Garrett. He spun and saw the snarling, open mouth of the seal before it lunged at him. The animal's weight easily toppled Garrett into the pool.

Ishmael's dark laughter invaded his mind.

He lied. Garrett thought as the cold encased him. His breath caught in his throat when the seal nipped at him, hooked its teeth in Garrett's pant leg and dragged him downwards.

Down, down, down. Garrett's mind ticked off the marks numbering the pool depth. *Five feet…eight…ten…twelve…twelving!*

Garrett took in his surroundings, darkness above and the greenish haze below.

The seal entered his halo of light. It watched him with sad black eyes.

I'm drowning. Garrett closed his eyes.

You're not. Said a grandfatherly voice.

Garrett opened his eyes. Found himself alone with not even the seal for company. *Who said that?*

Me.

You sound…

Ancient? The voice chuckled; a goodly sound, comforting and warm. *I like your voice too, young one, though in truth you're still finding it. Do not trouble yourself with Ishmael for now. A liar he may be, but the water is warm…isn't it?*

A sudden heat in his toes crawled up his body. He ceased fearing the water. His brain no longer panicked. And the water did feel warmer. *What's happening to me?*

Open your eyes, said the voice.

Garrett obeyed.

The stain of red no longer tainted the water. No darkness. No boundaries in this overpowering watery world. No edges for him to cling to. Garrett saw only an endless sea of blue, beckoning him to explore and revel in it.

Is this heaven?

This is your home. The voice said.

Garrett searched in vain for the voice's source.

Are you ready to come back?

I-I don't… Garrett slowly ascended toward the surface. *Are you the one Wilda spoke of?*

I am. The voice said, already fading. *Remember the wonder you felt upon meeting her—*

The water warmed the faster Garrett rose. The light brightened. *Cast away your fear of the scorned ones—*

Garrett closed in on the surface. *Twelve…ten…eight…*

Keep the memories of those you love safe within you.

Six…four…

Follow the one who turns his heart to stone, the voice said, barely above a whisper. *Help him to see—*

Four...two...one...

And follow your heart home.

Garrett opened his eyes. He lay on a soft mattress, a blanket draped over him, tucked in at the sides to keep him warm. A small window near the foot of the bed revealed night outside. A night-light, shaped like a dolphin, cast the silhouette of the animal on the far wall.

A low rumble beneath him gave Garrett cause to believe the room moved, like the time before his father died when they drove to Missouri in an old RV. He looked out the window into the night sky and black expanses of rolling lands.

Whoever had put him into bed had left him dressed but removed his socks and shoes. He found them beside his bunk. Garrett felt for his pockets in hopes of finding his cell phone.

Everything had been taken.

His head and body ached. Garrett rubbed his eyes. *What happened to me? Where am I?*

He remembered Sherriff Hullinger bringing him to the station. A marshal questioning him. Then...

The dwarf! Garrett sat up. *Lenny...*

Garrett rubbed his chest. Sore to the touch, but otherwise unharmed.

Why did he shoot me? Why bring me here? Garrett wondered as he looked around the unfamiliar room. The dolphin nightlight drew his attention. *Wilda.*

The mermaid—

No. Garrett's conscience argued. *Not a mermaid. She didn't like that word. She called herself a Merrow.*

Garrett thought back to witnessing her leap out of the Indianapolis

Zoo dolphin pool. Her gentle voice when she answered some of his questions and promised more answers to come.

I reckon someone'll come to call. He remembered her stately Southern twang. *You'll know 'em when you see 'em. Ask if they been Salted, or if they's born a Salt Child.*

Garrett swung his legs free of the bed and stood up. The floor rumbled beneath him. *Is that what happened? Did she send the dwarf?*

He supposed so. After all, Garrett had met Lenny at the same zoo earlier that day. Recalled Lenny had also yelled for him to stop and told him not to leave after the shark-man's tank exploded.

Did I screw everything up? Is that why Lenny and his friends came to the jail? To rescue me? Garrett pondered. *But if they came to rescue me why not say something? Why shoot me?*

His mind reeled from all the questions and scenarios he envisioned. He looked around the room for anything that might clue him in to where he was and why. Aside from the bed, he found only a small dresser with a mirror screwed into the wall and a picture tucked into the mirror corner.

Garrett took it and knelt to the dolphin nightlight.

He didn't recognize either person, but assumed them father and son. Both wore matching sweat suits that reminded Garrett of the onesie pajamas he wore as a kid, except these pajamas had hoods attached to the neckline. Unlike the bright red pajamas, littered with various superheroes Garrett recalled from his youth, these suits were pearl-white.

Garrett placed the picture back where he found it. Carefully, he slid open the dresser drawers one by one. He found them all empty. *What do I do now? Wait for whoever put me here to come back and ask why they took me?*

Garrett supposed he should try the door first. To his surprise, the handle turned easily enough and cracked open. *So I'm not a prisoner...*

He opened it further. Peeked out. To his immediate right, he saw an open door with a toilet and small sink. Across the aisle way, another door, this one closed. Garrett looked left, his eyes following the illuminating blue track lighting on the floor.

A pale light cut through the dark not thirty feet ahead.

He ventured out of the room, took a deep breath, then started up the aisle. Where the track lights ended, Garrett saw a giant windshield and empty highway rolling beneath it as they drove.

The driver loomed over the steering wheel.

Garrett put his back flat against the wall in hopes the dark might conceal him. He slid further up the aisle, inched closer to the light. He reached the edge. Peeked around the corner.

Lenny Dolan sat on a bar stool, his little legs dangling off the side, not even close to touching the floor. A glass of milk and half-eaten crust of bread sat on the remainder of a broken countertop. Lenny seemed not to notice the disrepair. He sat quietly among the wreckage, staring down at a notebook, his forehead wrinkled in deep thought.

"You..." Garrett said as he stepped around the corner.

Lenny's head jerked up, then relaxed. He snorted. "How ya doin', pal? Sleep all right?"

"I don't—"

"Sure hope so." Lenny resumed his study. "Real nice of Oscar to give up his captain's quarters for ya. Real generous, if ya know what I mean."

Garrett didn't. He looked around the room again.

"Hey. Ya speak any other languages?"

"N-no."

"Yeah, me neither." Lenny scratched his head. "Can't make any sense of this mess. The only one who—" Lenny cut himself off.

Garrett stepped closer to see what Lenny studied.

"Don't matta." Lenny closed the notebook and slipped it into a leather bag. "She's not here no more. So, kid…" Lenny winced. "Weava, I mean. That's ya name, right?"

"Yeah."

"Right. Sorry about shootin' ya back at the jail. Nothin' personal, ya understand. Just easier that way. Didn't have the kinda time back there we got now to do this sorta thing."

"What are you talking about?" Garrett asked, his voice raising. "Where are we? Where are you taking me?"

"Boss—" A deep voice came from the front. "You okay?"

Lenny raised a hand, but kept his eyes on Garrett. "Keep drivin', Paulie."

"What's he?" Garrett asked. "Your bodyguard?"

"Ya think I need one?" Lenny cocked an eyebrow.

"I don't know much of anything right now."

"Right," said Lenny. "See, that's what I'm talkin' about. We didn't have time to do this at the jail. No time to do the introductions." Lenny leaned forward, propping his left elbow on the counter and extending an open hand. "Name's Dolan. Lenny Dolan."

Garrett didn't accept the handshake. "I know who you are. The marshal told me."

"Oh yeah?" Lenny sat back. "What'd he say?"

Do I tell him? Garrett wondered as Lenny polished off the rest of his milk and rubbed the white moustache off his upper lip with the back of his sleeve.

"You tell me something first," said Garrett.

"Fire away."

"Where are you taking me?"

"What? It's not obvious? We're goin' fishin', boss." Lenny sat back in his chair and crossed his arms.

"Fishing." The bus driver said with a laugh. "You're killing me, Len."

"Shuddup, Paulie." Lenny said over his shoulder. He shifted in his chair and fixed his baleful stare on Garrett. "What'd the marshal say to ya?"

Tell him. See what he says. Garrett swallowed to wet his throat. "He said you and your friends had been moving around to different aquariums. That you were looking for something."

Lenny nodded. "Anything else?"

"Did you find it?" Garrett asked. "Did you find what you were looking for?"

"Yeah…" Lenny said after a long pause. "Yeah, I found it."

Garrett shrugged. "What was it?"

"*You,*" said a British voice behind him.

Garrett jumped forward. He turned around and found himself face to face with the teen from the picture. *He can't be any older than me, if he's even that old.*

"Oscar Collins." The teen smiled and extended his left hand. "Thrilled to make your acquaintance, Garrett."

Garrett shook his hand and let go as quick.

Oscar looked past him. Pursed his lips. "Lenny, is this how you treat all our guests? Eating in front of them and not offering a nosh?" Oscar shook his head and shooed Lenny off the stool. "Go on, then. Wake Ellie and have her put together some breakfast. You like eggs and bacon, Garrett?"

"Y-yeah."

"Right. I'll have some too, then. Go on, Len."

Garrett watched the dwarf huff down the aisle. He felt a hand on his back.

Oscar grinned back at him. "Come." He guided Garrett further up the aisle. "Sit with me. We've loads to talk on. Paulo, lights."

"Aye, aye."

The lights flickered on.

Whoa. Garrett looked around the room. *Did someone set Wolverine loose in here to sharpen his claws?*

Most of the leather chairs and couches had their fluffy insides exposed. Gash marks lined the mahogany walls. Bits of broken glass, wedged into the carpet, twinkled.

"Do forgive this mess," said Oscar like one personally injured by the sight. He shook his head. "*Vandals.*"

"Yeah, I guess so."

"Please," Oscar motioned for Garrett to sit on one of the unblemished cushions. He took his own seat in the opposite chair. "I expect this is all quite sudden for you. Can't imagine what it must feel like to wake in a new place amongst strangers. You must have a great many questions."

Garrett relaxed into the seat. "Yeah, I do."

"Inquire away," said Oscar. "Happy to shed light on anything I can."

"You said you were looking for…me."

"That's right."

"Why?" Garrett asked.

Oscar grinned wider, something Garrett didn't think possible. "You're special, Garrett. Surely you must realize that."

Garrett shrugged. "I-I guess I didn't."

Oscar's eyes narrowed. "Has no one ever told you what you are?"

You are a painted beauty, child. Garrett recalled Wilda saying to him. *Don't never let no one tell you different.*

Garrett shook his head. Laughed nervously. "If you're talking about my skin disorder—"

"No…no, you're quite a lot more than that. For instance, I'm only a Selkie." Oscar frowned. "Albeit a wealthy one, but you…you, Garrett, are a Salt Child."

Garrett sat up. "Can you tell me what that is?"

Oscar smirked. "I think it's better if I show you."

"O-okay. Show me."

"Well, I can't very well do it here and now. That's why we're going home. You do want to go home, don't you, Garrett?"

"No, I want to know—"

Oscar raised a hand to quiet him. "Not the home you know of. Your *real* home. Don't you want to see it?"

Garrett closed his eyes, pictured the endless sea of blue from his dream. The home the voice spoke of. Garrett opened his eyes and found Oscar watched him still. *Ask him.*

"Are you the one who came to call? Are you the one Wilda spoke of?"

Oscar smirked. "Of course I am."

CHIDI

HENRY LED CHIDI OUT OF THE CORNFIELD, HIS hand clasped around the back of her neck.

She did not fight it. *Better to let him take me away so Allambee and Zymon can escape.*

Chidi glanced skyward. The night felt darker here than most places, almost like the home she remembered as a girl. She loved the nights her father would build a fire and tell them stories.

Such times had long since been stolen away.

She pushed the memories away as they reached the gas mart.

The SUV that had been her escape lay flipped on its side between the fuel islands. The police unit Henry drove looked the worse for wear. Smoke drifted into the night sky from beneath the hood that had crinkled at the onslaught to the SUV.

Chidi offered a silent prayer for the remote location and time of night. Any persons chancing by to witness the horrors Henry left in his wake would surely join them. She no longer held any notion someone might happen along to rescue her. Such folk existed only in fairytales. Chidi knew only nightmares.

"Oh…man…" a voice came from inside the SUV. "What happened?"

Henry paused and stopped Chidi with him.

"I dunno," a second voice answered. "My head is killing me."

"You're bleeding bad, bro."

The door behind the driver's side opened. Gravity closed it again. A male voice cursed.

"Where are we?"

"I dunno."

The door opened again. Stayed open.

Henry squeezed Chidi's neck. Guided her forward as one of the teenagers peeked his head out like a gopher emerging from its lair. The teen's face had purple bruises and flecks of glass in his cheeks, but otherwise, he looked unharmed.

The teen surveyed the damage. "Whoa…Marrero, you gotta see this, man."

"What is it?"

"This cop—" The teen stopped short seeing Henry. He cursed again and climbed out of the wreckage.

"What, man?"

Henry shoved Racer's suit into Chidi's arms. He released his hold on her then ran for the SUV.

"Come on! Come on!" The teen atop the SUV pulled his friend up and out.

Mistake one. Chidi's mind ticked off. *You should have left your friend.*

Her conscience noted the irony of the thought. That she judged the teen so quickly when she had made the same error in the same night.

I might still be running. Right now.

Chidi stood by as Henry pulled the first teen, the white one, down off the SUV.

He slammed the teen against what was once the roof, now a wall since tipped on its side. Henry brought the black dagger to the teen's throat and held it in warning before the other one assaulted him.

"Get down," Henry commanded the other teen, the Hispanic one. "Or I keel your friend. Zen I keel you."

"Do what he says, Marrero!"

"F-fine, man. J-just chill, okay," said Marrero. "I'm coming down. Nice and easy."

Trust is a trap and loyalty its bait. Chidi thought as Henry shepherd both teens toward the police car.

Henry reached inside with his free hand and popped the trunk. He ushered the teens over, took a bundle of clear-coated zip-ties from the back.

I should have left them all.

"Your names," Henry said to the teens. "Now."

"B-Bryce T-Tardiff, sir," said the white one.

"And you?"

"Marrero. Juan M-Marrero."

Henry nodded. "Do as I say and you both leeve."

"Wh-where's our friend?" asked Tardiff. "Wh-what'd did you with Bennett?"

"I keeled 'im," Henry said matter-of-factly. "As I weel keel you if you don't leesin to me. *Chidi!*"

She hurried over as both teens took notice of her for the first time.

Marrero straightened like one not wishing a girl to see him frightened. Tardiff sniffled.

"*Oui?*" said Chidi.

Henry sniffed the air. Looked around the area. His eyes settled on an azure blue 4X4 truck with an extended cab parked beside the gas mart. "'Ere," he said to the teens. "Turn around."

"Wh-why?" Marrero asked.

Henry slapped him across the face.

Marrero whipped back, his face scarlet and snarling.

Henry stepped close, glared down at him. "*Do. Eet.*"

Do something! Chidi thought when both teens obliged Henry. *Tackle him. Punch him. Something!*

Chidi didn't move.

No. She thought, watching Tardiff weep openly and noting his friend seemed not far from it. *I can't count on them helping, even if I do surprise Henry.*

Her owner moved to sheathe his dagger, then paused. "Give me your 'ands."

Chidi lifted her arms. Her owner encircled a zip tie around her wrists and yanked the end so tight she feared her circulation might cut off.

Henry put his hand to the side of her face. Then he swung back to the teens. Zip-tied their wrists together. "Move." He nudged them in the back. "Come, Chidi."

She marched alongside them toward the blue truck with a roll-way top covering the bed.

Henry opened the tailgate and let it fall open. He patted the metal. "Up."

Tardiff shivered as he looked inside the dark hold. "No way, man. I'm not go—"

"Do it," said Chidi, surprising even herself for speaking up. "He'll kill your friend if you don't."

Henry grinned at her. "Ze girl speaks true. So…which weel eet be?"

"I-I'll go first," said Marrero. He walked steadily forward and slid onto the truck bed.

"Lie down," said Henry.

When Marrero obliged, Henry zip-tied his ankles together. He pushed Marrero further in and repeated the routine with Tardiff.

Chidi shrunk as Henry snatched Racer's suit from her, tossed it inside.

"Now you, my Chidi," he said.

Chidi swallowed the lump in her throat as she hopped onto the truck bed.

Unlike the boys, Henry placed his hand behind her head and gently guided her down. He tied her ankles together, though not so tight as her wrists, before placing something soft under her head. Almost like a pillow. *Racer's suit…*

Henry brushed her brow with his hand, leaned forward and kissed her cheek. Then he closed the tailgate, pitching his captives in darkness.

One of the teens was crying.

Tardiff, Chidi assumed. She perked her ears, listening for any sound of Henry waiting outside the truck bed to hear what she might say. She heard nothing. "Listen to me," she whispered. "Both of you. What—"

"Who are you?" Marrero asked.

"My name's Chidi Etienne."

"Wh-why is this h-happening to us?"

Chidi didn't know how to answer. *Why does anything happen to anybody? Did you take a wrong turn? Did I? Is that why I was taken?*

"We don't have much time," she said. "I need you to—"

"Why not?" Tardiff's voice was panicked. "Why don't have we much time? Is he going to kill us? Is that what you mean?"

"No," said Chidi. "If he wanted to kill you, he would have—"

"We're dead, Marrero—"

"*Listen to me,*" Chidi interrupted. "Whatever he says, you do it. No questions. No backtalk. If you want to live, do as you're told."

"That guy killed Bennett," said Tardiff. "*Bennett,* man. We've known him since like first grade—"

"Shut up, Tardiff," Marrero said, his voice cracked with pain. "You said your name is Chidi, right?"

"Yes."

"If that guy doesn't wanna kill us. Why tie us up?"

Again, Chidi stopped short. *How do I explain what this life is to them?* She had no answers for what Henry planned next, though she had a fair guess. Two teenaged males on the eve of manhood, according to Dryback standards, at least, Chidi knew both would fetch a fair price in the New Pearlaya slave market.

Or would Henry take them to his home instead? Make them work the fish and oyster farms. Henry didn't have much to his name, but two strong males would improve his fortunes. If he wanted to gamble, he might even test the fight in them. Use them for the pit games to challenge other owners in search of sport.

How do I tell them any of that without frightening them further?

The tailgate clanged open.

Sweet-smelling air with hints of wet grass and dirt poured in.

Chidi felt Henry's hands under her knees and the back of her neck. He tugged her out onto the tailgate. Lifted her, setting her right side up, then helping her touch down to stand.

The gas station attendant lay on the pavement, the rise and fall of his back signaling he yet lived. Henry bound the man's wrists and ankles and then lifted the larger man with a grunt.

Chidi marveled at Henry's uncommon strength, even for a Selkie, as he pushed the attendant into the vacated spot her absence had left behind. Then her owner bent over and picked up what resembled a folded, silvery tarp with black spots throughout.

A Selkie suit. Chidi's brain registered the make. *A Leopard Seal...Wotjek's.*

Chidi had the urge to cry then, even though she'd barely known Zymon's guardian.

"Come, Chidi." Henry led her around to the passenger side. "I weel not let you suffer as a common slave."

Henry opened both passenger side doors. Lifted her up into the back cab. "Lie down," he ordered.

When she did, he strapped the seat belt over her arms and mid-section, another across her legs and feet. She thanked the Ancients he at least did not strap the belt closest to her throat.

Henry hovered over her. He sat down between the seats, where passengers' feet should go. Then he laid his head on her chest like a child might against its mother. "I told you I would find you, Chidi." Henry whispered. "I weel always find you. I promise."

Chidi fought off a cold shudder and the urge to scream as Henry lifted his head. She watched him climb out. Close the door. She struggled against her bonds to no avail. Found she couldn't even move her fingers to push the button that might unlock the safety belt nearest her hands. Her thoughts drifted to the two teens in the back, the attendant who scorned her and Allambee.

Chidi had a flittering thought. She had not known any of them before this night. Perhaps the answer to Marrero's question was they might be deserving of such fates.

Did we all deserve this? She wondered. *Marrero and Tardiff? Are we all being punished?*

No. The answer came as quick. *No one deserves this.*

The driver's door opened and the seat tilted back. The engine fired.

None but Henry.

Chidi felt the truck set in motion, back up, then put in forward drive and gain speed. She swallowed. "Wh-where are we going?"

When Henry did not respond, Chidi thought his silence doubled as his reply.

Then, he spoke. "I keep my promises. Always."

"*O-oui.*"

"I go now to make good on one more," said Henry. "Who was it 'elped free you earlier zis night?"

*No...*Chidi bit her tongue. "R-Racer."

The truck swerved. Fishtailed in loose gravel before coming to a halt.

Henry threw the truck in park. The cab light flickered on, illuminating his face between the seats as he peered over at her. Any false hints of the sincerity he spoke with earlier vanished, replaced by a madman. "You know 'ow I feel about liars, Chidi."

She nodded.

"Who 'elped you?" Henry grabbed her trembling chin. Squeezed in what Chidi knew was only a modicum of his true power.

Give him the name. Give him what he wants.

Henry shook his head, a final warning before he resorted to other means. "*Who?*"

"Len..." Chidi croaked. "Lenny Dolan."

Henry grinned.

LENNY

LIGHT DAWNED AS PAULO DROVE UP AND OUT OF the tunnel, bound ever eastward on the Massachusetts Turnpike. Already, Lenny smelled briny hints of the ocean. It wouldn't be long until he would see it.

I'm comin' home, Pop.

"Whoa—" Garrett said from the back of the bus.

Lenny glanced over his shoulder and spied Garrett plastered to the glass, watching the downtown cityscape fade.

"That's Boston?"

"You've never been, I take it?" Oscar asked Garrett.

The abducted teen shook his head. "I've never been much of anywhere. My dad took me with him out on his rig once. Just to St. Louis and back. I always wanted to see more places."

Lenny tried to shut out Garrett's voice, the innocence plaguing his every word. Even Garrett's sheer happiness at witnessing a few skyscrapers and driving under overpasses annoyed Lenny.

The hefty girl seated next to him didn't help matters. All the respect Lenny thought he'd garnered from freeing Chidi and Racer vanished the moment he saw Ellie Briceño watching him. Indeed, her disapproval of her captain seemed to grow for every mile they drew closer to the Salt. Lenny knew she hadn't strayed five feet from Garrett since breakfast.

What's she think I'm gonna do? Lenny wondered. *Ask her to kill Oscar and have us all run?*

He snorted, both at the thought and to let Ellie know he read her disdainful look clear from the front of the bus.

"Where am I headed, boss?" Paulo asked.

Lenny leaned against the railing. "Oscar wants us to park at the pier."

Paulo snorted. "You mean he don't want Weaver to see where this little bus trip ends before it's too late."

Lenny nodded.

Paulo whistled. "Take in the sights. See some dead fish. Get Salted."

"He don't need to be Salted, rememba?" Lenny said as Paulo exited I-90 east and turned right on Congress Street. "He's a Salt Child."

"Lucky him."

"I dunno," said Lenny. "If he wadn't born that way, he wouldn't be here now."

"Sure he would."

"How's that?"

"Fate, boss," Paulo said. "Can't nobody hide from fate. She has her way with us whether we want her to or not."

Lenny folded his arms across his chest.

Paulo chuckled. "I know you don't buy into that talk, but it's true. Think about it. What're the odds a crew of Selkie catchers runs into an Orc on land? Oh, and that the Orc don't know what he is?"

"My good luck." Lenny scoffed. "And ticket outta here."

"Maybe." Paulo shrugged. "Or it's fate toying with you. My mother says—"

"Ah, would ya shuddup already? My Pop says a lotta crap. Don't make it all true."

No such thing as fate. A man makes his own luck.

Paulo raised his fingers from the steering wheel in show of surrender.

The radio hooked to the dash crackled. *"Oi? Anyone there?"*

"That's Tieran's voice." Paulo whispered. "What's he doing on the Hard?"

"Pick up, you sorry seadogs!"

Lenny stepped to the dash and snatched the radio up. "This is Dolan. Whattaya want?"

"I don't answer to no slaves, no nipperkins neither," said the voice. *"Put the lil' Crayfish on."*

Lenny clenched the receiver. "Ya master's busy…and ya talkin' to the captain. I'll ask ya again, whattaya want, Tieran?"

"I want lotsa things, your tongue included. Right now though? I want to know where you lot are. Can't strike out on me own until I finish me work. And I can't finish me work until I've got the bus and your haul tucked away, now can I?"

"So where are ya?"

"Boston Fish Pier, where else?"

Lenny glanced out the windshield as Paulo came to a halt. Stopped at the point where Congress Street ended in a T intersection at Northern Avenue, Lenny saw the Salt across the street.

We're here…

The bus lurched forward in a wide turn on a street meant for smaller vehicles. Horns blared. Drivers shouted obscenities.

Throughout it all, Lenny didn't take his eyes off the water. In a matter of hours, he would swim beneath the surface, bound for home and Crayfish Cavern.

Lenny glanced back at Garrett and found him grinning. *Not too late, Len.* He looked at Oscar. *Ya could still free him and send him on his merry way.*

That was his heart speaking though, Lenny knew. Weakness. To blatantly free Garrett now…

Oscar'd have me killed. Pop too.

Lenny steeled his mind as Paulo pulled onto the Boston Fish Pier and took up two parking spaces. The bus engine hissed at the momentary rest.

"Ah! Here at last!" Oscar said from the back. "Come, Garrett!"

"Open the doors, Paulie."

Lenny hurried off as they whooshed open. A collective scent of fish, gas, and salt smacked him in the face the moment his foot touched pavement. Lenny snorted his nostrils in an attempt to clear them of the smells.

It failed.

He focused on the trawler masts, swaying as their boats bobbed in the harbor. Air horns sounded in the distance. Men shouted out commands on the docks to others who argued back, all of them in hard accents akin to Lenny's own.

Lenny turned his gaze eastward. Buildings blocked his sight. He didn't need them gone to know what lay beyond. The lapping of waves by the dockside told him the Salt called his name. Some voice, deep and powerful, bid him return to that other world, the realm beneath the waves.

More than the voice, Lenny feared no small part of him desired the homecoming. Freedom existed on the Hard, but every Selkie knew of that other freedom, which existed only in the blue world. The kind even runners could not resist—the urge to swim, to cut through the water in a way no mere Dryback could ever experience.

Lenny fingered his hood then dropped his hand when the others exited the bus.

"Ah! Do you smell that, Garrett?" asked Oscar.

Lenny saw Garrett plug his nose. "Fish guts?"

"Opportunity," said Oscar. He clapped a hand on Garrett's shoulder. "Come. I'd like to show you my family stock and trade while the others ready our yacht."

"*Yacht?*" Garrett asked.

Lenny's earrings vibrated.

He's scared already? Paulo's voice entered Lenny's mind.

Lenny nodded. *But why?*

"You don't like yachts, Garrett?" Oscar asked, his voice calm and soothing.

Garrett shook his head. "I-I uh…I'm not a big fan of water either."

An Orc who's afraid of water? Lenny cocked an eyebrow as he surveyed the parking lot. *Oscar shoulda' thought this plan out a bit more. If Weava flips out here in the open, no way we get him back on board without bein' seen.*

Oblivious to Lenny's thoughts, Oscar patted Garrett's back. "It's a big yacht and quite safe, I assure you. We'll board soon enough. For now, won't you come with me and tour my father's business? It'll be loads more fun than the task I've set this lot."

Garrett nodded. "O-okay. Yeah, let's do that."

"Right," said Oscar. "Off we go then. Lenny, I believe Tieran is waiting for you. I rang ahead to let him know of our arrival. Do ensure all is ready on our return. I'll want to shove off immediately. Is that clear?"

"Aye."

"Good." Oscar smirked as he pulled Garrett away. "Shall we crack on, Garrett?"

Lenny's stomach turned as the pair walked toward the newly renovated buildings near the end of the pier. *This'll be over soon. Then ya can forget about him.*

"This is wrong," Ellie muttered.

Here we go... Lenny rolled his eyes.

"One of us should stay with him."

"Yeah?" asked Lenny. "Fine. I volunteer ya for the job, Elle."

"Why don't you do it?" She narrowed her eyes at him. "Garrett's your prize. Your ticket to freedom, right, Lenny?"

Paulo stepped between them, reached to touch her arm. "Easy, Ellie."

The big girl shrugged away.

"So you're on his side again?" she asked Paulo. "What happened to last night when we were alone? You told me this all felt wrong. That we should do something about it while we still could, Paulo. You remember that?"

"I—"

"Because I do," said Ellie, turning her stare again on Lenny. "And he knows it's wrong too."

"What I know is I gotta chance at freedom," said Lenny. "Maybe even for me *and* Pop. I know something else...ya woulda made the same deal if given half a chance."

Lenny's earrings flashed. *And ya almost did. If Oscar hadn't*

called me back inside the jail to help him, ya woulda been runnin'
free with Cheeds and Racer right now.

"No," said Ellie. "I wouldn't."

"I would…" said Paulo. "I'd make the same deal."

Ellie turned. "How can you say—"

"I would if it meant freedom for you," said Paulo.

"Ah, gimme a break with all this lovey-dovey crap, Paulie," said Lenny.

"Why?" Paulo wheeled on him. "Why is it okay for you to make a deal but not me?"

"Cause I'm talkin' about Pop," said Lenny. "Family."

Paulo loomed over his tiny captain. "I want her to be my family."

"Paulo…" Ellie sighed. "I keep telling you not to think like that."

"How come?"

Ellie hesitated. "I—"

"Ugh. The pair a ya are gonna make me puke," said Lenny. "Can we just get outta here already? I wanna get this over with and go home. Neva thought I'd miss the cavern so much, but after months on the road with the two of ya…"

Lenny left his crewmates without waiting for their response. Their heavier footsteps fell in behind him a second later, the pair of brutes allowing their captain the lead in the joyless reunion to come.

They found their owner's dockmaster, Tieran, in the southwest corner. A yacht bobbed near the pier, its pearl-white veneer gleaming in the sunlight. Lenny glared at the decal down the starboard side claiming the boat as *CRAYFISH I*, its letters emblazoned in gold.

A man in orange rubber waders and a black hoodie to match his equally dark and greasy hair strolled down the gangway, whistling all the way. Stopping near the end, he put a finger to his nostril and blew hard. A stream of green mucus shot into the ocean. He wiped the remains away with the back of his hand.

"Well, well, well. If it's not the lil' nipperkin, back from his—"

"Ya got keys for me, Tieran?"

"Slow down there, son. Mind who you're talking to and don't forget it."

Lenny frowned. "A dockmaster and auctioneer's got no power over catchas. Where's the keys?"

"I've more power than you'll ever know, *boy.*" Tieran spat. "Catchers or not, you're all just a gang of slaves."

"And all ya do is sell 'em," said Lenny. "Now. *The keys.*"

Tieran shook his head. "That's a sharp tongue on you. Make a fine trophy, I expect."

"Take it if ya can." Lenny stuck his tongue out and flicked it from side to side to make a popping sound as it struck either side of his lips.

Paulo and Ellie snickered.

Tieran reached for the dagger hanging at his hip. "You lot think this is funny, do you?"

"Aye," said Paulo.

"Wait till we get back under." Tieran said. "See what's there for you. I heard tell more than a lil' funny business happened during your haul. The sort that finds you dangling at the end of a rope, see."

"Wait," said Ellie. "What are you talking about? Heard from who?"

Oscar…

Tieran's smirk only confirmed Lenny's theory. "Aw, what's wrong, love? Not so funny now, is it?"

"What've you heard?" Paulo asked.

"I could tell you, I could," said Tieran. "But where's the profit in it for ol' Tieran, eh? Maybe I just make you sweat it out."

"Nah," said Lenny. "That's not ya style. Ya like to hear ya'self talk too much."

Tieran's grin broadened into a full on smile, full of rotted, yellowed teeth.

"So come on." Lenny urged. "Tell us what ya heard. Convince me to tell ya a secret a mine."

"You got secrets?" Tieran asked, bemused.

Lenny stepped closer. "Loads."

Tieran squinted. "Nah. I don't believe it. What's a nipperkin to know that ol' Tieran don't, eh? Nothin'. That's the answer to that, it is."

"I know we bagged an Orc."

Tieran barked a laugh. He cut it short when Paulo and Ellie didn't join in. His face grew serious. "Codswallop. That's what that is."

"Fine," said Lenny. "Wait till we get unda. I'll be sure and wave to ya before I leave the cavern with Pop…free Selkies, the both a us."

"You're a filthy lil' liar, you are," said Tieran. "And your brain's turned to muck if you think the Crayfish means to free you. I don't care if you caught a bleedin' pod a Orcs. The Crayfish don't give nothin' without he takes double for hisself."

"Ya, we'll see about that. I told ya a secret. Now gimme one."

Tieran stroked his whiskers. "All righ'. There's some guests been askin' on the crew what went looking for Marisa Bourgeois. I reckon they'll be plum tickled to hear you're back."

Lies. Lenny kept the thought. *Why would anyone care about our crew? No one knows we caught her.*

"Who?" Paulo asked. "Who are they?"

Tieran glanced down at his bare wrist. "My, my. Look at the time, won't you? I think it's best I shove off. The lil' Crayfish told me I could take one of you to help square the haul away. Think I'll take you." Tieran pointed at Ellie. "Maybe in more ways than one, eh?"

Paulo stepped forward.

Lenny stopped him.

Tieran grinned back, patting the translucent, coiled whip that dangled at his side. "That's righ'. You don't want none of this, do you, big fella? Call the skin off your back and sting you for days to boot. That's what my jelly whip'll do."

"You hurt her—" Paulo growled. "*Touch* her...you die."

"I'll die, sure. But it won't be this day, now will it?" Tieran reached into his pocket, drew a set of keys, and tossed them at Lenny. Then he leered at Ellie. "Always did like me a cow with a fair bit a meat on her bones. Come on with you, back to the bus. I mean to get this haul tucked away and meself snockered proper 'fore nightfall."

Lenny kept his hand on Paulo's stomach until the bus exited the parking lot. He noticed Paulo's earrings glittered the entire time. *Don't wanna include me in the conversation, Paulie?*

"Come on." Lenny tugged at his crewmate's Selkie suit. "Let's get her fired up. No tellin' when Oscar'll be back. Bet it's soon though."

"Why?" Paulo asked.

Lenny guessed the question came only as a poor man's attempt to delay time. *A love-struck idiot.* Lenny shook his head, waiting with Paulo until the bus had driven out of sight. Only then did Paulo budge.

Lenny walked up the gangplank. "'Cause he don't want Weava second-guessin' all this. Ya hear how scared he was back there?"

"Yeah," Paulo agreed as he untied one of the mooring lines from the dock and tossed the rope onto the boat. "Hey, boss. You think Tieran was telling the truth?"

"Nah. He's always been full of it."

"I dunno. Sounded serious." Paulo moved onto the next line. "Think it might be Henry waiting for us back home?"

So Paulie's thinkin' on it too. Lenny looked over the side. "Guy's a freak. Could be he tracked 'em quick. They escaped in one of them cop cars. Pop said most got trackers on 'em. Might be Henry used one to find 'em." Lenny frowned. "Plus, Henry'd move fasta than us in that slave ship we hauled here in…yeah. Guess it might be Henry."

"I hope so."

"Wha'?" Lenny asked. "Whattaya talkin' about, Paulie? Ya hate Henry as much as I do."

"Yeah." Paulo walked up the gangplank. He took the loose ends of rope in hand and coiled them. "But it's not him I'm hoping to see."

"I don't get it."

"Racer," said Paulo. "If Henry caught up to them, that means he found Racer."

Lenny fidgeted as Paulo bound the rope end over end, running them around his elbow and into the palm of his hand, each additional layer looking more and more like a thick noose.

"The pup turned runna," said Lenny. "He's not the first to—"

"I don't blame Racer for running. I blame him for the way he escaped." Paulo continued, his face scarlet. "Racer *hit* Ellie. Knocked her out cold, Len. He could've killed her."

But he didn't plan it, Paulie. Lenny kept the thought. *I did.*

"I hope Henry did find him." Paulo finished another loop. "Hope he brings Racer back too. When I get my hands on him…"

Paulo knotted the rope.

GARRETT

OSCAR STOPPED GARRETT OUTSIDE A BRICK BUILD-ing. He opened his arms as if to encompass the entire pier. "Tell me, what do you see?"

Garrett thought he missed something. "Buildings…the ocean?"

Oscar grinned. "My father loves to reminisce about this pier. How it looked when first he came. He'll talk for hours of men bustling back and forth, whether hauling fish or packing them with ice. Then Father would say, 'Boats! Boats, you can't imagine the number of boats, son.'" Oscar turned to the water. "Now, look at it."

Garrett spied only two—one of them, the yacht that Lenny and Paulo worked to untie from the dock.

"Nothing," said Oscar. "Nearly all the competition wiped away, thanks to my father's brilliance. Come. Let's have a look around shall we?"

Garrett followed Oscar's lead inside. Hung over the door, a chipped and faded crimson sign with a triangle of interlocking Cs emblazoned in gold lettering creaked in the breeze. Below the sign read *Crayfish Collins Co. est. 1883.*

A tiny bell signaled their entrance, yet no one stood behind the counter to greet them. A chalkboard listed the day's catch—flounder, salmon, tuna, and more Garrett never knew existed—along with prices.

The scent of fish bathed Garrett in its odor as he followed Oscar around the counter and through a series of doors. A makeshift inner office opened into a warehouse with grey, blue, and black plastic tubs stacked inside one another between hangar doors.

Garrett assumed they provided access onto the pier. He saw more tubs, packed to the brims with ice, aligned in rows down the middle of the floor. Each had neon green stickers placed upon the ice listing the fishy treasure kept fresh inside.

Far to the back, gaunt, unshaved men, hampered by their warm attire, worked in the freezers. Dirtied, orange waders covered their bodies from the chest down and ran over rubber boots. Stocking caps covered their hair and ears. Each of the men had a dark grey sweatshirt hood draped down their backs.

"You own all this?" Garrett asked as they passed an employee shoveling ice from the freezer into a plastic bin.

"I will," said Oscar. "Once I've proved myself to Father."

Garrett's stomach turned as Oscar led him past a conveyor belt where more men in orange waders gutted and cleaned fish. Twice, Oscar had to pull Garrett along or else leave him awestruck at how fast the employees wielded their knives. The two teens passed more fish—some headless, others with their heads attached but stomachs slit open.

"Prove yourself?" Garrett asked.

A few employees glanced up, but none would meet Garrett's eye.

"Aye," said Oscar. "It's all a bit complicated to explain. Suffice it to say I believe this will all be mine soon. After all, I've earned it." He spun on his heel. "Well, Garrett. Now you've seen it. What do you think?"

"It's uh…" Garrett glanced behind him.

Some of the employees they'd passed whispered to one another. All shut up and resumed their tasks upon noticing Garrett watching them.

"Yes, go on." Oscar urged. "Tell me."

Why are they so afraid?

"It's great," said Garrett. "You're pretty lucky."

"Luck." Oscar frowned. "You know, that's exactly the sort of answer I'd expect from Lenny. Has he been speaking out of line with you?"

"What? No…what do you—"

"Because if he has—" Oscar lowered his voice. "You need only say the word."

Garrett took a step back. "He hasn't said anything to me. No one has really. Just you."

Oscar's grin returned. "That's because I'm your friend, Garrett. Remember? I'm the one who brought you here. I'm the one taking you home."

"Yeah…about that. I have a couple questions."

"I'm sure you do. And I'm happy to answer them once we're asea. I expect Lenny and the others are ready for us by now. Come!"

Garrett hesitated. "I-I don't know about all this. I'm starting to think maybe…maybe I don't want to go."

"Listen to me, Garrett," said Oscar softly. "You're special. I promised that I would show you that, yes?"

Garrett nodded.

"Right." Oscar twisted toward his employees. "Attention everyone! Stop what you're doing."

All activity ceased.

"You all know me," said Oscar. "I want you to take a long look at my friend here."

Garrett winced under the attention.

"You all know what he is, I trust?"

What I am? A chill ran up Garrett's spine as each employee nodded. Some even removed their hats and placed it over their chests.

"You-" Oscar pointed to the nearest employee. "Have you ever seen Garrett before?"

The man cast his eyes downward. "N-no, m'lord."

M'lord? Garrett thought to himself. *Where'd you find this guy, Oscar, the Middle Ages?*

"Garrett," said Oscar. "Have you ever seen this man?"

"No…"

"Right then," said Oscar. "Tell Garrett what he is."

The man shuddered. "H-he…he's a-a…."

Oscar clapped his hands, startling the man. "Well, go on then, we haven't all day, do we? Tell him."

The man worried his hat in hand.

"He's an Orcinian—" a deep, confident voice came from the crowd.

The crowd offered a collective gasp and parted for an older, wiry man. Unlike his coworkers, the older man didn't shy away from either Garrett or Oscar.

"Fenton?" Oscar said. "What are you doing here?"

"Your father sent me when he heard about the-" Fenton looked at Garrett. "-friend, you decided to bring back."

"Whoa," said Garrett. "We-we're not friends."

"Garrett, don't be foolish. Of course we are." said Oscar. "And as for you, Fenton. I don't know why my father sent—"

"To bring you in the rest of the way," said Fenton. "And to make sure there's no more mistakes."

Oscar stamped his foot. "There haven't been any mistakes!"

Whoa, temper tantrum. Garrett fought back a laugh. He thought Fenton did too, if the smirk teasing his lips was any indicator.

"And even if there had been," Oscar continued. "My father will be overjoyed to meet Garrett and you know it."

"Not my place to disagree." Fenton motioned toward the warehouse entrance. "Shall we? Your father's waiting."

"Fine. But I want it known *I* found him." Oscar put his arm around Garrett's shoulder. "I brought him here. He's *my* guest. Understood?"

Garrett shrugged away. "Look, I'm not anyone's guest. Okay? I don't know even know how I got here. Sheriff Hullinger took me to the jail to answer some marshal's questions. Then Lenny, h-he shot me—"

"Lenny did?" Fenton asked.

Garrett nodded. "Th-then I woke up on some bus an-and he… Oscar…he said I was special. That he'd give me answers about what I am. But I don't care anymore. I just wanna go home." Garrett searched the employee faces. Willed one of them to speak up and say they'd help him. "I-I didn't choose to come here."

"I know, son," said Fenton. "Truly."

Garrett blinked. "You do?"

"Nobody chooses this." Fenton put his hands in his pockets. "But you're here now and I can promise you three things. You want answers? We can give you some. Tell you all about what you are. Help you figure that out. All right?"

"Y-yeah." Garrett said.

"Another thing I can promise you is that the one who shot you... Lenny." Fenton narrowed his eyes. "I'll deal with him."

Why do I feel like when he says deal with he means...deal with? As in...dead...sleeps with the fishes? Garrett shifted. "Wh-what's the last thing you can promise?"

"You're coming with us." Fenton took a gun out of his pocket and aimed it at Garrett's chest. "One way or another."

Garrett wet his pants.

"We can do this the easy way or the Salt way," said Fenton. "Your choice."

Oscar stepped in front of Garrett. "How dare you. Put that away. That's an order."

Fenton shook his head. "It's not your show anymore. That's straight from your father's mouth." Fenton waved the aim of his gun toward the door. "Time for a boat ride."

Oscar leaned his head around. "I won't let him harm you, Garrett. I promise."

Garrett doubted Oscar. He didn't doubt Fenton. The man's gaze never wavered and the ease with which he delivered his threats reminded Garrett of mob bosses in all the movies he'd watched over the years.

Reluctantly, Garrett followed Oscar. He lost any misguided hope he held of someone rescuing him the moment they exited onto the pier. Garrett didn't see a single person in their vicinity, no one to shout at for help. Instead, he listened to Fenton's heavy footfalls the entire way back to the boat.

Lenny awaited them at the dock.

Garrett didn't need to read lips to gather Lenny's reaction at who had joined their party.

"Whattaya doin' here, Boss Fenton," Lenny asked as they walked up the gangway.

"Shut your mouth, pup." Fenton growled. "Don't say another word."

Yikes. No wonder Lenny's such a grump.

The engines purred beneath Garrett's feet as he stepped aboard. The gentle shake of the ocean tipped the vessel back and forth. Lenny loaded the gangway with a thud.

The yacht drifted away from the pier.

Garrett's heart raced. *What do I do now?*

Fenton reminded him with a nudge in the back. "Downstairs."

"P-please." Garrett said.

"Ever heard of box jellyfish, son?" Fenton asked. "Cause that's the kind a venom I have loaded in this tranq. You want to find out how much it stings?"

Garrett shook his head.

"Downstairs."

Garrett stumbled over his feet as he followed Oscar toward the stairwell.

The engine thrummed as Paulo steered the vessel eastward, then throttled up and drove the yacht from the inner harbor toward the main channel.

Garrett lost his balance and fell against the railing. Ahead, he saw a few masts peaked here and there, but elsewise only blue skies and grey water on the horizon. Behind, the Boston cityscape dwindled.

"Keep moving." Fenton reminded him again.

The bottom of the stairs opened into a grand room with lavishness beyond anything Garrett had ever seen outside of TV. A tray of cold meats, cheeses, and crackers sat at the bar alongside several metal tins with steam rising off them. Garrett's stomach rumbled.

"Master Collins," said Fenton. "Join me on the captain's deck."

"I'll do no such thing," Oscar replied. "Garrett's my new friend and I mean to keep him company. I am a Collins, after all. Father wouldn't want it said I wasn't hospitable."

Fenton eyed Garrett warily.

"Go on, Fenton," said Oscar. "Garrett means me no harm, I assure you."

"Aye, aye." Fenton stepped out of the room and closed the door behind.

The door locked.

"Hey!" Garrett pounded on it. "Let me out. I need to go home!"

"We are going home," said Oscar. "We'll be there shortly, in fact, though I expect Fenton means to keep us tucked away in here until nightfall."

Garrett faced Oscar. "Wh-why are you doing this? Why did he lock the door?"

"We can't very well allow some passing fisherman to catch sight of you, now can we?" Oscar opened one of the metal tins and spooned himself a bowl of clam chowder. "Might as well enjoy a nosh in the meantime."

Garrett chose to focus on the fading sight of land. The ship had cleared the main channel, now in the lower middle of Boston Harbor. Islands lay to either side of their approach and beyond them nothing but ocean.

Is this really happening?

The floor rose and fell beneath him as the yacht gained more speed. The new sensation gave Garrett butterflies he might have enjoyed in any other circumstance. The walls closed in on him here, however, adding to his nausea.

Focus on something else...

Artwork adorned the walls. Not the cheesy and cheap kind, but paintings created by a master. Simple, yet elegant, all depicted marine life with complementary framings that spoke each received equal care in their appointments.

A pod of dolphins graced one painting - their natural grins evoking glee as they swam. Another depicted a heap of seals basking in the sun. Then a horrid one with hooked tentacles wrapped around a barnacle-encrusted whale.

The lone killer whale portrait entranced Garrett most. Beyond simply painting the magnificent creature, the artist had captured its essence - the raw power in its size, the beauty in its two-toned skin, the wisdom in its eyes.

A tickle in his toes whispered all the way up to his neck. "What am I?"

"Hmm?" Oscar mumbled as he slurped his soup.

"*What am I?*" Garrett faced him.

"Ah...back to that, are we?" Oscar dabbed at the corners of his mouth with a napkin. "First, I think it best you hear what you're not."

"O-okay..."

"You're *not* human."

Garrett thought back to his skin changing in the Tiber High pool. The same transformation it made at the Indy Zoo when the shark-man's tank burst. "So I'm what? A mutant or something like you?"

Oscar grimaced. "Only in my wildest dreams could I wield the power you possess. No, Garrett. Unfortunately, you and I are not alike. Do you see this?" Oscar reached for the pearl-white hood draped down his back. Held it up for Garrett to see. "Suit, coat, call it what you will. In truth, it's only a ticket, a pass that I might dwell in your world for a time. I'm a Selkie."

"And I'm not."

Oscar shook his head. "You're an Orcinian."

"You keep saying that." Garrett's voice rose. "What does it mean? Just tell me already! What are Orcinians?"

"*Murderers.*" Oscar leaned forward. "The finest killers in all the Salt."

LENNY

BOSS. PAULO SPOKE TO LENNY'S MIND. ANY GUESSES why Fenton's here?

Lenny shrugged. *Whateva the reason, it's not good.*

Buckets of blood, Paulo cursed. *I knew something wasn't right. Even back at the pier. Tieran was way too cocky. And when's the last time you saw Fenton leave the cavern?*

I dunno. Lenny tried to remember.

I do, said Paulo. *Never. He's been the head overseer since the Crayfish bought me and my mom. I've never seen him leave.*

That don't mean he's neva left, Paulie. Lenny replied. *Just means he don't get caught. 'Sides, it's not like the guy's gotta sneak around to get a swim in, is it? The Crayfish lets him do what he wants.*

I dunno, boss. Paulo patted the steering wheel. *I don't like this. Not one bit.*

Lenny didn't disagree. He'd had his fair share of run-ins with Fenton over the years, and the scars to prove it, but Lenny still believed an unspoken bond existed between his father and Byron Fenton. He didn't know why, of course, but Lenny understood Fenton had let him off the hook more times than not when catching the younger Dolan out for a swim after lockdown.

Have to ask Pop about it.

Paulo circled the tail of Deer Island, rounding his heading northeast past Little Faun, bound for the Boston North Channel.

Lenny looked eastward. He didn't see the lighthouse yet, but knew it lay in that direction. The waters would deepen shortly, greyer and choppier. The yacht rose and fell as Paulo throttled up again to bust through wakes of other boats returning to the harbor.

Not a few fishermen aboard the incoming trawlers glared at the yacht moving past.

Lenny recognized the look in those kindred spirits—worker's scorn for those who might wrongly perceive themselves of a higher station. The same look that crossed his own face whenever Oscar came around.

Paulo raised a hand to the fishermen.

Lenny knew Paulo meant the respectful gesture. He also knew it foolish.

The fisherman confirmed Lenny's belief when they spit off the sides of their boat and went back to work.

Lenny grinned. *They're workers, Paulie.* He thought on one of the many lessons his father taught him. *They don't give respect to nobody. Ya gotta earn it.*

His gaze wandered east again and he wondered how long it would be until he glimpsed the lighthouse.

Why, Len? Paulo asked. *Why would the Crayfish send Fenton for us? Why not your father instead? He's the one usually sent up.*

Wouldn't risk it, said Lenny. *Numba one, I'm already up here so what'd keep the two of us from runnin'?*

Your father would never run—

I know that, but we could if the Crayfish was dumb enough—and he's not—to send Pop ashore.

Right, said Paulo. *But why Fenton?*

I dunno! What in a blue hole do I look like? Ya think I got all the answers? Huh? Lenny rubbed his temples. *I don't. I'm in the depths with all this, same as you.*

Geez, Len, you don't have to go crazy.

Lenny sighed. *Look, I'm just ready for all this to end, ya know?*

You mean be free.

Huh?

The deal you made with Oscar, said Paulo. *You catch Weaver, Oscar sets you free, right? No wonder you can't wait to get back. All this—*Paulo pointed to the waters around them—*it all goes away for you when we get back.* Paulo grinned. *I'm going to miss you, boss.*

Shuddup, Paulie.

Yeah. Paulo chuckled. *I'll miss that too.*

Lenny stood up to stretch his legs.

"What's wrong, Dolan?" Fenton's voice came from behind him. "Lose your sea legs during your time ashore?"

Lenny smirked. "I didn't lose nothin', old timer. Brought ya back some prize, didn't I?"

Fenton scoffed.

"What's that supposed to mean?"

"I told August it wasn't wise sending you out." Fenton grimaced. "Too young and cocky. Like your father."

"Hey, my pop's the best catcha in—"

"All the Salt," said Fenton glumly. "So I've heard. You want to know something else? He's not happy with you either."

Lenny laughed. "Yeah, well, Pop's neva happy unless he's unhappy."

Fenton's face tightened.

Lenny stopped laughing. "What? We bagged the girl August wanted. Marisa Bourgeois, the uncatchable runna…ya rememba her, Boss Fenton?"

"I do."

"Good. We caught her. The Silksteala too."

Fenton remained unimpressed.

"Wha'?" Lenny said. "Whattaya lookin' at me like that for? Did ya not hear me or something? I brought ya all those prizes *and* an Orc. That's neva been done before."

"And for good reason." Fenton folded his arms.

"Yeah, but—"

"What do you think an Orc pod might do when they learn of a Selkie stupid enough to enslave one of their own?"

Lenny and Paulo exchanged a glance.

"They'll come for him," said Fenton. "Soon."

"Maybe they won't find out," said Paulo.

"They will." Fenton assured him.

"H-how do you know?"

Lenny knew the answer before Fenton spoke. "Tieran…"

Fenton nodded. "You know how he loves to run his mouth when he's drunk."

"Well, stop him," Paulo said. "Let me circle back right now. I'd love to shut him up."

"That sounds like mutiny to me." Fenton's voice rose. "Tieran's a freed Selkie. You're not."

Paulo dipped his head and focused on the wheel.

"I don't suppose you pups gave a thought as to how you'd bring your prize down to the cavern either, did you?" asked Fenton.

Lenny shrugged. "He'll swim down."

"Will he?" Fenton asked. "Or might he decide all that swims between him and freedom are a pair of young Selkies?"

Lenny leaned against the rail. "Son of a sea cook…"

"What?" Paulo asked. "I don't get it."

"Have either of you pups ever seen an Orc in open water?" Fenton asked.

Paulo shook his head.

"They're faster than us, more resilient, and outweigh all Selkies except for maybe your kind, Paulo," said Fenton. "They were made in the Ancients' image for Senchis's sake! I can't fathom what in a blue hole crossed your mind when you decided to bring that Orc back, Dolan, but you'll see this through or die trying."

Die?

"Boss Fenton," said Paulo. "If this is such a bad idea, why not let Weaver go? He seems like a good guy. I mean he wants to go home. Didn't he say so?"

"Only one way I know to ensure he keeps quiet." Fenton grimaced.

Lenny stood up. "Ya can't do that."

"What?" Paulo asked. "Can't do what?"

"Aye," said Fenton, rising to tower over Lenny. "What can't I do…slave?"

Lenny refused to back away. "Ya can't kill him. He's a kid that don't know no betta."

"You're right. *He* doesn't." Fenton's eyebrow twitched. "You did."

"Aye," said Lenny. "So take it out on me."

Fenton cracked a grin. "You truly are your father's son, Dolan."

"That's right." Lenny lifted his chin. "I am."

Fenton shook his head. "I never said that was a good thing."

Lenny relaxed, but only slightly, as the old overseer took his seat again.

"I've no plans to kill the Orc," said Fenton. "Honestly, we need him for when the others come looking for him. If they find him alive and well, might be they'll take him and go on their way. If our new Orc friend is dead, however…"

Lenny and Paulo exchanged a glance.

"Good," said Fenton. "You're catching on. If either of you want to live another day, you *need* him to survive the journey to Crayfish Cavern."

"Right," said Paulo. "That's no problem. He's an Orc. He'll swim down—"

"The kid hates water," said Lenny.

"Excuse me?"

Lenny nodded. "Says he can't swim."

Fenton laughed. "Marvelous."

"Buckets of blood," said Paulo. "So how are we supposed to get him down there?"

Lenny put his face in his hands, rubbed his temples. "Tranq him, maybe? Knock Weava out. Pull him down—"

Fenton raised his hand, halting Lenny. "Too risky. He might drown. August lost nearly a whole crop of new slaves employing the tranq method when he first began this business. It's not an option."

"Okay," said Paulo. "So we take him down the Gasping Hole—"

"Too small," said Lenny. "And I don't think Weava knows how to change all the way yet. If he freaks out—"

"He will," said Fenton. "They all do. You've seen their faces after."

Lenny shuddered and put the memories of new slaves fresh up

from the Gasping Hole out of mind. "So that's out. Tranqs are out. Whatta we supposed to do? Rent a submarine?"

"No," said Fenton. "From where I sit, you only have one option."

"*You,*" said Lenny. "Not we?"

"Aye. I'll have no part in it."

Lenny felt his guts twisting as Fenton laid out the plan. The situation he would be in should things turn sour. A part of him even wondered if putting him in such a scenario hadn't been Fenton's plan all along.

"Ya can't be serious with this," said Lenny, unable to contain himself.

Fenton's lips pursed.

"Ya talkin' about suicide!"

"Didn't you say the Orc doesn't know any better?"

"Yeah, but—"

"Then he'll listen to you," said Fenton. "After all, you're the only friend he has in the Salt, am I right?"

Lenny sighed. "I'm not his friend."

"You are now. Oh, and don't forget"—Fenton grinned—"you already told me that he would, how did you put it…keep his mouth shut?"

Lenny frowned. "Forgive me for not laughin'."

"Dolan," said Fenton softly. "Your fate is already linked to that Orc…as is your father's."

Lenny saw red.

"If Garrett Weaver escapes, drowns, or dies by any means," Fenton continued, "you and your father die too."

KELLEN

WHY HAVEN'T THEY OPENED THE DOORS YET?

Kellen stretched his legs from the poised position he had held for over an hour. Sweat dripped off the edge of his nose. The temperature had steadily risen ever since the walls stopped pulsing. Kellen assumed it meant the Selkies had parked and killed the engine.

What if they abandoned the bus? Left us to roast in here?

He pushed the thoughts away as quickly as they came.

They'll open the doors. He tried to convince himself. *Bryant said they would. We're valuable to them or else they would've killed us already.*

"Stay ready," Bryant whispered from a few feet away.

Kellen took up his crouched stance again; knee tucked under his waist, his other foot back, ready to spring forward and out the moment any bit of light shone through the locked hold door. He pictured his cellmate in a similar position at the opposite end.

However fearful Kellen may have once been of Bryant, he thanked God for the company now. The dark seemed not so claustrophobic while having someone to converse with. Bryant had kept his past shielded from Kellen's questions, as did Kellen to the marshal's inquiries. Elsewise, Kellen thought the pair of them had worked well together thus far.

Each had run their hands along the entire rectangular cell in case the other missed a crease in the metal paneling, or a loose screw to pry free. Kellen discovered two holes, one near either corner at the back wall, both wide enough for him to put his fingers inside. He found the opening smooth, like PVC piping, yet the tips of his fingers struggled to find where the tubes ended.

Probably letting air in, he deduced.

Their search turned up little else. Welded paneling. No screws, bolts, and barely any creases where the metal sheets fit together. Aside from the breathing holes, the hold door contained the only cracks.

When Kellen mentioned Oscar slammed the door closed from the middle, Bryant suggested they take up opposite ends. Doing so might allow them greater ease to spill out. Both hoped the Selkies might not expect them at the sides.

"What's the plan?" asked Bryant quietly.

Kellen rolled his eyes. "We've been over it a hundred times."

"Then you should know it by now. Now, the plan…"

"When the door opens, we lunge with our shoulders against the door to catch them off guard."

"And then?"

"Kill them," said Kellen. The answer rolled off his tongue as if he talked of shooting birds with his old pellet gun.

They're slavers. Kellen recalled Bryant's rebuke when first he wavered at such talk. *They're going to take us beneath the waves and make us theirs. Sell us to the highest bidder and work us until we die of exhaustion or worse.*

Kellen might have disagreed with Bryant had he not seen the transformations of seals into men back at the jail. Such a thing should not exist outside of movies and storybooks, yet Kellen witnessed it with his own eyes. Had watched Oscar shoot Richie Caspar in cold blood, take the others hostage, including the Lavere town drunk, Boone Merchant. All before shoving Kellen into the same dark hold that contained him now.

"You forgot something."

"No, I didn't," said Kellen defensively.

"Yes, you did." Bryant said. "Don't leave me behind."

Kellen smirked. Try as both might, neither had been able to release Bryant from his cuffs. Blinded by the hold's dark, he remained certain the marshal's wrists were bloodied and raw from the chafing he had given in the trying.

"I will if you can't keep up, old man."

"Don't be stupid," said Bryant. "We don't know where we'll be when they let us out of here. We do this and kill Oscar Collins, his daddy'll hire more catchers to find out who done the deed. I doubt it'd take them long to find out who we are. You said the Selkies lit the jail on fire too. Soon enough, the authorities will learn you're gone. You get away without me, you'll be headed straight to prison or the nearest ditch."

"How's that?"

"Bet they got your face on every news outlet there is right now. Two police officers are dead. A sheriff and a deputy marshal too. A couple cons missing, who do you think they'll point the finger at?" Bryant whistled. "Any self-respecting lawman would give their left nut to lay hands on you right now, Pinocchio. I won't even mention what the ones who don't respect the badge would do."

A lump formed in Kellen's throat.

"You need someone to hide you," Bryant continued. "Figure out a way to explain this mess if you ever hope to get your old life back. You leave me behind, you kiss all that goodbye."

"I won't leave you," said Kellen.

"See that you don't."

Kellen stewed, in silence, on Bryant's words.

"Kid…you hear that?"

Kellen tensed. He strained his ears to listen for the slightest sound; a door slamming, voices, even the low rumble of the bus engine firing anew would be a welcome relief from this waiting. He heard none of those.

The noise came from behind them, along the wall at the back of their cell. A scratchy sound, clearly outside the bus, and loud enough that whatever made it didn't care whether those inside heard or not.

"What is that?" Kellen hissed.

"Distraction," Bryant replied, his tone suggesting guesswork. "Trying to draw us away from the door and to the back instead."

Kellen's hands shook. "What if there's a door back there too? Hidden?"

"It's not. No creases for it to open by."

The noise came louder.

"Get ready," said Bryant lowly.

Lunge against the door. Kellen reminded himself.

The noise attached itself to the bus.

Spill out the side…

Sounded like metal grating metal, screwing on in clockwork fashion.

Kill them.

The noise vanished. The silence returned thick and heavy like a tomb.

What was that thing? What happened? Where did it go?

Kellen's calves ached. He tapped his toes against the floor, anything to ground the energy coursing through him.

"I don't like this," said Bryant.

For some reason, the admission frightened Kellen more than his silence.

The quiet did not last long.

A new sound emerged: soft and hissing at first, then…a drip. Then another.

What is that?

The drip became a trickle.

Kellen's jail sweatpants sagged, suddenly heavier around the knee…wet. He took his hand off the door and put it to the floor. Water wet his palm. *Oh no…*

The trickle became a faucet, the sound of water splashing against the metal base louder than the hissing had been.

Not breathing holes…

He spun away from the door and crawled to the back.

"Where are you going?" Bryant yelled.

"We have to plug the holes!" Kellen reached the back corner and fumbled around for the hole. Finding it, he tried to stop it up with his fingers.

The force came too great, the water rank like creek water siphoned off a main pool and left to still.

His first attempt failing, Kellen tried to block the hole with his hands.

The move created a geyser, spraying water in all directions, and still the flow continued.

"Bryant!" Kellen yelled. "I need help!"

"I'm not leaving this door," the marshal replied. "It's a distraction. They want us to move!"

Kellen no longer cared.

The water level rose over his legs, now halfway up his thighs.

It's filling too fast. There has to be more holes somewhere.

Kellen pressed his back tight against the ceiling.

The water continued to rise.

Plug the holes!

Kellen stripped his shirt off, wadded it up and shoved a sleeve inside the hole. Water pulsed through, impeded little by the makeshift stopgap.

The cold tickled Kellen's bare abs, a reminder it meant to overtake him still.

Another hole continued to gush and water pulsed from the hold bottom as Kellen crawled in search for the source.

Movement came harder now, slowed by the ascending water line.

Swim!

Kellen raised his head above the water line, cracked it against the ceiling. He opened his mouth to breathe.

Water rushed in.

Kellen spat it back out.

"Kid!" Bryant yelled.

Kellen ignored him. He angled his head sideways: one cheek pressed against the cool metal ceiling, the other wet by the water line. Kellen gulped each panicked breath of air. His hands scoured the wall for the water hole. Found it. *Plug the hole!*

He tried to slip his sweat pants off. Each attempt forced his head beneath water.

Choking and spitting, Kellen put his cheek to the ceiling.

The water rose further. Trickled in whenever he dared open his mouth.

Kellen flipped to his back. He sat on his knees and tilted his head, crammed his lips and nose to the metallic ceiling.

Water filled his ears, touched the corners of his eyes and continued to rise.

Open the doors. He prayed. *Please, God, open the doors!*

Light cut through the darkness and a sudden undertow yanked his legs out from under him. His back crashed against the floor as the hidden wave rushed him toward the door. Kellen opened his eyes to a swirling world of putrid green and dim light. He winced at the shock to his irises and moaned. Brackish, stale water filled his mouth.

Kellen choked it down as the surging water carried him toward the newly opened door. He saw roll bar cages outside and clawed for any kind of hold to stop.

The water prevented it.

The hold's sheet metal floor vanished and Kellen felt the exhilaration of a quick drop before he landed on a rubbery slide that flung him into a cage. He immediately threw up the water he had swallowed. It fell through the slatted cage floor as a constant wave crashed over his body and drained away.

Someone sputtered for air beside him.

Bryant, Kellen assumed, before retching again. His throat raw, head pounding, Kellen laid his cheeks against the bars as water subsided around him. His eyes adjusting to the light, Kellen opened them slowly.

Rust-colored iron bars encaged him. His legs dangled through the openings and, as Kellen looked down, he found his cage hung poised over a concrete pit. The stagnant water that had carried him out of the bus drained from his cage, pooling below in the pit. Kellen nearly threw up again at the rank odor.

Bryant coughed for air.

For the first time, Kellen glimpsed the man he'd shared a cell with. David Bryant looked older than Kellen would have initially guessed him to be, closer to fifty than forty. As Bryant crawled to his knees, Kellen didn't guess the marshal nearly as powerful as he sounded inside the dark hold.

Kellen felt something furry graze his arm. He looked to his right and into the eyes of a brown seal with long whiskers and pointed ears. The Cape Fur Seal stared at Kellen knowingly even as water cascaded around its body and emptied through the strainer flooring like a small waterfall.

"Ah." Kellen scrambled away.

The seal tilted its head quizzically at his surprise. Then Kellen saw the sealskin split down the middle, falling away and morphing into wet clothing, revealing the girl who foretold of his escape from the jail. *Marisa Bourgeois...*

"You..." Bryant said to her. "How did you get here?"

"I was in the cell next to yours," she answered. "It seems our paths are linked a little while longer, Silkstealer."

"Don't call me that." The marshal bristled. "You know damn well—"

Kellen winced at a banging further down the way – another of the bus holding doors being opened. Water spewed down the rubber slide attached to it, carrying out a Sea Lion and another familiar face.

Boone? Kellen thought back on his former cellmate from the Lavere County Jail. *Why would Selkies haul our town drunk here?*

The slide dumped both Boone and the Sea Lion into a neighboring cage. The animal positioned its body closest to the oncoming tide of water, almost as if it meant to shield the old man cowering in front of it. The Lavere town drunk had crunched his body into a ball. His hands, raised to protect his face and head, shook violently. Boone coughed for air as the water ebbed.

Kellen glanced around his new surroundings and found himself in a warehouse, large as an enclosed hangar for multiple airplanes. He smelled the sea, both fishy and briny. Gulls called somewhere outside and water lapped even closer. Not from the pit below, but nearby.

Opposite the bus, a mast gently swayed, the tip of it nearly touching the building's arched, sheet top ceiling. Dim fluorescent bulbs hung from the steel grated rafters like weak suns pitying any who chanced to happen upon such a wretched place.

"Well, well, well," came a man's voice. "Look what we have here, Silas. Looks like the lil' Crayfish made quite the catch on his first time out. Bagged his father a couple Selkie runners and a few mates to boot."

The speaker approached Kellen's cage sweeping away his black hair, long and greasy. His beady eyes greedily took in the situation. A coiled, translucent whip hung from one hip, a sheathed dagger on the other.

Kellen hated him on sight.

The man stopped shy of reach. "Ooh…and a pretty lil' lass to go with 'em. 'Ello, love." He said to Marisa Bourgeois. "Tieran Chelly's the name. What's yours?"

Marisa kept her silence.

"Quiet type, eh?" Tieran asked. "It's all righ'. Makes it more fun for ol' Tieran to tease answers outta you." His gaze flitted to Kellen. "And what's your name, lad?"

Show him you're not afraid. Kellen stepped closer to the bars. "Come in and find out."

Tieran pursed his lips. "Better watch out for this one, Silas. Defiant, he is."

"Right," said a fisherman along the dockside. Dressed in orange rubber overalls and a long-sleeved, hooded sweatshirt, the fisherman took a single glance at Kellen.

"Bah." The fisherman continued stacking wooden lobster pods. "That one won't keep me up nights. I'll wager swordfish put up more fight than him."

Tieran hocked a loogie and spat into the pit. He wiped his nose clean with the back of his hand. "Nah. He's a live one, this lot. A real fighter. I know the look when I sees it."

Good. Kellen thought to himself. *Then you'll know not to mess with me.*

Tieran chuckled, patted the coiled whip at his side. "Don't worry your pretty self, my son. Soon enough ol' Tieran'll take that fight righ' outta you. Then, you'll give me any name I like. Might be I decides to call you Bessie and you'll say, 'Yessir, Tieran, sir. Why thank you, sir.'"

Kellen glared back.

Tieran's eyes flitted away. "Who's this one, eh? What's your name, gov'nor?"

Bryant cleared his throat.

"What's wrong, ol' chap? Swaller a bit a water in there?" Tieran laughed.

"I'm U.S. Marshal David Bryant. I'm ordering you to release us right now."

Tieran's jaw jerked back and forth, as if weighting Bryant's words. "You hear this lot, Silas? We got a marshal on this haul. David Bryant's his name."

"Never heard of him."

Tieran shrugged. "Silas's never heard of you, mate. And we take our orders from the Crayfish and no one else. Righ'." Tieran clapped his knees and left them. "Best get this lot aboard 'fore the next catch comes in."

The next catch? Kellen wondered as Tieran left them and rounded the bus.

Bryant coughed beside him. "So much for our plan, huh, Pinocchio?"

Kellen ignored him. He stood up, his bare feet slippery on the bars. His legs felt weak at the crouched position the hold had limited him to. The cage did much the same, only allowing him to stand a few inches higher. Kellen surveyed the area.

Fishing nets were hammered into the exposed wooden wall sides. Kellen couldn't tell whether the nets hung there for storage or if they were some fisherman's idea of adding aesthetic value to the otherwise drab enclosure. A cleaning table stood nearby with heaped, day-old fish guts to judge by the smell.

The fisherman, Silas, didn't seem bothered with the prisoners or the fishy odor. He had stacked lobster pots ten high along the wall. A good deal more lay in a pile nearby, almost as if someone had dumped them there with little care.

"Edmund," Bryant said softly.

"What?" Kellen asked.

Bryant looked to make sure the fisherman didn't see, then pointed at the cage Boone cowered in. "That's Edmund…"

"No," said Kellen. "That's Boone. He—"

"Not the bum, boy. I mean the Sea Lion. It's my partner, Edmund."

Kellen looked again.

The Sea Lion waved its head up and down. Sat back on its hind end and covered its face with a long flipper.

Bryant nodded back then bowed his head.

"What are you doing?" Kellen asked.

"Letting him know I heard about Richie. His son."

Kellen looked on the Sea Lion with renewed interest. *He's one of them. A Selkie!*

The Sea Lion seemed to survey the area as Kellen had done. It paid particular attention to the rafters above. Then it looked back at them, growled suddenly, frightening Boone in the process, and stopped. Immediately after, the Sea Lion shook its head from side-to-side.

What's it doing?

"Right," said Bryant. "Listen, kid. Whatever happens next, Edmund doesn't want us to fight it."

"But you said they wanna make us slaves. Take us—"

"All of it true. Listen. Edmund's been through this kind of thing before and escaped. He's telling us not to fight these guys. Whatever they want from us, we lay over. Let it happen for now."

"What about our shot to get out?"

Bryant shook his head. "We missed it."

"No, you didn't."

Kellen wheeled and saw Marisa Bourgeois sitting in the corner of their cage. "What?"

"You didn't miss your chance."

"How do you know?" Kellen asked.

"I know because you will never escape, Kellen Winstel. The Salt has you in its sway now. An ancient and nameless voice sings your name, its melody dark and deep." Marisa's voice quivered. "These next few hours are the last you will ever walk upon these lands you call home."

"Don't listen to her," said Bryant. "She's nothing but a lying runaway."

A cold shudder ran through Kellen as he remembered Richard Caspar had said the same when Marisa Bourgeois predicted his death. Less than an hour later, Caspar was dead.

She's crazy. Kellen told himself. *Just trying to get under my skin.*

"All righ', gents." Tieran walked around from behind the bus, carrying what resembled a giant remote control in his hand as a black cable dragged behind him. Tieran paused shy of the cage, grinned at Kellen. "Up, up, up, and away."

Something whirred over Kellen's head. He looked toward the ceiling and a hydraulic pulley system of chains with hooks dangling from the ends. Tieran pressed another button and the hooks lowered until the ends clanged against the cage top.

"Righ' then." Tieran sat the control upon the lobster pot heap. "Shall we get to work, Silas?"

The fisherman threw his last trap upon the others and wiped his hands on his waders. He walked to a bright red steering wheel hooked onto the wall, and gave it a spin, unraveling a fire hose that piled neatly on the floor.

What's he need that for? Kellen wondered as Silas grabbed the head of it and continued on toward his cage. The wheel unraveled faster.

"Ready?" Tieran asked.

"Aye," said Silas.

Tieran looked at Kellen and Bryant each in turn. "No funny business now. You let ol' Tieran hook these chains up and I'll give you both a sweetie at the end. If not..."

Tieran shrugged then strode ahead.

What does he think he's doing?

Tieran reached the cage and climbed it.

Kellen looked past him at Silas.

The brawny fisherman with tats of anchors and topless mermaids never batted an eye as his partner reached the top, whistling all the way.

Kellen stepped to the corner as Tieran's boots dripped water and filth down through the open slats. He noticed Bryant shaking his head.

Don't do it. Kellen took the meaning.

Then he heard Tieran hock a loogie and spit.

Kellen's forehead felt wet. He wiped Tieran's mucus away and glared up.

"Whoopsie." Tieran grinned down. "Apologies, mate. I meant for it to go—"

Kellen threw his arms up through the slats and grabbed for Tieran's ankles.

A burst of water shot Kellen in the chest. Blasted him back against the bars.

The fire hose. Kellen's brain registered what had happened. *Silas has a water hose.*

Kellen lost his grip on Tieran's ankle, but would not give up the other. He pulled down, even as the surge of water forced him back.

"Oi!" Tieran shouted. "Get him offa me!"

"Let him go!" Bryant shouted.

Kellen would not. He twisted the ankle with all his might, reveling in Tieran's yelp before Silas shifted the water stream at his face. Red flashed his senses and he lost his hold on Tieran.

The stream grew stronger.

Kellen tried to block it with his hands. The water tore at his skin.

Silas shifted the stream to attack Kellen's groin.

Kellen yelped at the new blow. He curled up, as Boone had, shielding his vital parts.

The stream shut off.

Kellen shuddered, both from the cold and the onslaught.

The gangplanks thudded as Tieran climbed down. "What'd I tell you eh? Told you this one was a fighter."

Kellen sat up, his back against the bars. He cast a hateful stare on Tieran.

Silas snorted. "More like a whipped pussycat to me. You wanna take him out and learn him to listen?"

"Nah," said Tieran. "Not yet. I mean to have more fun with this one first."

"Suit yourself." Silas left to resume his other duties.

Tieran ambled back to the control he'd left behind. He picked it up, pressed a button.

The cage rattled. Jolted upward.

Kellen shouted at the jerky move and tried to find his footing.

Tieran laughed. "Till next time, love."

Up, up, up the cage rose with Kellen's legs dangling out the bottom and him straddling a pair of roll bars. His groin screamed at him to reposition himself. Kellen obliged, lifting his legs and sitting sideways across the bars. Now near the ceiling, he saw the massive hangar in its entirety.

The bus that carried them had parked atop a pier. Behind it, a large door presently closed. To the bus's left side, a trawler gently shook, anchored to the pier by ropes thicker than a grown man's thigh. A Crayfish emblem painted its bow, with *CRAYFISH II* marking its side. Kellen didn't see a *CRAYFISH I*, but he guessed it typically parked in the vacated expanse of open water beside the trawler.

The bow faced another closed gate, and a foot of air separated the choppy water from the bottom of the sheet metal wall. Daylight existed in the gap.

They drove through the night. Where am I?

Kellen's heart thudded when the hydraulics holding his cage in place reached its ending point. The cage swayed at the sudden stop, poised above the trawler. For a moment, Kellen feared the chains might break. When they held strong, he risked a peek downward.

What he saw made him gasp.

Other cages, like his, sat upon the trawler's deck and inside them, people. Most did not bother to look up. The few that did seemed not near as surprised as Kellen. Still more cages held seals and sea lions of varied sizes.

Kellen instinctively grabbed at the bars when the wench whirred and clicked, lowering his cage to join the others on the boat deck.

A pair of hooded deckhands appeared to guide Kellen's cage onto the trawler deck. They climbed atop his cell and mutely unhooked the chains.

Kellen froze, unable to even think of fighting them off. He searched the faces of his neighbors. Most seemed older than fifteen but younger than fifty, and nearly all were dark-skinned and foreign with few exceptions. A pair of children played a clapping game. He saw an elderly woman he thought might fall over dead at any moment.

Bryant rose beside Kellen. "Welcome to the real Pleasure Island, Pinocchio."

Kellen rushed the bars. "Let me out of here. Someone! Any—"

"*Shut up!*" one of the deckhands yelled back.

Kellen reached his arm through the bars, tried to grab the nearest fisherman by the leg. "Hey…listen to me."

The hooded fisherman slapped a long spear hook against the cage bars. "I said shut up!"

"Do as he says," Bryant whispered. "Lay over. Let it happen… for now."

Some of the others in cages watched Kellen. A few whispered in foreign tongues.

Look at the silly white boy, he imagined them saying, *losing his mind.*

Again, Kellen attacked the bars. "Let me out of here! You can't keep a person in—"

A punch in the gut stole his wind from him. Kellen fell, sucking for air.

The fisherman pulled the wooden end of his spear out of the cage. "Listen to ya pal there, boy, and it'll go easier for ya. Otherwise, I gotta bring Tieran over here. Ya don't wanna none of his whip, believe me."

How did this happen? Kellen sat down hard.

Bryant sat next to him. "I know you don't want hear it, but we need to listen to Edmund."

"What he needs," said Marisa. "You cannot give him."

"Oh yeah?" Kellen asked. "Since you're such an expert on me, why don't you—"

"You need freedom from your demons," said Marisa. "To cast off the hate your father seeded in you. The abandonment your mother crippled you with."

"I'm not crippled, you stupid bit—"

"Yes, you are," said Marisa, her tone resigned with sadness. "Crippled and blind to what could have been yours if you had only learned to show a bit of the same kindness and mercy you longed for yet never received. I pray you see that before the end."

Kellen snorted. "You're right, Bryant. She's crazy."

Kellen closed his eyes. Rested his head against the bars. *This isn't happening. Can't be happening.*

"Lemme outta here. I got my rights and I want me a phone call!"

I know that voice. Kellen sat up, hearing the whir of the hydraulic system and cage rattle above him again.

Inside the cage, Kellen saw Boone Merchant. The spindly old man's thin hair was plastered against his forehead and his clothes sopped water. The Sea Lion that Bryant insistently referred to as his partner sat next to Boone.

"Lower away," the fisherman called out.

"Hey, Mister," Boone yelled. "Mister! Cain't you lemme outta here? Someone done confused me for a seal and put me in here with one."

"It's a Sea Lion, Gramps," said the fisherman as he guided the cage down beside Kellen's. "Ya can tell by the flippers and the ears."

"Seal, sea lion, I don't care. I's s'posed to be in the drunk tank in Lavere County Jail, sleeping off this hangover. The sheriff hisself said I could stay there!"

The fisherman unhooked the chains. "Tell ya what. I'll let ya out when the sheriff shows up."

Boone nodded. "All right, then. You call up Sheriff Dick Hullinger and tell him I's here and waitin' on him."

"Whateva ya say, old timer." The fisherman counted the cages. Nodded. Whistled to his partner. "Let's get some lunch."

Kellen watched the two men walk away. Once they were gone, he went to the edge of his cage. "*Boone!*"

The scarecrow of a man grinned at Kellen. "Well, hot dog. You's in my dream too!" Boone chewed his lip, looked at the Sea Lion nuzzling his hand with its nose. "Well, would you look at that? This ol' boy likes me!" Boone pet the Sea Lion's head. "Sure do wish I could wake up. 'Spect I'll still have this hangover though."

"*Boone!*"

"Yeah?"

Kellen sighed. "It's *not* a dr—"

"Yes it is," Bryant interrupted, joining him at the bars. "This is all a big dream, Boone."

What is he talking about?

"Well, who are you, mister?" Boone asked. "Ain't never seen you before."

"My name's David. I'm a…a magician."

Boone's eyes went round. "Your last name Copperfield?"

Oh, God.

"Yeah," Bryant lied. "And I need your help, Boone."

"Well, shoot. You tell me what to do, Mr. Copperfield. Always did wanna meet you!"

Bryant licked his lips. "Okay, I want you to take hold of that sea lion's upper lip—"

"You want me to put my hand in that there seal's mouth?"

"Yeah."

Boone shook his head. "No, sir. I ain't never been around no seals before. What's to keep this ol' boy from biting my hand clean off?"

"He won't." Bryant promised.

The Sea Lion nuzzled Boone's cheek to get his attention, then shook its head as if to say it had no intentions of biting him. Then it yawned its mouth open wide.

Boone's jaw went slack. "Well, ain't he a smart one?"

"Do it, Boone," said Kellen. "Do what he says."

Boone did so warily. He winced at first touching the animal's lip, but the Sea Lion waited patiently. "A-all right," said Boone. "Now what?"

"Grab hold of his lip and tug up, then peel it back over the sea lion's head…think of it like taking a baseball hat off someone's head."

"Do what?"

"There's a man inside, Boone." Bryant coached. "You'll see."

Boone scratched his head with his free hand. "Don't reckon I know how you got some feller to fit inside there. Guess that's why I ain't no magician, huh?"

"Boone!" said Kellen.

"All right then. I'ma doing it." Boone pulled up on the Sea Lion's lip, then carried the motion over its head. Both he and Kellen gasped as the Sea Lion head peeled away like removing a hood.

The other prisoners took notice, whispering in foreign languages. One woman screamed. The rest watched with the same awed expression Kellen did as the changes swept over the Sea Lion's body, changing from skin to fabric.

In seconds, the Sea Lion vanished, replaced by a grizzled older man in what resembled a tannish, one-piece sweatpant suit with a hood draped down his back. The old man looked at Boone, nodded. "Thanks, partner."

"Holy crow." Boone fainted.

The other marshal from the jail. Kellen thought.

"Ed," said Bryant, extending his left hand through the bars to shake the older man's.

"Bryant." Edmund shook.

"How did…" Kellen sputtered. "How did you know to do that?"

"Told you he's my partner," said Bryant. "We've been at this awhile."

"You can wear the Salt form easily enough, pup," said Edmund. "It's the getting back that's the trick. Need someone to release you. Make you human again."

Kellen looked at the other seals and sea lions in cages. *They're all human inside? Waiting on someone to release them?*

"Sorry to hear about your son, Ed," said Bryant.

Edmund looked at Kellen, then back to Bryant. "This pup tell you all about it?"

"Yeah. Said Oscar Collins did the shooting."

Edmund nodded. "I mean to repay him for that. His no-account father too. Who was it bagged you?"

"Dolan. Came in while I was interviewing the Orc. Shot me with some kinda tranq," said Bryant. "I figure—"

"Look," Kellen cut in. "I get that you two are friends and all, but how about we talk about escape."

"There's no getting out of here," Edmund said grimly. "Not yet anyway."

"Why not?"

"You have a key I don't know about?"

Kellen glared at him.

"I thought not. 'Sides, I'm not going anywhere until I get my hands on Collins—"

"Ed—"

"And strangle the life out of him," said Edmund, his eyes glazing. "My face will be the last thing he ever sees. Then, we'll talk about escape."

"That's great," said Kellen. "*Perfect!* Let's just sit here and accept this."

"That's right."

"Well, I don't. Okay? *I don't!*"

Edmund sat with his back to them.

Kellen punched the bars.

"Ed." Bryant knelt with a groan. "Talk to me. Is there nothing we can do?"

Edmund nodded. "Wait…"

"For what?" Kellen snarled. "Those fishermen to come back and beat us up some more?"

"Wait to be Salted."

GARRETT

THE YACHT ENGINE HAD LONG SINCE QUIETED
and Oscar fallen asleep on a couch before Garrett heard the *click*
of the door lock opening.

Fenton stood outside it, harpoon gun in hand. He trained its
aim on Garrett. "It's time." Fenton jerked the harpoon at Oscar.
"Wake him up. *Now.*"

Garrett obeyed.

Oscar groaned. "Wh-what is it now? Time for breakfast already?"
He rubbed sleep from his eyes and sat up straighter upon seeing he
and Garrett were not alone. "Fenton?"

"You're to come with me, young master," said Fenton. "Your
friend too."

Garrett nearly spoke out to remind Fenton that he and Oscar
weren't friends. A second look at the harpoon made him think
otherwise. He followed Oscar's lead out onto the deck.

The moon shone larger than back home and the yacht's gentle
shake gave Garrett the impression the stars moved.

A lighthouse loomed in the distance, its swirling light warding
off the dark and fog.

Garrett surveyed the upper deck. A few men in sopping, hooded wetsuits stood watch. Two more occupied the captain's quarters where Garrett last saw Paulo. Like in the warehouse, he recognized none of these hooded men would help him.

Fenton nudged him toward the starboard side where the railing gate hung open.

Garrett took a step closer and peered over the side.

An inflated rubber life raft bobbed in the choppy water next to the yacht. Inside it, Lenny Dolan glowered with his arms crossed.

"Get in," Fenton commanded.

Garrett glanced over his shoulder. "Are you nuts? I'm not—"

Fenton dug the tip of the harpoon into Garrett's shoulder. "Get… in."

"Come on, Weava," said Lenny. "It's gonna be all right. Do what he says. Prove ya know how to listen."

Garrett trembled. "N-no. I-I can't…I can't s-swim!"

"Fenton," said Oscar. "What's going on? Why are you doing this?"

"Your father wants to make sure he's safe."

"*Safe*?" Garrett's voice cracked. "What do you even mean? I won't hurt—"

"Of course he's safe," said Oscar. "I spent the last several hours alone with him. Don't you think if he wanted to kill me he'd have done it by now?"

A sharp kick in the back sent Garrett plummeting into the raft. He nearly spilled over the far side. A wave crashed into the raft, wetting Garrett's face, soaking him. He tasted salt in his mouth. Spat it out.

"Whattaya gotta do that for, Boss?" Lenny yelled. "Weava's not gonna hurt nobody. Didn't I say so?"

"Following orders, Dolan." Fenton tossed the casting line into the raft next to Garrett. "I suggest you do the same."

The gate clanged closed and the yacht motor roared as it pulled away from the raft.

"No!" Garrett spun to reach for it. "Please. Come back!"

Lenny pulled him back. "They're not gonna listen."

"Let go of me!"

Oscar waved. "It'll be all right, Garrett. I promise! I'll see you at home soon!"

"Oscar," Garrett cried. "Don't leave me here!"

The motors thrummed, kicked up a fountain of ocean water, and headed off.

Garrett continued yelling even as the yacht became a speck in the darkness.

"I know ya not askin' for advice or nothin'"—Lenny lay against the rubber siding, hands behind his head, feet crossed—"but ya might as well relax."

"*You...*" Garrett glared at him. "This is your fault. You did this!"

"For what it's worth," said Lenny, "I neva thought it'd go this way."

"Oh, you mean stuck in a...a...a life raft in the middle of the freaking ocean?"

Lenny nodded. "Looks that way, don't it."

"It *is* that way!" Garrett collapsed between the inflated seats. Up and down the small raft bobbed. Garrett's stomach lurched each time. "Why, Lenny? Why did you bring me here?"

"It's a hard thing to understand. Harder still to try and explain it."

"Try. Might as well since we're going to die out here."

"Nah," said Lenny, fingering his black hood. "We're not."

Garrett thought back to the Indy Zoo and the shark tank. How he had seen Lenny transform. "Y-you can change."

Lenny nodded. "It's like Boss Fenton said. They wanna make sure ya safe is all."

"I don't get it. Why would I want to hurt anyone? I just want to go home."

"That's the spirit. Ya gotta keep that in mind from here on out."

"Why should I listen to anything you say?" Garrett asked.

Lenny shrugged. "I'm the only one out here to talk ya through what comes next, pal."

Garrett glanced at the choppy water. "Wh-what do you mean?"

"Ya know what I mean." Lenny spat over the side. "Time to get wet, Weava."

A wave rocked the raft.

"Ah!" Garrett's hands shot to either side of the raft for balance.

"A little water's not gonna hurt ya." Lenny mocked. "Not by a long shot."

"Shut up!" said Garrett.

The bottom of the raft bulged upward, then moved opposite the waves.

Garrett's eyes widened. "Wh-what was that!"

Lenny scrambled to the starboard side. "Hey, hey, *hey!*"

The little man leaned so far over Garrett feared Lenny might fall overboard.

Lenny didn't. Instead, he smacked the water. "Enough already, Paulie!"

Paulie? Garrett wondered.

Lenny kicked his legs against the side to leverage himself back into the raft. Falling into his seat again, he brushed seawater from his brow. "Ya know, not for nothin', but why don't ya get in the water? Make this easier on us all."

Again, the raft moved from the unseen presence below.

This time, Garrett saw sparks of light—both from studs in Lenny's ears.

"Hey!" Lenny yelled at the water. "I said enough. Give him some time will ya?"

The little man's earrings sparkled again.

What are those? Garrett wondered.

"Look, Weava," said Lenny. "Ya goin' in no matta what. Might as well be ya choice."

Garrett shivered. "Are you nuts? That's the *ocean*, man! Did you not hear me back at the pier? I…can't…swim!"

"Yeaaah." Lenny looked Garrett up and down. "I don't think that's gonna be a problem."

Garrett spied something dark surface ten away from the boat. It growled and snorted, then disappeared beneath the waves again. "Wh-what the heck was that!"

Lenny scrambled for the side again. "Paulie! Stop scarin' the kid!"

"Wh-who are you talking to?" Garrett asked. "Th-there's no one out here. No one but us."

"Ya sure about that?"

Garrett hesitated, but glanced over the side at the choppy water.

Lenny's earrings flashed again as he donned his black hood. "Time's almost up. Ya gonna jump in or not?"

"No way I'm going in the water," said Garrett. "Not a chance."

Lenny frowned. "Ya really wanna know why Boss Fenton had us bring ya out here?"

"Us?" Garrett watched Lenny take something from his sweatshirt pocket that caught the moonlight.

Is that a knife? Garrett recoiled to the furthest reaches of the raft.

"'Cause there's only one way to get back," Lenny said. "Sink or swim time, Weava."

"I can't swim."

"Ya can…and ya will."

"I'm telling you—" Garrett's voice cracked. "I *can't* swim!"

"All right." Lenny plunged his dagger into the raft side.

"No!"

A sudden *hiss* of escaping air drowned out Garrett's cry.

Lenny stabbed at the raft again and again, widening the first hole and creating new ones even as water spilt over the side.

"Stop!" Garrett yelled, reaching for Lenny, not daring to cross the empty space of raft between them. Fear huddled him to his side where air pressure remained.

"See ya in the Salt, Weava!" Lenny pocketed the dagger. Then the little man began to change. The black hood melted over his face. The sweatshirt enveloped his arms.

Garrett's screams didn't stop Lenny's changes. Within seconds, a tiny seal with white circles across its black backside shared the raft with Garrett. The seal motioned its head toward the water.

"G-go away!" Garrett shouted.

Again, the seal looked toward the ocean.

"Leave me alone!"

The seal growled, then slipped out of the raft into the water.

Alone, with the ocean waves pounding the raft sides, Garrett immediately regretted his claim. "Lenny…" Garrett whispered. "Lenny, come back."

Please come back. Don't leave me alone.

Ocean water overtook Lenny's side of the raft and rushed toward him. Garrett tried to stand.

The move dipped his end of the raft, hurried the water and pooled it at his feet.

Garrett sat down again. "Is anyone out there? Please. Help me! *Help!*"

Again, something nudged the raft from underneath.

What is that thing? Garrett's imagination conjured up the shark-man at the Indianapolis Zoo. His scythe-like tail swaying back and forth and his jagged teeth patiently waiting to rend Garrett apart.

He glanced at the water, steadily overtaking his end of the raft, then leaned over the side as it reached his knees. Garrett thrashed at the ocean in a poor attempt at paddling.

A black seal head porpoised not ten feet away.

Is that…Lenny?

"Wh-what do you want me to do?" Garrett asked.

The seal lay on its side. Used its flipper to smack the water.

"No…"

The seal barked several times. Clacked it jaws.

"I can't!" Garrett cried.

The seal growled, then disappeared again.

Where did he—

The raft upended beneath Garrett, toppled him backward into the ocean.

No! Garrett opened his eyes. The salt stung them. He vaguely saw shadows encircle him, darting in and out of what little moonlight penetrated the watery surface.

Kick! Kick!

Garrett tried, but went nowhere. Blackness swirled in his mind as he spun to decipher up from down. He choked again, his lungs begging for air. His brain ordered him take a breath.

Salt water filled his mouth.

Garrett swallowed it down involuntarily.

A comforting itch started in his toes, worked its way up his shins.

Garrett swallowed another mouthful of salt water. Then another. And another.

The cold disappeared as the itch sped up to his waist.

A seal with white circles on its skin swam inches from Garrett's face. *Weava.* Lenny's voice echoed in Garrett's mind. *Why are ya still changin'? Why haven't ya stopped?*

Garrett's arms lazed to his sides. The tickle moved faster. Enveloped his fingertips.

Weava! Stop changin' already. Ya've gone far enough!

Garrett's mind screamed for air.

The itch invaded his head. Fiery warmth quaked through him. His tongue felt fatter, wider. Teeth elongated. His panic vanished, replaced by an eerie calm. Confident awareness. How had he not known which way was up or down before? Light or no light, the ocean held no such secrets now.

Then he heard.

The currents sang to Garrett. Told him east from west, north from south. The slightest change in temperature whispered how far he need go if desiring air. The pressure around him spoke to the depth at which he hung. More importantly, he knew not one, but two seals swam nearby.

Garrett opened his eyes and saw them.

One had a black hide with white circles adorning its back. Another loomed at least ten times the size of the Ringed Seal.

Garrett keyed on the smaller one—the one daring swim closest to him. His lower body moved instinctually, parting the water with ease.

Buckets a blood…Weava, w-whattaya doin'?

The fear in seal's voice sent a giddy rush through Garrett's being, waking a stronger, primal one deep within him.

Catch him, the primal voice whispered. *If you can…*

Garrett laughed at the small challenge. A shrill call emanated through the water. A second later, he had a clear mental picture in his mind's eye.

The bigger seal, a Southern Elephant, dove for deeper waters.

That's right. Swim away. Make this fun. Garrett chuckled. Again, a piercing sound echoed away and returned seconds later with a new picture—a boat headed for the shoreline with the lighthouse, a nautical mile away. He knew of other boats, further out, but there all the same.

How do I know that? Garrett heard his own voice, weak as Lenny's had been.

The motors, the stronger, primal voice returned. *Can't you hear them, moving in and out of the harbor?*

Garrett recognized the foreign stirrings did not belong in his watery world. This world belonged to him and his kind.

Hey, Weava! Can ya hear me in there? It's me, Lenny!

The primal mind pushed the voice away. It laughed another shrill call through the water, reverbed away, and returned with a new mental picture. It showed the smallest seal floated near the surface.

Watching him.

Waiting.

Alone.

A singular thought crossed the primal mind.

Food.

LENNY

BOSS, SAID PAULO. WE NEED TO GET OUT OF HERE!

Lenny tried to wish away the image of the eight-ton animal Garrett Weaver had become.

Boss...

Shuddup, Paulie. I got this.

No, you don't, said Paulo. *He's too far gone. Let's go!*

I'm not goin' anywhere. Lenny focused on the Killer Whale, its locked gaze, tail swishing up and down. He tried to recall the first time he had changed, the feeling of another mind inside his own, wrestling for control.

Weava! Can ya hear me in there? It's me, Lenny!

A shrill call pulsed through the waters around him.

Boss, did he just—

Echolocate, Lenny finished. *Yeah.*

The Ringed Seal's mind begged Lenny to swim away from one of the Salt's deadliest predators. He fought off the impulse.

He's gone, Len, said Paulo. *The Orc mind's taken over.*

No! I can get him back.

You're only a seal to him now, said Paulo. *What if he eats you?*

Lenny shuddered as he stared down the animal fifty times his size. He snorted, focused his mind on the human image of Garrett.

Listen to me, Weava. Ya gotta control ya Orc mind! Ya still ya'self in there. Don't forget—

Swim fast, little seal, said Garrett, his voice cold. Primal.

The Killer Whale shot forward, crossing the distance in seconds. Its mouth yawned wide.

Lenny dove.

The Killer Whale surged above him. Its wake tugged at Lenny's body. It took all his strength to fight for deeper water.

Lenny kicked harder. *Paulie. Little help here!*

What am I supposed to do?

We gotta hand him off, said Lenny. *Tire him out.*

Orcs are seawolves. Paulo mocked. *You don't just tire them out, Len!*

Lenny tilted his head, tipped his fore flippers downward, careened through the water with the Killer Whale close behind.

I'm on my way back up, boss.

Lenny tired. Knew the Killer Whale gained on him with each passing moment. *Ya neva gonna be big, son.* Lenny recalled another of his father's mantras. *So ya gotta be fasta or smarta if ya wanna survive.*

Lenny angled his nose up and rocketed toward the surface. He shot out of the water in an arcing leap with the Killer Whale right behind. Lenny tucked his head the moment he reentered, somersaulting his body.

The Killer Whale's speed carried it over him, missed.

Move, Len! Move! He reminded his flippers as the Killer Whale circled wide.

The waters pulsed with echolocation. A second later, Lenny heard chuckling in his mind. He spun and saw the giant swimming straight at him. Lenny's seal instincts urged him dive.

Patience...He recalled his father's first rule.

The Killer Whale never slowed.

Now!

Lenny dove. His hind flippers brushed the Killer Whale's jaw as the predator again shot overtop him. Again, the Killer Whale's wake tugged at him. Lenny fought to swim free of it.

The Killer Whale shrieked at the near miss, the noise pulsing through Lenny's mind.

His seal body slowed, its motor skills dulled by the echolocation. *Wake up, Weava!*

I see you! Garrett's primal voice taunted Lenny, hidden in the dark waters but growing louder.

Control its mind, Weava. Lenny thought as his fate sliced through the water, bound directly for him. *Control it!*

The Killer Whale opened its mouth.

The ascending Southern Elephant Seal closed it, like a boxer connecting with an uppercut. *Wake up, Weaver!* Paulo shouted. *Boss...*

Lenny's senses returned. He swam at the Killer Whale, even as it shook off the blow and shifted focus to Paulo. *I'm comin', Paulie.* He dodged the Killer Whale's tail and made for the dorsal fin, nearly as tall as Lenny's human form.

Weava, Lenny called out to Garrett's mind as he struggled to reach the Killer Whale's grey saddle patch. *Just...a bit...furtha...* Lenny latched claws sharp enough to hack through glacier ice into the Killer Whale's dorsal fin.

The beast screeched in pain. It bucked and spun in an attempt to shake off the pest on its back.

Ya name's Garrett Weava! Lenny dug his seal nails in tighter. *Now...wake...up!*

Lenny bit into the dorsal fin.

GARRETT

AHH! GARRETT SCREAMED.

He tried in vain to swat at the thing biting his back. More annoying than painful, it refused to go away. *Why can't I reach it?* Garrett next attempted craning his neck to see what the thing was. That attempt failed too. *Ugh, why does it feel like I'm wearing a neck brace?*

Weava, ya alive in there?

I know that voice. Garrett's mind swam with faces. Memories. *Lenny? The dwarf...the seal!*

Garrett opened his mouth to speak.

Salt water filled it.

Choking, Garrett spat it out.

Easy, Weava, said Lenny. *Calm down before I lose ya again. Listen to my voice and just...picture me in ya head. What I look like.*

Garrett imagined the little man sitting in the raft with him—Lenny's mop of brown, curly hair, his black hood with white circles on it, and the way he transformed into a seal. *Why am I doing this?* Garrett thought.

That's it. Lenny spoke in Garrett's mind. *Just like that!*

Wha-how did I...you can hear me?

Betta than that. I can see ya.

The pain in Garrett's back ebbed. A moment later, a Ringed Seal swam inches in front of his face, its doe-like eyes inquisitive, head cocked.

Whoa! Garrett thought. *This is so cool! Am I dreaming again?*

The Ringed Seal shook its head. *Nah. If ya were, that girlfriend a yours woulda been here instead of me.*

The seal gave a flick of its foreflippers, swooshed away and performed a pair of backflips.

No way, said Garrett. *This can't be real. You can't be a person and a seal.*

The seal swam closer. *This from the guy who said he couldn't swim.*

Garrett's throat clenched. He gagged on more salt water.

Weava, said Lenny. *Ya all right in there?*

A-air. Garrett's mind spun. *N-need a-air.*

He swam for the surface.

That's not the way, the primal voice whispered.

Garrett continued swimming.

The water's turned colder, the voice continued. *Feel the pressure increasing?*

Garrett slowed at the realization. Though slight, he felt the changes the voice spoke of. *Doesn't matter.* He continued swimming in the same direction.

Weava! Lenny called. *Where ya goin'?*

I-I n-need to b-breathe.

Then ya might wanna surface. Lenny snorted. *I hear there's air up there. Do ya'self a favor and follow Paulie.*

The largest seal Garrett had ever seen ascended from the blackish depths like a giant grey balloon. *Hey, Weaver.* Paulo's deep voice echoed in Garrett's mind. *Up is this way.*

Garrett thrashed at the water to follow the seal.

Lenny's laughter filled his head. *Weava, let ya big animal brain do the swimmin'. It knows where to go.*

But I—

He's right, the primal voice said, stronger now. *Let me.*

Garrett relaxed as the confidence again washed over him.

The current song returned. Unlike before, however, Garrett experienced the newness like an equal, his mind twinning with the primal one. He suddenly knew the ceiling between water and sky existed ten feet in the opposite direction. *I've been descending the whole time…*

Mmm-hmm, the primal mind calmly agreed. *And we don't need air yet either, but if you insist.*

Garrett angled his nose upward, felt his lower body glide into position. Then he kicked.

Whoooaaaa! Garrett screamed as he zoomed past both seals and shattered the watery ceiling. He noted the sudden dryness, the foreign atmosphere, and worse, gravity. He twisted to the side and flopped hard back into the ocean, splaying small waves in opposite directions with his massive weight.

He laughed and released the shrill call of echolocation again. A second later, a mental picture revealed both seals swimming toward him.

Ya still ya'self in there, Weava?

Garrett pictured the dwarf in his mind. *Lenny!*

Hey, whattaya know, he still remembas my name, said Lenny. *Guess we're all right, Paulie.*

Garrett lifted his head above the surface, took a deep breath of air. *Lenny, how is this possible?*

Well, it's like this. When a Mommy Orc and a Daddy Orc—

Wait. What's an Orc? Garrett asked.

The Ringed Seal turned its head toward the Elephant Seal. *Ya believe this kid, Paulie? And here we been told Orcs were smart all these years.*

It's not his fault, Len, said Paulo. *Listen, Weaver, you're a—*

The Ringed Seal swam forward and slapped its larger cousin. Both opened and closed their mouths, almost like talking to one another, yet their voices didn't fill Garrett's head anymore.

What's going on? He asked them.

The Ringed Seal, Lenny, swam closer to him. *Rememba what I told ya up top about needin' to make sure ya safe?*

Yeah, said Garrett.

Right, well, we gotta do that first. Then I'll tell ya what an Orc is.

But Len, I told you I would never hurt—

You wouldn't, but the uh—thing—ya are right now would if ya lost control again. So listen up. Close ya eyes and tell us what ya look like.

Why?

Just do it.

Garrett closed his eyes. *This is so stupid.*

Now tell us. Lenny coached. *Whattaya look like?*

Garrett pictured himself in front of a mirror. *I have dark hair... brown eyes...I guess I'm taller than a lot of my classmates.*

Uh huh, keep goin'. What about ya skin?

Garrett tensed. *What about it?*

Tell us what it looks like.

I-I have a disorder...v-vitiligo, said Garrett, imagining his varied skin tones. The splotchy paleness covering his ears, nose, and forehead, almost like his tan had been seared away by fire.

Garrett opened his eyes and found both seals watching him. *Why am I telling you this? You know what I look like.*

The Elephant Seal turned its head toward its smaller companion. *It's not working, Len.*

Ya think I don't see that? The Ringed Seal clacked its jaws.

What's not working? Garrett asked.

Don't listen to him, said Lenny. *Picture ya'self with legs, Weava.*

I already did that, Len—

Do it again!

Why? Garrett asked. *Why do I have to do any of this?*

Rememba those guys on the boat?

Len, said Paulo. *Don't.*

No, no, said Lenny. *He wants to know, well, here it is. If that son of a sea cook, Fenton, comes back, sees ya like this, and ya don't look safe, he'll kill ya, all right?*

Garrett shuddered. *Wh-what?*

That got ya attention, huh? Good. 'Cause he'll kill me, Paulie, and my pop too.

B-but why? Why would he kill—

'Cause the Salt's a hard ol' world, Weava. Best get used to it, said Lenny. *Now, ya wanna know what's happenin' to ya? I'm tryin' to help! So...just...listen, would ya?*

O-okay. What do I do?

Picture ya'self with legs.

Garrett obeyed. He imagined his thin, practically hairless, chicken-like legs and the light-skinned patches that streaked down them.

Nothing, boss, said Paulo.

Think harda, Weava! Focus on the itch.

Garrett closed his eyes tighter, focused so hard on his legs that his head shook. Exhausted, he raised his face above the water and exhaled. *Did it work?*

The Ringed Seal surfaced nearby and swam over to him. *Nah. Gotta try something else.*

What about running? Paulo asked. *That might help.*

Might help? Garrett asked.

Well, I don't know, said Paulo. *I'm not an Orcinian.*

I don't even know what an Orcinian is!

All right, calm down, said Lenny. *It's our first time tryin' to talk somebody through changin' too, ya know.*

But I saw you change earlier, said Garrett. *In the boat! You went from human to seal—*

Ya not a Selkie, said Lenny. *It's different. We gotta have our coats. Ya can change by thinkin' about it. You're a Salt Child. Ya belong here.*

And you guys don't?

Nah, said Lenny. *We're kinda like…permanent guests.*

Garrett puzzled over Lenny's meaning. He didn't like the sound of it, but Paulo seemed to think Lenny's connotation hilarious.

What about ya girlfriend? Lenny asked. *What was her name again?*

Sydney, Garrett replied. He imagined her worrying when she hadn't heard back from the thousand texts she'd undoubtedly sent him.

Yeah, Sydney, said Lenny. *Picture those nice, sweet legs she's got on her.*

Garrett found thinking of Sydney's legs far easier than imagining his own. He thought back to tennis matches—her white skirt, pasty white legs. The way she attacked the net when she sensed her opponent's weakness.

Garrett's toes went numb. The itch returned, working up his shins.

That's it, Weava! Lenny said. *Keep it up.*

The image of Sydney vanished.

No, no, no. Garrett fought to retain the idea of Sydney as the itch receded to his toes. *Why is this so hard?* He thought to himself. *How many times have you daydreamed about her legs, Weaver? Now you can't even picture her face? Get it together, dude!*

Weava, said Lenny. *Whateva ya thinkin' on, it's not workin'. Come up with something else.*

I'm trying, Lenny!

Think about sports, Paulo suggested. *Athletes. Football. Baseball.*

Garrett's mind drifted from Sydney to sitting alongside his mom at an Indy baseball diamond when he was ten. The sun crisping his skin and how careful he had been not to let the back of his legs touch the scalding metal bleachers. He remembered complaining of the heat. His mom promised ice cream once the game ended. Then the crowd cheered as the newest batter walked to the plate. Watching the bat slice the air with several practice swings, young Garrett forgot all his earlier wants.

The itch continued up his shins. Still, it did not distract Garrett from the memory—one he had relived time and again these past few years.

He remembered the pitcher being afraid of the batter. That he threw the ball wide and outside each time. *Ball one.* Garrett recalled the referee's loud voice over the crowd's collective sigh. *Ball two... Ball three...*

The itch reached his waist, continued up his stomach. His head dipped beneath the water. A large seal appeared beneath him to steady his suddenly shaky legs. *The seal...Paulo...*

The fourth pitch went high and outside. The batter swung anyway. Garrett remembered the ball chirping off the bat's end and soaring toward the outfield. The left fielder waving his glove in frustration as the ball cleared the fence with no chance of being caught. Garrett recalled standing with the rest of the crowd, the need to climb the top of the bleachers to see the batter round the bases. All of it to the tune of the crowd's cheer...

Keep goin', Weava.

Garrett reached to scratch his neck. His human nails dug at human skin, cold to the touch, yet warmth spread through him. *What is happening to me?* He wondered as the itch continued up his scalp.

Unlike other batters who made extravagant shows of crossing home plate, Garrett remembered the red-haired giant took the step in stride. His teammates clapped him on the back, yet he passed through them with the smallest of grins, his gaze set on the boy in the bleachers. Garrett recalled jumping off, caught in the strongest pair of arms he ever knew. *Will I ever be as fast as you, Dad?*

The comforting itch washed over the top of Garrett's head, then vanished.

When those little chicken legs of yours grow a bit, his father had answered. *You'll be faster than I ever was.*

Garrett opened his eyes and found the Ringed Seal staring back.

Ya did it, said Lenny.

CHIDI

THE SALT SCENT GREW STRONGER WITH EACH passing mile.

Chidi shifted uneasily. Her back was sore from limited movement, her wrists and ankles numb from the constricting zip ties. Still, she took comfort in the fact she laid upon cushioned seats, worn and unforgiving as they were, rather than being bound in the truck bed like the others Henry enslaved.

She had dozed on and off throughout most of the journey. Even now, the truck engine's thrum suggested she return to sleep. Chidi wouldn't. Whether triggered by Racer's sacrifice, or Henry's words she belonged to him, a carousel of nightmares haunted her each time she nodded off.

Chidi remembered her father would soothe her when she awoke from such night terrors as a little girl. He had told her the bad things in her dreams could not harm her. Such words rang false now, as did his claims he would never allow any evil to befall her.

He didn't know what would happen, she reminded herself.

Chidi craned her neck to see out the truck cab windows. Skyscrapers, a few interstate signs, but no indicator of which coastal state Henry drove in.

Henry angled the rearview. "We weel be there soon, *mon amour.*"

She turned her gaze away from him as the truck slowed to a crawl. Stacked container cars loomed outside the window alongside motionless cranes. She assumed they were near a dock, confirmed a moment later by the sounds of gulls.

Henry drove beneath a faded crimson sign with the words *Crayfish Collins Co. est. 1883.* He stopped the truck near a barbed wire gate and rolled the window down.

A long-faced man approached the window. He glanced at Chidi, then Henry. "Right. How much for the girl?"

"Do you know who I am?" Henry asked.

"Nah," said the fisherman. "Don't guess I do. But if ya here, that means ya lookin' to do business."

"I am," said Henry. "But not weeth you."

The fisherman chuckled. "Look, pal, I dunno—"

Chidi heard a scuffle, a gasp, then a thud.

The overhead cab light flickered on.

An alarm dinged as Henry exited the truck and left the door open.

Chidi shifted to look outside. A man dressed in orange waders and a black hoodie lay sprawled across the pavement, unconscious. She watched Henry approach a barbed wire fence that read Private Property: No Trespassing. He unlatched the roller gate and pushed it open.

A rundown warehouse lay ahead. Near the top, a Crayfish emblem bathed in the milky glow of a security light. *The Crayfish... we're going back?*

Chidi lay down upon seeing Henry turn from the gate. He climbed inside the truck with nary a word, put the vehicle in gear, and cruised ahead. Chidi tried telling herself Henry would only revisit Crayfish Cavern to collect the second half of his payment for protecting Oscar. Her heart knew it for a lie. *Lenny…*

The brakes squealed to a halt moments later. Henry laid on the horn until someone tapped his window.

"Hey! What's up with the noise, buddy?" the man asked. "Ya tryin' to draw attention on us or something? Who are ya?"

"Henry Boucher. I bring gifts for the Crayfeesh." Henry nodded in Chidi's direction.

The fisherman poked his head inside and grinned down on her. "Why, she's a pretty one isn't she?" The man disappeared. "Ya said ya name was Boucher?"

"*Oui.*"

"Boucher…Boucher…"

Chidi listened to papers ruffling.

"Yeah," said the fisherman. "Ya not on my list, pal. Can't let ya through. Dockmaster's orders."

"I see," said Henry. "Tell *Monsieur* Tieran I have a message for 'im."

"Ya know, Tieran, huh?" The fisherman chuckled. "Ya look the type he does business with. Still can't let ya through. Why don'tcha gimme ya message and—hey, how did ya get past our man back at the gate anyway?"

"Ze same way I weel pass you if you don't do as I say. Now, fetch your master, seadog."

Do what he says. Chidi wished to tell the fisherman. *Please.*

"No need to get nasty, pal," said the fisherman after a lengthy delay. "Just doin' my job."

"Tieran," said Henry. "*Now.*"

The fisherman sighed. "All right. Gimme a sec."

Chidi listened to Henry mutter in French as they waited. Five minutes later, a knock came at the window. A weasel-faced man stood outside it. Chidi smelled the booze on him even from the back seat.

"Well, well, well," the man slurred. "If it's not me ol' pal. All righ', Henry?"

"*Oui.*"

"Righ', tell me then, what can I do you for? Gotta shove off soon to keep on schedule. It's a special haul I got, or so said the lil' Crayfish. I expect his father'll be wantin' to see 'em soon." Tieran belched. "So come on. Out with it. What've you got for ol' Tieran, eh?"

"Two pups. A fat man. A few coats," said Henry.

"Righ', but that's all for the Crayfish." Tieran leaned against the truck to keep from falling over. "I got a full boat inside, and I'm not in the business of handing out favors. So...I ask you again, mate. What's in it for ol' Tieran?"

"I weel give you the truck."

"This ol' beater?" Tieran laughed. "What am I to do with it? Drive it off the pier and hope it sprouts flippers? Nah...you want a ride to Crayfish Cavern with us to sell slaves, I needs one of 'em for meself. That's a bargain, it is."

Henry shrugged. "You can 'ave the fat man."

"Nah," said Tieran. "I want one of the pups. The Crayfish has a sale on soon. Plans to put on games for his guests. Might be I could use a pup in the pits."

"Take my offer." Henry insisted.

Chidi listened to Tieran hiccup.

"One slave's better than none, eh?" Tieran sighed. "Drive me truck inside and park it on the pier. We'll have your haul unloaded and be off." Tieran left the window. "All righ'! Open it up, lads!"

A metal door in desperate need of oiling screeched open. The truck shuddered beneath Chidi as it pulled ahead toward the light. The wheels left smooth pavement for the *rat-a-tat-tat-tat* as they transitioned onto the pier's wooden planks.

Henry killed the truck engine. A minute later, he helped Chidi exit the driver's side door.

Chidi leaned against the truck bed to stretch her legs, then surveyed her surroundings.

The warehouse was cleaner and more organized than most others she'd seen in her time with Henry. A trawler bobbed gently alongside the pier. Cages littered the deck. Most of those inside had hollow eyes. They took one look at her bonds then resigned themselves back to listless stares.

A few still kept a flicker of life. One of them, an athletic teenager with a shaved head, stood in his cage, hands on the bars, eyes watchful of everything happening on the pier. She didn't recognize the teen, but gasped when his cellmates stood. *The Silkstealer and Marisa Bourgeois...together? How did they end up here?*

"All righ'," said Tieran. "Get this haul unloaded and shove off! We got a schedule to keep!"

Chidi vaguely heard the tailgate clang open as Henry let it fall. Instead, she found herself drawn to Marisa.

The elusive slave grinned at Chidi.

"Please!" one of Henry's captive teens yelled behind Chidi. "I'm not supposed to be here—"

"This guy kidnapped us!" said the other.

"Quiet, you lot!" Tieran yelled back, flogging the teens with the butt of his whip.

With the teens unloaded, Henry removed the Selkie suits he'd skinned from the back of the truck and tucked them under his arm. He took Chidi firmly by the bicep and led her toward the boat. She followed his lead without quarrel, noticing Marisa's sad gaze followed her.

Henry leapt across the divide and onto the boat, then reached for Chidi.

She managed the jump without help.

"So strong..." Henry took her by the arm and led her near a series of cages, drawing close to Marisa's. *But if Marisa is here,* Chidi thought to herself. *That means Lenny and the others have already come back! They'll be down in the Cavern waiting for us.*

"Henry!" Tieran shouted. "Give us a hand, will you?"

Chidi watched the fisherman struggle with the gas station attendant. The man had somehow stolen away a fishing spear from one of the guards and swung it wildly back and forth whenever anyone came near.

"Don't move," Henry commanded Chidi before leaving.

"Hello again, Chidi..."

Chidi turned and found Marisa Bourgeois grinning at her.

"My heart is happy to see you again."

"H-how did they catch you?" Chidi asked.

Marisa shrugged playfully. She stepped closer to the bars of her cage, eyes twinkling. "Why did you let me escape at the zoo?"

"I—"

"Bryce..." said the Silkstealer's teen cellmate. "Marrero, hey. Bryce, over here!"

Chidi glanced over her shoulder and saw Henry's teen captives. *They know each other?* Chidi frowned as taskmasters dragged the teens she'd coached into the truck bed down the pier, both captives fighting and yelling all the way.

"Quiet!" One of the fishermen struck them upside the heads before shepherding them one after the other onto the boat and into a nearby cage.

*Three teens who all know one another...*Chidi processed. *What are the odds?*

A pain in her gut warned she had missed something. She didn't have long to contemplate.

The platoon of fisherman had overtaken the attendant. Tieran held the man's face to the ground with the heel of his boot while his lackeys kicked the attendant into submission.

Chidi glanced away as Henry strode up the dock, scowling. He leapt onto the boat and, without a word, jerked her further up the deck and into the captain's quarters that reeked of day old coffee and cigarettes. A radio crackled with Coast Guard updates and weather advisories.

"Chidi?"

Chidi twisted around. *Ellie?*

The heavyset girl sat on a leather couch behind the captain's chair, her hands bound around a silver mast pole running from floor to ceiling. She shook strands of loose hair from her eyes. For a moment, Chidi thought her friend genuinely happy to see her. Her shoulders sagged a second later when Henry took the Selkie suits from under his arm and placed them on the table in front of her.

"Where eez Dolan?" Henry asked.

"Not here." Ellie eyed the bloodstained suits. "G-gone home to

Crayfish Cavern with Oscar and the Orc. Tieran kept me behind to help with the new haul."

"Then what are you doing in 'ere?" Henry asked.

Chidi knew the answer, even as she eyed the bruises on Ellie's cheeks and neck. She recognized them for the same bruises she oft bore after fending Henry away. Chidi guessed Ellie more successful in her bout, however. Not for the first time, Chidi wished she had the larger frame and strength Ellie carried.

The cabin door slid open before Ellie answered.

Tieran strolled in. Behind him came a tall, broad-shouldered man dressed in a threadbare trench coat. His greenish-gold eyes found Chidi and he grinned easily, revealing pointed teeth that glinted razor sharp. "Hello there," he purred as his gaze worked up and down Chidi's bodice.

Henry stepped in front of her.

Tieran cleared his throat. "Righ', Henry, this is, uh—"

"Ishmael." The guest gave a curt nod. "Call me Ishmael."

Ishmael opened his coat. Scars and tattooed numerals lined his bare, muscular chest and abs. What resembled grey tights began at his waist, covered his parts and ran down his legs, ending at his ankles.

He's a Salt Child. Chidi thought.

"Like what you see?" Ishmael chuckled at her staring. "Wouldn't be the first to say so. Nor will you be the last, girl. Want to know what these marks mean? Come over and I'll whisper it in your ear."

Chidi didn't budge.

Tieran sniggered. "Met Ish in the pub tonight, I did. Said the Crayfish invited 'em to the auction soon to come. Thought he'd get a first peek at the new crop by buyin' me drinks." Tieran slurred.

"Smart one, that. He saw you lot come in and fancies your lil' darkie."

"Indeed," said Ishmael to Henry. "How much you will have for her?"

"She eez not for sale."

Ishmael smirked. "You really don't know who I am, do you?"

"I don't care," said Henry. "She eez mine."

A lump formed in Chidi's stomach as the two haggled over her with no regard that she stood in their midst.

"For now," said Ishmael.

"For always." Henry drew a dagger from his Selkie pocket.

Ishmael laughed. "Is this one for sale, Tieran?" He jerked his thumb toward Henry.

"'Fraid not. Henry's a freed Selkie, he is. Owner too."

"Shame," said Ishmael. "Not met many Selkies with his boldness. I like that in a slave."

He's a madman, thought Chidi. *They all are.*

"Wait till the auction, sir," said Tieran. "Might have a fighter or two in this new lot for you. Let you know which after I test 'em."

"Aye. See that you do." Ishmael turned to leave.

"No need to run off, sir," said Tieran. "You can ride up here with the captain."

"Kind of you," said Ishmael. "But I know when I'm not welcome."

Chidi glanced at Henry, his gaze locked on Ishmael, blade ready to strike.

Ishmael looked on Chidi a final time. "I'll see you again, lovely."

She shivered as he stepped out the door and slid it closed.

"He makes me nervous, that one." Tieran collapsed into the captain's chair. "It's the Nomad blood in 'em. Savages, all, the lot of 'em."

"Why do you do business with zem?" Henry asked.

"About the only ones you can sell to nowadays. Word on the currents is the powers what be in the capital plans on outlawing slavery soon."

Henry snorted. "And soon Selkies weel rule the world."

Tieran laughed. "Aye. That'll be the day, mate. Guess I don't buy into all that bollocks we hear outta the capital anyway. Them rich Blowholes still need girls for their beds and boys to fight in the pits. Sometimes t'other way around, eh?" Tieran chuckled. "Been that way since the dawn of time, I guess. Don't see it changin' much."

Tieran stood. Stretched. "Righ'. Best get back to work. See me down in the cavern and I'll buy them skins off you. Gotta check with the Crayfish first and find what he's willing to pay."

Need. Chidi hated the word as Tieran left the cabin, whistling. *Need girls for their beds.* Anger coursed through her, yet she found herself powerless to give it an outlet even as she stared down the man who oft spoke of his need for her.

I have a need too, she thought, watching Henry. *And one day, I'll show you how bad I need to see it through.*

Henry remained ignorant of her loathing. He placed his dagger on the table as he stepped around the table. "Ellie." Henry bent to kiss her cheeks. "So good to see you again. Allow me to show you ze geefts I bring for your master." Henry reached for the Selkie suits and unfolded them across the table, one by one. "Zis one I took from a Leper—"

Wotjek, Chidi thought. *His name was Wotjek.*

"And zese two from Lions. One at ze jail, and zis one"—Henry tapped the smaller tannish coat—"I skinned from your friend, Racer, right after I keeled 'im."

"N-no," Ellie squeaked.

"*Oui*." Henry sat next to Ellie and placed his arm around her broad shoulders.

No. Chidi thought, her feet rooted to the floor.

Henry took a strand of Ellie's hair, wrapped it around his fingers. "I know what you did to 'elp my Chidi," he said lowly.

Ellie's face pained.

"I know zat ze nipperkin planned eet." Henry twirled Ellie's hair tighter, tugging her ear closer to his mouth. "Would you like to learn what else I know?"

"G-go to hell." Ellie said.

"In time, perhaps, but not yet."

Ellie quivered, the metallic jingle of her cuffs reverbing up the pole. Her wrists pulled at the tiny chain links, begging for release, as Henry secured his grip on her further.

"I know zat you weel do all I ask. Zat you weel tell your master eet was Dolan who set Racer and my Chidi free. Won't you, Ellie?"

Say yes. Chidi willed her crewmate. *Please. Say yes.*

"I-I will," said Ellie.

"Good," said Henry. "Because if you lie to me, Ellie—" Henry picked his dagger off the table and placed its tip at Ellie's throat "—I add your suit to my collection."

GARRETT

GARRETT CLUNG TO PAULO'S SEAL NECK, THE STINK of wet fur entrenched in his nostrils, as waves crashed over them.

Two feet away, the Ringed Seal popped its head above water.

"I did what you asked," Garrett yelled over the waves. "Now tell me why!"

Had to see ya control the changes, said Lenny. *Needed to know it before takin' ya to Crayfish Cavern. Ya done good, Weava. Real good.*

"So now what happens?"

Ya change back into an Orcinian. Then we go!

"I don't know what an Orcinian is!"

Yes, you do. The primal voice returned, called out his lie. *You've always known. Now, you believe.*

"T-tell me." Garrett begged of Lenny. "Tell me what I am."

An Orca, said Lenny. *You're a Killa Whale.*

Yesss. Garrett closed his eyes and slipped off Paulo's back. *That's what I am.*

He allowed himself to sink, no longer fearing his inability to swim. No longer afraid to drown. He pictured the painting on Oscar's boat - the mammoth size, the raw power, the overwhelming awe of sighting such a majestic beast.

The itch returned in his toes.

No. Garrett willed his eyes open. *I want to see it.*

He found himself naked, his clothes rent to shreds from the last transformation. The changes had already begun, his feet black and flipper-like. They conjoined at the ankles and he felt a drag akin to nails drifting up his shins. Goose pimples rose in its wake like a trail for the blackish hue to follow. It overtook his shins, knees, and thighs. All expanded, like an airless balloon hung from the end of a tap and filled with water.

Garrett nearly cried. *This is so cool!*

A sprint of white emerged near his groin and raced up his stomach and chest, even as the black weaved in and out about his ribs to form an hourglass pattern around it.

Garrett watched his biceps flatten. The changes continued down his forearms and his fingertips melded together, rounding into giant black paddles.

The itch worked up his neck, enveloped his head and face. He imagined the splotches of white around his ears expanding into what he previously thought of as a Killer Whale's eyes. Garrett pictured the white streak up his chest, continuing to his throat and encasing his lower jaw. He felt his teeth round, mouth widening. The ocean spoke to him again.

And now we are truly one, the primal voice whispered ere vanishing to the recesses of his mind. Garrett grinned inwardly. *Lenny. I'm a Killer Whale!*

An Orcinian. Lenny ventured closer.

Garrett's mind raced with the new senses. He laughed and listened to the shrill call echo away. It returned a moment later with mental pictures of the waters around him. Garrett kicked his tail, spun, then dove. He laughed frequently, receiving new x-ray-like images each time.

Wow! Garrett said. *I feel like I can hear and see everything.*

That's great, Weava, said Lenny. *Glad ya happy.*

Happy? I'm stoked, dude! Garrett cut through the waters. His Orca mind sensed fear in both seals as he zoomed past. The thought elated him. He laughed again and performed a slow, wide angle before returning to Lenny. *This is so sweet. Lenny, what else can I do?*

Huh?

I can change into a freakin' Killer Whale, man! What other powers do I have?

I dunno. Ya gettin' on my nerves though, said Lenny. *Count that as one.*

Nah, said Paulo. *Everybody has that power.*

Shuddup, Paulie, said Lenny. *All right. He seems safe enough. Let's head home.*

I don't want to go home now. Garrett swam away, diving and rising. He fired off more echolocation blasts. The returning image showed Lenny and Paulo swam northeastward toward a rocky island. Garrett gave chase again.

Whoa. Stop doin' that, will ya? Lenny barked.

What?

Oh, I dunno. What would ya do if ya was a seal and a Killa Whale swam right at ya?

Right, sorry. Garrett tried to quell his excitement, even as a thousand questions raced through his mind. *Lenny, how long can I hold my breath?*

The Ringed Seal ascended. *I look like an Orcinian to ya?*

No.

Then how would I know?

Forget Lenny, Paulo said to Garrett. *He's always mad his suit's limiting.*

How do you mean?

He's made for cold weather and ice living. Len's claws are sharper than mine, but he's not built for power. Plus, he can only hold his breath about five minutes. Me? I can dive for two hours.

Whoa! Garrett said. *That's crazy.*

Eh, it's what my suit's made for, said Paulo. *I'm a brute—deep diver and security, mostly. I got nothing on you though.*

So how strong am I?

Strong. Paulo laughed. *I got to know some of your kind when I lived in the capital. They were mostly good to me. That's Rezzies for you though. The ones like you, the Trannies—*

Wait. Garrett slowed. *What'd you call me? I thought you guys said I was an Orcinian.*

You are, said Paulo. *There's different types. Rezzies are the nice ones. They mostly eat fish, maybe some squid here and there. Trannies though.* Paulo whistled. *They're the ones Selkies like me and Len have to watch out for.*

But—

Buckets a blood, said Lenny. *Enough with the questions already. Ya gonna have to wise up to make it down here, Weava. Ya want some advice? Here's a tip. Selkies and Orcs? They don't mix. Not eva.*

Why not? Garrett asked.

Ya spend much time with cows and chickens back home?

No, why would I—Garrett stopped at the realization of what Lenny alluded to. *You're saying my kind...eats...Selkies?*

It's what I hear.

Garrett gagged. *How could they? It's not only murder, it's…it's—*

Survival of the fittest, said Lenny.

Just be glad you're an Orc, said Paulo. *You're kind of at the top of the food chain. Nobody wants to mess with your kind.*

Yeah, look at ya! Lenny barked. *Ya the size of a friggin' bus. Who's gonna get in the way of that body ya got?*

Not to mention Orcs always travel together in pods, said Paulo.

Then why am I alone? Garrett wondered.

Oh, and hey, don't listen to everything Len says, said Paulo. *That whole bit about Orcs eating Selkies? It's not true.*

It is so, said Lenny.

It's not, said Paulo. *The Rezzies I knew in the capital were in the Painted Guard. They beat a few Selkies up from time to time, but they never ate them.*

Sure. Not that ya saw, said Lenny. *They do it, Weava. Mark my words.*

Paulo shook his bulbous seal head. *Don't listen to him, Garrett.*

Paulie, all I'm sayin' is how do ya know they didn't eat 'em when ya weren't lookin'?

For the same reason you'd stop if a fish you snagged spoke, said Paulo. *Real seals…they don't talk. If it's a Selkie inside though, you can bet they'd beg for their lives the second they noticed an Orc on their tail. Ancients know I would.*

What if the seal isn't paying attention? Garrett asked.

Bam! Lenny somersaulted and slapped Garrett's side with a fore flipper. *Ya just another Saturday Selkie special. My pop said he saw a runna get laid out once by an Orc pod. Sent the Selkie flyin' in the air and popped his insides out. Killed that runna on the spot.*

So that's why you guys were worried about me. Garrett shivered. *Man, I can't believe you even got in the water with me after hearing that story.*

It's not like we had a choice. Paulo chuckled. *But now you know why I swam for deeper waters when you did your little changeover for the first time back there.*

Garrett relived the moment the Orca mind took over. How it viewed chasing the Ringed Seal—*Lenny,* Garrett reminded himself—as a game. He shuddered at the thought of what might've happened had he not come to his senses. *This is insane.*

That's the Salt, said Paulo. *And it's why Fenton told us to make sure you were safe before bringing you home to Crayfish Cavern.*

Garrett surfaced for a quick breath and spied the lighthouse near. *Is that where we're going? The lighthouse is your home?*

Sort of, said Paulo. *You'll see it soon. We're almost there.*

Paulo, how did you know I was a…um…a—

A Trannie?

Garrett laughed.

What's so funny?

That word means something waaay different on land. Garrett chuckled. *How do you know the difference between a Rezzie and a—*Garrett sniggered—*a Trannie?*

For starters, Rezzies aren't usually chasing me. Not that you have to worry about that sort of thing. Paulo sighed. *An easy way to tell is your dorsal fin. Trannies have pointed ones, kind of like Nomads. Rezzie fins are rounded over. That's about all I know of Orcs though. Like Lenny said, our kinds don't mix much.*

We're here, said Lenny. *Take a breath before we dive, Weava.*

Garrett surfaced and exhaled. He had never seen a lighthouse in person before. Somehow he recognized that tall tower as the last sentinel of civilization. The unknown existed beyond—and, more importantly, below—the swirling light.

Garrett trembled at the prospect.

The Ringed Seal swam closer. *Ready?*

Yeah, said Garrett.

You sound nervous, said Paulo.

I guess so, Garrett acknowledged. *What if where we're going is too deep? What if I can't hold my breath?*

You can, said Paulo. *The tunnel is only about thirty feet down. Easy enough for an Orc.*

Yeah, said Lenny. *Follow the big guy, Weava.*

The Ringed Seal dipped below the water, followed by the Elephant Seal.

Garrett took a final lingering look at the lighthouse, and then descended. With visibility nil, he echolocated and pinged the two seals. The returning image revealed jagged, rocky outcroppings at varying depths, sure to dissuade any boats from venturing too close to the island. Garrett gave another flick of his powerful tail and caught up to the seals.

The waters darkened the deeper they dove. Twice, Garrett accidentally nudged Paulo with his Orca beak.

The Elephant Seal grunted in response.

Here we go, said Lenny.

Garrett fired off another burst of echolocation, learned the tunnel was wide enough to accommodate his size, but only just. Long and dark, the primal mind told Garrett the passageway descended. How far it went his Orc brain couldn't estimate.

Do it, Garrett willed himself on. *You've come this far.*

He swam forward. Ten feet inside, the walls seemed to close in on him. Garrett kicked hard to speed ahead.

Whoa! Not so fast, said Lenny. *Ya wanna smash us into the walls? N-need...o-out.*

We're almost there, Weava. Look ahead. See the waters lighten?

Garrett did. Still dark, but less so than the near pitch he currently found himself in, the light offered some minor relief to his claustrophobia. *Y-yeah.*

Focus on that.

Garrett stayed close to both seals' tails, pushing them to swim faster.

The tunnel floor bottomed out, then quickly rose and brightened. Another flick of his tail and Garrett exited the passage into open water again. An echolocation burst revealed cavern walls, unlike the open ocean in which he'd first transformed.

Garrett ascended for the surface with the pair of seals flanking either side of him. *Wh-what're you guys doing?*

Makin' sure nobody panics at an Orcinian showin' up unannounced, said Lenny.

Paulo chuckled. *Bet the dockworkers ran for the mansion when they saw his dorsal fin.*

Garrett surfaced and exhaled, drinking in the air. He looked up and gasped. *Whoa.*

He gaped at the walls curved to form a giant dome. Geode crystals, purple and green, twinkled at him from high in the cavern ceiling. Stalactites hung like sparkling stone icicles. Some looked thick as pillars, others thin and brittle. A few of their tips even broke the water's surface.

Garrett completed his turn.

A dock stood fifty yards from them with lit braziers entrenched in each post. Whitewashed, wooden buildings with thatched roofs stood beyond the dock.

It's like a whole other world! Garrett thought to himself, following Lenny's lead inland.

Beyond the whitewashed homes, a pathway led up a stone hill. At the peak, a mansion carved from the cavern walls towered over all. The sight stole Garrett's breath away. He desired nothing more than to walk the steep incline, touch the home, and search for what treasures surely lay inside.

"Garrett!" a voice yelled.

Garrett looked for the source. He saw Oscar run to the end of the dock, near pitching over the edge in his excitement. Behind him, a troop of men in hooded Selkie suits escorted a corpulent man, dressed in the same regal attire as Oscar, a pearl-white Harp coat.

Fenton flanked the obese man. So too did a dwarf who bore a striking resemblance to Lenny. Both escorts stopped when the fat man did, all well short of the dock's end.

Paulo, who's the fat guy?

August Collins, Oscar's father, said Paulo. *And don't let him or anyone else hear you call him fat. He doesn't like it one bit.*

Weava, said Lenny. *When we get to the dock, let me do the talkin'. Probably betta if ya change back too.*

Garrett stiffened. *What if I can't? I've only done it once. What if I—*

Think about whateva ya did last time and you'll do fine. The Ringed Seal blinked. *Well…come on! Change already.*

Garrett swam close enough to the docks to grab hold once in human form and keep from sinking. He nearly laughed when seeing a few of the hooded guardians step back. With his ribs brushing the barnacle-encrusted pillars, Garrett closed his eyes and recalled the memory of his father's baseball game.

The itch returned.

Garrett hugged a wooden pillar the moment his arms returned. The barnacles tore at his skin, but still he hung on, even upon feeling Paulo rise beneath him again. Garrett reopened his eyes.

August had stepped to the edge of the dock, his flabby arm draped around Oscar's shoulders. "So, this is Garrett Weaver. The Orc my son deemed it wise to bring home."

"Y-yes, sir," said Garrett.

"*Sir*?" August's voice peaked. "Oh, I do like you already. It's been, well, certainly never, since I met a well-mannered Orc. Wouldn't you agree, Fenton?"

Garrett fought off a sneer as he looked on the man who'd kicked him off a boat and trained a harpoon on him not an hour ago.

"Aye," Fenton agreed.

"Hello again, Garrett." Oscar waved.

"H-hi Oscar."

"Told you everything would be all right, didn't I?" Oscar said. "Father, might we take Garrett up to our home?"

"Oh, yes, of course," said August. "He's no doubt tired after such an arduous journey as you all have led him on. Fenton?"

The old overseer whistled at the hooded guardians. "You three. Help him out of the water."

The men near fell over one another to obey.

That's weird. Why do they all seem so afraid? Garrett glanced back to the tunnel's underwater entrance.

"Thinking of leaving us so soon, Garrett?" August *tsk*ed. "That won't do at all. You don't want to be rude, after all. Come, we've warm clothes for you, a cozy bed, and Fenton will direct the cooks to prepare anything you'd like."

Garrett turned back to the guardian's open hands. He ignored their aid and pulled himself from the water, onto the dock. He heard another splash, followed by a thud.

The Ringed Seal had joined him on the deck. It snorted its nostrils at the guardians and opened its mouth to hiss. *Rememba what I said, Weava,* Lenny's voice filled Garrett's mind. *Let me do the talkin'.*

Garrett didn't argue. Hunched to hide his nakedness, someone draped an itchy blanket about him. He glanced up and into the scar-lined face of a little man.

"Th-thank you," said Garrett.

"Declan." The little man nodded in reply, then stepped back as Fenton helped Garrett to his feet. "Declan Dolan."

"There," said Fenton, rubbing Garrett's shoulders and pulling the blanket tight. "No hard feelings, I trust? Had to be done."

Schyeah right.

"All right, Garrett?" Oscar pushed forward, grinning.

Garrett nodded.

"Fantastic! Let me show you around!"

August thrust his arm out, halting his son. His eyes narrowed. "Oscar said you've never changed, er, transformed, before. Is that correct?"

"N-no, sir. Never."

August rubbed at his turkey neck with the back of his hand. "Then how is it you've done it now so easily. Where did you learn?"

"L-Lenny helped me. Talked me through it, I guess."

"Ah." August's gaze flitted to the Ringed Seal. "Yes, I see. Friends now, are you?"

The seal arched its neck to look up at Garrett, its head cocked to the side.

"N-no, sir," Garrett said to August. "Not friends. He helped me is all."

"Father," Oscar said. "Would you like to join Garrett and me?"

August's face broke into a wide grin. "Of course, son. He is our guest, after all, aren't you, Garrett? I'll not have it said Crayfish Collins wasn't hospitable." August laughed. "So let's be off, boys. Back up the hill where we'll have good food, conversation, and warm beds after."

August clapped Garrett on the back and waddled up the dock.

Garrett followed after, yet stopped upon seeing not all in the party joined them.

Both Fenton and Declan had remained behind.

Garrett eyed the handful of hooded guardians encircling the two seals.

"Come along, Garrett." August lifted a meaty hand from Oscar's shoulder and motioned with equally fat fingers for him to follow. "Don't want that chowder to grow cold."

Garrett shifted his attention to the dock and his seal companions. *What do I do?*

The Ringed Seal barked. Nodded its head up and down.

All right, Lenny. Garrett thought. *If you say so.*

Garrett turned his back on Lenny and set his sights on the stone mansion.

KELLEN

KELLEN LISTENED INTENTLY AS HIS FRIENDS detailed the story of their arrival. He fought the rising fear within him, wary of showing weakness in his surrounding company.

"Wait," said Kellen. "If you guys are here, what happened to Bennett?"

Marrero and Tardiff exchanged a glance.

A chill shot up Kellen's back. "Where's Bennett?"

"He was with us at the zoo." Marrero shrugged. "That's the last thing I remember before the French dude knocked me out."

"Yeah," said Tardiff. "And he wasn't with us in the car wreck either."

"Then he's dead," said the elder marshal, Edmund.

Kellen glared at the opposing cage. "You don't know that. Maybe he was with them and he got away. Or—"

"I'm not gonna argue with you, kid," said Edmund. "Believe what you want."

"Bennett...*dead?*" Tardiff's voice broke. "That can't be, man. He can't be dead."

Marrero sat down hard, eyes glazing over.

The same weakness threatened Kellen. He glanced up the dock at the balding man who kidnapped his friends. Kellen drowned the weakness with his anger. *It was you that did it.* He thought of the Frenchman. *I know it was you.*

"His name's Henry Boucher," Bryant whispered to Kellen. "Bounty hunter and small-time slave owner. Had a dossier on him for a long time now. That old boy's mean as they come."

"So are we, Silkstealer."

"Ed," said Bryant. "Stop calling me—"

"Henry's the one who took my boy's suit," Edmund spat. "If he's here, Collins can't be far away. Henry's the muscle paid to watch Daddy's little darling."

Kellen heard a thud as Tieran tossed the mooring lines onto the boat and stumbled aboard.

"All righ', Silas. Shove off!"

The trawler engine belched the scent of fuel and black smoke as the engine thundered to life. Kellen winced at the sudden noise, as did the other captives in the surrounding cages. The doors of the warehouse screamed open on their rusty hinges and a gust of sea wind howled through.

The trawler stuttered ahead.

Kellen saw the black pitch of night before Tieran threw a rope line across the deck. A blue tarp whipped over the cages, simultaneously covering and blinding them.

"Maybe we should yell for help," Tardiff suggested.

Bryant shook his head. "Boat's pretty loud."

"Aye," said Edmund. "And you can bet what ears might be listening are on the Crayfish's payroll. Don't have to pay night shifters as much to look the other way either."

Tardiff threw himself at the edge of his cage. "Help!" He batted at the blue tarp. "Hel—"

A wooden rod smacked the top.

"Quiet in there, or I'll have your tongue out!" Tieran hissed.

"Is he serious?" Marrero asked Kellen and the marshals.

Edmund answered with a blank stare.

"H-how do you know?"

Kellen took the silence to mean Edmund had seen more than his fair share of tongues taken. He took a deep breath. "So," said Kellen. "How do we get out of this?"

Edmund sighed. "I already told you. We wait—"

"To be Salted, I know. When does that happen?"

"Hang on," said Marrero. "What does that even mean?"

The two marshals exchanged a glance.

"Well, come on, tell us," said Kellen. "Give us some clue. It's better than not knowing anything."

Edmund humphed. "Be careful what you wish for, pup."

"The kid's right," said Bryant. "They might as well know."

Edmund clenched his jaw as he looked each teen in the eye. "In the olden days—"

"I'm not looking for a history lesson, Grandpa," said Kellen. "How far back you taking us?"

"How far back you want to go, pup?" Edmund growled.

Kellen glared back. "Just tell me what I want to know."

"Hey." Bryant spun Kellen around. "You wanna see home again? You best listen to Ed."

"Go on," said Tardiff. "Tell us. I'm listening, even if Kellen won't."

Edmund sucked his teeth. "In the olden days, Salted's what sailors called the most experienced among them. For instance, my partner, Bryant, over here would look at little pissants like you boys and direct you to me if you had any questions. 'Ask Ed,' Bryant might say. 'He's Salted.'"

"So it means you know a thing or two," said Kellen.

"It means the Salt tried to drown me and I fought for air," Edmund replied. "I'm hardened. Salted. The testing time is coming, pups. We'll see if you're this lippy afterward."

I'll be around. Kellen knew. *Doesn't matter what it is. I'll make it.*

A corner of the tarp ripped back. Tieran held the edge of it in hand as he grinned down at the captives. "That's righ', lads. It's almost time." His drunken gaze meandered to Kellen. "You ready to get Salted too, mate? Ready to put on the last coat you'll ever wear?"

"*Tieran!*"

Kellen saw the bearded fisherman from the warehouse stride across the deck.

"Wha'?" Tieran said. "Something to say, Silas?"

"Leave them alone. They're scared enough as is."

"I'll do as I like," said Tieran. "Need I remind you, I'm the Crayfish's dockmaster and auctioneer—"

"We're not on the docks," said Silas. "Or the auction block. I'm captain of this ship. Ya do as I say, or I'll toss ya in myself and let ya swim to the Graves."

Tieran sneered and let the tarp fall closed again.

Kellen listened to his heavy boots clomp further up the boat. Then he punched the bars.

"That's right, pup," said Edmund. "Get mad. Might help you live longer."

"What did he mean?" Kellen demanded. "The last coat you'll ever wear?"

"You a slow learner, pup? Need me to spell it out for you?"

Tardiff shook his head. "You want us to believe if we wear one of these…hoodie, pajama sweatsuit, things you and some of these other guys have on that we can't take it off again? That it would kill us?"

"Aye," said Edmund. "That's what I'm saying."

Marrero snorted. "That's stupid."

Kellen thought back to the Lavere County jail, watching Henry Boucher saw the hooded suit off the dead marshal. *They're never getting me in one of those suits…*

"Kell, you believe this old geezer?" Marrero asked.

"You'll wear one," said Edmund.

"No," said Kellen. "I won't."

Edmund sighed. "Kid, if you'd seen what I have in my lifetime, you'll beg them to put the coat on you when the time comes."

"How's that?" Kellen asked.

"Because where they're taking us—" Edmund shook his head. "A suit like this is the only chance you've got of seeing the shore again."

"Ed," said Bryant. "You hear what the captain said about where we're going?"

"Where?" Kellen asked.

"The Graves," said the elder marshal. "It's an island off the coast."

Bryant cursed. "This isn't happening. Not to me, Ed. Not after—"

"Calm down, Bryant," said Edmund. "It'll be all right. You're the Silkstealer, remember?"

"What is that?" Kellen asked.

"Not a that, a *he*," said Edmund, nodding in Bryant's direction. "The Silkstealer's a boogeyman known throughout the Salt, right? A mass murderer of Selkies and a living nightmare to Silkies."

Mass murderer? Kellen looked at his cellmate skeptically. *This guy?*

"I wish you'd quit calling me that," said Bryant.

"I wish you'd start owning it," Edmund replied harshly. "Makes you valuable. Might be they even put you on a tour as a spectacle, rather than put you in the pits. You're just like these boys, except you should know better. All of you need to wake up to the position we're in. It's every man for himself now. Make no mistake. You find a chance to get away, take it."

Kellen saw fear in his friends' faces and fought not to let it overtake him too. "You said we're going to the Graves. You ever been there?"

"Heard about it," said Edmund. "Rumor has it the Crayfish likes to make an impression on his new property. Sounds like we're going down a Gasping Hole, fellas."

"Why do I not like the sound of that?" asked Tardiff.

"You boys are in your prime," said Edmund. "Strong. You'll be fine if you do what they say. For now at least."

"I'm done with that," Kellen whispered. "Soon as they unlock this gate, I'm going out swinging."

Edmund grinned. "That's the spirit, kid. Remember that if you survive the Gasping Hole."

The old man shuffled to the back of his cage and sat down. He laid his head back against the bars, stared at the tarp in angry silence.

Kellen waved his friends over. "Look," he whispered. "I don't care what these guys say, they let us out of here, we fight."

Marrero nodded.

"And go where?" Tardiff asked. "In case you didn't notice, Kell, that bit of water we saw…I'm thinking that's the ocean!"

"Your point?"

"There's no ocean near Indiana, idiot. God knows how far we are from home. Are we in California? Florida?"

"Nah," said Marrero. "Too cold for either of those. Gotta be somewhere further north."

"Who cares where we are! In case you didn't notice"—Kellen grabbed the bars of his cage and rattled them—"we're not exactly guests here, Tardiff. What do you think's going to happen when we get where they're taking us?"

"I dunno," said Tardiff. "And you don't either!"

"Yeah? Well, I know a place called the Graves, and going *down* whatever a Gasping Hole is, doesn't sound great. Plus that French guy who brought you in...he killed Campbell at the jail."

"No way..." Tardiff sniffled. "So w-what do we do, man. How're we gonna get out of here?"

"We fight." Kellen looked around the cages. "There's three of us and the two marshals."

"What about Boone?" Marrero asked.

Kellen glanced at the Lavere town drunk. Boone had sat with his back against the bars upon waking and hadn't said two words to anyone since. Kellen wondered if the old man thought himself still in a dream where men morphed into seals.

Kellen turned back to his friends. "He can't help us. Probably just get in our way."

"Count me in too..." The beefy man who Kellen had seen brought in with Tardiff and Marrero stood in his cage, his meaty paws grasping the bars. "You get me outta this cage and I'll strangle the first one I get my hands on."

Kellen grinned. "Done. All right, that's six of us to what...five, maybe six, of them?"

"Sounds right," said Marrero. "So what do we do, Kell?"

"First one out grabs the guard with keys and—"

"Are you nuts?" said Tardiff. "What if they have guns, man?"

"Look where we are, idiot." Kellen glanced around the deck at the surrounding cages. Found people watching him, new hope in their eyes. A few had stood, their hands drawn into fists. Kellen gathered they didn't all understand him by the way their faces scrunched, but he knew they understood what he planned.

"We're in freaking cages, Tardiff," said Kellen. "They're taking us somewhere by boat and they killed our friends for God's sake! I think we either fight now or—"

A foghorn sounded.

"All clear, mates!" Tieran shouted.

"All clear!" a voice even further away answered.

The engine shuddered beneath them.

We're here. Kellen swallowed hard. Butterflies swarmed in his gut even as nervous energy coursed through him. He glanced around the cages at his companions. Marrero had donned the same murderous look he often had before stepping onto the wrestling mat back home. Tardiff anxiously nodded at Kellen. The trucker popped his knuckles.

Be the leader. Kellen prepped himself. *Show them what it means to be a man.*

Kellen heard the tarp pulled away.

Tieran held the end of it in hand. A towering shadow loomed behind him and at the top, a swirling light. It alone warded off the pervading darkness.

A lighthouse? Kellen continued searching the area.

"That's righ'," said Tieran. "Get a looksee around, ladies and gents. There's no way back—"

"Quiet, Tieran," Silas boomed. "And get them off my ship."

"Will do, your lordship." Tieran bowed and nearly tumbled over the side. He laughed at himself, then whistled. "All righ', you sorry seadogs, get 'em off the captain's boat."

"Wait! Mister! I got a secret for ya!"

Kellen spun.

Boone stood at the end of his cage, scraggly arm waving for attention. "Mister!"

What's he doing?

"Hey, mister!"

Tieran jumped down onto the deck, giving a wide berth to the cages as he made toward Boone. "What're you on about, then?"

"Wonderin' if ya wouldn't mind makin' a deal?"

No. Kellen thought, watching Boone's eyes round at the sight of Tieran removing a flask from his pocket.

"And why would I wanna do that?" Tieran asked.

Boone licked his lips. "Well, mister, I got quite the secret for ya."

No! Kellen glared at the old man. *Shut up, Boone.*

"Righ', give it up then."

"No, sir, ain't the way deals work."

Tieran laughed. "You're too much, mate. So what you want for this lil' secret?"

"Well, I heard tell you's takin' us somewhere I don't rightly wanna go. Sheriff Hullinger never did keep me behind bars very long. Think I've seen enough for now, so I'd like ya to set me free," said Boone. "Want your word on it."

Like he'd honor his promise. Kellen thought.

Tieran took a swig of his flask. "Set you free?"

"Yessir," said Boone. "You let me outta here and I'll tell you my good secret."

"Done." Tieran stoppered his flask and pocketed it. He removed a set of keys and opened the gate.

Kellen's heart rushed at hearing the lock unlatch. He anticipated Edmund rushing the cage, grabbing Tieran like they had planned.

The elder marshal remained huddled in the back as his cellmate exited.

Tieran closed the gate and locked it. He put his arm around Boone and leaned on the old man to keep from falling as the trawler shook in the ocean's wake.

"Well, I'll be!" said Boone, stepping up on the gangway. "This here's an island, ain't it? What'd ya wanna bring us all the way out here for?"

"Don't you worry yourself about that. You're a free man, now," said Tieran. "So, let's have that secret."

Kellen's chest pounded as Boone looked squarely at him.

"Well, mister. Them boys is plotting against you."

Tieran's drunken gaze wandered over the cages and faces. "Which boys?"

No...

"Him," Boone pointed at Kellen. "Him and them others from around town. They's waiting on you to cut'em loose outta them there cages. Then they's gonna backstab you and your fellas."

Tieran glared at Kellen as he reached into his pocket again. "Is that so?"

"Yessir," said Boone. "Reckon they're gonna get out—"

Tieran pulled something black from his pocket and pointed it at Boone's head.

No! Kellen closed his eyes.

A gunshot echoed across the night sky.

The immediate splash and screams in the surrounding cages were silenced by a second gunshot.

Kellen opened his eyes.

Tieran held his gun in the air. "Anyone else have a secret they'd like to share with ol' Tieran, eh?" He pointed his aim at Kellen. "You lot still plan on running?"

Kellen shook his head, lifted his hands in front of him. "D-don't shoot me."

Tieran chuckled. "Nah, mate. Sounds like the lot of you wanted to fight, eh? That's all righ'. The Crayfish'll have big plans for you and your pals." He pocketed his gun and gave another whistle. "Righ'! Get 'em off the boat and step lively with 'em!"

A score of men in hooded suits bounded up the gangway, each with a coiled whip hanging off their person and a wooden baton in hand. Scars littered their extremities. All bore brands of a Crayfish—some on their necks, others on the back of their hands. They clanged their clubs on the cages as they went down the rows, unlocking one at a time.

One unlocked the beefy man's cage, and Kellen watched him come out brawling.

Three of the hooded men descended on him with their clubs, knocked him woozy to the deck less than a minute later.

"Get 'em on his feet, then!" Tieran shouted.

Another hooded man threw a bucket of seawater in the beefy man's face.

Kellen winced as the man howled.

"Wakey, wakey," one of the captors joked.

Kellen backed to the corner furthest from the mayhem as two men pulled the beefy man to his feet and half carried, half dragged, him down the gangway.

Another unlocked Marrero and Tardiff's cage. "Out with ye!"

Edmund walked out of his own accord and Marrero set his jaw before allowing himself to be led next.

"No," said Tardiff, huddling to the back. "This isn't real…"

"Out with ye!" the hooded men growled from the opening.

"*No!*" Tardiff hugged his arms around the bars. "Please, I want to go home!"

The hooded man entered the cage and pried at Tardiff's arms.

"No…please!"

Kellen saw the captor reach for his club. *Now!* He found himself suddenly on his feet, arms reaching through the bars, punching at the hooded man. *Get his club!*

"Kell!"

Strong arms tugged Kellen away.

"Let go, kid," Bryant said.

"No!"

Bryant lifted Kellen off his feet and yanked him free of the bars. They fell as one to the floor of their cage. Kellen struggled for his own release as a hooded man clocked Tardiff. A loud *pop* suggested he broke Tardiff's arm.

Kellen shrunk at the sound.

"Kell…" Tardiff screamed as a pair of men finally pried his hands loose.

"What's wrong, boy? Ya want ya mummy and daddy? They can't hear ya now."

"Marrero…" Tardiff cried.

"It'll be all right," Marrero yelled.

Kellen knew it wouldn't be as they dragged Tardiff away.

"Do what they say," Bryant commanded in his ear.

I'll kill them. Kellen rocked back and forth as his cage unlocked.

"On ya feet!"

Bryant stood and offered an open hand to help Kellen stand.

Show them you're not afraid. Kellen accepted Bryant's hand and was promptly yanked to his feet. *Don't be like Tardiff. They're hazing you, that's all.* Kellen convinced himself. He glared at the hooded man. *Just hazing.*

"What're ya lookin' at, seadog," the man shouted.

Kellen stood tall, straightened his shoulders, and strode past Bryant out of the cage.

"Oooh, look at that one!" one of the captors catcalled. "A right brave one, ain't he, Tieran?"

"Bah, see how he fares when facing the Gasping Hole."

Yeah, we'll see. Kellen clenched his fists and tried not to fall as he found his sea legs. He peered over the side. Choppy ocean water gleamed darkly as white swells crashed over the island rocks.

He thought the island aptly named. The whole of it seemed dead beneath the lighthouse's ghostly swirl. The jagged rocks and large boulders conjured unmarked gravestones in Kellen's mind as he followed the line of captives toward the lighthouse. Each time a rock made him slip, he winced, half expecting a corpse to rise and snatch him below.

Kellen glanced behind him as the sea crashed around them. He saw no second island. Only the ocean and the boat that carried him to this island Tieran named the Graves.

"Keep movin'," another hooded guardian yelled. "No time for sightseein'!"

Kellen stepped into the lighthouse's shadow and across the open door's threshold into a dim, reddish light. Two spiral staircases stood before him—one ascending, the other...

"Down ya go," said his captor. "Mind ya keep both hands on the rail else ya pitch over the side."

Kellen peered down the staircase into nothingness, the same sort of overpowering darkness his basement held back home. The same black pitch his father banished him to as a kid whenever he tired of welting him with the belt.

Kellen heard moaning below, crying and pain also. He swore his father's voice echoed up the stairs with the other sounds.

What's wrong, Kelly? Thought I raised you to be a man, not a little girl. You scared of the dark? Want your whore momma?

It's only steps, Kellen prodded himself along. *Just going down a flight of stairs.*

He reached for the railing, the coldness of it seeping into his sweating palms. The floor of it shook and squealed as he stepped onto it. Kellen shut his eyes and took a deep breath. He descended.

The stairwell swayed from side to side as if desiring to toss him into the abyss.

Get down them steps, Kelly. Quit your crying. Your momma's not gonna save you.

Kellen took another step. Another. Hand over hand he guided himself down the circular stairwell, the cries and moans intensifying with every step taken, the clangs of others following him down. He snorted at the musty smell.

This is what a crypt smells like. His imagination ran with him.

Kellen took another step, tried putting out of mind the constant thought of dead things living behind the slats to grab his ankle. Down and down he went until his hands found only air and feet discovered no more steps.

Kellen opened his eyes. The walls had broadened and pale,

greenish light illuminated the circular room and concrete sides. Ahead, the other captives formed a line, bound for another doorway. Some trembled. Others buried their faces in the shoulders of loved ones, or even strangers. It didn't matter now. Most of those Kellen saw cried. Others seemed lost, deadened to their bleak surroundings already.

Kellen steeled himself. *Show them you're not afraid.*

The line steadily shuffled forward.

Behind him came the noise of skittering feet down metal steps. Kellen glanced behind him.

Tieran reached the last step and stumbled toward the front of the line. "Righ', listen up, you sorry sea-rats, if ya hope to see tomorrow. You're about to go down the Gasping Hole. This is where we learn which of ya listen and which of ya die."

Kellen stepped out of line to see where it ended. He felt a sharp tap on the shoulder.

"Back in line," said a guard, holding his baton aloft for Kellen to see.

Kellen obeyed.

"Now," Tieran continued. "When you get in the water, keep hold of the rope, and swim as best you can. Don't fight. I'll say it again. Do. Not. Fight. Less'n you wanna learn what it's like to breathe water out your earholes."

Another clamor came from the stairwell. A moment later, the Frenchman, Henry, strode past leading a black girl by the arm. Another girl, thicker and taller, followed them. All three wore one-piece hooded suits like Tieran and the guardians did.

They each vanished through the doorway.

"When you feel air on your face, take a breath quick like," said

Tieran. "You'll be taken back down right after so be sure and hold your air in. Do all that and we'll see you on the other side. Do it not, and you're off to Fiddler's Green."

Kellen glanced behind him. "What's Fiddler's Green?" he whispered to Bryant.

"The afterlife for Salt folk. A heaven of crystal clear waters they can swim in peace," said Bryant. "I don't plan on finding out if it exists or not."

Kellen faced front. *Me either.*

They continued their slow march forward, the sounds of splashing and struggle increasing with each step. Only a couple people stood in front of him now and Kellen swore he heard lapping water and woeful voices from within.

The wooden door opened, squeaked on its rusty hinges.

"You three with me," said the doorman.

The two in front of him took a step back.

Show them. Kellen continued his reminder, his only defense against the fear pulsing in the back of his mind. He shouldered past the pair in front of him to be first through the door.

A wooden baton slapped the side.

Kellen stopped.

"Quite the brave one, aren't you," Tieran said. "Righ'. I'll take this one down."

The doorman's gaze wandered. "Tieran…"

"I said I'll take this one." Tieran clucked his tongue. "Never seen no one so eager to go down the Gasping Hole…think you're special, do you?"

Kellen kept his focus on the open door, the sound of lapping water clear now. *Show them.*

"Hey!" Tieran tapped Kellen's back shoulder with his baton. "I asked you a question, boy. Think you're special?"

"No."

"Mmm. Special *and* a liar, my favorite. Go on with you, then." Tieran motioned. "March through them doors."

Kellen stepped over the threshold. More of the pale green light lit the smaller room of likewise bare surroundings. Kellen tensed at what lay in the middle—a circular pool with a sheer surface of black. To his mind, it almost looked like a giant well.

A seal surfaced and snorted for air.

Kellen stepped back.

"What's wrong, boy?" Tieran chuckled. "Scared of a lil' ol' seal?"

Another seal leapt out of the water onto the concrete deck. It shook its head and body like a wet dog might, sprinkling water everywhere. Both seals glanced at Kellen. One turned toward the other, almost as if they spoke to one another.

Show. Them. Kellen faced Tieran. "What do we do now?"

"Get in the water. Find out."

Only hazing. Kellen spun on his heel and strode for the pool. *Like twelving.*

One of the seals barked.

Still Kellen walked on, until he reached the edge of the pool. Kellen glanced down at the black water. For a moment, he thought of the pool as a big septic tank, the kind that once overflowed in his basement. Unlike the tank back home, however, this one gave no hint as to how deep it went.

"Go on," said Tieran.

Kellen jumped in. The icy water punched him in the gut. Stole his breath away. Goosebumps relayed up and down his body. Kellen surfaced for air, gasping, already shivering.

"Cold, is it?" Tieran laughed. "Just you wait, boy. It only gets colder from here."

Tieran tossed a lasso of rope in front of Kellen's face. "Put that under your armpits. Remember what I said. Don't fight if you want to see tomorrow and don't loose yourself of the rope till we reach the other side. You won't find your way back, I promise you."

Kellen took hold of the rope and lifted it over his head. His teeth chattering, he put his arms through and pushed the rope under his armpits. Then he tightened it. Kellen glanced up as Tieran donned his hood.

Then Tieran changed. His face transformed into a seal, his nose and mouth bulging outward. He fell to his hands and knees as they became flippers.

Kellen wanted to scream. The cold prevented it.

A moment later, the seal that was Tieran crashed into the water. It surfaced near Kellen's face, barked, then took the end of rope in its mouth.

Wha-what's it do—

The seal dove, its hind flippers broke the surface. The last thing Kellen saw before his rope harness yanked him below.

Down, down, he went.

His body instinctually fought to surface.

The rope harness warned against it, tugging, pulling him deeper.

Kellen opened his eyes. Salt stung them, swirling black with bubbles.

Air! Kellen's brain cried out. His mind swam, attempting to learn where the surface lay.

The rope harness loosened.

Kellen swam forward. Bumped his face into rock, scratching his forehead and left cheek.

The seal suddenly appeared in front of him. It bit the rope again, tugged down.

Don't fight. Kellen recalled the reminder. *Swim with him!*

Kellen flipped and furiously kicked to follow the seal.

Down, down, down they descended, angling right here, left there, and the water growing colder with every stroke.

White spots popped in Kellen's mind.

He continued to kick.

The rope harness tugged upward.

Kellen followed it. Without warning, he breached the surface. Cool air kissed his cheeks.

"*Huuuuuuh.*" He gulped down the foul-tasting air, savoring each deep breath. He opened his eyes, but saw nothing. No indication of how large the area might be. He thought to call out and hear an echo.

The harness tugged him back under.

Again, Kellen kicked and swam, his ears popping as they twisted this way and that, always descending. His air waned, heart thudded. The harness tugged upward.

Kellen clawed for the surface, snorting firewater as his body ached for air. He breached, coughing and gagging, thankful to suck down any hint of oxygen.

Seconds later, the harness tugged at him again.

The cold wore on his body. His limbs lethargically kicked and pulled at the water as the harness yanked him further below.

Let it be over. Let me drown.

The harness refused to let him quit.

Blackness overtook his thoughts.

He felt sleepy. Wilting.

Salt water filled his nostrils, trickled into his throat.

The harness tugged upward.

Kellen's throat relaxed.

Water gushed in.

And then he breached to cool air upon his face. Kellen immediately vomited mouthful after mouthful of seawater, his body wracking the liquid from his lungs. His head pounding, Kellen was vaguely aware the harness tugged him through the water. He opened his eyes.

The sight made him dizzy.

He closed them and let the cold waters numb the throbbing in his head.

Suffering surrounded him. Strangers sobbing, others gasping for air as he had done.

Kellen risked seeing again.

The dark heavens glistened with sparkly light.

Are those...stars? Kellen's vision cleared with each new breath.

The harness went limp.

Strong hands lifted under his arms and dragged him up and out of the water.

Kellen transfixed on the sparkling lights.

"Sit up, boy—"

Edmund?

"You'll feel better."

Kellen did. His head swooned at the sudden movement and he began to tip.

Again, someone righted him.

"Easy now."

"St-stars," said Kellen. He shifted to see the elder marshal, beads of water caught in his grizzled beard. "I see…stars."

"Not stars."

"What?"

"Look again."

Kellen did. What he thought the heavens, now he saw ended in stone. Long, thin rock pillars descended from the ceiling like fangs with diamonds trapped throughout.

"Wh-where are we?"

Edmund grimaced. "Welcome to Crayfish Cavern, kid."

LENNY

LENNY WATCHED TASKMASTERS SURROUND PAULO.
With Garrett gone, they ceased their pretense. Each took whips
off their belts, though none dared crack them yet. A few looked
toward the Crayfish's head overseer in wait of orders.

Fenton turned his cold gaze on Lenny. "Get these fools out of
their coats."

Fingers touched his nose. *Pop?*

"Open ya mouth, pup," said Declan.

Lenny obliged him.

Declan jerked hard on Lenny's upper lip to release him from
his Salt form. The cavern's cold seeped into Lenny's human skin
moments later. He fell shivering on the dock and noticed Paulo
had likewise been released from his Elephant Seal form. Heavy
steps clomped closer.

"Captain Dolan," said Fenton. "Our Lord Master Collins sent
you to capture a slave girl. Instead you bring him an Orc calf."

"I caught the girl too." Lenny dared look Fenton in the face. "I—"

Declan backhanded Lenny. "Boss Fenton's talkin', boy."

The sting in Lenny's cheek smarted from the lesson. *Don't say
nothin',* Lenny took the slap to mean. *Give Fenton what he wants.*

"Your son has a lot to learn, Dolan," Fenton said.

"Aye, Boss," Declan replied. "Stubborn and hot-headed. He'll learn betta."

"So you've said for a number of years now..." Fenton's gaze flickered back to Lenny. "And how is it a newly made captain caught not only Marisa Bourgeois, but an Orc calf?"

Keep ya mouth shut. Lenny's cheek throbbed. "I'm my fatha's son."

Fenton frowned. "Proud of your accomplishments, are you?"

"Aye, sir." Lenny stood up. "Ya said Bourgeois was uncatchable—"

"Of course I did," said Fenton. "She wouldn't have been much of a prize for Master Oscar to recapture and boast of otherwise, would she?"

Lenny smarted from the sarcastic tone. "Whattaya mean?"

Fenton shook his head. "Did you truly believe Master Oscar was sent on his first hunt with even the slightest chance he might return empty-handed?"

Lenny's stomach churned as Fenton continued.

"That our Lord Master would truly entrust the safety of his only son to an unproven lot of catchers? Let alone the rather small hands of an ill-made, nipperkin captain?" Fenton *tsk*ed.

"Maybe we was unproven before," said Lenny. "Not now. I didn't just catch Bourgeois and the Orc. I caught the Silksteala too."

The other taskmasters laughed at such a claim.

Fenton quieted their laughter with a raise of his hand. "The Silkstealer? That haunted boogeyman of Selkie children lore?" he asked skeptically.

"Aye," said Lenny. "Wait till Tieran gets here. See for ya'selves what I done."

"What you did," said Fenton. "Did your crew not help?"

"Aye," Paulo said. "We did."

"I see," said Fenton to Paulo. "And were you ordered to abandon your mission, in lieu of what Captain Dolan apparently thought of as a much more enticing target, or did you disobey Master August's orders willingly?"

Lenny glanced at Paulo as his large friend hesitated to answer.

The surrounding taskmasters had unfurled their whips. One even swished the ends of tattered leather across the floor, no doubt eager to swing and call screams from the brute before him.

Lie, Paulie. Lenny's earrings flashed. *Tell him I ordered it. They didn't break these whips out not to use 'em.*

Paulo glared at the Selkies around him. "I did it willingly."

Lenny sighed.

"A noble answer." Fenton shifted back to Lenny. "And where is the remainder of your crew, Captain Dolan? I recall seven were sent out, yet only the two of you and Master Oscar have returned."

"Tieran kept Ellie behind," said Lenny. "Henry abandoned us when his slave girl ran off."

"Abandoned, you say?"

"Aye," said Lenny, unsatisfied when Fenton's face gave no hint as to his feelings on the matter. "Ask Oscar if ya don't believe me. He'll tell ya the same."

"I'll do that," said Fenton. "But that's only six catchers accounted for. I believe you were assigned a sprinter, a pup. Where is Racer?"

Lenny's chin dipped. "He ran off with Henry's girl."

Fenton's gaze flickered to a hooded taskmaster. "Fetch the pup's father and lock him in the stocks. We'll make an example of him soon, along with these two—"

The deep bellow of a conch-shell horn echoed throughout the cavern. It sounded a second time. *A warning?* Lenny looked toward the main entrance, along with all those standing at the dock.

A pair of triangular-shaped dorsal fins breached the surface, the two swimming side-by-side.

"*Nomads…*" a taskmaster whispered.

The pair of fins approached far faster than anything Lenny had ever seen swim, trailing white V's in their wakes. Their dorsal fins dipped beneath the surface twenty feet from the dock. Seconds later, two short-fin Mako Sharks exploded from the water, soaring high above, transforming as their arch reached its apex. Their sickle-fin tails split in two to form human legs. Arms burst from their pectoral fins like hands shoving through tight sleeves. Both finished their conversion to human before landing upon the dock and taking a knee.

Lenny backed into Fenton as both Nomads rose to their full height. Their human legs sheened bluish-grey, retaining their Nomadic hue, and their human toes were webbed. Sinewy muscle cleaved to their lean chests and arms. Tattooed runes and symbols lined their extremities. Lenny thought their markings familiar, but struggled to place where he had seen such patterns before.

The shorter of the two wore a triangular patch, carved from a seashell, over his right eye.

Lenny forced himself not to look away as the lone eye's gaze fell on him. Something in Lenny's core whispered that eye peered deep inside his soul, and he exhaled when it glanced away.

The one-eyed stranger finished his slow surveillance of those amongst the dock and mumbled in a Nomadic tongue.

His companion stepped forward, arms open. "Greetings," said

the stranger, his voice clear and distinct. Eyes sharp. "I am called Quill. This is my brother, Watawa." He motioned to the one-eyed Nomad. "The Open Shell."

"Our master's greetings to you also." Fenton stepped around Lenny. "Forgive my ignorance. You have the look of Nomads, yet you stand before us, breathing our air. Never have I seen such a feat. H-how is this possible? Who are you?"

Lenny saw Watawa sneer before mumbling again in the Nomadic tongue.

Quill seemed to find his brother's words humorous. "Do you believe in the Ancients, Selkie? That they gifted this realm equally to their Salt Children, both Merrow and Nomad?"

"Aye," said Fenton.

"We are their bastards." Quill's grin revealed pointed white teeth. "Call my kind what you will. The scorned ones, the in-betweens, the unloved, it makes no matter to us. We are the Unwanted."

Declan stepped forward, brushing Lenny aside.

"I've heard of ya kind," said Declan. "It's said the Sancul king wove his black magic over Merrows ravaged in the Nomadic War. Made 'em birth half-breeds as an insult to both the Merrow king, Darius Longbeak, and the Nomad high chieftain, Standing Reef."

How does Pop know all that? Lenny wondered.

"An educated slave…" Quill bowed his head to Declan. "Impressive."

"I might say the same for half-breeds," Declan replied.

Lenny grinned when his father's response coaxed a laugh from Quill and the smallest of smiles from his one-eyed brother. *Tell 'em, Pop.*

"It remains our hope your master would forgive our father's

heathen shark blood in favor of our gentle dolphin mother's," said Quill.

"Our Lord Master cares little for the blood running in your veins," said Fenton. "So long as you bring anemonies with you. Have you come for the auction?"

"Perhaps," said Quill. "The Ancients granted my brother a vision. In it, Watawa saw a crayfish hoarding numerous bounties, greatly desired by our enemies. Our chieftain, No Boundaries, sent us to learn what treasures your master keeps hidden in his cavern."

"Your pardon, sirs," said Fenton. "Our master is but a poor trader—"

Watawa's lone eyed squinted and he mumbled in his native tongue.

"My brother names you liar, Selkie," said Quill. "Yet I think you only misspoke. Please…continue. You were saying your master is poor?"

Lenny saw beads of sweat forming atop Fenton's balding head. *Betta think of something fast, boss.* Lenny nearly grinned, having never seen the head overseer at such a loss for words.

"Aye," said Fenton, finally. "Poor compared to owners in the capital. His stock is in the trading of slaves. Not caverns and titles. Nor does he hoard secrets or anemonies."

"Wiser minds than my own have said all that glistens is not silver and gold," said Quill. "We heard your master's auction mentioned on the currents. Perhaps we'll stay and find the treasure from my brother's vision there."

Slaves as treasure? Lenny scratched his head. *These two must not a been to many auctions before.*

"I'll inform Master August immediately," said Fenton. "In the meantime, please allow Declan to show you our master's hospitality. You shall have a warm bed—"

Watawa mumbled.

"We should like to accompany you to see your master." Quill stepped forward. "Now."

"O-of course." Fenton bowed away, his earrings flashing.

Buckets a blood. Lenny thought to himself. *Wish I knew what orders he's sendin' out to everybody right now.* He imagined Fenton attempting to contact anyone near their master with a warning of the Nomad intrusion.

Lenny snorted after Fenton led the brothers away, escorted by most of the hooded guardians he'd brought to the dock.

Declan gave him an immediate scolding glance.

Sorry, Pop. Lenny said. *Neva seen Fenton so nervous. Those two are—*

Cold, iron manacles pinched around Lenny's wrists. He looked into the face of the one who shackled him. "Pop?"

"When are ya gonna learn, pup?" Declan whispered.

"Pop, I don't—"

"Ya heard Boss Fenton," Declan addressed the few remaining taskmasters. "Get 'em both outta here."

A guardian tugged at Lenny's hood.

Lenny held his ground. Glared at his father. "Ya'd send ya only son to the stocks?"

"Nah," Declan replied. "I'm sendin' a captain who didn't do what he was told and lost a Selkie in his charge because of it." Declan glanced at the taskmaster. "Take 'em to the stocks till Boss Fenton decides what he wants done with 'em."

Lenny seethed as the taskmaster pulled hard. His father's earrings flashed.

Ya did good out there, pup. Declan's voice filled Lenny's head. *But the penalty for losin' one a ya crew is twenty lashes.*

I know what the penalty is. Lenny put his back to Declan and followed the taskmaster's lead toward the stockyard.

Then why'd ya come back? Declan asked.

I'm a Dolan. Lenny stepped off the docks onto a sandstone path that led between the small guest homes August provided his guests and buyers.

Yeah, ya are, said Declan. *Ya comin' back like this proves ya mettle. Might be Fenton gives ya less of the lash for the haul ya brung in.*

Might be? Lenny humphed. *He shoulda set me free by now.*

How's that? Declan asked.

Part a the deal I made with Oscar. Said if I caught the Orc for him, he'd gimme my freedom. Thought between that and the reward August promised—

A hand clapped Lenny on his shoulder. Whipped him around.

"Ya enslaved that boy?" Declan growled.

"He's no boy, Pop. He's an Orc—"

"An innocent *boy*," said Declan. "Orc or not. He's no runna. Ya can see it in his face. And ya brought him here on a…a promise? From Oscar?"

Lenny fumed when the taskmasters sniggered. He shook away from his captor. Stepped closer to his father. "I wanted to get us outta here."

"We're Dolans."

"Yeah," said Lenny. "We don't run. I know. This wouldn't a been runnin', Pop. We was gonna swim outta here, free and clear, with marks from the Crayfish to prove it."

"Boss Fenton was right. Ya still have a lot to learn, pup." Declan shook his head. "It's not only about runnin'. We don't leave others behind."

Lenny clenched his fists. "At least I—"

"*Dolan!*"

Lenny spun and saw Henry Boucher's snarl before the larger man knocked him to the ground. He curled into a ball as Henry pummeled him.

"Stupeed nipperkin," said Henry. "Told you I would—"

The rain of Henry's fists stopped, replaced by a different scuffle.

Lenny risked a peek.

Henry lay a few feet away, clutching his throat, coughing to catch his breath. He sneered as he climbed to his feet.

A shadow blocked Lenny's vision. His protector wore a black suit with white circles throughout. The same Ringed Seal suit Lenny wore.

"Stay away from my son," Declan growled at Henry.

CHIDI

CHIDI WATCHED HER OWNER RISE AND CHARGE Lenny's father. Henry slashed and stabbed, his attacks brutal and rapid.

The little man moved with surprising quickness.

I don't believe it. Chidi thought as the elder Dolan dodged rather than countered, always a half step ahead of Henry.

"Get him, Dolan!" The surrounding taskmasters cheered the fight on. "Whip that Lepa!"

"Kill him, Declan," Ellie whispered.

Chidi's heart urged she allow herself to be caught up in their excitement. A pit in her stomach bid otherwise. Still, as the bout raged on, Chidi saw something in Henry's face she had not witnessed often—frustration.

Henry sneered, then bull-rushed Declan.

Again, the little man danced away, a hair's breadth from Henry running him through.

"Call ya'self a catcha, do ya?" Declan taunted as he sidestepped another of Henry's swipes. "Seems to me all ya good for"—he dodged again—"is catchin' little girls."

Henry allowed the force of his last attack to carry through, finding only air where Declan had stood. He slashed behind him blindly.

Yes! Chidi thought as Declan caught Henry's wrist, twisted, and forced the larger man to take a knee. In one swift movement, Declan pried the dagger free and caught the hilt of it under Henry's chin.

Chidi saw her owner's head snap back from the blow.

The crowd roared approval as Declan dropped his knee onto Henry's ribs, eliciting a gasp from his opponent. With a flick of his wrist, Declan flipped the blade and had its tip hovering over Henry's throat.

Kill him, Chidi thought. *Please, kill him.*

"Pipe down!" Declan addressed the crowd.

Chidi gasped when they obeyed. *He commands so much respect.* She thought, gazing past the two fighters and noticing the tiny captive, made safe by the protection of his father. To her mind, Lenny Dolan seemed as shocked as she at how the events had unfolded. Their eyes connected.

Chidi saw his shoulders sag. Chin dip.

Henry coughed, drawing her attention. "Weel you keel a free man, slave?" He leaned his head to the side. Spit blood. "I theenk not. Else your owner would keel you and your fool son."

"Ya plan on killin' my boy?"

"No," said Henry. "I would skin 'im first."

Declan chuckled. "He's not worth the trouble it'd bring ya."

"What deed you say?"

Declan stepped back, positioned himself between Henry and Lenny. "Ringed suits sell cheap in the capital. Guarantee ya'd find a betta deal down there if that's the type a suit ya lookin' for."

"I don't want a Ringed suit," Henry snarled. "I want 'is." He pointed at Lenny.

"Oh, ya mean Master Collins's property?" Declan asked. "'Cause that suit and my pup belong to him."

Henry's thin lips pulled tighter.

"Don't think Master Collins'd be too happy findin' out some two-bit owna came into his cavern and skinned one a his slaves," said Declan. "'Specially a captain from one a his catcha crews."

Chidi suppressed a grin. She looked across the way and learned Lenny didn't bother hiding his. *Like father, like son.*

"Like I said, Ringed suits go cheap in New Pearlaya. Lepa suits like yours though…" Declan *tsk*ed. "Pricey. Especially all the way out here in the shallows, right, fellas?"

Chidi saw understanding dawn in her owner's eyes as the elder Dolan paraded around, drawing Henry's attention to the surrounding ring of hooded taskmasters.

"Yeah," said Declan. "I hear buyers all the time askin' Master Collins if he's got any Lepa suits he's willin' to sell off. Betcha some buyers'd pay double too, if only to save 'em a trip to the capital. Now, if only Master Collins knew where to get a suit like that…"

Greed oozed around Chidi as the taskmasters, all bearing shoddy and worn Common Seal suits, eyed Henry's silvery hood.

Declan stopped his march, feigning ignorance. "Anyone know ya down here, Henry? 'Cause with that accent ya got, I'd guess ya a long way from home." Declan knelt and placed Henry's coral dagger on the stone floor, then kicked it over. "Still wanna talk about skinnin' my pup?"

The elation Chidi had felt melted as Henry picked his dagger up and pointed its tip at Lenny. "'E must pay for what 'e deed."

"He will," said Declan. "If he's done anything wrong, that is."

"'E freed my Chidi. Punish 'im."

Declan shook his head. "Don't work like that. Boss Fenton's the head overseer. Up to him what punish—"

"*Now*," Henry demanded. "I weel see 'im pay now!"

"Boss Fenton—"

"Send someone to fetch 'im," said Henry. "I weel not leave until I see zat nipperkin pay."

Declan folded his arms across his chest. "Ya want Boss Fenton so bad? Go get him ya'self. He's on his way up to Master Collins mansion right now."

He knows. Chidi marveled at Declan's defiance. She had yet to meet an overseer who took kindly to an outsider's demands. Those she'd witnessed give such ultimatums often ended up with the opposite reaction they originally intended.

"Chidi," Henry shouted.

Her legs compelled her step forward. "Aye, master?"

"Find Fenton," said Henry dryly. "And eef you fail to bring 'im, ze skin I would flay from ze nipperkin's back, I take from yours instead."

Chidi felt the others watching her. She focused on Lenny most. The iron shackles around his wrists. Placed upon him, she guessed, for his part in helping her and Racer escape.

Refuse, a tiny, brave voice whispered inside her. *Stand your ground and take the beating Henry promises in Lenny's stead.*

Henry vanquished the voice with a single word. "Go."

Chidi looked once more upon Lenny Dolan. His mop of curly hair, the stern demeanor he tried so hard to maintain. She honed on the sadness in his eyes most of all, the pair of them narrowed in regret at her. *I'm sorry, Lenny.*

Chidi sprinted away along the sandstone path through the small commerce square, past the storehouses and the oyster farms.

Slaves in cages beside the auction block stood up as she angled northward, bound for the mansion atop the hill. A group had already begun the ascent.

Chidi stopped beside a whitewashed guesthouse. Squinting, she noted the pair of bare-skinned backs distinguished from the mass of grey Common suits surrounding them. *Those look like Nomads...*

She near jumped when hearing the slap of footfalls across the driftwood porch behind her.

"Well, well, well. Look who found me..."

Chidi turned.

The broad-shouldered beast of a Salt Child leaned against the porch's frame. He had shed his trench coat for a long-sleeved shirt, sewn of violet sea-grass. The seeming tights he wore resembled chaps; white along his inner thighs and crotch, grey overtaking everywhere else.

"Come to learn what these marks mean after all, girl?" Ishmael unhooked the shells used to keep his shirt closed. The chest of it pulled open, revealing innumerable scars lining his pectorals. Ishmael grinned. "Come inside with me. I'll tell you all about them."

Chidi shook her head. "M-my master sent me—"

"Did he?" Ishmael hopped off the porch and reached Chidi before she thought to move. "How kind of him to send me such a beautiful gift. Remind me to thank him later."

Chidi shivered as Ishmael ran his fingers along her shoulders and up the back of her neck.

"You know, I don't normally lay with Silkies," he whispered. "They bore me. Oh, but when I saw you on that pier…" He sighed as he stepped back to look her full in the face.

Chidi flinched when he reached out to stroke her cheek.

Ishmael chuckled. "You're right to fear me, girl. Only fools do not." He dropped his hand from her face. "So…you've tracked me down to learn how I earned these scars, have you?"

"P-please, sir. My master sent me to fetch the Crayfish's overseer," said Chidi. "H-he'll beat me if I don't return."

"Would you like it if I beat him instead?" Ishmael grinned broadly to show Chidi his pointed, razor-sharp teeth. "Perhaps I would eat him after."

"Y-you're a Nomad?"

"Half," said Ishmael. "Else how would I breathe your air? Let others tell you what they will about the ignorance of savages. I found them wise enough to recognize me as one of their own, despite my Merrow mother's blood. They even granted me a name. I am Red Water of the Bull nation."

Chidi's eyes widened.

"Ah. That's more like it." Ishmael laughed. "You've heard of me then?"

"Aye," said Chidi, bowing her head.

"And your master? Has he heard of my Nomad name?"

Chidi nodded.

Ishmael placed his finger under her chin, gently lifted it.

She stared into his greenish-gold eyes.

"Good," said Ishmael. "Then he will know I always get what I want. Carry out the errand he sent you on. Then give him a message from me upon your return."

"A-aye, sir." Chidi stammered. "What message?"

"Tell him Red Water will have you."

"Sir," said Chidi. "My master—"

Chidi trembled in Ishmael's grip as he placed his free hand roughly over her mouth.

"I *will* have you, girl. The next time we meet, you will belong to me," said Ishmael. He shoved her away. "Now go. Deliver my words to your master."

Chidi ran.

KELLEN

"KID." EDMUND SLAPPED KELLEN'S CHEEKS. "LISten to me. We don't have much time. Remember what I told you up top about fighting?"

Kellen brushed away the water droplets falling from the old marshal's beard. Though the ceiling glittered with the promise of enchantment, the illusion vanished the moment Kellen sat up. A ring of hooded men guarded the perimeter, many of them bearing lit torches that danced shadows on the stony cavern walls.

He pinched his nostrils to shut them of the scent of muck and vomit, only to discover the odor clung to his own skin. Kellen threw up at the realization.

"It's all right, kid. You'll get used to the slave stink."

Kellen dry heaved as Edmund patted him on the back. He swooned, but caught himself. Forced his eyes to remain open and stare at the cracks in the cavern floor until the world stopped spinning.

"Remember what I told you," said Edmund. "Fight. It's the only chance you've got of escape. You *have to earn* a suit."

Shivering, Kellen rubbed his shoulders to warm them. "Wh-where's my friends."

Edmund shook his head. "Can't worry about them right now. Listen—"

"*Where's my friends?*"

Edmund hung his head.

Kellen climbed to his feet. He surveyed the rocky area as a seal surfaced in the small inlet pool Edmund had dragged him from. Bryant surfaced behind the animal, gasping for air.

Where are you guys? Kellen continued his search as Edmund waded in to retrieve his partner.

A handful of people lay on their backs, chests heaving as they caught their breath. Others puked seawater. A few meandered toward the hooded men, begging in languages Kellen had never heard. The hooded men turned them all back, some with words, others with a strike of a baton.

"Kell!"

Marrero! Kellen saw his friend across the pool, sitting on his knees with a seeming corpse laid in front of him. Kellen's gut panged with recognition. *Tardiff...*

Marrero waved Kellen over, then resumed giving their friend CPR.

Kellen ran to their side, slipping on the wet rocks at the last. He fell beside Marrero.

Tardiff didn't move.

"Wh-what happened?"

"I don't know, man," said Marrero. "He wasn't breathing when they brought him up. I tried giving him CPR but...he just...he..."

Kellen shoved Marrero away. He gently tilted Tardiff's head back to clear his airway, bent to breathe life back into his friend's mouth. Tardiff's lips felt cold and slimy as Kellen gave him quick, short breaths. *Come on, Tardiff...come on...*

"They left him, man…" Marrero said. "I saw them bring him up. He just…just hung there…like, dead…"

Kellen pulled away, put all his weight into pumping Tardiff's chest. *Come on…*

Marrero sniffled. "Th-they left him…"

"No!" Kellen lost himself raining fists on his friend's chest.

Tardiff never batted an eye. Never coughed. Never took another breath.

His strength drained from the Gasping Hole, Kellen tired quickly. He fell back, staring at Tardiff's corpse, tears welling.

What's wrong, Kelly? A shade of his father's voice haunted him. *Need to have a little cry?*

Kellen closed his eyes. Steeled himself against the fear and sadness.

"He's dead…isn't he?" Marrero asked, panting. "I kn-knew it. He's dead. Oh my God, Kell, Tardiff's dead. And B-Bennett. And Bo-Boone. Th-they're gonna kill us too, man. We're gonna die down here."

Kellen shuddered. "No…" he whispered.

"Wh-what?"

"No," he said again, louder, drawing strength from the words. "I'm not."

Look at him. Kellen pulled away, forced himself to gaze on Tardiff's body a final time. *Tardiff always was just a whiny little pussy. Not like me. That's why I'm still here.* Kellen glared at Tieran as the weasel-faced man approached. *That's why I'll get out.*

"Too bad your mate didn't listen…" said Tieran. "Might not've—"

Kellen leapt up swinging.

Tieran stepped away and caught him upside the head with the

butt of his whip. He unraveled it with a flick of his hand and cracked it for good measure.

Kellen winced at the loud snap.

"Have your attention now, do I?" Tieran addressed the crowd. "I've my eye on each and every one of you lot. You step out of line, look at me in a way I don't like…" He cracked the whip again. "You'll get a lil' kiss from ol' Tieran."

Kellen inched backward, joining Edmund and Bryant.

"I don't care where you're from, or who you were before," Tieran continued. "*This* is your home now. You don't like it? Try to run?" He cracked the whip.

"Hey!" The beefy man stood. "You can't get away with this. It ain't—"

Kellen barely saw Tieran flick his wrist.

The end of the whip snapped, its end drawing a thin line of red across the beefy man's cheek.

As the big man fell to his knees, holding his cheek, Tieran held the whip aloft. "This is the only language you know from now on. You'll obey me and my lot, or we'll have the skin off your backs. You don't speak. You don't go nowhere. You don't even die unless I give my leave!"

Tieran lowered his whip. "Order up in two lines, now. Gents on the one side. Ladies on t'other. Step lively!" Tieran flicked his wrist, cracking the whip anew.

Kellen surprised himself with how fast he and the others obeyed.

"Righ', now follow the leader!"

Kellen traipsed after the beefy man in front of him, following the stuttering torchlight near the front.

Hooded taskmasters marched alongside them. All wore one-piece clothing that resembled threadbare snowsuits. A few kept careful watch, the others seemed to him as dispirited as the ones they guarded.

Now away from the Gasping Hole, the scent sweetened, albeit still foul and fishy. To Kellen's left, only cavern walls. On his right, large pools of water with people hip-deep, shoulders hunched, as they raked in nets hand over hand. High atop a stone hill, Kellen saw a small castle, carved from the cavern walls. *What is this place?*

Tieran halted them not much later.

Kellen saw no reason why. He glanced over his shoulder. Marrero stood behind him with Bryant and Edmund in line after them.

"Kell…" Marrero hissed. "What's going on?"

Would've thought a wrestler like Marrero would know to size up an opponent before making a move, Kellen thought as Tieran paraded down the line. *Get your mind right, Marrero, or else you'll end up like Tardiff.*

"Bend your ears, you sea-rats. As lord dockmaster and auctioneer, it's my lot to sort you in the way I see fit. Some of you'll stay with us, others moving on directly. If I tell you the block, step to the right. Those bound for the pits to the left."

Kellen shivered as Tieran barked out orders.

"Block," he said of a woman and a girl Kellen assumed as her daughter.

Next, he looked to a man with dark hair and heavy eyebrows. "Pits."

Down the line Tieran went with his orders. Kellen found himself guessing which would be sorted where. He deciphered Tieran sent the hardiest amongst them to the pits, those with children, elderly, or otherwise weak, went to the block.

Kellen's legs shook at each sorting called out, watching Tieran draw closer to him. His teeth chattered by the time Tieran reached the trucker.

"Oi," said Tieran, clapping the beefy man under the chin with the butt of his whip. "Well, now aren't you a big fella. You belong to me. The Crayfish means to throw some games for his company soon. Best find out how much fight there is in you beforehand, eh? *Pits!*"

Tieran grinned as the beefy man stepped to the left. It faded when he looked on Kellen.

"Ah, if it's not the bravest amongst the lot." His gaze wandered across Kellen's face and body. "Handsome and fit too. Whether the fields or the brothels, you'd fetch a pretty price at market, son, but I'll warrant you earn Master August more another way. *Pits!*"

Kellen stepped to the left as Tieran moved on to inspect Marrero.

"Righ'," said Tieran. "Pits for this one, but see that he don't get tossed in willy-nilly with the rest. He still belongs to Henry, he does. Man's already lost one to the Gasping Hole today. You can bet he'll blame me for it too. Best make sure this one sees the games or else."

Marrero quickly stepped to the left and joined Kellen, bumping shoulders in the process.

Kellen sighed, grateful he and Marrero wouldn't be split up, or at least for the moment. He listened as Tieran continued down the line, ordering Bryant to the pits, Edmund too due to his already owning a suit.

Still, Kellen felt relieved to see the elder marshal join them on the left. The sorting ended sooner than Kellen anticipated. He found himself watching the line on the right continue their march southward down the boardwalk.

Tieran gave him little time to wonder where the others ended up. "Righ', lads, this way!"

Kellen traipsed after him with the remaining handful of men and teens sorted with him. They followed Tieran westward and approached a narrow geode tunnel of purple crystals.

Whoa, Kellen thought as he followed the line through. For a moment, he forgot his predicament, lost in the sparkling shine the crystals emoted when reflecting the hooded guardians' torchlights. Nearby, a bowl-like shelf, fashioned by a combination of time and constant drips, provided a steady trickle.

Tieran stopped to dip his fingers in the bowl, then touched them to his forehead and ran his fingers down his face. Each of the guardians did the same. So too did Edmund, the lone captive to partake in the ritual.

The end of the tunnel opened into an area large enough to accommodate half the Tiber High School swimming pool. A row of rusted and barnacle encrusted cages lined one wall. Five hooded men with lean, starved frames occupied them. All stepped to the edge of their cages. Their hollow faces neither surprised, or glad, to see Kellen and the newest arrivals.

At the center, the cavern floor ended suddenly into another pool of equal size to the Gasping Hole. Its water held the same blackish veneer.

A wooden door creaked and swung closed as torchbearers shut the captives inside.

"Now," said Tieran as he walked to the far wall. "Time to see what you lot are made of. In the testing pool with you." Tieran cracked his whip.

Kellen warily stepped forward as torchbearers ushered he and the others onward.

"Did you not hear what I said?" Tieran yelled. "Get that one outta line! He belongs to Henry!"

"Kell!" Marrero cried as hooded men pulled him away from the group. "Where are you taking me?"

Kellen stepped after him.

"He'll be fine," Edmund growled, stopping him. "And so will you."

Kellen watched as they locked Marrero in a cage.

"Righ'," said Tieran. "Get in, I said. We've not got all night, do we?"

"Boss Tieran," said a torchbearer. "You want us to pull the old Selkie too?"

Tieran approached Edmund, lifted his chin to inspect him better. "Nah. Maybe he did earn his suit, once. Don't mean he gets to keep it now. Let's see if this runner still has fight in him. Toss 'em in."

Edmund didn't wait to dive in. Bryant followed suit.

Get in there and fight. Kellen jumped in feet first, desiring to learn the depth. His feet grazed a needle-like, rocky bottom of razor-sharp stone. Kellen gazed up at the glow of torchlights above the surface. He estimated the pool no more than twelve feet deep.

A crossing shadow broke his vision, startling him, and vanished.

With a hard breaststroke, Kellen ascended. He surfaced near Bryant and the beefy man. Where Edmund swam, he didn't know. Other men bobbed around him, a few desperately trying to reach the edges and climb out.

Hooded men stepped on their hands and laughed.

"I'll lay five anemonies on him," one of the hooded men motioned toward Bryant. "The rest of this lot are rotten."

"The runner's who I'll take, Tieran," said another. "Wherever he disappeared down to."

"That old geezer?" a third hooded man laughed. "Nah. The big man's who I want. What about you, Tieran? Who's your pick?"

Kellen watched Tieran's gaze fall on him.

"That one. Said it from the start, I did. Ol' Tieran knows a fighter when he sees it."

"Aye, he looks a strong one, he does. But can he swim?"

"Time to find out." Tieran stepped to the edge of the pool. "Righ', listen up you lot. Let ol' Tieran school you on the difference between dogs and rats. Dogs got fight in 'em, loyal beasts and easy to train. Rats though…we drown rats. Time to learn which of you's is which. This is a simple pool, with simple rules. All you lot gotta do is reach the other side and make it back."

Swim to the other side and back? Kellen nearly laughed as he looked on the length of the pool. *It's like a hundred meter swim…*

"Oi," Tieran called. "What you waiting for? Get swimming now."

Kellen ducked under the water, placed his feet against the wall, then kicked off the side. He remained underwater as long as he could, cupping his hands and pulling himself forward. He surfaced near the middle of the pool and swam freestyle, hand over hand, losing himself to his competitive nature. Leaning his head to the side for a quick breath, he saw no other swimmer close.

He heard cheers and applause coming from behind and, for a moment, almost believed he was back in his high school's pool. Placing his face again in the water, he opened his eyes but saw only blackness.

How am I supposed to know when to flip turn?

A few strokes later, his hand slapped the rocky siding, slicing his palm.

*Ah...*Kellen winced and halted. His torso drifted under him as he treaded water to stay afloat.

"What you stopping for, seadog?" Tieran yelled from the far side of the pool. "Move on. I got good monies on you!"

Kellen glanced back the way he'd swam and gasped.

Bryant had barely passed the halfway mark. His eyes wide, but determined, he sidestroked onward, always keeping his focus on what lay behind him.

Kellen saw why.

The waters at the far end churned frothy. Few of the others tossed into the pool with him had even made it a quarter of the way. Most struggled to hold onto the tiniest outcroppings along the stony wall. Blood streaked down their arms, their faces round with terror as water splashed around them.

What the...

"Kell!"

Marrero? Kellen blinked water from his eyes.

"Kell, swim! Hurry!"

He saw the cages beside Marrero empty, the doors unlocked and open. *They let those prisoners out...*

Another man in the water screamed as he tried in vain to climb the wall. A black backed seal leapt from the water and knocked the man back into the water. The hooded guards above jeered at the man as he resurfaced, coughing and waving before the seal dragged him below the surface.

"What you waiting for?" Tieran yelled at Kellen. "Make it back here and I'll get you a coat, lad!"

A coat? Kellen thought back on Edmund's words. *You have to fight. Have to earn—*

Something wet and rubbery brushed Kellen's thigh.

He yelped as a seal poked its head above the surface and hissed at him.

Kellen punched the animal, more reacting than thinking. He threw his face back into the water and pushed off the side, scissor-kicking as fast as he could.

A vice clamped round his ankle.

"Ah!" Kellen moaned as he lifted his head above the surface.

The vice tugged him back below.

Biting me. Kellen gagged on salt water. *A seal is biting me.*

Again, Kellen kicked. This time, he connected, the ball of his foot striking what felt like a smooth, wet stone.

The vice relented.

Kellen fought to surface. He had reached the middle of the pool. Saw chaos continuing in the waters ahead. *What do I do?*

A shadow leapt over him, splashing back into the water right in front of his face.

"Kid!"

Kellen glanced back the way he'd came and saw Bryant clinging to the far edge.

"It's Ed, kid," said Bryant. "Follow him!"

*Ed…*Kellen thought back to the deck of the ship and Edmund's changing with Boone's help.

A seal barked at Kellen. He turned and saw it bound directly at him, mouth open.

A Sea Lion porpoised beside him and lunged at the other animal, both snarling as they took their fight below the surface.

Ed! Kellen thought as they disappeared under. *He's clearing the way for me!*

Again, Kellen swam forward, coaxing all the speed he could muster out of his limbs. Taking a breath, he saw the beefy man's face red, bare arms squeezing a seal in a chokehold.

Shut it out. Kellen dipped his face back in the water. *Focus. They don't matter.*

Another breath and he saw a man clawing to maintain his grip on the cavern wall as a seal leveraged its weight to drown him.

"That's righ'!" Tieran yelled. "Come on, lad. Keep swimming! Win ol' Tieran his monies!"

"No," yelled another hooded man. "Stop him, seadogs!"

Kellen lifted his head and saw the starting point not ten feet away. *I'm going to make it—*

A seal reared its head and hissed at him.

Screw you. Kellen lunged forward, hugging his arms around the seal's neck and alligator rolling to the top. He lifted his head out of the water to catch his breath, then kicked free of the animal and swam for the wall, slapping the rocky side hard the moment he reached it.

A sharp whistle pierced the air.

"All righ', lads. Time to pay up!" Tieran crowed. "And get the rest of 'em outta the water."

The seals who fought the captives in the water ceased their battles and leapt one after the other onto the deck. The Sea Lion jumped up last.

Treading water, Kellen watched as a hooded man reached for the Sea Lion's mouth and took hold of its upper lip, then tugged back toward the skull.

The Sea Lion head peeled away. The body morphed and its skin transformed to clothing. Edmund stood on his human legs a moment later. He glanced at Kellen and nodded.

Yeah. Kellen thought. *I'm still here, old man.*

Another seal moved toward the hooded guardian.

"No!" said Tieran. "They don't get freed tonight, nor eat neither. Not after that worthless show. Back in the cages with you lot." He cracked his whip at the seals. "Call yourselves seadogs, do you? Can't even lick a new crop a slaves. How're you supposed to compete in New Pearlaya, eh?"

The seals slopped their way back to the cages. Most of the men surrounding Kellen coughed. Others cried as they clung to the side, shivering.

"Drag these sorry rats outta my sight and get 'em down to the block," said Tieran. "Not wasting a coat on 'em."

"You don't want any of them, Boss Tieran?" a hooded man asked.

"Keep that one on the far end." Tieran pointed at Bryant, then the beefy man. "And that fat lot Henry gave me. Might be a worthless swimmer, but at least he's big."

Kellen watched Tieran look down on him and grin. "And this one here."

Tieran knelt and extended an open hand toward him.

Kellen took it and was pulled up and out. His muscles trembling from the cold and the fight, he collapsed onto the stony floor.

Tieran clapped him on the shoulder. "Good show, that. You done well for yourself in there." He slapped Kellen's cheeks to garner his attention. "You'll do it again too, won't you?"

Kellen nodded.

"Good boy." Tieran pet Kellen's wet hair. Whistled at his companions. "Need to find this one a proper coat. He's earned it."

GARRETT

GARRETT LOOKED ON THE COLLINS MANSION with equal parts dread and fascination. The stonework intricacies alone boggled his mind. Lit torches cast their flickering lights against black-stained Crayfish emblems, carved near every window and doorframe, as if daring any who entered to forget who owned the mansion.

"Come along then, boys." The master of Crayfish Cavern clapped Garrett on the shoulder. "I have a hunger for wines, cheeses, and the great tales of my son's first hunt."

Garrett didn't pretend to care about the hunting portion, but the thought of food wrestled a groan from his belly.

The hooded guards who accompanied them from the dock rushed to open the great wooden doors, the weight of them calling a creaking echo.

August opened his hand invitingly toward the mansion.

Garrett ventured in.

Lush rugs of soft sea grass extended down the open hall. Garrett hesitated to walk on them until Oscar burst ahead without so much as bothering to wipe his feet. Candelabras, with arms shaped liked octopus tentacles to hold the tallow candles, lined the long hall.

Above, stone arches with draperies of deep crimson hung from rafter to rafter, almost like parachutes.

"Like those, do you?" August asked. "A salvaging crew of mine discovered them in an old trading shipwreck. I scarce thought they'd dry out so easily, but…" He shrugged gaily. "Good as new and priceless to boot. What are they again?"

"Chinese, 2nd century, sir," said one of his attendants. "Of the Han dynasty."

"Ah, yes, yes, of course. You'll have to forgive me, Garrett," said August. "When one acquires so many ancient relics, he can hardly be expected to recall all the dates and facts."

Indeed, every nook and cranny of the mansion seemed a museum, to Garrett's mind. Stacked paintings with golden frames leaned against walls. Decorative ewers of varied shapes, sizes, and colors that he dared not go near. High-backed chairs of polished wood engraved with sigils Garrett had never seen before.

Walking down the long hall, Garrett caught glimpses of every room, each more extravagant than the last. One room had nothing but pirate flags and weapons adorning the walls—daggers and dirks, swords, axes, and scimitars. The next room held guns and long rifles, pistols, and even a corner with stacked cannonballs.

"As you can tell, I'm quite the collector, Garrett," said August. "I've always been fascinated by treasure. Even as a pup, I was always finding things to keep. Ah, here we are."

Garrett followed August into a large dining area where Oscar slurped steaming soup at one end of a table of polished black wood. "An old sailing mast I had split down the middle and sanded down," August added helpfully. At least twenty high-backed chairs lined the rectangular table, each bearing the Crayfish emblem, claws pointed up and open, as their head centerpiece.

Older men stoked the massive fireplace. Above its mantle hung the same crest of interlocking Cs that Garrett had seen back at the Boston pier. Lady servants in drab, hooded dresses stood with their heads bowed near the table. *What is this place?*

"Do look up, Garrett," said August. "You're missing the best part."

Garrett obeyed and gasped at the sight. He had seen geodes before, the largest the size of a basketball. None anywhere close to the scale he looked on now.

It's bigger than the courthouse in town.

The dome-shaped geode ceiling gleamed deep violet. Light from the torches seemed to send endless waves of color across its crystals. Garrett near wept at the sight.

"Never seen anything like that in all your days, have you?" asked August.

Garrett shook his head. "No, sir."

August barked a laugh. "I'll never get over that. Did you all hear him? He called me sir."

"Aye, m'lord," the attendants answered as one.

"Me!" August said again, as if they didn't hear him. "A Selkie."

"Aye, m'lord."

August laughed again before ushering him toward the table.

Garrett had scarcely sat down before an attendant appeared with piping hot soup to place before him. It reeked of seafood, but he spooned a mouthful despite himself. Briny and rubbery, he swallowed it down nonetheless, so as to not insult his hosts. Fortunately, more attendants placed rolls and cheeses next. Garrett plunged into them.

"Hungry are you?" August asked. "That's good. Always like to see young lads eat. Makes you strong. Then one day, you wake up and look like me."

Garrett chuckled as the whale of a man heaped bread and cheese upon his own plate.

"Wine," August called and had his cup instantly attended. "Now, Oscar, my boy, regale me with tales of your epic hunt. I would hear how you crossed paths with Garrett."

Garrett listened intently to Oscar relaying his story to August. As Oscar complained about Lenny Dolan and whined of mistreatment, Garrett learned it had been Lenny that first found him and convinced Oscar of his worth.

Whatever that means. Garrett thought as he reached for his flagon to wash down more of the foul soup. He hesitated even as he brought the cup to his lips, seeing the rubies embedded in it. Garrett caught August watching him rather than listening to his son. Not wishing to offend, he drank down the sour liquid.

A servant took the cup and filled it before Garrett had a chance to place it on the table.

He continued picking at the food as Oscar droned on and noticed August slumping in his chair, one thrice the size of the others ringed round the table. Only when Oscar mentioned the Nomad at the Indianapolis Zoo did Garrett see a flicker of life return to August's previously gay demeanor.

"A Nomad, you say?"

"Aye, father. A Great Hammer."

"Hmm." August stroked his jowls. "But how did a Nomad end up there? Garrett, did you see him too?"

"Y-yes."

"And did he speak to you? Say anything at all?"

Garrett shook his head.

"Curious…" August's gaze wandered. "Very curious."

An attendant suddenly rushed the table, her seashell-shaped earrings shimmering as she whispered to August.

The Crayfish's eyes went wide. "Hide them both. Quickly!"

Servants descended on Garrett, ushering him stand. *What's going on?*

"Take your hands off me," Oscar cried. "Father!"

"No time, son. We've no time. Hurry!"

A servant forcefully led Garrett around the table, toward a tapestry that took up nearly half the wall. Garrett noted the seaside setting, mermaids lain out upon the rocks with scaly tails, though he saw people too. Most dressed in hooded suits. *They're Selkies,* Garrett thought.

"Father, let go!" Oscar whined as August dragged him toward the drapery.

"Open it," August commanded.

A servant reached behind the tapestry. A second later, the servant's hands flew over a dangling rope, tugging it down, hand over hand. The tapestry rolled upward on squeaking wheels.

A hidden entrance!

August flung the doublewide doors open, revealing a steep, spiraled staircase of stone.

Garrett snorted. *Augh. What is that smell?* It hinted of gym locker room and rotted fruit. He also knew he would not risk descending the steps to find out. *No telling how deep that goes.*

"No time!" said August. "Quickly, now!"

Garrett heard laughter. Saw August's face pale.

"Do you see what I do, Watawa?" asked a voice teeming with confidence. "It seems our presence here is unwanted."

Garrett peeked around the Crayfish.

A pair of strangers stood at the end of the table, watching them. Their lean bodies, fierce demeanor, and tribal tattoos conjured Native American pictures Garrett had often looked at in history class. Still, though both had raven hair, black as pitch, their skin seemed too pale for Garrett to believe them Indians.

"Nomads..." Oscar said, his voice full of wonder.

"Only half, boy," said the taller of the two strangers. "But enough to suffice."

The Nomad with a lone eye cocked his head upon seeing Garrett. Muttered gibberish.

The other smirked. "My brother, Watawa, asks why the Crayfish would hide such a prize as this away?" His gaze shifted to Garrett. "Our greetings to you, Orc."

"My name's Garrett."

The Nomad grinned, revealing a pair of dimples previously hidden. "And I am Quill. Tell me, how is it an Orc comes to sup with a Selkie slaver?"

"A guest," August said merrily. "Only a guest."

"And like to be a permanent one, if the tales I've heard of you are true, Crayfish." Quill paced toward Garrett.

What's he doing? Garrett stood, frozen, as Quill circled round him. Eyed him up and down.

"What do you think, brother?" Quill asked. "Is this Orc the treasure we've come for?"

Watawa shrugged.

"H-he's not for sale," said August.

"Sale?" Garrett asked. "Wh-what do you mean? What's for sale?"

Quill smirked. "You have no idea where you are, do you, Orc?"

"Excuse me," said August. "Uh, what did you say your name was again?"

"You heard me the first time," said Quill.

"Ah, yes, well, I realize common courtesies are often lost on Nomads—"

Garrett heard Watawa mumble.

"Peace, brother," said Quill. "Let the Crayfish finish. Surely this one is not so foolish as to insult his guests. Especially emissaries sent by No Boundaries."

August swallowed hard. His hand reached for a chair to lean upon. "Did you say…"

Quill chuckled. "You've heard of our chief then, I take it."

"A-aye." August quivered. "Everyone's heard of him."

"Indeed," said Quill. "Then you will know he is quick to reward those generous to him. Faster still to punish those defiant of his wants."

August's eyes flitted between Garrett and Quill. "I-I can only give you what I own."

Quill laughed.

"What?" Garrett heard himself ask. "What's so funny? What is he talking about?"

"The Lord Crayfish thinks we're come to take you, Orc," said Quill, looking to August again. "But that would only bring the Painted Guard upon us…"

Watawa mumbled.

Quill's eyes found August. "My brother says you've already sent for them."

"How can he…" August blinked. "Aye. The moment I heard the news. I-I want no trouble with my business."

"What you want and the trouble you find is of little consequence to us," said Quill.

"Wait," said Garrett. "What's this…Painted Guard…thing."

Quill's gaze fell on him. "Which of the five oceans are you from, Orc?"

"Five?"

"Aye. Which?"

Garrett looked to Oscar for the answer.

The Crayfish's son scarcely noticed him. Too busy watching the Nomads, mesmerized.

Garrett found Quill staring at him, his eyes like piercing daggers.

"He's not from the Salt," said Oscar. "I found him ashore."

"Son!"

Garrett trembled as Quill's gaze narrowed on Oscar.

"Did you? Where?"

Oscar opened his mouth to speak.

Garrett heard a struggle outside the dining hall. A moment later, a girl in a cream-colored and hooded suit burst through the doors.

I know her. Garrett thought. *Where have I seen her before?*

"Chidi?" said Oscar. "How did you get—"

Garrett tensed as a trio of hooded guards came through the doors after her.

The girl nimbly dodged them, and ran for Fenton. "Please, my lord!" She fell at Fenton's feet, panting for air. "You must come quick."

"Chidi!" said Oscar. "How did you get here? Where's Henry?"

Garrett thought the girl must have felt him staring. She glanced away the moment she saw his face, like one ashamed.

"A-at the dock," Chidi panted. "He bids you come down…had a fight with…Lenny."

"A fight." Oscar's voice perked. "I'll come with you. I'd love to watch Henry beat the blubber out of the nipperkin. Though I expect to have some harsh words with Henry myself."

Garrett heard Watawa mumble. He moved aside as Quill stepped past him, closer to Chidi. *What's he doing?* Garrett wondered as the Nomad knelt beside her and placed his fingers under her chin.

Chidi's lip quivered as Quill bid her look up.

Watawa mumbled again, yet this time Garrett swore his tone sounded different. Quieter. Thoughtful.

"Who are you, child?" Quill asked.

"That's Chidi," Oscar sneered. "She's a runaway and Henry's whor—"

"Watawa," Quill said softly. "If that whelp speaks again…take his tongue."

Garrett heard a blade drawn from its sheathe. He nervously glanced at Watawa, saw the one-eyed Nomad pointed a long knife in Oscar's direction.

Oscar shrunk behind his massive father.

"Now," said Quill to the girl. "Who are you?"

"Chi-Chidi, my lord."

School…The front office! Garrett remembered. *She was there when Sheriff Hullinger led me out.*

"I am no lord," said Quill. "Only an Unwanted. Like you…"

Garrett saw the Nomad look back at him.

"And you, Orc."

Stop calling me that. Garrett thought to say. Seeing Watawa and his long knife made him keep his silence.

"P-please, sir," said Chidi. "Please let me go. My owner will beat me if I delay."

Quill nodded. Glanced at August. "You own this girl?"

August vehemently shook his head. "I hired her master to protect my son. He insisted she be allowed to accompany him."

"Why?"

"To keep his bed warm, I shouldn't wonder," said August. "Look at her. Beautiful and dark. I should welcome her into my own bed if Henry would allow it."

Dude. She's standing right there. Garrett grimaced. He searched the faces of those around him. None seemed as disgusted as he at the way August spoke of Chidi.

"And this…Henry…" said Quill. "He would not allow it?"

"Wouldn't hear of it," said August. "No matter how much I offered for the girl."

Watawa mumbled again.

Quill nodded. "I should like to meet this Henry."

"Yes, yes, of course," said August. "I'm throwing a dinner party tonight. Henry will be invited of course, as will all the buyers for tomorrow's auction." He hesitated. "A-am I right in assuming you and, uh—"

Garrett watched August lick his lips as he glanced to the other brother.

"Ah, um," August wrung his hands. "Will you both do me the honor of attending also?"

"Aye," said Quill, helping Chidi stand. "We should like that. I can hardly remember the last time I was hosted by a crayfish."

Watawa chuckled.

"Pl-please, sirs," said Chidi. "My master—"

"Yes, yes, you must needs return to Henry," said August. "Fenton."

The grim-faced Selkie stepped forward. "Aye, master."

"Do see Chidi down to the dock and…uh…" August reached behind him. "Take my son with you."

"As you wish, master." Fenton bowed away.

The gazes of both Nomads lingered on Chidi as Fenton escorted her and Oscar out. Only when the doors had closed did they exchange a look before facing the Crayfish.

What do they want with her? Garret wondered.

"Might, uh, might I offer you both some refreshment?" August asked. "Some clam cakes? Perhaps a spot of grog?"

"No," said Quill. "But we should like to spend some time alone with your Orc."

It took Garrett a moment to realize they talked about him. "Me?"

Quill nodded. "My brother and I remain curious how an Orc calf came to this cavern. Especially one who can't seem to recall which of the five oceans he's from." He glanced at August. "Of course, you don't mind if we tour your home? Perhaps have a room to speak with him in…alone."

August's triple chin wiggled as he shook his head. "N-not at all. I should warn you, however, the Painted Guard—"

"I assure you we'll be gone before they reach your cavern."

Garrett looked to August for help and saw in the Crayfish's face he would find none. Garrett glanced at where the hidden door lay. Wondered if he might reach it in time and slip through the doors, find a way to lock the brothers from following.

"Fond of tapestries, Orc?" Quill asked.

Garrett shook his head. *He's messing with me. Knows what I'm thinking.*

"Uh," August cleared his throat. "Perhaps you would be comfortable in the library. There's a great hearth—"

"My blood runs warm enough, Crayfish," said Quill. "I have little need for your fires. But a library…that I have always enjoyed. It will suffice our needs."

"Very well."

Garrett thought August clapped at the servants in such a manner he would do anything to rid himself of the Nomads' company.

"Shall we, Orc?" Quill asked.

Like I've got a choice. Garrett thought. He followed Quill and one of August's servants out of the dining hall. Glanced back to see August wringing his hands. Then Watawa stepped in Garrett's line of sight. The one-eyed Nomad's stern expression warned Garrett should follow his brother's lead.

Garrett did.

The servant led them through a series of stone corridors. Trickles of water ran down the walls, almost like the cavern was alive and the trickles its lifeblood. More paintings hung on the walls, all of them picturing marine life and mythological sea creatures. Garrett scarcely had time to look at them with Watawa bringing up the rear, matching him step for step.

A pair of heavy oaken doors loomed at the end of the hall. Garrett gasped as the servant opened them both and led the group into the library.

"Quite the collection," said Quill, stepping into the room.

Garrett followed, his head swiveling at the sheer number of books, scrolls, and other treasures hoarded by August Collins. Model ships tucked inside glass bottles, their sails proudly displaying their colors. Garrett took one of the smaller bottles in hand, marveled at the detail with which the ship inside had been constructed. *How do they get these things in there?*

A fire crackled in a hearth taking up near half the wall and a driftwood log popped as it burned and shot sparks of red.

Garrett replaced the bottle on the shelf. He noticed Watawa at the far end of the room, fingering the book covers, head tilted to the side to better read the title works. His brother seemed to have already found a large tome he might enjoy.

Quill threw regal quilted pillows off an equally regal, cushioned couch that looked like it too belonged in a museum. He opened the tome, leaned forward to smell the pages. "Do you like books, Orc?"

"Yeah," Garrett answered. "Comics mostly...superheroes and stuff."

"I know nothing of superheroes," said Quill. "What are their stories?"

Garrett shrugged. "All kinds, I guess. My mom thinks they're just about fighting and cool weapons, but a lot more than that happens in them."

"What more?"

"Lotsa stuff. Standing up for what's right. Choosing whether to use their power for good or not. My favorite's Batman." Garrett looked at Quill. "You'd probably like Aquaman."

Watawa muttered gibberish as he resumed his search.

Garrett saw Quill's cheeks clench. "My brother says you jest with us."

"N-no." Garrett put his hands in front of him. "Sorry. It-it was only a joke. Honest."

Quill licked his finger then turned the page of the tome in

front of him. "The Crayfish's son said he found you ashore." He glanced up. "What were you doing there?"

"I live there," said Garrett. "I-I'm not from here."

"Clearly," said Quill. "Had you been, my brother and I might have killed you by now."

Garrett's laugh died in his throat. "W-why?"

"You're an Orc."

"B-but I haven't done anything to you."

"You haven't." Quill's eyes flashed. "Your kind has."

Garrett backed into a bookshelf. "P-please…please don't hurt me. Whatever my…kind…did. I'm sorry for it."

"Calm yourself. If I wished you dead, you would be," said Quill. "Can it truly be you know nothing of your kind? Nothing of the realm beneath the waves?"

Garrett shook his head. "Only what the dolphin-lady told me at the zoo."

He saw Watawa perk, leave the books he'd been searching and stride toward his brother, muttering.

Quill gave a reply in the same foreign gibberish before rounding on Garrett again. "Tell us more of this dolphin-lady. Was she old, or young? Did you catch her name, by chance?"

Lie. Garrett thought, disliking the way the brothers looked on him, especially Watawa. The Nomad's lone eye squinted and his lips moved as though he intended to speak, yet no sound came out.

"What was her name, Orc?" Quill pressed. "Tell us true."

"W-Wilda," Garrett noted his answer pleased the brothers.

Quill leaned forward. "And were there others like her at this… zoo? Any like you?"

Garrett took a deep breath to calm his nerves. "I saw a shark-man," said Garrett to the same pleasing recognition in the brother's faces. "H-he broke through his tank to get to me."

"Did he?" Quill chuckled. "And what did he look like? What type of shark?"

Garrett thought back to the darkened exhibit, the flat panel of acrylic and the giant inside. "A Hammerhead...A big one."

"And his skin?" Quill grimaced. "Black?"

Garrett nodded. "How did you know?"

Watawa again leaned toward his brother, whispered.

Quill muttered gibberish back. "My brother wishes to learn how you knew the girl in the Crayfish's dining hall...Chidi."

"I-I don't know her."

"Truly? She seemed to know you."

"I-I'm pretty sure I saw her once at my school, but—"

"Your school is on the Hard?" Quill asked. "Ashore?"

"Yes."

Quill leaned back on the couch, his demeanor ponderous. "And your home...how far is it from here?"

"Why?" Garrett asked. "Could you take me there? Will you take me home?"

"No," said Quill. "But you will tell us how to get there."

Garrett felt Watawa's lone eye focus on him again. He swallowed hard, suddenly cold, and in his heart, knew full well the Nomad brothers would not be denied an answer.

LENNY

Lenny sat upon an uneven boulder, his legs and hands outstretched. He had the odd thought he must resemble a table, tipped on its side with its legs facing straight out. The wooden stocks binding his wrists and ankles limited his mobility. Lenny fought his bonds to stretch his back. He guessed it had been near an hour since Henry sent Chidi to fetch Fenton.

They'll be back soon. Lenny knew. *Pop tried his best, but even his delay's not gonna stop what's comin'.*

Lenny glanced up and found Henry staring back, confirming his suspicions.

Henry had scarcely moved since sending Chidi away. He had raged a little while after, but no amount of obscenities, taunts, or demands stirred Declan from Lenny's side. He sat next to his son even now, stroking the head of his pet sea otter that nestled its head against him.

The two Dolans had scarcely said three words to one another since the fight. Lenny didn't know where to begin. He also knew Declan would say little, and less with Henry so near. Not for the first time, he cursed Henry's smarts in demanding Declan separate Lenny, Paulo, and Ellie and have their earrings removed to keep them from devising a story to back one another for when Fenton eventually returned. Now, without his earrings to mind-speak, Lenny found himself alone with his thoughts.

He hated it.

Ever since seeing Chidi and Henry, a single question ran circles in his mind. *Where's Racer?*

His conscience warned he already knew the answer. Lenny refused to accept it. He envisioned various scenarios where Henry only cared about recapturing Chidi. That the crazed Frenchman might have allowed the others go free.

If that's true, why does Henry have a bundle of sealskins with him? Lenny's conscience argued. He recognized the makes of all three suits—two Lions and a Leper. *One a those was the marshal's from the jailhouse.* Lenny recalled. *The Lepa suit though...could that be Wotjek's?* Lenny couldn't remember what kind of suit Zymon Gorski wore.

Racer made it, he convinced himself. *Him and the boy, Allambee. They're out there. Free.* He tried again to stretch his back from the cramped position the stocks forced him to hold.

Lenny growled when the pain refused to go away.

"Uncomfortable, nipperkin?" Henry chuckled. "You weel be soon. Once Fenton arrives."

"Maybe he's not comin'," said Lenny.

"'E weel," said Henry. "Sooner or later, 'e weel come. Ze Crayfeesh owes me."

"For what?" Declan asked.

"*Monsieur* Oscar promised to double my fee for 'elping capture ze Orc."

"Uh huh...he promised to free me too." Lenny rapped his knuckles against the wooden barriers holding him prisoner. "Guess I should get up and swim outta here, huh?"

"You are only a slave," said Henry. "Stupeed of you to believe 'im."

"When ya got nothin', whattaya got to lose?"

Henry frowned. "Zere is always something to lose."

"What've ya eva lost, Henry?" asked Lenny. "Besides the anemonies Oscar promised ya?"

A shadow crossed Henry's face. "Ze Crayfeesh *weel* pay me."

"Rememba ya said that when he knifes ya in the back."

Henry waved away Lenny's words. Then he stood and backtracked toward the docks, muttering in French.

Lenny waited until he gauged Henry out of hearing range. Then he elbowed Declan. "Pop."

"Hmm?"

"Thanks."

Declan glanced up from his otter. "For what?"

Lenny sighed. "Savin' me back there. From Henry."

"Why ya thankin' me for? Like I done ya a favor or something."

"Ya did, Pop. He woulda killed me if not for ya steppin' in."

"Might kill ya still," said Declan. He pushed the otter away and looked Lenny full in the face. "I'm not always gonna be there, pup. Whatta I always tell ya, huh? Ya neva gonna be big, Len, so ya gotta be—"

"Fasta or smarta if ya wanna survive," Lenny finished. "I haven't forgot."

"Then ya didn't listen too good."

Lenny's brow furrowed. "Huh?"

Declan looked around to see if anyone listened. He leaned close.

"Ya let 'em go, didn't ya? Chidi and Racer. They got to ya somehow. Made ya feel sorry for 'em so ya turned 'em loose, right?"

"I did what I thought ya would in my place."

"Yeah?" Declan frowned. "What ya didn't do was ya job. Rememba the last thing I told ya before ya left, or did ya forget that part too?"

"I rememba," said Lenny, his voice rising. "Told me to catch the girl and bring my crew back safe."

"So why didn't ya?" Declan's tone rose to match Lenny's. "Why can't ya eva just listen to me, Len?"

"I dunno," said Lenny. "Why didn't ya tell me the truth, Pop?"

"About what?"

"Bourgeois. Ya told me ya'd heard of her before in the trade towns. That loads a catcha crews had been sent for her and all of 'em came back empty-handed. Fenton said it was a fake hunt." Lenny sighed. "Why'd ya lie, Pop? Why not tell me the chase was a…a… fake? Something to make Oscar feel—"

"Important?" Declan said quietly.

"Yeah…"

"Ya told Henry when ya got nothin', ya got nothin' to lose," said Declan. "But when ya got nothin', ya got nothin' to give neither."

"Pop…"

"All these years down here, only thing I could give ya was advice." Declan shook his head. "Prepare ya, best I knew how, for what's out there, swimmin' the Salt. Master Collins made ya a captain." Declan paused to compose himself. "Ya think I'd take that away from my boy?"

"But Pop…" said Lenny. "Why didn't ya at least tell me ya knew her?"

"I don't," said Declan. "Neva heard of her before ya were sent out."

"Why'd she have a picture of ya then?"

"Picture?"

Lenny nodded. "Found it in a notebook we lifted off her. She drew it."

Declan scratched his head. "How did she—"

"Ah-ha!" Henry crowed. "You weel pay now, Dolan."

Both Dolans turned their gaze toward the docks.

Fenton marched through the square at the head of a column of slaves, all brought to witness the punishment to come. Taskmasters surrounded the group, ensuring none slipped away. Familiar faces blended amongst the crowd—catchers Lenny had known all his life, including Paulo's mother. The others he assumed worked in the Collins's mansion; those who had learned it best to keep their heads down after a lifetime of whippings for daring to look others in the eye.

Lenny cursed upon seeing the white sheen of a Harp suit to Fenton's right. Its bearer grinned eagerly, near skipping to the stocks.

Oscar. Lenny sneered.

"Endrees," Declan said to his otter. "Go home."

The animal scampered away as the throng approached.

Lenny honed on Chidi, bringing up the rear, noting she refused to meet his eye line. *I don't blame ya, Cheeds.* He wished to speak his mind. *Ancients know I'd neva believe ya meant to get caught.*

Henry fell in beside her, his earrings flashing.

Must be yellin' in her head. Lenny thought when Chidi winced. He sighed and listened to the quiet shuffling of feet as the horde spread around him to witness.

Fenton stopped well short of the stocks, Oscar a shadow by his side.

"Where is your crew, Captain Dolan?" Fenton asked.

Declan rose. "Henry demanded they be separated, boss. Worried they might talk to one another."

"They would 'ave." Henry shoved toward the front. "Slaves are liars."

"I'll determine the truth here," said Fenton. He glanced at the taskmasters closest to him. "Bring me his crewmates."

Lenny watched them scurry off to do his bidding.

"Life in the Salt is harsh for our kind," Fenton addressed the crowd. "And fear our constant companion. We gather here on this Blue Monday not only to give thanks for our Lord Master's protection and the Salt life he gifted us, but as a reminder of the penalties for disobeying him." Fenton narrowed his eyes at Henry. "Sir, Captain Dolan informed us you abandoned your mission—"

"Lies," Henry spat.

"A point Master Oscar agreed with." Fenton finished.

Lenny nearly choked. *Oscar stood up for me?*

"He also called me a fool." Oscar said. "Don't think I've forgotten, Henry."

"What say you to these claims, sir?" Fenton asked.

"I admit eet," Henry said. "I called the leetle Crayfeesh a fool."

"Fenton!" Oscar grit his teeth. "Are you going to let him call me that again?"

Lenny hid a grin.

"Sir," said Fenton. "I remind you, Master Oscar is your employer—"

"Aye," said Henry. "And 'as yet to pay me what's owed."

Oscar crossed his arms. "You don't get paid for abandoning me. What if they'd killed me after you left? What then?"

"I would not be 'ere," said Henry. "But you are alive and well. Ze girl I was 'ired to catch has been captured. So too was ze Orc you 'ired my services for."

Lenny heard a collective gasp from the crowd, whispers of an Orc in Crayfish Cavern. He saw the catchers amongst the crowd look on him with newfound respect. A few of the older ones, Paulo's mother included, shook their heads. *Like ya wouldn't do the same.*

"Silence!" Fenton commanded, *thwack*ing his waist-high, razor shell cane on the cavern floor.

"I weel not be silent," said Henry. "I weel be paid."

"You abandoned—"

"To reclaim Crayfeesh property 'is nipperkin set free!"

The crowd parted as the taskmasters returned with Paulo and Ellie, escorting them to the center where three repurposed masts had been erected in a line. Chains and shackles dangled from holes in the tops of each.

Paulo glared at Lenny as the taskmasters took hold of his wrists and shackled him to a mast. A taskmaster pulled the chain taut, raising Paulo's arms over his head, forcing his belly against the wooden pole. Another taskmaster repeated the procedure with Ellie.

Lenny grimaced as he looked on his crewmates, chained only a few feet apart from one another. *It should be me there. Not them.*

"You have proof of your claim?" Fenton asked, calling Lenny's attention back to the matter at hand.

"Aye." Henry shoved Chidi forward. "Tell 'im what you told me."

No. Lenny thought, watching Chidi stumble. She picked herself up and met his gaze. Lenny saw her reddened eyes before she looked away.

"I-it's true," said Chidi.

"Speak up, girl." Henry snarled. "Let zem all hear what ze son of Declan Dolan deed."

I'm a stone. Lenny repeated to himself as he listened to Chidi confess how she became free of her bonds. That Ellie had been in on the plot and he the mastermind. He watched Paulo's face turn scarlet as Chidi mentioned Ellie and Lenny knew him too stupid to keep such a weighty secret and kept the brute ignorant of their plan.

Henry smirked.

Two can play this game, pal.

"She'll say anything Henry tells her too." Lenny interrupted Chidi's confession. "Look at her. She's shakin', Boss. Whatsamatta, Cheeds? He gonna beat ya if ya screw up ya lines?"

Chidi's face melted in shame.

Sorry, Cheeds. We're not on the Hard no more. Gotta look out for ourselves down here.

"I'm inclined to agree with Captain Dolan, sir," Fenton said to Henry. "Forgive me, but your slave certainly seems frightened by you. One can only imagine—"

"Ask Ellie," said Henry.

"I beg your pardon?"

"Ask…*Ellie.*"

"Very well," said Fenton. "What do you say of these charges, Ellie?"

Ellie placed her forehead against the wooden mast. Her shoulders heaved, chains rattled.

"Ellie—" Fenton's bushy eyebrows raised. "Did your captain order you to free your crewmates?"

Come on, Elle. Lenny willed her. *Back me up.*

"N-no," said Ellie. "Racer hit—"

"Liar!" Henry cried.

Lenny sighed in relief. When he looked up again, he caught Paulo glowering at him. *He knows what I did.* Lenny realized. *That Ellie's lyin' to protect us.*

Oscar laughed. "Did you honestly expect a slave to admit herself guilty, Henry? Now who's the fool?"

Henry traipsed to the whipping masts, his right hand drifting into his Selkie pocket. "Remember what I promised you, Ellie?"

Lenny straightened. *No...*

Henry drew his coral dagger free of the pocket, raised the blade above his head.

Lenny heard a loud crack near his ear. A second later, he saw Henry yanked off balance by the whip wrapped around his wrist. He pitched backward, losing the grip on his dagger. Lenny glanced to his left.

Declan held the whip, his face stern as he stared down his adversary.

"Seize him," Fenton roared.

No! Lenny's heart fluttered. *Not Pop.*

His panic melted when the taskmasters instead took hold of Henry. The Frenchman fought to free himself of their grip, snarling and raging.

"Ellie," Fenton said quietly. "What did he promise you?"

"That if I didn't agree with Chidi, he would..." Ellie's voice cracked. "He would skin me like he did R-Racer."

Lenny reeled at the admission. He imagined the innocent young catcher as he had last seen him at the jail, his eagerness to follow the plan and gain his freedom. Lenny's thoughts drifted to Henry, peeling the suit off the deputy marshal, Richard Caspar. His stomach twisted at the notion Racer endured the same end. Lenny fought down the urge to retch and give Henry a point to argue his guilt.

"Is this true?" Fenton demanded.

"Aye," said Henry. "I keeled 'im. Eez eet not a penalty for runners to die?"

"I decide the penalties here," said Fenton. "Guards. Take this fool from my sight."

Henry shrugged free of his captors. "I 'ave not been paid!"

"You shall receive it after the auction tomorrow."

Henry glared at Lenny. "I would see 'im punished first."

"You forfeit that right when you slew the Lord Crayfish's property without leave," said Fenton. "Now go. Unless, of course, you would rather be tied to the masts with your crew?"

Henry glowered at Fenton as he left, stopping only to jerk Chidi to her feet and drag her behind him toward the guesthouses.

Fenton waited until both had gone before continuing. "Declan?"

"Aye, boss?"

"Has Racer's father, Ansel, been taken into your charge?"

"Not yet," said Declan. "Sent some men to fetch him from the oyster fields already. Should be here soon."

"Very good," said Fenton. "See him brought to the gallows at first light."

"Aye, boss." Declan bowed away as Fenton addressed the crowd.

"All of you know full well the penalty for running. Each of you has been brought here to serve a purpose. To shirk your duty and abandon your fellows is to sentence them with death. Racer knew the consequences of such an act. He stood in our Lord Master's sight and said the words. Should any slave not return—"

"Let my loved ones pay the price," the crowd echoed as one.

Fenton nodded. "Tomorrow, the father will hang for the son's crime. Let this be a lesson to you all."

My crime. Not his. I'm the one who turned 'em all loose. Lenny glanced at Declan, studied his features that he knew by heart. Imagined Declan being led to the gallows in his place. *What've I done, Pop?*

"Ellie Briceño," Fenton continued. "Paulo Varela."

Lenny listened to the chains of his crewmates rattle as they maneuvered themselves to look on Fenton. "Aye, boss," they answered together.

"Your lack of vigilance allowed one of your Lord Master's slaves to escape. The penalty is twenty lashes." Fenton glanced away. "Taskmasters, to your work."

Two men emerged from the crowd, freeing the loose ends of their whips from their coils. They paced ten feet away from Ellie and Paulo and stood their ground.

Lenny shifted. *No...*

"Boss Fenton." Paulo called.

"Yes?"

"I'll take it all, sir. Both my penalty and Ellie's."

"Paulo, no," said Ellie.

I keep tellin' ya to forget about her, Paulie, Lenny wanted to tell Paulo, despite knowing what his friend's response would be. *Can't ask a Brazilian to give up on love.*

"A noble gesture." The old overseer's eyes squinted at Paulo. "You love her, pup?"

"From the moment I saw her, sir."

Fenton nodded.

"No." Oscar stepped forward. "That's not how it works. You can't decide to take her faults on."

Fenton cleared his throat. "Master—"

"I said no." Oscar wheeled on Fenton. "My father owns you, slave. That means I own you too. Do as I command, else I'll have you take their punishment and then some."

Lenny cursed Oscar when the old Selkie wilted before the little beast.

Fenton lifted his gnarled hand then let it fall.

The twin cracking of whips came instantly.

Lenny winced as Ellie howled and hugged the mast, a thin line of red streaking across her back.

"Leave her alone," Paulo shouted as the whips lashed again.

Lenny's wrists and ankles pulled at the edges of his wooden confines. He heard Paulo grunt as the whips cracked a third time. Saw the brute try and lean himself nearer Ellie to shield her from the blows. The chains halted his goal.

"*Harder,*" Oscar ordered.

Another crack and Ellie cried out again.

Paulo stood on his tiptoes. The move allowed him to bend his wrists, grab the chains. His face turned red as another lash called sealskin and blood from his back.

Paulie, whattaya doin'? Lenny gasped with the crowd as the product of slave owner selection inched forward, blood running from his wrists down his arms.

The mast top quivered.

"F-Fenton," said Oscar. "What's he doing?"

Lenny noted the aged overseer's mouth hung open as the whips sounded anew.

"*Paulo!*" Ellie cried.

Paulo's face turned purple. His shoulders trembled and he

released a feral roar Lenny swore Bostonians could hear on the mainland.

The mast top shook and then leaned.

Paulo's chains laxed and he fell across Ellie, shielding her with his girth.

Save for the sobbing of Ellie and Paulo's mother, Lenny had never heard Crayfish Cavern so silent.

Paulo's back shuddered, a crisscrossed maze of red rising and falling in wait for the next blows to fall.

Son of a sea cook, Paulie. Lenny marveled at the tipped mast. His astonishment vanished when he saw Oscar stride toward the taskmasters.

"Lay on!" Oscar screamed. "What are you standing there for, idiots? I said lay on."

"No…" said Fenton quietly.

"*What?*"

"Their punishment already given them will suffice."

Oscar shook his head. "When my father—"

"I shall personally inform him of my decision, young master." Fenton glanced at the mast. "Your father would not wish such an incredible beast ruined by more lashings." Fenton whistled at the taskmasters. "Free them both and see them well attended, especially the bull. I warrant these two will make a fine pair for breeding. Their offspring should fetch our Lord Master quite a fortune."

We all shoulda ran. Lenny thought as they released Paulo from his chains. His crewmate remained conscious, though he leaned heavily on the taskmasters as they led him away.

Ellie stood without help.

Lenny thanked the Ancients for that little mercy, even as she cast a sad glance at him before she too was led away. *Take care of him, Elle.*

"Now it's your turn, nipperkin."

Lenny stared down Oscar. *I shoulda killed ya first chance I got. Henry too. Then we'd all be out there, free and safe, watchin' each other's* backs.

But then it'd have been Pop in my place, his conscience argued. *Paulie's ma and some poor schmuck hangin' for Ellie too.*

"Aye," said Fenton. "Captain Dolan, you've been accused of freeing your crewmates—"

"And releasing more than a few new slaves I caught for Father," Oscar said.

"Do you deny these accusations?" Fenton asked.

"Aye," said Lenny. "Why would I let anyone go? To come back and see my friends beat for it, huh? Have ya punish me too? They're all—"

"You sniveling little liar." Oscar said. "I say he's guilty."

"And I can find no fault in Captain Dolan's reasoning," said Fenton. "He completed the task your father set him and brought new slaves. The same twenty lashes will suffice."

"No," said Oscar. "My father said we were captains, but they always followed his commands instead of mine. They loved him more than me. I saw it in their faces, Fenton."

Maybe if ya weren't such a brat.

"Young master, please."

"They would follow him anywhere. I know they obeyed him in this." Oscar said. "He planned it, Fenton! He's *always* planning something."

Like how I'd love to strangle ya? Lenny stared down his owner's son.

"Master Oscar," said Fenton. "That is hardly a reason to wish him—"

"I want him punished!" Spittle flew from Oscar's mouth. "Not locked in the stocks. Not twenty, not even one hundred lashes. I will see his little feet dance in the air as he pulls at the rope, begging for one last breath. I want him hanged!"

Lenny watched Fenton weigh the option of continuing his argument.

The overseer's shoulders sagged. "Very well," Fenton sighed. "He will hang..."

Oscar grinned smugly.

"...but not by the neck."

Lenny's face paled.

"What are you playing at, Fenton?" Oscar asked. "That's the only way to hang a slave."

"No, young master," said the old overseer. "There is another way."

CHIDI

HENRY SHOVED CHIDI ACROSS THE THRESHOLD of the guest quarters lent to them.

She retreated into the corner while her owner paced the floor, raging in French of the terrible things he would do if Lenny Dolan were in his charge. For now, she remained silent, fearing Henry's fury would only heighten when she relayed the message the half-blooded Nomad, Ishmael, ordered her give.

Henry plucked the cork stopper from a rust-hued bottle of grog and tossed it. He placed the lip to his mouth and upended it.

Chidi listened to him guzzle it down. She had rarely seen him drink, but when he did…

She recalled with distinct clarity it wouldn't be long before he looked to her as an outlet for his madness. Her eyes searched the room for a place to hide. A door to wedge behind until Henry tired or passed out from the liquor.

The bottle shattering on the driftwood floor made her jump. She spun and caught Henry leering at her. He wiped the last traces of alcohol from his lips with the back of his hand and started toward her. *Please, no…not again.*

A knock came at the door and it opened without the guest

waiting for an answer. Tieran stood in the entryway. He grinned slyly. "This a bad time?"

"*Oui*," said Henry. "Get out."

Tieran strolled in. "Sorry, mate. Just come from the testing pit, I have. Impressive new lot you and the nipperkin brought back." Tieran helped himself to the liquor stores and poured a shot. "I'll warrant they'll fatten all our purses tomorrow. Might even be one or two make it a month on the reef circuits."

Tieran took the shot down easily, then poured himself another.

"I've come to pick up those extra suits you brought back."

"Buy," said Henry.

"Sorry?"

"You've come to *buy* the suits. Not pick up."

"What do you take me for, Henry?" Tieran feigned offense as he took the second shot. "Always been fair with the trade, I have. So come on, let's see 'em."

Chidi slid away to the opposite wall as Henry took the hooded suits off the bed and unrolled them across the dining table. Tieran picked up the silvery suit, a twin to the hooded garment Henry wore.

"A Leper suit, eh," said Tieran, unfolding the suit to inspect it. "Don't see these much outside the capital. Who'd you kill for it?"

Wotjek. Chidi thought back on Zymon Gorski's brave protector.

Henry narrowed his eyes at Tieran's question.

"No offense, mate," Tieran chuckled nervously. "Don't matter to ol' Tieran where you got it, now does it? How much you want for it?"

"A thousand anemonies," said Henry.

Tieran whistled. "A pretty price for a pretty suit, that is. Don't suppose you'd do four hundred and I'll toss in this ol' thing?" Tieran tugged at his worn Common Seal hood.

Henry stepped closer. "A thousand."

"All righ', all righ'." Tieran backed away. "No need to get nasty. Can't blame ol' Tieran for tryin' now, can you? As it happens, I know just the pup for this coat. With a suit like this, he's sure to earn his keep."

Chidi saw Tieran give a sideways glance to the other two suits.

"How much for the pair a Lions?"

The thought crossed Chidi's mind to mention both already belonged to the Crayfish. The one Racer's, the other Chidi remained certain Henry had picked up after she had escaped at the jail.

"Four 'undred," said Henry. "Each."

"You drive a hard bargain, mate. But it's your lucky day." Tieran removed a leather pouch from his waist, untied it, and reached in. He produced a handful of coins and pocketed them. Then he tossed the pouch to Henry.

Chidi listened to the doubloons jangle against one another as her owner caught it.

"His lordship told me to pay whatever you asked." Tieran grinned. "Told me to keep the lot left over."

Henry sneered. "Give me the rest."

"That's not how deals work, mate," said Tieran, as he gathered up the suits. "'Specially not down here. I'll give you another tip though. Only seems fair after what you done for me." Tieran jiggled his pocket to make the coins rattle. "You'd do well to take what monies you still got, that lass a yours, and light outta here while you both still got suits on your backs."

"Why?" Henry asked.

"Your girl's a beaut, she is." Tieran nodded at Chidi. "Nomads round these parts are known for ravaging pretty lil' Silkies they fancy. You got one of the worst with his mind made up on having her."

"Ishmael…" Chidi whispered.

"Aye," said Tieran. "Champion of the reef circuit pits, he is. Won me a fair bit a coin when I bet on him in the capital arena too. He's one a them Bull Sharks. Their lot's worse than Whites, to my mind. Whites are bigger, sure, but pound for pound, there's nothin' like a Bull in a fight."

"'Ave you ever been in a fight?" asked Henry.

"Mostly bet on 'em. That's what I do. Done all righ' for meself too, I don't mind sayin' it." Tieran grinned. "So you can believe it when ol' Tieran tells you, there's no Bull like Ishmael neither. I heard it said the Nomads took him as one of their own, even on account of his Merrow mother's blood. They call him Red Water. Don't have to be a smart one to figger why. After you done seen one of his fights, it's all that left behind."

Chidi thought on the scars Ishmael had shown her. She glanced at Henry, knew him smart enough to recognize he would be outmatched in a bout with a Salt Child like Ishmael.

"Anyway." Tieran shifted his focus to Henry. "Run into him on the way over, I did. Said he gave your lil' bird a message for you. Told me to give you the same if'n I saw you first. Says he'll be taking her off your hands, mate. Next time he sees you, that is."

Chidi shivered.

"Might be I'd be willing to run her over to him, if you like," said Tieran. "If the price is right, that is."

"Where eez 'e now," asked Henry.

"On his way up to the Lord Master's mansion, I'd guess. The Crayfish loves to entertain his guests the night 'fore an auction, especially the ones what are here to buy. I'll warrant those half-bred Nomads want to see this new lot fight 'fore they pay. Blood 'em early, that's what the Crayfish'll tell ol' Tieran tomorrow. Anything to drive the price up." Tieran laughed. "You'll be staying for the auction too, I expect. Won't you?"

Why does he care? Chidi wondered. She thought the Crayfish's auctioneer seemed jittery when Henry did not answer.

Tieran stepped to the threshold, paused. "I take it you won't have me escort your lil' lady to Ishmael then?"

"Get out!" Henry threw the empty bottle of grog and missed Tieran's head by an inch.

"Will do, sir. Can't blame ol' Tieran for tryin' now, can you?"

Chidi hated the way the Crayfish's auctioneer looked on her before closing the door. A man like that knew only greed, she knew, and Chidi harbored little doubt he had not come for the suits alone. Her owner seemed of the same mind.

Henry paced to the amber-colored window, peeked out to watch Tieran's departure. His lip curled and he muttered curses in French.

This won't end well. Chidi thought as he sat down upon a rickety chair and produced his coral dagger and a whetstone from his Selkie pocket. His hand flashed back and forth and Chidi tried to control her breathing as the dagger's edges sang, each note making it sharper. She swore Henry struck his blade against the stone harder every time he glanced at the door, almost as if he awaited Tieran's next entrance.

She could not say how much time passed before he stopped, but estimated near a half-hour. Then Henry tucked both dagger and stone away and stood, unconcerned that the chair tipped over and cracked its back in two.

"We are leaving." Henry stepped to the door.

Chidi hung back.

"Are you deaf, girl?" Henry snarled. "I said we are leaving."

Chidi nodded and hurried out the guesthouse after him. They darted from house to house, looping ever wider to go unseen from those at Lenny's trial. *Where is he going?*

Once past the houses, she followed Henry's lead along the narrow paths through the oyster fields. Henry never stopped until they reached the easternmost part of the cavern, far from the crowded docks. She guessed them somewhere south of the Gasping Hole they'd arrived through. Chidi saw no one around and the only landmark a lone storehouse she recalled passing not a few hours ago.

She had paid little attention to the shack at the time, but fear mounted in her as Henry approached its locked door and used the tip of his dagger to pick the lock open.

The lock clicked free.

Henry pocketed it and nudged the door open.

Goose bumps raced up Chidi's arms and legs as she looked on the blackness awaiting them.

Henry plucked a torch free of its mounted holding beside the door to ward off the dark. "Come, Chidi."

She obeyed, fearing Henry's wrath more than the shadows cast by the flickering orange flames. Chidi stepped into the shack.

Henry's torch revealed the outer siding as a ruse to what truly lay inside. No mere shed for storing tools, nets, or the like. Chidi saw the cavern walls shaped like hourglasses leading to a winding tunnel.

"H-how did you know this was here?" Chidi asked.

"I deedn't." Henry ventured further in. "I needed only a place to 'ide you away until after ze auction. I'll not 'ave some Nomad take my Chidi."

So this will be my prison. Chidi took in her surroundings with greater interest. The walls here were unlike those outside the shack. These were rougher, unsmoothed by time and pressure.

It's a mining tunnel! Chidi realized. *But where are all the tools?*

"A shack would 'ave done nicely." Henry continued deeper into the tunnel. "I like zis better."

They followed the winding path until it branched in a Y.

Left or right? Chidi wondered.

Henry chose to go right. The walls sloped inward the further they went and soon Chidi found herself forced to turn sideways to fit. She thanked the Ancients when the side tunnel dead-ended near thirty yards later in a pool, its waters so still Chidi thought it a black mirror.

Henry thrust the torch at her. Only after she took it did he don his hood and transform into his Salt form.

Chidi shivered as the Leopard Seal slipped into the pool. Circled the perimeter as if in wait of a predator below. Henry dove so suddenly that she thought a Nomad or something more sinister still had caught him. She backed away from the edge, torch quivering in her sweaty grip.

Henry's seal head breached a moment later, swam for the edge, and slipped out of the pool. The top of his seal head split in two, torn like a perforated edge, as the changes swept down his back until he stood on human legs.

Chidi sighed, wished she had the power to change at will like Henry and other freed Selkies had. "Wh-what was down there?" she asked.

"Nothing of note." Henry snatched the torch from her.

She followed him back to the Y and into the tunnel branching left off the main. Unlike the previous passageway, these walls widened as they went. The rock face of them was chipped, this tunnel handcrafted.

Henry stopped, cursed before continuing.

Chidi followed warily. She heard shuffling ahead and not from Henry. Her pulse quickened as the low ceiling opened into a larger room and Henry's shadow cast across the far wall. Hesitantly, she stepped through the threshold and looked on what had made Henry curse.

Chidi gasped as Marisa Bourgeois stood tall in the iron cage she'd been locked away in.

"What are you doing 'ere, slave?" Henry asked.

"Waiting for you." Marisa grinned.

"Lies." Henry spat.

"Aye," said Marisa. "In truth, I wait for someone else. The Lord Crayfish ordered me hidden away the moment my presence was made known to him."

"Why?"

"Why have you brought Chidi?" Marisa chuckled. "To keep others from seeing her."

"You know nothing of my reasons," said Henry.

"I know many things." Marisa replied with a calmness that prickled Chidi's arms anew. "Most of them secrets. Would you like me to share yours, Henry Boucher?"

Henry scoffed.

Chidi saw Marisa's head cock to the side.

"Should I tell Chidi why you will never let any harm befall her?"

Marisa asked. "How you loathe the very sight of her, but cannot bring yourself to end your suffering?"

Henry's face paled.

Marisa smirked. "Should I tell her about—"

"*Stop.*" Henry choked. Wiped the corners of his eyes with the back of his hand. "Stop…"

Chidi sighed, not realizing she'd been holding her breath. *How does she know all this?* Her gaze flickered to Henry. *What does she know of him?* Then came a thought more haunting still. *What does she know of me?*

Henry grabbed Chidi by her bicep and led her to the iron cage opposite Marisa's. In moments, he picked the lock with his coral dagger, then ushered her inside.

"Wh-what are you—"

"*Shh-shh.*" Henry shushed her as he closed the gate and reclosed the lock. "Eet's only for a leetle while. Till tomorrow when I collect what's owed. We weel leave after, I promise you. Off for home, far from this miserable den of liars and thieves."

Chidi looked into his eyes. Normally hard and unforgiving, now she saw them weary and concerned.

"You are mine, Chidi," Henry said softly. "I would never let anything 'appen to you."

Chidi backed to the furthest reaches of her cage.

Henry frowned. He turned to leave, then seemed to think better of it. Kneeling, he pushed the bottom end of the torch through the slat openings enough to support the weight. "A present for you." He stood and looked on Chidi again. "I know you despise ze dark."

Chidi saw his shoulders sag as he left the cage, almost as if he expected a thank you, or for her to beg him not to go. He never bothered address Marisa again, did not even glance at her, as he vanished back through the tunnel the way they came. Chidi thought to call out to him as a test to see if he yet lingered in the shadows.

She didn't. Instead, Chidi looked on the torch's flame. All that fought off the darkness Henry rightly surmised she hated.

"Why did you let me go, Chidi?"

Chidi shifted away from the flame and lost herself in the gaze of Marisa Bourgeois.

"You never answered me on the boat," said Marisa. "Tell me now."

Chidi hesitated. "First tell me what you know of Henry. I've never seen him look like that before. What did you say to scare him so?"

"I know many things about many faces," said Marisa. "I would wrong them by spilling their secrets. Even one as wretched as he deserves his secrets kept."

"But you just said—"

Marisa smirked. "What I said feared him…isn't that what you wanted? For him to feel some small measure of what you live with in his shadow every day?"

Chidi shook her head. "I want to be rid of him."

Marisa's eyes searched the empty cavern around them. "And we are."

"For now. He'll be back…he always comes back."

"I gave you what you wanted, Chidi Etienne," said Marisa. "Now give me something in return. Why did you let me go at the zoo?"

"I-I wanted to go with you. I thought…"

"We might run together?"

Chidi nodded.

"We will," said Marisa. "Some day. The Ancients sang it to me."

"The Ancients are all but forgotten."

Marisa nodded. "It is as you say. But there are still a few who believe."

"I've heard the Ancients' songs many times, but never once did they sing words." Chidi sat down in her cage, her back against the bars.

"Yes, but you sense them, no? Feel their power stir something in you?"

Chidi tried recalling the last time she'd seen an Ancient. Massive beyond compare, the shades of a mystic world forgotten and neglected. Their long, haunting melodies the sole reminder of the wisdom and goodness lost once their legacy passed to Salt Children.

"All I feel is sadness," said Chidi.

"I too know of grief." Marisa sat down in her cage. "Such over-powering sadness. It near drove me to make an end of myself."

Chidi leaned her face between the bars. "Why didn't you?"

"Why let sadness win?" Marisa answered.

Chidi wiped her eyes. "Did the Ancients teach you that?"

"No. I learned that truth for myself. As you will."

"I don't understand. What truth?"

"*Daar is altyd 'n keuse.*"

There is always a choice, Chidi translated. She shook her head. "You're wrong."

"Am I?"

"We have no choice in this." Chidi tapped the bars of her cage.

Marisa shook her head. "Our choices led us here, as those we have yet to make will lead us out."

Chidi sat up straighter.

"We are in the waiting time," said Marisa. "With harder currents still to swim."

"H-how do you know?"

"The Ancients have sung me countless songs, one loudest of all. In that melody, I heard many voices." Marisa smiled. "Yours is my favorite."

"Why?"

"Can you not know?" Marisa mocked playfully. "Your spirit, Chidi. A goodly one that brings hope to others."

"Hope? There is no hope in this place." Chidi shook her head. "And my spirit is broken."

"It will not always be so. You swim a different current than the others." Marisa's voice cracked. "Theirs is littered with much pain and death."

Chidi hesitated to ask her next question. "A-and mine? Wh-what do you see for me?"

Marisa grinned broadly and her eyes glazed. "Tears."

KELLEN

"YOU DID WELL TODAY, KID," SAID EDMUND. "MIGHT even make it out of here alive."

Kellen leaned his head against the cold, rough bars of his cage. Marrero shifted behind him. The cage would have fit the pair of them comfortably enough. Grouping the three older men—Edmund, Bryant, and the beefy man—inside with them voided the option of lying down.

Kellen's muscles ached from sitting in the cramped quarters. His attempts to stretch only led to more rubbing shoulders with Edmund.

Unlike their human counterparts, Kellen's seal opponents slept piled atop one another in the neighboring cage. He caught whiffs of their dank, wet fur each time one moved to shuffle the pile. Kellen plugged his nose. His eyelids felt heavy. Chin nodded.

He slapped himself awake. Each time he closed his eyes, dead faces swelled in his mind. Kellen thought he would gladly trade his sadness for fear of the unknown again. *At least there had been action when Tieran brought me down the Gasping Hole and into the pits. Better than this waiting.*

"Kid," said Edmund. "Did you hear me?"

"Mmm-hmm…"

"Then buck up."

"What are you, my freaking dad or something?" Kellen asked. "Trying to coach me up? I don't need your praise, old man."

Edmund chuckled. "Sound like my son, Richie."

"I'm not your son," said Kellen. "He's dead. Remember?"

Bryant shifted. "Watch your mouth, you little—"

"It's okay," said Edmund, shifting his attention. "He's right. My son is dead."

Kellen smirked, glad to take his anger out on someone rather than stew in it. "Maybe you should've taught him to be a man and he'd be here instead of me."

"That what your daddy did for you?" asked Edmund. "Make you a man?"

"I'm still alive, aren't I?"

"For now," Edmund acknowledged. "Maybe I should've been harder on Richie. 'Course there's always a tradeoff. If I had been, he might've turned into a little prick like you." Edmund shrugged. "Guess then I wouldn't miss him so much though. Think your daddy misses you?"

"I don't care," said Kellen.

"Then I'm sorry for you."

Kellen sat up. "What'd you say?"

"Your daddy wronged you," said Edmund. "He might've made you into a survivor, but that don't make you a man. You got hate in your heart? That's fine. It's what's fueling me now too. My son meant everything to me. Only reason I'm still going is to avenge him. That's what a man does, *boy*. He rights the wrongs in the world."

"Guess I should've had a dad like you," said Kellen snidely. "Bet you would've bailed your son out of jail if he called, huh? I wouldn't even be here if mine had."

"You're bailed out now," said Edmund. "That's something, I guess."

Kellen snorted. "Yeah. I traded one jail cell for another. At least back in Lavere it didn't smell as bad."

"Don't get comfortable. We won't be here long."

Marrero pulled away. "So what happens next, old timer. You said you've been here before."

"Not here. Not this place. But if it's anything like the others, you'll be Salted soon." Edmund lifted his hood for Kellen to see. "Put on the last suit you'll ever wear."

Kellen stared at the tannish hood. Imagined what it would be like to transform. *I wonder if it hurts.*

"And that'll help us get out of here?" Marrero asked.

"Give you a better chance."

Marrero shook his head. "I don't get it."

"We're too far underwater to reach the surface on one breath," said Kellen.

"Bingo." The old Selkie yawned. "But if you pups wanna try swimming the Gasping Hole without a suit, well, it was nice knowing—"

"Quiet," said Bryant. "Someone's coming."

Kellen sat up straighter.

A glimmer of torchlight made its way steadily through the tunnel. Its bearer whistled.

"Guess what ol' Tieran has, you sorry seadogs."

Kellen sneered as the auctioneer made for the cages, carrying several bundles of what looked like clothes in the crook of his arm. *Laundry?*

Tieran handed off his torch to a hooded guard. His eyes fell on Kellen. "It's your lucky day, pup." He motioned the guard ahead. "Bring 'em out."

Kellen stood, along with his cellmates, as the guard unlocked the cage. He thought it funny he ever believed them willing to fight for their freedom not a few hours previous. None of his cellmates showed a whiff of struggle in them now. *You're all a bunch of wusses.*

His conscience reminded nothing stopped him from fighting the guards as Kellen stepped out of the cage. Nearby him, Tieran kneeled and unfurled one of the bundles, a one-piece suit flecked with silver specks and a black hood. *It's a Selkie suit.*

Kellen shivered upon sighting a pair of black metallic rods. *What's that attached to the ends?*

"Aye, I'd be shaking in me own boots if I was you. Shaking with excitement, that is." Tieran grinned. "It's not everyone gets Salted with a Leper coat. Doing you a favor, I am. See you don't forget it if the Lord Crayfish rewards you." Tieran glanced at the guards. "Take his clothes off."

"No." Kellen slapped a guard's hand. "Get away—"

A strong rap on the back of his head brought Kellen to his knees, his mind spinning black and red. Someone kicked him and he fell to the floor. A guard put their knee in his back, pinning him. Cold steel pressed against his skin and his clothes were shorn off.

"Get off of me!" he yelled.

"Not yet." Tieran knelt. "First I want to play me a lil' game I learned on the mainland. Ever play something called 'would you rather', boy?"

Kellen sneered. "Screw you."

"Nah." Tieran sucked his teeth. "This is how the game's played.

I give you two options. You pick the one you like best. So if I asked you, would you rather have a Leper coat, or have me drag you through the Gasping Hole again, I'd figure you'd choose a coat, see?"

"So give it to me," said Kellen.

"You'll get that, sure. Earned it, you did, but that's not the option in question. I've a different one for you …" Tieran smirked. "Hand or foot? Which would you rather?"

"Wh-what do you mean?" Kellen shook.

"Just what I asked," said Tieran. "I'm feeling a mite generous today so I figure why not let you choose. So…will it be your hand, or your foot?"

Kellen recalled with distinct clarity a video once shown in his history class. One of the few things he had stayed awake for. A slave had escaped and when the bounty hunters tracked him down, they gave the slave such a choice—a means to keep him from running ever again.

Whatever I say, he's going to chop it off. Kellen trembled, his breathing labored.

"Which will it be, lad?"

Focus! Kellen tried to quell the fear in him. *I can't run without a foot. Can't escape.*

"H-hand."

"Righ', then," said Tieran. "You heard the lad."

Kellen writhed and bucked as a hooded guard stretched Kellen's arm in front of him.

Tieran stepped on his wrist. "Quit moving."

Kellen saw a lit torch in Tieran's hand. In the other, Tieran held one of the long, black rods to the flame. Its tip glowed orange as Tieran took the rod away from the fire.

What is that thing? Kellen suddenly found he had more fight in him.

"I said, quit moving!" Tieran handed the torch to a guard. "Don't want ol' Tieran to make a mess of it now, do you?"

"Get that thing away from me!"

"Would you rather have it on your head?" Tieran lowered the end of the poker toward Kellen's face, the hot metal shaped in the form of a crayfish.

"No…" said Kellen. "

"Quit movin', then. Won't tell you again."

Kellen fought back his fears, obliging. Opened his hand and placed his palm flat on the cavern floor.

"No worries, lad. It'll only tickle for a minute."

Tieran plunged the poker against the back of Kellen's hand, branding him.

Kellen howled at the fiery pain and sound of sizzling flesh. He opened his eyes and looked on the crayfish brand seared into his skin.

Tieran took his foot off Kellen's wrist. "Douse him and see him dressed."

One of the guards threw a bucket of tepid salt water on Kellen's hand. He winced at the new burning, curled into a ball.

The guards yanked him to his feet.

"Next!" Tieran called.

The cage door swung open and Kellen briefly saw the guards pull Marrero out before guiding him away. One of them lifted the silver-speckled suit in front of Kellen.

"Put this on." The guard threw it at him.

Kellen caught it with his unburned hand. It felt soft and fuzzy, almost like cotton, and not at all like he expected. Nearby, Marrero screamed. Kellen found his friend clutching his left hand as the guards lifted him.

"Next!" Tieran yelled.

Bryant walked out of the cage of his own accord.

"Oi!" the guard called Kellen's attention. "I said put it on."

Kellen looked down on the coat. The back of it had been cut, almost like someone had forgotten a zipper should be sewn in. He lowered the suit's opening to his knees and slipped his leg inside. *It feels like pajamas.*

He put his other leg through, then stood and ran his good hand through the right sleeve.

Nearby, Bryant growled alongside the sizzle of burning skin.

Kellen closed his eyes. He winced and groaned as he slipped his branded hand through the other sleeve, finding cool air at the opening. He sighed as he relaxed his grip. Again, he looked on his left hand, now forever ruined with a crayfish emblem.

Kellen made a fist, wincing at the pain, drawing on the hate.

Then something tickled up his back.

He spun, thinking to see a guard with a feather, but no one stood behind him.

The nearest guard was ten feet away, aiding others dress Marrero in a hooded suit of tannish-gold.

Kellen tried looking over his shoulder to see his back as the warm tickle continued its slow and steady ascension. It stopped at his neck. Thermal heat pulsed through him and he moaned in ecstasy.

Kellen almost laughed, the memory of pain from his hand nothing compared to the strength, such glorious strength, seeping into his limbs.

He saw the opening on Marrero's suit stitching itself together, almost like the suit had a mind of its own and meant to heal itself. Marrero moaned with the same pleasure Kellen experienced as the tickle finished near his neck.

Kellen swung his arms back and forth, reveling in the warmth and freedom he had taken for granted before being locked in a cage.

"This is awesome," said Marrero.

Kellen watched Bryant don a tannish-gold suit that resembled Marrero's. Unlike the teens, however, Bryant cried as his suit sewed itself about his body.

What's up with him?

"Stop, stop," Tieran said. "Put him back in."

Kellen saw a guard had the beefy man by the arm to lead him from the cage.

Tieran pushed the beefy man back in and slammed the gate home. "He don't belong to the Crayfish. He belongs to me. Does it look like I've the monies to buy me slaves a suit?"

"No, boss."

"Righ', and even if I did, this one hasn't earned it. I oughta skin Henry for pawning this lug off on me. Leave him." Tieran swung back to Kellen and the others now wearing suits. "All righ', you sorry seadogs, time for a swim. Off to the pit with this lot."

A guard took Kellen roughly by the arm.

Kellen shrugged him away. "I can walk."

He strode toward the testing pool with both Marrero and Bryant beside him.

"Don your hoods," said Tieran as they drew close to the edge.

Kellen reached behind his shoulders and pulled the hood up to cover his ears and head. He heard the cage door swing open behind them and glanced back to see Edmund led out.

Kellen thought the old marshal came willingly enough, but looked as though he too had been crying.

Edmund stopped beside Bryant and touched the arm of his suit.

"You," Tieran pointed at Edmund. "You been here before. Show these pups how it's done then."

Edmund nodded and donned his hood. Then his body changed.

"What the…" Marrero gasped.

Kellen watched, fascinated, as Edmund fell to all fours, the sleeves extending over his hands and feet, then transforming into sea lion flippers. Kellen's nose wrinkled when Edmund's hood closed over his face and bulged outward, sprouting whiskers. The changes completed in a matter of seconds and a Sea Lion looked on them all sadly.

I'm going to do that too. I'm going to change. Kellen thought of the strength pulsing in him. He looked at the guards and Tieran. *Then I'm going to swim back out the Gasping Hole.*

"How-how did he," Marrero hyperventilated. "Wha-what did he…"

"He's a Selkie, lad," said Tieran. "Like the lot of you are now. So get a good look at him cause the pair of you"—Tieran pointed at Marrero and Bryant—"are just like him."

"I'm a…I'm a…"

"A Sea Lion," said Tieran. "And there's worse suits, believe you me. Now, close your eyes, lads, and think about the animal. Picture him in your head and keep it there. You'll feel something funny in you, sure, but don't lose the thought, see?"

Bryant's hood drifted over his face. His body transformed the same as Edmund. Marrero's changes came slower, his eyes widening and stopping the transition nearly as soon as it had begun.

"Keep the picture in your head," Tieran reprimanded. "No good being some sort of halfsie."

Kellen watched as Marrero finished the metamorphosis; a trio of Sea Lions where his cellmates had stood. The one who had been Marrero barked.

Kellen closed his eyes and pictured the Sea Lion in his mind's eye. He felt nothing.

"Nah, nah," said Tieran. "Won't do you no good."

Kellen opened his eyes. "What do you mean? It worked for them."

"They're Sea Lions. You're not."

"What?"

Tieran grinned. "Your suit's far and away better than theirs. You ever see a Leopard Seal?"

Kellen shook his head.

Tieran frowned. "Did you meet Henry? A no good Frenchman who—"

"Yeah," said Kellen. "I remember him."

"Good," said Tieran. "'Cause your suit's like his."

Kellen closed his eyes and thought back to the jail. He remembered the silvery seal with a snake-like head that ripped out Officer Murphy's throat, recalled the seal's bloodstained teeth and its cold, black eyes.

A killer. That's what I am. Kellen thought. *That's what I'm going to do to Tieran.*

The cold air on his face vanished entirely, warmed as his hood lengthened past his nose and sewed itself shut. He kept the thought of the Leopard Seal in mind and was pulled to earth, dropped to his knees as the tickle sped through his body. Kellen swore his tongue felt looser, longer, and he ran it over his teeth, now pointed and wicked sharp.

*Yes. We're Lepers...*a primal voice whispered. *That's what we are. Fear us.*

Power surged through him and Kellen whipped his seal head back. His satisfied moan became a hiss and his tongue licked the air. Kellen opened his eyes.

The smallest Sea Lion backed away.

He snorted at it. *That's right. Stay away.* Kellen thought, looking at all three Sea Lions and the guards with newfound confidence. *None of you have what I do.*

"Righ'," said Tieran. "The games are tomorrow and you lot need all the practice in these new bodies you can get. Into the pit with you."

Kellen hissed. *Come make me.*

Tieran chuckled. "Been at this a long time, I have. Don't let that seal mind convince you to try and pull one over on ol' Tieran."

Kellen showed Tieran his jaws. Roared.

A wire noose wrapped around Kellen's neck and tightened. He gurgled as the guards dragged him toward the pit and dumped him over the side.

Kellen hit the water on his back and felt the wire release. His seal mind reminded him to flip, swim for the surface. His body instinctually responded and did it for him.

Whoa. Kellen thought as he peeked his head above the water line.

Tieran looked down on him from the edge. He motioned to the guards. "Get the others in."

The three Sea Lions joined Kellen in the pit, splashing beside him. He growled at Tieran.

"Now, now, I'll have none of that," said Tieran. "Did you a favor, I did. Now do me one. Get used to that new Salt body of yours. The games'll be here before you know it, come morning. Best be ready to earn your keep, else I'll pluck that pretty suit off your back." Tieran backed away from the edge. "Righ', lock 'em in for the night, lads."

Kellen saw the guards walk the edge of the pit, dragging a thick rope net over the top.

No! He barked.

The guards continued their work until the rope net covered the pit entirely. Then, they left and took their torches with them, leaving the sea lions and Kellen to the dark of Crayfish Cavern.

LENNY

"CAPTAIN DOLAN," FENTON ADDRESSED LENNY. "Master Oscar would see you hanged for freeing slaves—"

"Even though he's got no proof of it." Lenny earned a disapproving glance from his father.

"But our Lord Master Collins is both generous and fair. I do not believe he would wish a newly made captain hanged without evidence, especially one with a pedigree such as yours." Fenton nodded in Declan's direction. "However, you lost a member of your crew, which does warrant a punishment. Since you are a captain, it stands to reason you should bear the harshest sentencing of all."

"He's going to hang you," Oscar nearly sang the words.

Lenny shut his ears of the taunt as he awaited Fenton's judgment.

"Lenny Dolan, the Ancients will decide your guilt or innocence. Guards"—Fenton looked up—"see him keel-raked immediately."

Lenny slumped as far as his wooden confines allowed, scarcely hearing anything but Oscar's giggles as taskmasters swarmed him. The rusted lock popped open and the wooden beams released. Rather than help him stand, one of the larger taskmasters lifted Lenny from the stone and carried him through the throng of slaves bound for the dock.

Declan shoved through the crowd to keep up, his bum leg hobbling him. "Ya gonna be all right, son."

They're gonna drown me, Pop. Lenny's eyes welled. *Drag me from one corna of the cavern to the other.*

They passed the racks of wet seaweed hung to dry for the next morning's take to the Boston markets. Lenny closed his eyes. Tried listening to the sound of waves lapping, yet he only heard the footfalls of taskmasters and slaves echo off the same rotting boardwalk he would soon pass under.

Lenny stared at the glittering stalactites, recalled happier times from his youth when Declan taught him to use their alignments as a map.

"Saddle the seahorses!" Oscar called as they neared the furthest dock, the one in most need of repair and staging point for the keel-raking to come.

Several taskmasters dove in to carry out Oscar's command.

The Selkie carrying Lenny knelt and set his bare feet to the cold, wet boards.

Lenny shivered as a taskmaster emerged with a rope to bind his wrists, then tossed the other end of rope tossed into the ocean.

The rickety pier shook beneath him, the water frothy from a struggle beneath the surface.

A seahorse stallion, large as any Lenny had seen on land, raised its violet head above the surface, black eyes mad, nostrils flaring. Its furious neigh echoed throughout the cavern as the Selkie taskmaster slipped a harness over its mouth and yanked its head below again.

Another seahorse, yellow with orange rings about its body, bucked the Selkie on its back while other taskmasters dove in to help restrain their master's prized steeds.

Slave children nudged one another, gleefully pointing at the beasts seldom released from their underwater stables. Tieran had arrived and ventured along the dock taking bets with Merrow buyers come out from their guest homes to watch the spectacle. Their gambles not on whether Lenny would survive the keel-raking, but if the initial jolt from the stallions would rip his stunted limbs from his body.

Declan stepped into his line of sight. "Rememba what I told ya?"

Lenny gazed up the boardwalk, ten feet in front of him, knowing he would shortly be dragged under it. He had only seen a keel-raking twice and, staring up the boardwalk now, he thought it little wonder neither of the condemned had survived. The length of track ran almost the entirety of the cavern with the far end taking a sweeping angle to the right, curving back into itself to rejoin the main line, as if the architect modeled its form as a long, wooden P.

He glanced down at the space between the barnacle-encrusted pillars.

The watery black hole the stallions would pull him through yawned wide, eager to devour its newest victim.

"Hey!" Declan called his attention. "Rememba what I told ya?"

Lenny shook his head.

"Ya was neva gonna be big, Len. Today it's gonna save ya life."

"How?" asked Lenny. "Nobody survives keel-rakin'."

"They weren't as small as us. Weighed more." Declan placed his hands on Lenny's shoulders. "Ya gonna make it, Len. I know ya will."

Lenny felt a pinch as a taskmaster pinned his hood to his back, preventing him from changing into his Salt form once below the surface line.

"Don't wait for 'em to pull ya. Understand?" Declan asked.

Lenny opened his mouth to speak, then stopped when Oscar strolled onto the pier.

The younger Collins glanced at the churning water. "The horses certainly are eager today, wouldn't you agree?"

"Aye," said Lenny, steeling his voice. "Ready to get this ova with. Same as me."

"Soon enough." Oscar's gaze flitted to Declan. "I do hope the pair of you have said your goodbyes."

"My son's innocent. He's gonna make it."

Oscar laughed. "Just like a nipperkin…more height than sense. Guards. Take him away."

"No need." Declan sidestepped the guards. He glanced at his son. "Rememba what I said."

I will, Pop. Lenny thought as Declan limped away and stood next to Fenton.

"Any last words?" Oscar asked.

"Yeah," said Lenny. "Why ya doin' this?"

"Do you remember the Shedd?" Oscar asked. "That…all-important post…you assigned me to take?"

Lenny did. How he had given Oscar a fake position to keep him safe and, more importantly, out of the way. "Oscar—"

"You all laughed at me that day."

Lenny shook his head.

"I know you did," said Oscar. "Henry told me."

"Ya gonna take his word on it? The guy who left ya behind?"

"I remember how stupid I felt," said Oscar, "standing there amidst Drybacks, all of them beneath my station, only to learn you…a *nipperkin*…was laughing at me."

"I neva laughed at ya," said Lenny.

"You would say that now. You would say anything for me to halt this sentencing. Then, later when you'd be around your friends, you'd laugh at me again."

"Oscar—"

"Laugh at how stupid I was to believe you." Oscar stepped closer. "Know this, you little swine. I'll be the one laughing today. When you're yanked off the pier, I'll laugh at the stupid face you make before you hit the water. When you're under the pier, I'll be laughing at the thought of your inhuman form bouncing from pillar to pillar, your ribs crushed at every smack. And when they pull your bloated carcass from the water…I'll be laughing still."

Oscar turned up the pier to walk away.

Lenny knew he should keep his silence. That anything he said to bruise Oscar's ego might bring his madness upon Declan. He glanced at the space beneath the pier. Thought of Oscar laughing.

"Ya know," said Lenny. "Not for nothin', Oscar, but ya got issues."

"Goodbye, Lenny Dolan," Oscar sneered. "I shan't miss you at all."

And I shan't miss the stupid way ya talk. Lenny sighed as he looked down at the outlines of massive, colorful seahorse bodies, mismatched against the blue. He recalled the first time he'd dove to look on his master's steeds as a child. How the beasts of beauty and burden towered over his Salt form even then. Lenny had secretly held a wish to ride one from that point on, knowing it could never be.

Oddly, a giddy rush overtook him as he watched the seahorses now, the loose rope tying him to them growing taut, then lax as the taskmasters fought to restrain them.

The rope! Lenny thought back to his father's words. He remembered the keel-rakings he'd witnessed and how the condemned seemingly resigned themselves to their fates. The surprise in their faces as Fenton whistled. How they were torn from the pier in the seahorse's initial burst.

Lenny focused on the rope. *Don't let 'em pull ya.*

When it laxed again, Lenny stepped to the edge of the pier, near the point of falling off. His fingers trembled on the coarse, wet threads. He forced the fear away and squeezed the rope. *Fasta or smarta.*

His breathing ragged and quick, Lenny chanced a final look at his father.

Patience, son. Lenny imagined Declan's voice mentoring him still. He took a deep breath as wetness stained his cheeks. *Focus.*

Fasta. Lenny closed his eyes, leaned forward, and dove from the pier. Fenton's whistle sounded before he struck the water and Lenny swore his shoulders popped at the immediate whiplash.

The cold of the North Atlantic against his human skin nearly punched the air from his lungs. His eyelids were ripped back, his vision swirling blue waters mixed with red from the Salt sting.

Spinning, spinning, spinning, he knew, his mind dizzied from the constant pressure changes. His body swung up and down, swayed left and right. His left foot smacked a pillar and sent him spiraling anew as the unrelenting power of twin steeds pulled him onward.

Smarta! He vaguely noticed the colored tendril-tails of the seahorses. Focused on the yellow one with bright orange rings as he swayed in their wake. *Gotta get closa.*

Hand over hand, Lenny attempted to pull himself closer to the steeds, every inch a struggle. He lost his grip when they unexpectedly veered right. The rope burn ripped through his hands at the quick stop and pull. He reached the end again, all his progress lost.

The turn. His conscience suggested. *Ya reached the turn.*

Darkness swirled in Lenny's mind. His lungs cried for air. Arms went numb and jelly-like, his strength waning.

Gonna...drown...Pop.

Something brushed his foot, moving up the side of his right leg, chest, and then neck. Whiskers and rubbery skin tickled his cheek.

Lenny tucked his chin and opened his eyes. *Endrees?*

His father's sea otter had attached itself to him. The otter wiggled its weasel-like nose. Then it nipped at him between the shoulders. The otter's weight slithered off a moment later.

Lenny thought he saw the otter with the tip of his hood in its mouth. He felt the familiar material slipping over his ears and head, the otter helping him don the Selkie hood.

Endrees squeaked at him.

Lenny guessed its meaning. He pictured the Salt form he had never before desired so badly. The black back, the white circles, sharp claws. He felt the changes sweep over his body and the rope binding his wrists slide easily off his now tinier flipper paws. His vision cleared as the seahorses swam further up the tunnel.

Endrees appeared before him, paws folded. The otter squeaked, then ascended.

Love ya too, ya dirty rat. Lenny ascended. His seal nostrils breached the surface. Lenny drank in the oxygen and thought the stink of Crayfish Cavern never smelled so sweet.

Endrees chirped at him, then dove and swam after the seahorses.

Gotta face the music, eh? Lenny followed his father's pet, watching Endrees rise and fall, spin and zag, as if its otter brain wouldn't decide which direction it most enjoyed.

Lenny chuckled. Wondered how he had ever begrudged the love his father showed the pet.

The water lightened as they neared the end and it struck Lenny then he had no way of exiting his suit. No one to free him of his Salted form.

Endrees doubled back, stopping an inch from Lenny's seal face. Blinking its beady eyes, the otter swooped in and hooked its sharp claws in Lenny's mouth.

Ah. Lenny winced as the otter darted upward and back. The Salt changes reversed, his seal body melting away and human form returning. The water seemed suddenly heavier, darker, and his mind panicked at his sluggishness. Lenny opened his eyes and found Endrees suspended in front of him. *Thanks, pal. Promise I'll make it up to ya.*

The otter wiggled its nose again, then did a back flip and swam away like helping Lenny had been little more than a game.

Lenny kicked his human feet and struggled for the surface. Breaching, he sucked in air again. The seahorses neighed nearby and churned the water as the taskmasters struggled to stable them again. Lenny swam toward the shoreline, reveling in the surprise and shock that swept the faces of those come to witness his execution. None seemed more surprised than Oscar Collins.

"How did he…"

Lenny made a point to chuckle as his feet found ground. He waded up the stony shore, onto the boardwalk, searching for the one face he wanted to see more than any other. There, he saw the rarest of sights: his father grinning.

I made it, Pop.

Declan nodded at him.

"It seems," Fenton Fenton cleared his throat. "The Ancients have deemed you innocent, Captain Dolan."

"Aye, boss," said Lenny.

"No!" Oscar said. "He can't have...how did he..."

"Whose laughin' now, pal?" said Lenny.

"Test him again!" Oscar wheeled to face Fenton. "With one horse this time."

Lenny clenched his fists.

"No," said Fenton. "I will not."

Oscar's mouth fell open. "What did you—"

"You wished him tested against the Ancient's will, young master," said Fenton. "He has been. Even your father would say—"

"Let's speak to my father about it then, shall we, Fenton?"

"Very well," said Fenton. "Though I believe he's retired with his guests for the evening. We shall speak with him on the morrow."

"Fine," said Oscar. "But I want him locked in the stocks."

Lenny stepped forward. "Boss—"

"Haven't I already told you he plotted the whole escape, Fenton?" asked Oscar. "What do you think he'll do if we leave him free to wander tonight? Why would he stay when he faces keel-raking again on the morrow?"

Lenny's gut panged as Fenton looked on him sadly.

"Guards," the old Selkie sighed. "See Master Oscar's order carried out."

"What in a blue hole is this, Boss?" Lenny exploded. "Ya know it's not right what ya doin'."

"Son," said Declan quietly.

"Why don'tcha test that son of a sea cook, Oscar, huh?" Lenny asked.

"You treasonous little whelp." Oscar's face turned scarlet. "I'll see you—"

"What? Keel-raked?" asked Lenny. "Ya gonna do it again anyway, right? I'm done keepin' my mouth shut, ya piece a—"

"*Lenny!*" Declan silenced him. "Keep ya mouth shut."

Strong hands took hold of Lenny.

"Get offa me!" He struggled to fend off the taskmasters. His fight mattered little in the end.

One wearing an Elephant Seal suit threw Lenny over his wide shoulder.

Lenny kicked, but found only air, as the taskmaster carried him through the crowd, bound for the stocks. He felt the crowd watching him, another spectacle to cap off the day.

"This iddn't right!" Lenny shouted, past the point of caring. "The Crayfish talks about bein' fair? Look what his son's done to me!"

The younger slaves whispered, a few going so far as to glare at the taskmasters behind their backs. The elder slaves moved away from the dock. Without Fenton and Oscar ordering them to follow, the crowd dissipated, as if Lenny's words might taint them too.

Only one followed his captor back to the stocks.

His face masked in typical stoicism, Declan Dolan limped along the path. He said nothing when the taskmaster locked Lenny's limbs inside the stocks.

"Sorry, Declan," said the taskmaster. "Following orders."

Lenny saw his father nod as the taskmaster lumbered away. Only once they were alone did Declan look him in the eye.

"Couldn't keep ya mouth shut, could ya?"

"Somebody had to say something," said Lenny.

"Boss Fenton did."

"Are ya freakin' kiddin' me, Pop? He's the one had me keel-raked. Fenton—"

"Gave ya a chance to survive," said Declan.

Lenny snorted. "Whattaya talkin' about?"

"Oscar wanted ya hanged. Woulda seen it done too if he'd gotten the chance to talk with his fatha." Declan crossed his arms. "Boss Fenton made sure that didn't happen. He gave ya a shot at fightin' back."

"Keel-rakin' me…" said Lenny. "That's fightin' back? That's how ya see it?"

"Ya still here aren't ya?" Declan's voice rose. "Didn't ya see Oscar's face when ya came up outta the water?"

"I saw it. I also heard him say to keel-rake me again."

"Yeah? Guess ya missed the part where Boss Fenton took up for ya again. Only reason ya sittin' here and not back in that tunnel right now is 'cause he put his neck on the line for ya. But then ya had to go and run ya mouth off!"

Declan sat down hard, ran his fingers through the same coarse hair he'd passed onto his son.

"Why can't ya eva just *listen* to me, boy?" Declan sighed.

"Pop…" said Lenny, his voice quiet. "Whatsamatta? Wh-why do ya sound so nervous?"

"The things ya said back there—" Declan shook his head. "Ya threatened an owna. Put ideas in people's minds about what's fair and not. The Crayfish won't let it go. Can't let it go."

Lenny sat up straighter. "I don't understand, Pop."

"They're gonna kill ya, son." Declan groaned as he stood. "And nothin' Boss Fenton says'll stop 'em this time."

"Pop…" Lenny called as his father limped down the boardwalk. "Where ya goin'?"

"Gotta think on something, alone. See if I can't figure a way to get ya outta this mess."

"But ya said nothin' Fenton can do will stop'em."

"Aye," said Declan. "I said *he* can't."

GARRETT

GARRETT'S STOMACH GRUMBLED AS HE RECALLED the Nomad brothers' promise to August they would finish with him by dinner. *How many people live in your town? Are there any more who look like you? What did Wilda say to you?* Garrett had answered the same questions countless times in the hours since leaving the dining hall. Yet for every answer he thought pleased Quill, the next sent the Nomad back to his brooding.

Quill watched him even now in such a way that Garrett recognized a new line of questioning to come.

"Look," said Garrett before giving the Nomad a chance. "I've told you everything I know, okay? I don't have any more answers."

"But you must know—"

"I don't know! Okay?" Garrett exploded. "I don't know anything. I don't know why I'm here. You keep calling me Orc. Saying Wilda is a Merrow and you're a Nomad. When are you going to understand I don't know what any of that means?" Garrett sat back. "I thought it was cool to change and swim, but now I wanna go home."

Quill shook his head. "You can't—"

"I *know*," said Garrett. "That's the only thing I do know."

"An Orc who doesn't presume to know everything…"

Garrett turned toward the new voice.

A beast of a man stood in the library's entryway. Scars lined his body and a belt hung at his waist with knives and a long sword.

I've seen him before…but where?

"I don't believe I've ever met such an Orc." The man's gaze fell on Garrett. He grinned, revealing pointed teeth. "But the whispers are true. The Crayfish hides one in his cavern." He looked to Quill. "It seems the Unwanted are not the only unwelcome guests here."

Garrett saw Watawa's lip curl as he mumbled.

"Peace, brother," said Quill.

"Peace?" the man scoffed. "Since when have you ever desired that?"

"You wrong me. I have always aspired for peace, Ishmael," said Quill, a smirk teasing his cheeks. "If only my enemies would grant it on my terms."

Ishmael threw his head back with a hearty laugh. "You haven't changed a bit, old friend."

"Nor you."

These guys know each other? Garrett wondered as the two of them clasped forearms.

"When I heard a pair of Makos had come to this cavern," said Ishmael, "one ugly as sin and the other near handsome as myself, I knew it could only be the bastard boys of Blue Breaker."

Though Quill grinned, Watawa did not seem to share his brother's sentiment.

Ishmael sighed, shaking his head as he picked at the books on shelves. "Knew I would find you in a library," said Ishmael to Quill. "Always did have your head in a book when your father would've put a sword in your hand."

Quill nodded. "And yet I recall giving you several scars."

"Aye. More than I gave you…but many things change with the passage of time." Ishmael's hand moved faster than Garrett's eyes followed. He snatched a dagger from the eel-skin belt it hung from and whipped it to the ready. "Should we dance again?"

"We are guests here," said Quill. "It would be rude—"

"You and your codes. They're only Selkies." Ishmael sheathed his dagger. "Well, if we're not going to fight, might as well drink. You!" He pointed to a servant girl. "Bring grog for me, my friends"—his gaze wandered to Garrett—"and this poor, despicable creature."

Garrett glared at him.

"Ooh. I misspoke. It's a feisty devil," said Ishmael. "Were you anything but an Orc, I should like to buy you. Should I show you what I do to Orcs?"

Garrett saw Ishmael again reach for his dagger.

"Peace, Ishmael." Quill stopped him. "Let the Orc alone and let us drink to old times. He's only a lost calf anyway. No honor in killing him."

"There is always honor in killing Orcs." Ishmael's eyes flashed. "Or have you forgotten what they did to your father?"

Watawa appeared from nowhere. "You forget your place, Red Water."

Whoa, thought Garrett. *He can speak English?*

"Watawa," said Ishmael easily. "Still swimming in your brother's wake, eh?"

"I swim the currents the Ancients sing to me," said Watawa. "My brother listens to their songs, as should you…*traitor.*"

Ishmael unsheathed his dagger, slowly this time, allowing its blade to screech. He held it aloft for all to see. "Now it is you who forget your place," he spat. "Call me traitor again and I take the only eye you have left."

These dudes are gonna kill each other. Garrett's heart thudded against his chest as the three Nomads stood motionless, each waiting for the other to move first.

The library doors echoed open as the servant girl bore a cask of wine and silver cups into the room.

"Saved by a Selkie," Ishmael laughed, sheathing his blade. "It seems the Ancients love you after all, priest."

The scarred Nomad snatched the tray away, pouring the wine even as he returned to join the others. "To old friends," he toasted, then drank down the contents of his cup.

Quill followed suit. Watawa did not.

"What's wrong, Open Shell?" Ishmael asked. "You used to have a great love for the grog. I remember more than a few nights watching you swim circles."

"I partake no longer," said Watawa quietly.

"Your Ancients require that, do they?"

"No. I have the choice."

"Well, here's to your Ancients and your choices." Ishmael poured another cup. "As for me, I choose dinner. Saw a bunch of giggling, Blowhole buyers gathering in the dining hall. Thought I might find you first rather than be left among them. Shall we be off?"

"Aye," said Quill. "I too have a fearsome hunger."

"For Orc?" Ishmael grinned at Garrett.

"Conversation," said Quill. "I've heard rumors of Bulls warring against the Great Whites. Perhaps I can convince you to speak with your cousins and have them turn their bloodlust elsewhere."

"A Bull's lust goes wherever there is blood. It matters little to us whose blood it may be," said Ishmael, downing another cup. "But you have your father's silver tongue, no doubt, so I'm sure you will convince me before the night is out. Perhaps I can finally convince you to bed one of the Crayfish's Silkies. There's a pretty black one I've my eyes on. Perhaps she has a sister."

Garrett squirmed, repulsed by the easy way Ishmael spoke.

Quill, however, seemed to take it in stride. "Very well. We'll sit to dinner and wage our words, and in the morning—"

Ishmael waved Quill's words away. "In the morning I'll have a headache the size of an Ancient and you'll remind me what I agreed to. I know your works."

Quill grinned. "Shall we be off then to have our war of wits and words?"

"Aye. Might as well get this over with." Ishmael drained another cup. Wiped his mouth and looked at Garrett. "Can't say that I've ever drank with an Orc. Don't mean to start tonight. The sight of you makes my stomach turn."

The feeling's mutual, jerk. Garrett thought to say.

"I will stay with him."

Garrett saw Watawa stand tall.

"I don't suppose the Crayfish would like the rumors of an Orc enslaved in his cavern confirmed." Watawa glanced at Garrett. "Unless you would rather go and be stared at and whispered about all night."

Garrett thought back to the hooded men at the Boston pier, how their eyes followed him. He imagined listening to Ishmael's vile talk and taunts for another hour or two.

"No," said Garrett. "No, I'll stay."

Watawa nodded. "Girl," he said to the servant. "Bring us food, please."

"*Please*?" Ishmael mocked. "The son of Blue Breaker…"

Ishmael shook his head as he left the room, hugging the bottle of grog.

Quill nodded at his brother, then followed Ishmael out and closed the doors.

Garrett sighed. *Thank God they're gone.*

"Alone at last…"

Garrett turned. "Y-you speak English."

"Aye," said Watawa. "You seem surprised."

Garrett nodded.

"I spent many years talking. My wits scrambled with grog." Watawa frowned. "I have since learned to listen. Forgive my brother his many questions. His heart lays heavy with the need for answers no one can give."

"W-what kind of answers?"

"Those to the questions we all have…what would one do if given a chance to change the past? Can one right the wrongs they made? Can one ever be truly forgiven?" Watawa walked to the couch his brother had sat upon and took a seat. His gaze found Garrett. "What do you think?"

Garrett swallowed hard. "I-I don't know."

"A wise answer," said Watawa. "Perhaps the wisest of all. My brother has yet to learn this. He cannot accept the value in the unknowable." Watawa's lone eye squinted. "I sense my brother's unease in you. Many questions lay on your heart, yes?"

A shiver ran up Garrett's back. "Yes."

"Ask them," said Watawa. "And I will give you what answers I can."

Garrett drew a blank. *Come on, idiot. Think!* He thought back to Wilda and tried recalling the questions he so desperately wanted to ask her, yet he thought only of Lenny, changing in the boat, and talking him through his own changes from Killer Whale into human form.

"Why am I like this?" Garrett asked. "What is this world—"

"And your place in it?"

Garrett nodded.

Watawa glanced at the tome on the table in front of him. The same Quill had left behind. "Has anyone told why you and I, Orc and Nomad, aye, and Merrows too, why we are all Salt Children? What that means?"

"No..." Garrett walked to the couch and sat opposite the one-eyed Nomad. "No one's told me anything."

"Long ago, when the Ancients ruled the Salt, peace existed amongst the four races." Watawa turned the tome for Garrett to inspect. He pointed at a Blue Whale. "The Ancients."

Garrett stared at the mottled grey complexion of the giant beast. Massive beyond compare, the largest being on the planet.

"And the younger races"—Watawa pointed to a Great White Shark and a Striped Dolphin—"who seemed but children compared to their wisdom."

Garrett thought back to meeting Wilda at the Indianapolis Zoo, her silvery hair and wrinkled skin. He remembered the Nomad and his dreadlocks, like black and silvery snakes. *Younger races?* Garrett wondered of the shark and dolphin images. *How old does that make the Ancients?*

Garrett stared down upon the page. The bottom corner was torn off. "What was that?"

"The fourth race, the Sancul." Watawa shook his head. "Powerful as the Ancients and enemy to them and their Salt Children. They are gone from this world now, banished to the abyss. One morning"—Watawa continued before Garrett could ask more about the Sancul—"as the four rulers swam together, they happened upon a creature near the surface."

Watawa flipped the page.

"A man?" Garrett asked.

Watawa nodded. "The Ancient asked his fellows what should be done with this new being. The Nomad thought it unnatural for a creature to struggle to swim. He suggested they take mercy on the beast and kill it."

Garrett stared at the Great White's pointed teeth and its cold eyes that gave nothing away. No hint that it felt anything at all. He shuddered with the memory of standing in the Nomad's presence at the Indianapolis zoo. Remembered flinching when its dead, black eyes gazed upon him.

Watawa pointed to the dolphin. "The Merrow swam closest. Youngest of all the races and ever one to follow the Ancient's lead, she thought to befriend the Man and learn if it could be taught."

Turning the page, Garrett saw the next one had been ripped out. "The Sancul?"

"Aye," said Watawa. "The Sancul sensed an eagerness in Man, a bottomless hunger to match its own. It warned Man would be reckless, for how else should such a creature find its way so far into the Salt with no means of returning home?"

Garrett listened to a log pop in the fire. He settled deeper into his cushion.

"The Ancient acknowledged the Sancul's claim, yet took the

advice of the Salt children. It showed mercy by carrying Man to shore that he might live. Then he asked Man to come every day to see if it might learn what the Merrow would teach."

"And the Sancul?" Garrett asked.

"Retreated to the depths…and waited." Watawa turned the page. "Soon Merrow and Man were inseparable, but Man quickly grew sad. It desired the Salt Children to come ashore and see its home. The Nomad believed no creature should exist in two worlds and refused."

Garrett couldn't tell if he detected disappointment in Watawa's tone, or some small manner of respect at the Nomad's refusal to Man's offer. He hesitated to ask, fearing Watawa might quit his historical account if Garrett bothered him with too many questions.

Watawa turned another page and cleared his throat. "The Merrow volunteered, curious to see these new lands. Fearful for one of its Children, the Ancient said it too would go ashore, but warned the Merrow doing so would change them both forever. That once a being chose to live in two worlds, it must return to both forever."

"And they did go," said Garrett. "Right?"

"Aye," said Watawa quietly.

On the next page, Garrett saw plumes of sea spray at the surface, shot skyward from the blowholes of the whales and dolphins.

"And to this day, until the end of days, both Ancient and Merrow must return to the surface for life."

"And Orcs," said Garrett, recalling his own need to surface. *I want to know about those like me!* Garrett fought the urge to beg answers from Watawa. "Y-you forgot about them."

"They had not yet come to be." Watawa returned his focus to the book. "Upon their return, the Merrow relayed all she had seen to the Sancul and the Nomad. The Sancul grew even more distrustful of Man and envious of a world beyond his reach. He ordered his subjects to the far north and south to bring down the ice caps and flood the world with Salt."

Garrett looked on the next page filled with drowned men and women. He quickly turned it.

"But the Ancients and Merrows again took mercy on Man," said Watawa neutrally.

Garrett smiled as he looked at the illustration of men and women seated on the backs of whales. Others held onto the dorsal fins of dolphins. *That's so awesome. I'll bet the Orcs helped too.* He thought before recalling Watawa's mention Orcs hadn't come to exist yet.

"They kept Man afloat until the Salt gave way to the Hard again. The Ancient warned Man away to keep him hidden until justice was wrought on the Sancul for attempted genocide. But the wily Sancul claimed his actions were only to protect the Salt and its Children. Ever merciful, the Ancient thought it little coincidence the Salt had five oceans, yet only four races. It deemed Man should be welcomed as the fifth race and the Sancul's punishment a means of providing Man with Salt life."

Garrett flipped the page and gasped at the number of seals and sea lions lain out upon the rocks. "Selkies…"

"Aye," said Watawa grimly. "The Sancul wisely accepted the decision, but suggested Man be given a lesser form. It warned the Ancient that to give Salt life, Salt life must also be taken in equal measure, for nothing comes without cost. In its desire to keep the peace, the Ancient agreed and set the Sancul to its task."

Garrett looked on the next page with horror. The seals and sea lions from the previous page now lay dead, their bodies stripped of their coats. Men stretched the sealskins upon racks to dry while women wove the heads into closed hoods.

Watawa frowned. "The Sancul had rightly judged the dark desires in man's heart to swim amongst the Salt Children."

That's horrible. Garrett thought, flipping to the next page where seals and sea lions swam underwater.

"Soon the Salt teemed with Selkies and harmony existed for a time," the one-eyed Nomad continued his tale. "Pleased with his decision, the Ancient commissioned a city built, half on the Hard, half in the Salt to solidify the union amongst the now five races."

Garrett saw a gleaming city next, set half upon a beach of white sand, the other in crystal green waters. The caps of its ivory towers resembled golden conch shells. An illustrious city bursting with wealth and beauty leapt off the page, the artist having captured the city's utter magnificence in great detail.

Whoa. Garrett thought. *How do I go there?*

"But it was not to last," said Watawa.

Garrett gaped at the hundreds of boats crewed by men in Selkie suits. Seal heads in the water and hind flippers above the surface as their owners dove.

"Soon the Nomads cried to their high chieftain of hunger. They claimed Man fished and plundered with no regard for the Salt Children. That Man reviled them, yet loved the Merrows. The Ancient refused to hear their claims, holding to the belief Man was inherently good."

The Ancients must not have known many then. Garrett frowned, thinking on all the chaos and negativity the news invaded upon him daily. Terrorist acts, students with guns, political scandals. Garrett shook his head. *How did the Ancients not see it coming?*

"The Sancul knew better. Playing to the greed he rightly guessed in them, he taught Man the true riches of the Salt lay not in fish, but in something larger…"

Garrett near wept at the next page. *So much for the goodness in Man.*

Boats circled around whales with enough harpoons that Garrett imagined them as living pincushions. Except even he knew as he looked upon the page there was nothing alive about these animals. The artist had depicted men cheering aboard the decks. Others walked along the behemoth's back to stick it with more harpoons.

"Then one morning, the Sancul brought news to the Ancient king." Watawa paused, his head bowed low. "Man had lured his son into the shallow and killed him. They stripped his body bare for the blubbery riches and the rest they left to rot upon the Hard."

Garrett didn't linger on the hulking bones of a Blue Whale, turning the page after a mere glimpse. The next revealed the once great city, now ruined and afire.

"In his rage, the Ancient ordered the bastion of unity sunk and all inside drowned." Watawa paused. "But the Sancul suggested a different fate for Man. 'Death would be quick,' he said to the Ancient. 'But to pay for his crimes through servitude…'"

Garrett gasped at the illustration of men in hooded suits, chained together as they worked in dark caverns. He thought of Lenny and Paulo, wondered where they were and what life must be like for them. *Is this the way they live?*

"All was not lost, however. The Merrow alone refused to forego her trust in Man. She vowed to live among them as proof not all were killers," said Watawa. "The Sancul had other plans. He followed the Merrow and maimed her, leaving her to drown in Salt."

Garrett stared in awe at the young dolphin-lady, sinking below the surface. *She's beautiful.*

"Her faith was rewarded," said Watawa, straightening as he turned the page.

Garrett smiled at the sight of the seals and sea lions surrounding the dolphin lady. One rose under her, reminding Garrett of how Paulo had kept him from sinking. "They saved her…"

"Aye. The Selkies swam the Merrow to shore and nursed her back to health. She returned to the Ancient king and told him of the Sancul's betrayal, thus beginning the War of the Ancients."

"H-how did it end?"

Watawa turned his lone eye on Garrett, squinted. "The way all wars finish."

Garrett winced at the next page; the ocean's water turned crimson with bloated corpses floating near the surface—sharks, dolphins, whales, and seals.

"In the end, the Ancient king, Senchis, defeated his enemy. He had his rival's body cut into five pieces and sunk in the deepest parts of the five oceans as a warning to the Sancul supporters never to rise again."

Garrett looked on the tattered remains of the torn out page where he assumed pictures of the Sancul had been drawn. *Why is he telling me all this*—Garrett glanced at Watawa and saw the Nomad's lone eye squint—*if the Sancul are all gone?*

Watawa looked away. "The Ancients had won the war, but grew sad as the years passed. They watched Man spread and devour, just as the Sancul had warned, and tired of the bickering between Merrow and Nomad. The Ancients decided they had lingered too long in this world and felt, like the Sancul, the time for their rule had passed. They would retreat into their Salt forms, never to return."

"But what about the Orcs?" Garrett asked. He swallowed hard, seeing Watawa's cheek twitched. "W-what about those like me?"

Watawa's face tightened. "When the Ancients made known their decision, both Merrow and Nomad cried the wars would begin anew as each wrestled for control of the Salt. The Merrow begged the Ancients stay, for without them, the Salt would surely descend into chaos once more.

"The Ancient took pity on its favored Salt Child. Her beauty and innocence swaying him against the barbarous acts he knew full well the Nomad would commit. However, the Ancient again warned the Merrow that no decision comes without cost. That what she asked of him may indeed be Merrow's undoing. The Merrow readily agreed to the consequences, fearing the Nomad's bite more. And so the Ancient used what little magic remained in the world to give her a gift, a protector."

Nervous energy swelled in Garrett as Watawa turned the page, revealing the portrait of a Killer Whale.

"Orcs..." Watawa said, his voice near a growl. "Near powerful as an Ancient, smart as the Merrow, and deadlier than Nomads. Created to keep peace throughout the Salt."

"And they did, didn't they?" Garrett asked, hearing the eagerness in his voice. Proud that he hailed from a line of peacekeepers. "My kind kept the peace?"

Watawa shook his head.

The library doors opened with a loud echo. A servant girl stood in the doorway.

"P-pardon, m'lords," she stammered. "The Lord Crayfish asked that I secret the umm..." She glanced at Garrett.

"The Orc," said Watawa.

"A-aye," said the girl. "He asked that I show you to your room, m'lord. He does not wish you seen by his guests."

"What if I don't want to go?" asked Garrett.

"Do as you're bidden, Orc," Watawa squinted at him. "Else your decision reflect poorly on your friends. Your being here, as it is, brings them much trouble."

"I didn't ask them to bring me," said Garrett. "And I don't have any friends down here."

Watawa squinted. "You do, however low they may be thought of. They are friends to you nonetheless. So go now…the Ancients are not done with you, Garrett Weaver."

Garrett felt a tingle up his spine. "How did you know my last name?"

"Only once my eye was plucked, did I begin to see. The Ancients have shown me many visions, one clearer than all."

Garrett hesitated. "Wh-what was it?"

"An ancient loom, sunk below the waves. Behind it stands an Orc calf, passing the shuttle back and forth through the tapestry," said Watawa quietly. "A weaver to bind all threads together."

"Me?" Garrett swallowed hard. "But I…I don't even know how."

"You've been weaving all your life." Watawa grinned. Then he headed for the door.

Garrett followed. "Wait!"

Watawa stopped. "Yes?"

"Will I see you again?"

"If the Ancients will it." Watawa touched his forehead with his left hand, then his chest, and made a wide sweeping arc with his hand open. "May they bless you and the currents you swim."

Garrett watched him leave.

The servant girl remained in the doorway, head bowed low.

Garrett stepped forward. "D-did you say you were going to take me to my room?"

"Aye," she said and spun on her heel. "This way, m'lord."

M'lord? Garrett followed her out of the library.

Though shorter than he, the girl walked quick enough that Garrett found himself double-timing his strides to keep up. He didn't exactly see her face fully, but gathered they were of a similar age when she glanced back to see if he kept up. *She's pretty too*, he thought, as the girl led him down a series of halls he'd not yet been through, and then up a flight of stone stairs.

Unlike the rooms below, Garrett found the doors closed on this level. He followed the servant to the furthest room at the end, waited as she produced a silver key from the pocket of her drab dress. Only then did Garrett notice she had no hood. *She's not a Selkie.*

The locked door clicked open and the girl entered the darkened room. A moment later, the dim glow of flame struck to candle. Garrett crossed the threshold and saw it a simple room, but regal. A giant bed with its four wooden posts carved in the form of squid tentacles.

Wicked…

The girl hurriedly stepped away when Garrett crossed to look out the window. He took in the whole of Crayfish Cavern far below—the pier, the boardwalk, and even open still ponds far to the east.

A fire crackled behind him. The servant girl stood beside the newly lit hearth, trembling.

"What's wrong?" Garrett asked.

"Nothin', m'lord," she said in a tone that suggested otherwise. "My Lord Crayfish says I'm…I'm a gift for you."

Garrett kept his gaze fixated on the stone floor. "I don't understand."

"He says I belong to you for the night. To...to do with as you will."

Garrett thought back to Ishmael and his vile speech about bedding and the pretty black girl he'd had his eye on. *This is insane. What do I say?*

"H-have I displeased you, m'lord?" she asked, her voice plagued with fear. "Oh, please say I haven't."

"No...No, I just..."

Garrett looked up, truly seeing her for the first time. Her skin pale as the white chowder, hair black as the Nomads had been. *She can't be much older than I am...*

"What is this place?" Garrett asked, more to himself than the girl.

"Crayfish Cavern, m'lord."

"No, not that. This *place*." Garrett shook. "You being sent here for me as a...a..."

"A gift, m'lord."

"Right! I mean, how messed up is that?" Garrett asked. "You're what? Fifteen, maybe sixteen?"

The girl's head forehead wrinkled.

"You don't know how old you are?" Garrett asked. "Your age?"

"No, m'lord."

Garrett sat down on the bed. "Hey...it's all right...I won't hurt you. You can look at me."

"Aye, m'lord." The girl continued staring at the floor.

"Look at me."

She dared a look, then glanced away.

"I won't hurt you," said Garrett. "I promise."

The girl looked again on Garrett, her gaze holding. "Aye, m'lord."

"How did you get here?"

"Boss Tieran…bought me in the capital and brung me here."

"The capital?" Garrett asked. "What's that? Where?"

The girl hesitated.

"It's okay," said Garrett. "You can say anything. Promise."

The girl nodded. "You…you are a strange Orc, m'lord."

"Yeah." Garrett scoffed. "I'm starting to think that's not a bad thing."

He looked to the girl for confirmation, but her face gave nothing away. "So what do we do now?"

"The Lord Crayfish said I am yours for the night."

That's all she knows to say. Garrett thought. "Do you, uh, do you want to stay?"

"M'lord?"

"I mean, not for any…y-you know…" Garrett blushed. "What would happen if you went back to…wherever it is you came from."

The girl trembled. "Boss Tieran will show me the lash if I've displeased you."

Maybe someone should beat Boss Tieran. Garrett kept the thought. He sighed. "Then stay…please."

The servant girl looked up again. "M'lord?"

"Stay with me. I don't wanna be alone." Garrett rose from the bed. "Here…you can have the bed. I doubt I'll sleep much anyway."

The girl stepped toward the bed slowly.

She thinks I'm messing with her. Garrett backed away from the bed, closer to the fireplace. He lay out upon the hard stone floor, close enough to feel the fire's warmth, and listened to the covers rustle as the girl climbed into the bed.

298 ～ AARON GALVIN

Garrett sat up when she began sobbing. "Are you okay?"

"A-aye…"

You sure don't sound like it. Garrett lay back down.

"Th-thank you…thank you, m'lord. F-for your kindness."

"You're welcome," Garrett said so softly even he barely heard himself acknowledge her. Then he closed his eyes and listened to the fire pop, wondering how he had ever gotten himself into this mess. Then came a worse thought. *How do I get out of here?*

CHIDI

CLOAKED IN ABSOLUTE DARK, CHIDI SAT WITH her back against a cavern wall. The light from Henry's torch had burned out long ago, or was it a few minutes? Chidi desperately clutched at the torch and touched her fingers to what had been its flamed tip, now cooled.

Awhile then, she decided.

Across the way, Marisa snored softly.

Chidi thought to scream, wake her, and have someone to talk with. At least it would pass the time until Henry came to collect her like he'd promised. She had little doubt her owner would follow through. *He always keeps his promises.* She fought the notion he abandoned her to endless dark and conjured the many promises Henry had kept.

Chidi always found it hardest to ward off the newest memories. Burying the dead faces deep in her mind took time and effort and she struggled with the discipline of it now. She kept seeing Racer, lying in an open field. Pictured Wotjek sprawled on the floor of the gas station and relived Henry's threat to Ellie.

Just because he hasn't killed her yet, doesn't mean he won't. Her conscience warned. *Henry always keeps his promises.*

She feared for Lenny then, too, the master planner who had given her freedom for a moment.

And I betrayed them both. Chidi sobbed. *They gave me freedom and I brought them death.*

Not all of them, a quiet, inner voice reminded her. *Allambee is free.*

Yes. Chidi clapped a hand over her mouth to stifle her sobs. She thought on the last thing Zymon Gorski had told her and the fear in his voice. *You know fear already. Have lived with it in that other world and survived this long. You are the only one who can save us now. Will you do that, Chidi? Will you save our lives?*

"But who's going to save mine?" she cried at the darkness. "Who will save me…"

Deep in the tunnel, orange light dawned.

Chidi stood up, watched the light bob as the torchbearer meandered through the snaky tunnel.

"Endrees!" a hard voice called out. "Get back here, ya sorry excuse for a sea rat."

A shadow darted across the floor, bound toward Chidi.

No, no, no. She backed to the edge of her cage.

A sea otter poked its nose through the iron slat, wiggled its nose, and chirped at her.

"Endre—Buckets a blood…how'd ya get in here?"

Chidi glanced up. *Is that…no! It can't be.*

The torchbearer stood at the tunnel's edge, his stature small, belying the giant shadow he cast against the cavern wall.

For a moment, Chidi thought Lenny Dolan must have escaped the stocks and come to rescue her. As the little man neared, she saw it only a trick of the light. "You're…"

"Declan Dolan. You're Henry's girl."

"Chidi…"

"Right," said Declan. He glanced down at the hunk of bread and cup of water he'd carried in his other hand. He sighed. "Boss Fenton didn't say nothin' about ya bein' locked in here. I don't have any food for ya. No water neither."

"It's all right. No one knows I'm here. They can't know I'm here," she added quickly. "If Henry finds out…o-or Ishmael."

"Relax, girlie. I don't wanna see ya get in trouble. Long as ya don't say nothin', I won't. Far as I'm concerned, ya wadn't here when I brought Miss Bourgeois over there her dinna."

"Th-Thank you."

Declan nodded, then shifted toward Marisa's cage.

"Wait!" Chidi reached through the slats. "Please."

"What?"

Chidi's mind raced for something to say, a compliment, a lie, anything to keep Declan from leaving and taking the light with him. The dam behind her eyes nearly burst when the only thing that mattered came to her. "I-I'm sorry."

Declan sighed. "For my boy?"

"Yes." Tears trickled down Chidi's cheeks. "I'm so sorry. I—"

"It's all right. Wadn't ya fault."

"But I-I lied." Chidi fought to breathe. "To everyone."

"Ya did what ya had to. Just like Len."

Chidi looked on Declan's wizened face and found kindness that belied the hard exterior his son fought so hard to maintain. "I don't understand. The things I said…they'll punish them. Lenny too."

"They already did. Keel-raked him."

Chidi gasped, fell to her knees. "No…then he's…he—"

"He made it."

"Lenny's alive?" Chidi sobbed. "How?"

"He's my son. He can figure his way outta anything." Declan's gaze honed on Chidi. "Len freed ya, didn't he?"

Chidi hesitated.

"Thought so." Declan smirked. "Mind if I ask how ya talked him into it?"

"I didn't…Ellie and Racer freed me. They said it was Lenny's plan."

"Well, whattaya know. Maybe he's learnin' after all." Declan chuckled. "So ya neva said nothin' to him? Didn't suggest it? Promise him something?"

Chidi shook her head. "I don't know why he did it."

"I do." Declan said. "There's this story I told him about these two catchas, one of 'em old, the other comin' into his own. Anyway, one day, as they reach the top of a hill, they look down and see a bunch a runnas sittin' around a fire. The pup looks up at the old catcha and whispers, 'Let's run down and scare 'em. They'll scatter. Maybe we can catch us one to take back.'"

Chidi leaned closer as Declan continued.

"The old catcha shakes his head at the pup. Then he says, 'Let's *sneak* down and get 'em all.'" Declan sighed, glanced down at the otter nuzzling against his legs. "Told Len that story I dunno how many times…Neva knew he listened to it."

"I don't understand," said Chidi after a long pause.

"My pup's learnin' to think on his own," said Declan. "Steppin' outta my shadow to become his own man…all any good fatha wants for his son."

Chidi smiled.

"His plan almost worked too. Settin' a few of ya free, but comin' back with his mission accomplished…Smart." Declan winked at Chidi. "He'll do betta next time."

"Declan Dolan…"

Chidi saw Marisa Bourgeois standing, watching them both from her cage.

"All these years…hearing your voice…seeing your face in my dreams," said Marisa, her voice full of reverence. She bowed her head. "It's a privilege to finally meet you."

Declan's warmth faded. "My pup said ya drew a picture a me."

Marisa nodded.

"How'd ya know what I look like?" Declan asked. "I neva seen ya before in all my life."

"The Ancients sang your face to me. Set my path to cross with yours that we might leave this place together."

"I'm a Dolan." Declan crossed his arms. "We don't run."

"Today you do," said Marisa softly.

The otter squeaked. It nipped at the ankles of Declan's suit, tugging him toward Marisa's cage.

"Whattaya doin', Endrees?" Declan lightly kicked the otter away.

The animal scurried to join Marisa, then promptly chirped at its master.

Marisa reached her arm through the slats. "The Ancients would have you see, Declan."

Chidi thought the elder Dolan seemed hypnotized as he approached Marisa. *How is she doing this?* Chidi wondered. A pit in her gut urged her cry out. "Stop…Don't!"

Her voice seemed to call Declan from his trance. He stopped short of Marisa's arm, glanced back and forth between she and Chidi.

"Don't…" Chidi cautioned. Her mind curious to know what Marisa would tell Declan, her soul fearing it.

"Boss Fenton said ya was a fake runna," said Declan to Marisa. "That he only sent my pup and the others lookin' for ya to build Oscar's ego."

"Then why am I locked in here?" Marisa answered. "Far from the Nomads who arrived unannounced and uninvited?"

"Tell me."

"A feeble story for feeble minds," said Marisa. "In truth, the Crayfish trembles even as we speak in his mansion bought and built with the blood of others. He knows your son brings much trouble on this cavern, but which problem to face first? The Orc? The Nomads?" Marisa chuckled. "Those with power are quick to act on what they perceive the largest of issues, yet it's often the smallest which brings their demise."

Chidi gripped the iron bars of her cage, curiosity trumping her fear.

"The Crayfish *knows,* Declan, as you do. And you also." Marisa glanced at Chidi.

"What?" Chidi asked breathlessly. "What do we know?"

"The Salt will have its due."

Chidi's heart fluttered as Marisa continued.

"The Ancients sing our names from shore to shore. We defy them at our peril." Marisa looked on Declan again. "Take my arm, Declan Dolan. Learn what would they ask of you."

The elder Dolan seemed skeptical, to Chidi's mind, yet he clasped his small hand atop Marisa's forearm. Declan's head whipped back, eyes open wide, the moment Marisa flexed her grip, and his body quaked like one caught by stinging jelly nets.

Chidi saw Marisa release her hold.

Declan fell to the stony floor, gasping. "H-How did ya…"

"You understand now?" Marisa asked. "You see? Know what must be done."

What did she do to him? Chidi wondered as Declan climbed to his feet and approached Marisa's cage.

He unsheathed a hidden dagger from his Selkie pocket and put its tip to the door. A moment later, the lock echoed off the cavern floor.

Marisa pushed the gate open and stepped out.

"My son…" said Declan. "He—"

"Cannot know," Marisa replied. "Did you not say a father's want for his son is to find his own way? Lenny will discover his."

Chidi saw Declan nod. He glanced over at her. "Is she comin' with us?"

Marisa shook her head.

"What? Why not?" Chidi asked. "Please. Take me with you!"

"I'm sorry, Chidi," said Marisa. "Our paths must diverge a little while longer."

"They don't have to. You could take me with you. Right now!"

"Yours is a different work to do," said Marisa. "For now, I leave you to it."

"But—"

"Chidi," said Declan. "Tell Len, I…I'm proud of him…"

She noticed the torchlight made Declan's eyes glisten.

"Tell my boy I love him," Declan's voice broke. "He won't understand why I left…but do that for me, will ya, Chidi?"

Marisa put her hand to Declan's back.

"Endrees…" the elder Dolan said as he strode toward the passageway. "With me."

The otter followed its master to the tunnel's mouth, both vanishing into the dark.

"No!" Chidi cried. "Declan! Come back."

"Chidi." Marisa approached her cage and passed the torch between the slats in the same manner Henry had done. "Be strong, Chidi. The waiting time is almost ended."

Then she, too, abandoned Chidi to the hidden hollow.

Chidi continued screaming at Marisa, long after both she and Declan had gone. She had no tears left to cry, but anger aplenty. She kicked and punched the cage, staining its bars with blood from her knuckles and toes. Exhaustion forced her collapse and she stared numbly at the tunnel mouth, wishing either Declan or Marisa had at least done her the favor of killing her.

She could not say how much time passed before she heard the echo of someone's approach, but her torch's light had waned to a flicker. Chidi didn't bother looking to see who came for her, knowing it must be Henry.

"What the…How'd you get in here? How did she…"

Chidi glanced up at the familiar voice.

"Oh no…" Tieran's eyes rounded at the sight of Marisa's empty cage. "No, no, no."

He ran to the cage. Entered like he half expected Marisa to have learned a way to make herself invisible and hid there still.

Chidi listened to him curse and rant. *Fool.* She thought. *He's forgotten I'm even here.*

He remembered a few minutes later. "How'd you get in here?" Tieran demanded.

"Henry."

Tieran sneered. "Let her go, did he? To get back at the Crayfish for what's owed him?"

"Aye," said Chidi, the embers of anger stoked anew. "Henry and Declan Dolan."

LENNY

LENNY GRUNTED AS HE LIFTED HIS FOREHEAD from the stocks. Sleep eluded him, not only because of his forced position. He had witnessed a commotion of catchers and taskmasters several hours previous and not a word given as to why. At first, he had thought it maybe Orcs come to gather Garrett. He saw none, however, and gathered they'd been sent out when none returned from the docks.

Morn had not yet graced Crayfish Cavern and all but the largest braziers had reduced to embers, awaiting slaves to feed their flames anew.

A groan from the prisoner opposite him made Lenny give silent thanks to Fenton. The old overseer had at least allowed Lenny his Selkie suit to ward away the natural cold of Crayfish Cavern. A grant not awarded his fellow convict.

The taskmasters had brought Racer's father, Ansel, to join Lenny in the stocks not long after Declan departed the previous night. Lenny recalled them stripping Ansel of his suit, a worn and lowly Common, leaving his dignity to a loincloth. Shoulders twitching, wrists and ankles rattling against his confines, Ansel winced as he straightened and shook the reedy blond hair from his eyes.

The pair had said little with a taskmaster left to keep watch. Lenny saw the same taskmaster now slumped against the whipping masts, head tilted back and snoring softly.

"My boy...Racer," Ansel's voice sounded haggard. "He run off, didn't he?"

"Aye." Guilt washed over Lenny as the father looked on him with the same brilliant gaze Racer had inherited. *'Cause I told him to.*

Ansel nodded. "That why you're locked up?"

"Some of it."

"Not right." Ansel winced again. "Hope you can forgive my boy, Captain Dolan. Racer...he always has looked up to you."

"Think ya mean looked down," said Lenny. "Nobody looks up at a nipperkin."

"My son does. Ever since he was a pup, it's all he'd talk on. Becoming a catcher like you Dolans." Ansel paused. "Smart, my boy. Always knew that'd be best. Better life than slaving in the fields like his old man. I knew it too, you see?"

Lenny shook his head.

Ansel grinned crookedly, even as his body trembled from the cold. "Might be a field slave, but I know a thing or two. A catcher's life, why, it's the only way my boy would ever have a chance of living free. Escaping." His grin faded. "Mighty sorry his running landed you here, sir."

"I'm no sir," said Lenny.

"Yes, you are. You is a captain, sir," said Ansel quickly. "Like your daddy."

"Pop's known throughout the Salt. A legend."

"Legends take time to grow. Might be yours is just getting started."

"Some start I'm off to." Lenny rattled his wrists against the stocks.

"Oh, I dunno. I'd heard it in the fields 'fore they brought me here your crew caught an Orc," said Ansel. "Never been done before, they said."

And shouldn't a been this time. Lenny glanced at the Collins mansion and wondered how Garrett fared. His thoughts drifted to the yard beside it and the gallows soon to welcome its next victim.

Ansel sighed. "Gonna hang me soon, I guess."

Lenny knew the older Selkie's sentence true yet he couldn't think of how to respond.

Ansel craned his neck, the answer existing in the silence between them.

Lenny too glanced up to the twinkling high above.

"Did my son see stars?" Ansel asked.

"Aye." Lenny recalled the many times he'd yelled at Racer during their hunt, how often he woke to the sound of Racer rising in the night to step off the bus and gaze at the heavens. He imagined Racer and grinned. *Stupid pup.*

"That's good," said Ansel. "Always did wonder what they'd look like. All I could ever tell him was the stories my daddy told me. He was in the Dryback's navy once, my daddy. Used to say there was nothing in this world like seeing stars cast out over the Salt." Ansel looked at Lenny. "You think there'll be any in Fiddler's Green?"

Lenny honed on the twinkling stalactites. Knew the beauty in their small light was nothing when compared against that which they feebly attempted to emulate. He closed his eyes, conjured a memory of pink skies turning violet before fading into a black backdrop with too many tiny lights to count. A shiver ran through Lenny as he reopened his eyes.

"Aye," he choked.

"Me too. Them and clear green waters you can see forever in." Ansel glanced at the ceiling again. "Not like here."

"Ya scared?" Lenny asked without thinking. *Course he's scared, ya idiot. Weren't ya about to bawl ya eyes out back before ya got keel-raked? Whatsamatta with ya?*

"Probably should be," said Ansel. "Guess Fiddler's Green might only be a place somebody made up. Might be I'm headed for the Abyss instead."

"That don't scare ya?"

Ansel shook his head. "Can't be worse than here."

Things can always be worse. Lenny thought of another Declan mantra.

"Guess I'll find out soon enough," said Ansel. "Not that I'm ungrateful, sir."

Lenny sat up. "I don't understand."

"You're not a father. I was your age once. Told myself I'd never settle down. What good was love when the masters could snatch it from you? And they did." Ansel's voice cracked. "I watched Master August sell my oldest boy. Didn't say two words neither. Too afraid he'd take my others from me. Then I came home from the fields one night and learned he'd done the same with my little girl. Never did get to say goodbye."

Lenny hung his head low as Ansel continued.

"That's how they keep us. Shackles and stocks, cages and nets… not one of 'em strong as love." Ansel collected himself. "I told Racer that night, you ever get the chance to run, boy, you do it. He argued, of course."

Lenny glanced up.

"Good boy, my son." Ansel smirked. "Knew his momma or me would pay for it if he ran. I told him not to think on it. That I'd go to them gallows a happy man knowing one of my children ran free. I'd swim them warm waters of Fiddler's Green waiting on him to come tell me stories about all the things he'd seen and done on the Hard...mostly I'd wanna hear about stars."

Lenny sniffled. Tried to conceal how Ansel's words affected him.

Ansel didn't bother hiding his emotions. "Sir...can I ask you something?"

"Y-yeah," said Lenny.

"How'd he do? Racer...he a good catcher?"

Lenny forced himself not to look away. "Aye. Saved my life."

Ansel gasped. "He did? My boy?"

"Aye." Lenny bent his neck to wipe his cheeks on the shoulder of his Selkie suit. He felt horrible directly after when he looked back to see Ansel still shivering. "I...uh..." Lenny cleared his throat. "I had our target cornered when a Lepa came outta nowhere."

"No..." Ansel said.

Lenny nodded. "Had me and one a my crew dead to rights. This Lepa moves in on us, then *wham*—" Lenny smacked his palm against the stocks. "All I see is this...uh...bundle of tan and blond take the Lepa out. Racer...he popped up grinnin'. Taunted that Lepa. Can ya believe it?"

"I can." Ansel's face broke. "I sure can, sir. I can see it."

"Aye," said Lenny. "Then he fended the Lepa off while the rest a us escaped."

"My boy...my brave boy." Ansel grinned again, eyes gleaming. "Thank you, sir."

"Don't thank me," Lenny's voice rose. "If we hadn't needed to get the Orc back, I woulda chased ya son down."

"I don't believe that," said Ansel softly. "The taskmasters who brought me here…they said you was keel-raked for helping my boy and that you lived cause the Ancients knew you was innocent. I know the truth of it though. The Ancients let you live because you're a good man. Just like your daddy."

Lenny hung his head. "The Ancients didn't have anything to do with it, pal. I woulda drowned like all the others if it weren't for Pop's sea rat. Helped me pull my hood on and get Salted…" Lenny sighed. "Hated that pet all my life. What're the odds, huh?"

"Don't know much about odds," said Ansel. "But I know sea otters have a mind of their own. Had me one as a boy. Real sickly thing I nursed back to health. My daddy warned against it. Said you can't train the wild out of them." Ansel cracked a grin. "He was right."

"Sea rats." Lenny shook his head. "Always worried the thing'd gnaw my face off as I slept."

"Thing is…" Ansel said. "After our owner sold me away from my family, that otter of mine was the only thing that kept me going. Bedded down beside me at night, barked to warn me before Nomads swam near…"

Ansel grinned, lost in his memories.

"Used to tell myself the Ancients sent him to me," Ansel continued. "Something to keep watch over a little boy sold away from his family. You know he didn't leave me until I found my wife?"

"Lucky," said Lenny.

"Aye. Best friend I ever had, that otter. Rotten little thief that he was." Ansel chuckled.

Lenny found it hard not to join in his fellow's recollection, though Ansel quieted a few moments later.

"You set my boy free that he might live, Captain Dolan. I think maybe the Ancients sent your daddy's otter so you could too."

"Why would the Ancients care about me?" Lenny asked.

Ansel's eyes glistened. "Why wouldn't they?"

The reply stopped Lenny cold. *I'm a slave,* he thought to say. *A nobody.*

Ansel spoke before he could. "Them same taskmasters what brought me here, they…they told me what really happened, you know. They said my…my boy's dead."

Lenny's shoulders sagged as Ansel glanced at the stalactites to compose himself.

"Some bounty hunter in your crew killed him. Brung his suit back as proof and sold it to Tieran for a little profit."

"Taskmasters lie," said Lenny. "Every slave knows that. I'd lay anemonies Racer's out there, runnin' free."

"Might be. I'll learn the truth of it soon enough." Ansel looked on Lenny sadly. "I don't blame you, sir."

"Ya should. I didn't do nothin' to help ya son."

"You did," said Ansel. "I know you had a hand in it, sir."

"Stop callin' me that. I'm not no sir or captain, all right? Captains don't get locked up if they do their job, bring back runnas, and their crew. I didn't do that. Nothin' I do helps nobody."

Ansel bowed his head. "I'm grateful, sir," he said quietly.

"Why? They're gonna hang ya soon, pal. Ya forget that? Gonna stretch ya neck 'cause I didn't do my job. I didn't bring ya son back. I might've got ya both killed 'cause of it!"

"Aye."

Lenny slumped as far as the stocks would let him.

"Maybe my boy is dead," said Ansel. "I don't know. Don't want to either. But even if he is…" Ansel paused. "At least he tasted freedom for a little while. That's more than I could ever give him in a lifetime down here."

Lenny steeled himself as Ansel's gaze honed on him.

"If you didn't have a hand in his escape, I'm grateful you didn't bother catching him to bring back. But if you did help him…if you set my boy free." Ansel's eyes welled. "May the Ancients sing your praises, sir. I hope they bless you and yours until they call you to swim the green waters."

"I—" Lenny cleared his throat. "I didn't free Racer."

"All right, then." Ansel smiled. He looked away, toward the boardwalk and approaching footsteps.

Lenny expected to see Fenton round the corner with a host of taskmasters to take Ansel away. He didn't expect Paulo among their company.

The brute stood a head taller than those he walked alongside. Even then, Lenny knew Paulo hunched a bit, wincing occasionally, as he carried a bucket of water and plate with the scrapping of week old bread and dried seaweed. *Whattaya doin' here, Paulie?*

The taskmasters attended their work silently, much the same as Fenton. The old overseer never bothered look on Lenny. Indeed, it seemed he left that right to Paulo alone.

Something's wrong. Lenny thought as his crewmate glowered at him.

Ansel groaned when released from the stocks. The taskmasters helped him rise and supported him upon his initial stumble. He politely shrugged away from their grip, determined to walk of his own accord.

The taskmasters gave Fenton a wary look, but he merely gave a slight shake of his head to warn them off.

Lenny noticed Ansel's head dipped between his shoulders, as if time and backbreaking labor had worn away his neck. Even as his body shook, Racer's father did his best to stand straight without revealing his pain.

"Ansel," said Fenton. "Are you ready?"

"Aye, boss."

Fenton stepped aside and motioned toward the boardwalk.

The two convicts shared a final, parting look and then Ansel strode for the boardwalk, head held high. The taskmasters fell in behind the condemned, along with Fenton. Not one gave Lenny a parting glance, or uttered a single word.

Ansel turned the corner, never to be seen again by Lenny Dolan.

Lenny lay his forehead against the block, closed his eyes and offered his father's prayer.

"Feeling guilty?"

Lenny straightened. "Paulie…"

"Don't Paulie me," said the brute. "You're no friend of mine."

"Whattaya mean? Of course I—"

Paulo shifted around, revealing the freshly bandaged wounds crisscrossing his back. "This what friends do for each other?"

Lenny opened his mouth to speak. Thought better of it as Paulo faced him again.

"Or am I too big and stupid to understand?"

"Ya not stupid, Paulie."

"No? Why'd Chidi say that then?" Paulo stepped closer. "Why did Ellie get to know the plan, but not me?"

"No time." Lenny confessed. "It all happened so fast, I…"

"You could've told me later. After."

"I coulda'…but I didn't."

Paulo's cheeks turned scarlet. "Why?"

"If ya didn't know, ya didn't have to lie." Lenny omitted the part where it had been Ellie's idea to not clue their crewmate in. "Ya was neva any good at lyin', Paulie—"

"Right," said Paulo. "Never had any need to with you around. Makes me wonder what else you've lied to me about."

"Nothin', Paulie. I swear—"

"What? To the Ancients?" Paulo shook his head. "They let you survive keel-raking, but I know you aren't innocent. Ellie told me everything last night. Never thought I'd say this, Len, but Oscar was right. You're always plotting something. Can't plan your way out of this though. And Declan's not here to protect you anymore."

Lenny's body went numb. "Whattaya mean? Where's Pop?"

"Gone."

Lenny laughed. "Yeah right."

"It's true, Len," Paulo said somberly. "Taskmasters are saying he busted Marisa Bourgeois out and took off with her."

"I don't believe ya. Pop would neva run. We're Dolans."

"Seems all you Dolans are nothing but liars then."

"Don't talk about Pop like that." Lenny bristled.

Paulo shrugged. "Believe what you want. He's gone though. I know you had to see all the catcher groups sent out earlier. Some taskmasters too."

It's a lie. Paulie's mad. That's all. Tryin' to get a rise outta me.

"Heard the Crayfish lost his mind when they gave him the news," said Paulo. "Sent out everyone he could spare to find the two of them. He's offering five thousand anemonies to whoever brings your father back."

"Oh yeah?" Lenny sneered. "Then why aren't ya out there with 'em?"

"Fenton wouldn't allow it. Doesn't trust me, or Ellie, anymore. Said we won't ever be sent out again. Now we're breeding stock for the Crayfish."

Lenny snorted. "Looks like ya got what ya want then. Get to be with ya girl after all."

"Yeah, lucky us." Paulo's tone dripped with sarcasm. "Forced to do things no one should have put on them. Then we're supposed to watch any babies we have sold away. All because of you."

"Me? I'm not the one who ran."

"No, but you told Racer to."

"Yeah?" Lenny asked. "And who's the one who talked about it with him all the time, huh? That was you, Paulie. Rememba?"

"I remember Ellie bleeding." Paulo sneered. "Holding her head in my lap after she'd been knocked unconscious back at the jail. All part of your plan, right?"

"Nah." Lenny studied his former friend, the anger resonating off him, his defensive stance. "But ya wouldn't believe me now anyway."

"Nope." Paulo looked at the bucket of water he'd brought and the food. "I'm supposed to feed you. Boss wanted Ellie to do it, but—"

"What? Ya thought I'd talk her into freein' me or something?"

"I don't know what to think about you anymore." Paulo's forehead wrinkled. "I do know you're not going anywhere soon. With Declan gone, you're in the same boat Ansel was…"

I'm not. Lenny thought to himself. *The old man's given up. I haven't.*

"They're going to hang you, Len," said Paulo. "String you up because your father ran. All these years, him filling your head with that crap about Dolans won't leave people behind. Dolans don't run."

"Don't talk about my Pop like that, Paulie."

"What's wrong? You don't like being lied to?" Paulo kicked the water bucket over, then he smashed the bread between his meaty paws and let the crumbs fall across the stone floor.

Lenny glared at Paulo, his insides pulsing with hate.

"They're going to hang you, Len." Paulo wiped his nose with his forearm. "And I'm going to watch and not feel anything."

GARRETT

GARRETT WOKE TO A DOOR SLAMMING AGAINST the cavern wall.

"Morning, Garr—" Oscar's jaw hung open as he stood in the entryway. "What are you doing on the floor when there's a perfectly good bed?"

Garrett sat up. His back screamed with stiffness and he groaned as Oscar strolled into the room and jumped on the bed. Garrett half expected the servant girl to scream. Then he saw she wasn't there. *Thank God.*

"So what are you doing on the floor?" Oscar asked again.

"Bed was too soft."

"Ah, yes, well, sorry about that. Did you enjoy the gift my father sent you last night?" Oscar winked. "She's still learning the finer points of her trade, but I thought you should at least have some company since father so rudely didn't invite you to dinner. You'll simply have to forgive him. He's set in his ways and doesn't understand the benefits of having an Orc at our table. No worries though, I've since convinced him otherwise."

Garrett stood, stretched. "What do you mean?"

"You're to have breakfast with us this morning. Now, in fact."

Oscar grinned. "Come on. Let's not keep father waiting. He can be quite irritable if he goes too long without food."

Garrett followed Oscar out of the room and back down the long hall. He wondered when the servant girl left and how she slipped out of his room without waking him. *Probably for the best,* he decided, not knowing what he might have said had she been there when he woke.

After a few turns and a brief walk, Garrett followed Oscar onto a veranda with stone parapets. He saw a wooden platform constructed below the veranda and off to the side. Garrett wondered what it might be for, thinking of it as a small stage a band might play on.

August already sat at the table, snacking on crab cakes smeared with tartar sauce.

Garrett nearly retched at the smell as he and Oscar joined the owner of Crayfish Cavern.

"Ah, Garrett," said August. "Lovely to see you again. My sincerest apologies regarding last evening. I near lost my wits at the sight of those Nomads. Beastly, I tell you." August leaned forward. "I'm told you spoke with them at length?"

"Yeah," said Garrett as a servant placed a bowl of soup that reeked to high heaven.

"How did you find them?" August leaned forward. The tabletop dipped. "Fascinating, I shouldn't wonder. They and their ilk are nothing but heathens, after all."

And you're not? Garrett kept the thought. "They were okay, I guess. Two of them anyway."

"No need to tell me the one who wasn't." August laughed. "If Ishmael weren't such a frequent customer, I should have him thrown out. The other two…" August shuddered and hurriedly reached for another cake. "Quite a different matter altogether."

Garrett glanced at the soup in front of him. *Am I supposed to eat that?*

"But enough of Nomads and savagery," August continued. "I'll bet you're wondering why I've asked you here to breakfast with my son and me this glorious morning."

"Yeah," Garrett answered, happy for any excuse that might keep him from eating. He saw Oscar helping himself to bits of everything, with an appetite seemingly large as his father.

"Excellent," said August. "You might be unaware of this, but I thought it appalling when I learned my brave boy was bringing home an Orc. Meaning no offense, of course," he said quickly. "But I saw only complications to my business when the Painted Guard inevitably becomes involved."

Garrett thought to cut in and say he still had no idea who or what the Painted Guard was, but August blathered on with little regard that his guest might be confused.

"Last night, however," August reached across the table and grabbed hold of Oscar's shoulder. "My dear son opened my eyes to a new world of possibility. A world where Orc and Selkie might partner that our business might flourish."

Why do I get the vibe I don't like where this is going? Garrett wondered as both father and son looked at him greedily.

"To think I'd ever have an immortal guarding my cavern." August dabbed at his eyes. "I admit even I had not thought to dream so large."

"Wait…" said Garrett. "What do you mean…immortal?"

"Ah, yes," said August. "Technically, you're right. I suppose you're not *really* immortal since you can be killed. Semantics." August reached for another cake and popped it in his mouth.

"No, hang on. You said I'm immortal?" Garrett asked.

August swallowed. "Surely someone must have told you by now."

Garrett noted Oscar as surprised as his father.

"Ooh, I do love this game." August clapped. "Tell me, Garrett. How old do you think I am?"

Garrett studied him.

"Go on, go on," said August. "Oh, and spare no regard for my feelings, please. Come on...out with it."

Garrett shrugged. "Fifty?"

August squealed. "Quite wrong, of course, but I thank you for the compliment."

"Okay," said Garrett. "So how old are you really then? Fifty-five?"

August beamed. "Older."

"Sixty?"

August shook his head. "Older," he said gleefully.

"No way," said Garrett. "I know you guys think I'm dumb, but I'm not *that* dumb. You can't be more than sixty."

"Quite a lot actually," said August. "Call it five hundred sixty."

"Yeah right."

August chuckled. "I don't blame you for not believing. The Ancients know I didn't either when I was a boy." He sighed. "In truth, it doesn't seem that long ago when I discovered the secret of delaying death."

This is so stupid. Garrett sat back. "All right, I'll bite. What's the secret?"

"Like you need it." Oscar scowled at him.

"Son, please," said August. "It's not often I get to tell this story, let alone to a Salt Child. You'll ruin my breakfast if you give any more away."

"Sorry, Father." Oscar returned to his soup.

"Now," said August. "Where were we?"

Garrett slouched in his chair. "The secret to immortality."

"No," August cautioned. "Not immortality. Beneath this suit, why, I'm only a man. Take it from me, and I should naturally age. Die, right from the start, actually, if the one stripping it from me weren't a Salt Child. In that way, I suppose one might say all Selkies remain slaves to their suits." August stroked the sheen of his coat. "Ah, but inside its threads, the only elixir mankind will ever find to truly ward off death."

Garrett sat up. "What do you mean?"

August smiled. "Even as a boy, I was ambitious. My father was a rich man and powerful too. We lived happily for a time in our grand estate in southern England, all the niceties of the times within our reach. We had everything, or so I thought."

Lucky you. Garrett thought as August continued.

"My father had not yet reached forty when the sickness found him. Some type of pox, I recall." August frowned. "He sent for the brightest physicians in our country and from others too. Each and every one of them brought the same news…nothing could save him."

August took another cake in his hands. This one he did not eat, however. Merely kept it in hand and looked at as if it were a mirror to his past.

"Day after excruciating day, my father withered whilst meaningless servants flaunted their health about him. For two years, I watched him die, bed-ridden and mad out of his mind. Only a boy, and yet I already feared death unlike my fellows who naively thought the invincibility of youth should last."

August plopped the cake into his mouth, hardly chewing before swallowing down the pastry.

"With father gone, I spent his fortune examining any whisper of a chance to beat death, or at least stave it. So many stories." August shook his head. "Vampires and werewolves, elves and fairies, all of it bollocks. I had resigned myself to death when a servant girl mentioned a man in her homeland, Ireland, of whom it was said never aged."

Garrett saw a dangerous glint in August's eye and a smirk teasing the corners of his lips.

"She took me to her village and I met with many of the locals. The elderly spoke in hushed whispers of how the man had been the same age when they were wee girls. I bid them take me to him and to leave us alone. To my surprise, I found him forthcoming with information. He was nearing the end of his time with the suit, you see." August looked at Garrett for the first time since beginning his story. "But of course you know nothing about that either, do you?"

"No," said Garrett. "One of Nomads told me Selkie suits were made with Salt Child blood."

"Indeed," said August. "The inventor implanted a bit of irony in this dark gift to humanity. At the time, I thought it quite silly. Only now do I understand the maker's inspired genius."

"I-I don't understand."

"The old man told me Salt Children never considered us their equals. What good is ruling if you have no one to rule over?" August chuckled. "And what good is a mortal slave to those who know nothing of death? Drybacks should be dead and gone in the blink of a Salt Child's eye. Hardly any time for us to learn our place and be put to work."

August's belly jiggled as he sighed.

"No," he continued. "The maker knew better. By mixing a Salt Child's blood with the skin of this mortal creature." August tugged at his hood. "The maker extended our life, but did not give us an immortal life to match his own."

"Sooo you won't live forever," said Garrett.

"The same question I asked the old man." August smiled. "He warned the suit staved aging for only a hundred years. After that, the suit loses its power. It must be gifted to a new owner to work its dark enchantment anew."

"But why would someone give that up?" Garrett asked.

"To wear the suit is to become its slave," said August. "Most are happy to shed the yoke after a lifetime of servitude in the realm beneath the waves."

"Servitude?"

"Aye. Who else to wait on Salt Children? Fetch their food and wine. Clean their homes and build their cities. All this and more the old man, Conroy," August hesitated. "Funny that I still recall his name after all these years." August shook off the memory. "He had been press-ganged by a pod of Orcinians to carry out the will of the royal families. After years of Salt slavery, he somehow managed to escape, though I never did tease the story of how out of him. Too busy staring at his coat."

August reached for another of the cakes, his eyes widening as he stared on its rich frosting.

"Conroy told me he had tired of the Salt life," said August. "Had come ashore and started a new family. Still, he knew to remove the coat himself would surely kill him and so his Selkie suit continued its magic. It kept him alive while he watched his family pass on.

He begged me then to kill him and burn his suit after." August's eyes narrowed. "Even as I told him I would, I knew he recognized it for a lie. He warned me immortality was a curse, but what did I care? I had witnessed the ones I loved suffer and die. I had no wish to follow that path."

Oscar slapped the table, surprising Garrett. "And so you killed him! Didn't you, Father?"

"Aye," said August. "I granted that one request. His suit I kept. I donned it quickly and made for the sea, entering those frigid waters and changing for the first time. At first, there was only dark. The old man had tricked me, I thought. Then I heard."

Garrett noted a new energy in August's voice. He thought back to the one in his own head, the Orca's, and how the oceans sang to him when first he changed.

"I lost myself in the swimming. Soon I ventured further out and deeper." August shook his head. "Foolish. I had forgotten all Conroy had said to me. Soon, I found myself enslaved by the same Salt Children he warned me against."

"You were a slave?" Garrett asked.

"Aye, twice actually. The first time I escaped with several others." August's lip curled. "But there was a traitor in our midst. A group of catchers found him and teased our whereabouts from him before his death. They captured the rest of us easily, and back into slavery I went."

"But you escaped again," said Oscar proudly.

"Aye," August continued. "And the second time I was not so naïve as those I ran with."

"Father killed them," said Oscar.

Garrett looked on August with new understanding.

"Aye," said August. "I did what was necessary. My time in Conroy's suit wore thin and I knew I must procure a new one."

Oookay. Garrett squirmed. *I'm sitting with a serial killer and his son.*

"And it was then, taking their suits from them, I learned the most important lesson of all."

"Wh-what?" Garrett hesitated to ask.

"That I was capable of much and more," said August. "Tell me something, Garrett. You wish to go home, yes?"

Garrett nodded.

"Would you kill to go home?"

Garrett's throat parched. August had asked the question so easily, as if asking Garrett if he wanted to go to the movies. "N-no. I wouldn't kill for anything."

"Not yet," said August. "But what if I told you that someday, perhaps soon, you would."

Garrett shook his head. "No, I wouldn't."

August grinned as he stood and stepped to the edge of the veranda. "Come, Garrett. There's something I'd like to show you."

Garrett balked upon noticing a host of guards had silently slipped onto the veranda to join them.

"Come along," said August. "I have other matters yet to attend this morning."

I don't have a choice. Garrett thought as he stood from the table.

His chair screeched as a hooded guardian pulled it away and escorted him to the edge.

"Fenton," August looked down toward the wooden stage. "As you will."

Garrett saw Fenton lead an older man, naked save for a loincloth, onto the stage. A hooded guardian tied off a rope as he joined them and Garrett suddenly knew in his heart what the driftwood beam above the stage would be used for. He choked at seeing a noose thrown over the beam and watched Fenton tease it down over the older man's neck then tighten it.

"Ansel," Fenton's voice boomed. "Your son, Racer, said the words. By the laws of New Pearlaya, should any slave not return…"

"Let my loved ones pay the price," said Ansel.

Fenton nodded. "Have you any last words?"

Garrett saw the older man glance up at him and those on the veranda. Their eyes connected for a moment before he looked away.

Ansel straightened, his gaze fixed on August Collins. "Send me off to Fiddler's Green. I want to see my boy again."

Garrett cried openly at the defiance in the condemned and he wondered how a man could stand so proudly while staring death in the eye.

"No!" said Garrett as Fenton guided Ansel to the edge and placed a black hood over his head. "What are you doing? Stop!"

Garrett closed his eyes when Fenton placed his hand to Ansel's back. A moment later, he heard the rope snap tight. Garrett fell to his knees, gasping at the constant creaking.

"The Painted Guard will come to collect you soon," August said. "But I think you want to stay in my cavern and protect me and my son. That's what you'll tell them anyway. Won't you, Orc?"

Garrett glared up. "N-never."

"Oscar…"

"Aye, Father?"

"Where did you say Garrett was from again?"

"Some place called Indiana. Pretty far inland too. Can't remember the town exactly, although I expect Lenny certainly would. That nipperkin never forgets a thing."

"We'll have to ask him, then," said August. "After all, I imagine you'll want your loved ones brought here to join you, won't you, Garrett?"

"No…" Garrett thought of his mom. "You can't…"

"I can do anything I like," said August. "Did you not listen to my story? I learned much that day I took my fellows' coats…that I would do *anything* to survive and protect my family. That lesson's served me well in my profession. You're a bright Orc. Will you learn this lesson too? Or will you make me show you how serious I am?"

"I…I…"

"That worthless vermin you saw hanged…little more than krill, to my mind. He did nothing wrong. His boy ran. Desired freedom more than his father's life," said August. "So what do you think I might do to someone who defied my wishes? Hmm?"

"Please…"

August leaned closer. "I will send a crew to bring me your family this very day should you not do as I ask."

Garrett threw up.

"Getting the point, are you?" August asked. "Good. When the Painted Guard arrive to collect you, what are you going to say?"

Garrett's head swooned with thoughts of his mother. He broke down, sobbing.

"What will you tell them?"

"I-I…"

"Say the words, *Orc,*" said August. "Convince me."

Garrett looked at August through blurry eyes. "I want to stay…"

"Excellent." August clapped Garrett on the shoulder. "See, Oscar?

Don't ever let it be said you can't teach an Orc a new lesson. Right, then, we have an auction and games to attend. Guards! See this Orc locked away until the Painted Guard arrives. I want him cleaned and fed too. He's looking a bit peakish."

Garrett's legs threatened to give out.

The guards kept him upright as August and Oscar left.

"Oh," August turned back. "And you will eat, won't you, Garrett? I noticed you didn't touch your breakfast. After all, we don't want the Painted Guard thinking you've not been taken care of. I'll not have it said Crayfish Collins isn't hospitable."

KELLEN

KELLEN LANGUISHED IN THE PIT. HE REMAINED certain if he could transform back into his normal self that he would find a way to unhook the net strung above him. For hours, he had pictured his human face, hands, and body.

Nothing worked.

Why can't I change back? He snorted bubbles.

His Sea Lion cellmates did little to help. The two he guessed as Edmund and Bryant huddled together at one corner. The smaller one Kellen figured as Marrero had swam near him once. Kellen had lost control of his seal mind and lunged at what he viewed as prey. Marrero hadn't dared swim back over since.

Kellen and the seal's mind had fought much of the night for control over their shared body. Even so, he enjoyed allowing the seal mind take over from time to time, if nothing more than because it too hated. Hated that it had been outsmarted by man and couldn't find a way to loosen the nets. Hated that Kellen kept fighting it back into submission. It lingered at the back of his mind even now.

Kellen knew it would only be a matter of time before the Leper mind fought free again.

He glanced up at the nets to focus both their minds on a common enemy. He had tried several times to leap from the pit. Snatch the net in his jaws and let his seal's weight carry it down. Each attempt left him weaker and scarcely budged the net.

Must've tied it down somehow.

And so Kellen waited with only his hate and the seal mind to comfort him.

When do we hunt? The seal endlessly wished to know. *When do we eat?*

Soon, Kellen would remind it, picturing Tieran Chelly's face, imagining what he would do if given half a chance.

Light flickered above the nets. Someone whistled.

"Wakey, wakey, eggs and bakey. How many of my seadogs are still alive?"

Tieran. Kellen heard a low rumble in his seal throat at the thought.

Tieran appeared at the edge, along with a host of hooded guards, and he dipped his torch low toward the pits to light the dark waters. "Well, well. All still alive." He sighed as he looked on Kellen. "And I half thought you'd take the rest of 'em out. Might be you don't have the fight in you after all."

Kellen opened his mouth and hissed.

Tieran grinned. "That's the spirit. Just in time for the games too. All righ', lads," Tieran motioned to the guards. "Auction's starting soon. Might be a couple there wanna buy some fighters. String 'em up."

Kellen shrunk as the nets fell. He dipped below the water to miss being struck on the head. His seal mind warned to dive deep and swim away. Kellen ignored it and surfaced, peeking his nostrils for a quick breath.

Guards patrolled either side of the pit, harpoons in hand.

What are they doing?

Kellen detected movement in the water. He ducked below again.

Down, Kellen thought to his seal brain. His body responded and he tucked his nose and dove with a quick swish of his hind flippers. Kellen descended to the bottom, but the noise source eluded him. He searched for the three Sea Lions, but did not see or hear them anywhere.

Still the scratchy noise continued.

Swim! his seal mind commanded.

Kellen fought it off. Waiting, suspended in water. Watching.

He realized too late the seal mind had the right of it.

The rope net swooped in out of the darkness.

The seal mind took over, spinning to swim the opposite direction.

Swim under it! Kellen immediately pivoted and dove. Then he saw his mistake.

The net bottom lay heavy on the pit floor, weighted by stone. Still it came on, water sieving through the open bits.

Up and over! Kellen ascended, his hind flippers swishing rapidly to build speed. His nose broke the surface and he leapt. Mouth open and snarling.

The net loomed before him, stretched high above the surface.

Kellen's momentum carried him into it. He smacked the net, his flippers wedging through the openings and hanging him there. He bucked and writhed, but the struggle served only to entangle him further.

The smallest of the Sea Lions also hung in the nets near him. It barked in his direction.

Marrero! Kellen searched for a weak spot in the net, finding none. The ropes, stretched tight and creaking, ran up and out of the pits. They tied off at a winch near the ceiling and descended to a massive wooden spindle manned by six hooded guards that walked it like a merry-go-round to draw the net in.

The weight of his seal body pulled at his joints. Kellen barked in agony.

The net neared the end of the pits where the remaining two Sea Lions, Bryant and Edmund, waited. Ropes from the bottom finally pulled up, scooping the Sea Lions into the same net entrapping Kellen and Marrero.

A hooded guard guided the rope net over to the main floor with a hook. Those at the spindle reversed their walk and the net lowered, jolting Kellen's joints with each bumpy increment until the net touched the cavern floor. Kellen hung his head and moaned at the instant relief in his seal appendages.

He didn't bother to fight back as the guards peeled the net away. One knelt beside him with a knife and sawed at the rope wrapped round Kellen's hind flippers.

"No, no, no." Tieran pulled the guard back by his hood and took his knife. "You'll ruin the net, fool."

Tieran held the knife in front of Kellen's face. "Open your mouth."

Kellen growled.

"I said open your mouth. And if your jaws so much as quiver when ol' Tieran takes hold of you, I'll have you thrown back in the pits still wearing this netted mess. Drown you, it will."

Reluctantly, Kellen obeyed.

Tieran reached forward and took hold of Kellen's upper lip, then peeled it back.

Kellen thought it should hurt, but it instead reminded him of taking a ball cap off his head. The tickle returned and the changes from seal to human swept over him in reverse like shower water streaming down his back. The cavern's natural chill kissed his forehead and cheeks again. In seconds, Kellen lay in human form with the net draped over him.

He easily pulled his feet free and untangled his arms. Gingerly, he used his right hand to ensure the left passed easily out of the net. He sneered at seeing the crayfish emblem freshly scarred on the back of his hand. Brownish blood pooled at the edges, but elsewise it looked bruised, purple and black.

"Ah," a nearby voice yelled. "Ah, ah!"

Kellen found Marrero human again and guessed his friend screamed while watching the Sea Lion face melt away into Edmund's human one. Kellen opened his mouth to tell Marrero to shut up. A wire noose drew tight round his neck.

Kellen reached to pull it away.

The guard holding the pole end lifted, forcing Kellen to stand, or suffocate. He heard others gasp and saw the same maneuver surprise Marrero and Bryant.

Edmund alone did nothing to fight against the noose.

"All righ', lads," Tieran crowed. "Step these sorry seadogs in line and get this lot down to the pier. On with you now!" He cracked his whip. "Double time!"

Another group of guards ushered the seals and sea lions out of the cage neighboring the one Kellen had occupied. The beefy man came next, his face red and purple, as two guards escorted him from the end of their long poles.

Cold iron grazed Kellen's neck, nudging him onward.

"Move," said the guard holding him prisoner.

Kellen walked forward, falling in behind the beefy man. He glanced back and learned Marrero came next, with Edmund and Bryant not far after. He followed the line through the geode tunnel. They angled south, headed the way Kellen had seen the others go after the sorting, bound for what Tieran had called the Block.

They stopped at what Kellen thought a rickety shed, half the size of his dad's pole barn. An old man in a hooded Selkie suit awaited them, his face set in grimness.

"All righ', Boss Fenton?" Tieran addressed him. "What you here for?"

"One of the Lord Master's guests has asked for some…companionship. I'm told you've locked her away for safekeeping. I assume you have a key?"

"Aye." Tieran produced a key from his Selkie pocket and handed it over. "But I'll warn you. This won't go over well."

Fenton frowned. "Your job is to sell slaves, not give unrequested advice."

"Righ'," said Tieran. "I'll keep on then, yeah?"

"That would be wise." Fenton turneded the latch and vanished inside the shed.

Tieran cracked his whip. "You heard Boss Fenton, lads. Keep on with you now, keep on!"

The pole nudged Kellen in the neck again. "Move."

Kellen trod along, his head on a swivel taking in the new surroundings. He didn't know what he searched for, but thought it important to remember all he could. Any clue that might help him escape.

He found little helpful.

Cavern walls existed to his left, and pond fields to his right. Workers waded waist deep in still ponds, shucking pearls from oysters. Others had thatched bundles on their backs, piled high with wet seaweed as they picked it fresh and tossed it in their packs.

Kellen followed the line westward toward small, whitewashed homes. He heard voices as they continued the march. Small at first, they quickly became a roar upon nearing the homes.

Kellen looked left, out over the open waters where men and women casually bobbed without the aid of any floatation devices. They laughed and drank from silver cups with rubies and sapphires. A few pointed at him and the others in his group. Kellen marveled as those in the water swam inland without the use of their hands, all far faster than he ever imagined a person capable of swimming.

One leapt from the water, a man with a dolphin tail.

Kellen gasped as the tail split in two, forming human legs that shone wetly like bluish-grey tights.

Marrero screamed behind him. "What the—"

"Quiet!" the guards silenced him.

This is insane. Kellen thought as they passed through the crowds. At first, he thought them normal people, albeit dressed weirdly. The longer he stared, he knew them anything but human.

Some of the women wore weird swimsuits of various patterns, some swirled white and grey, others with stripes. Others, including the men, wore shirts woven from sea grass, their colors neon bright.

Kellen took note nearly all bedecked themselves with jewelry— pearl necklaces, gold medallions, and the like. An eel shawl draped low over one woman's shoulders, and a man teased its owner with the eel's lax jaws.

The noose round his neck hastened Kellen along.

Some of those in the crowd stepped close to him, touched his shoulders and thumped his chest. The guard charged with him stopped to let the people crowd around him.

Kellen made to smack their hands away.

The noose constricted and another guard slapped iron manacles around his wrists, belting them around his waist.

Emboldened by his shackling, the crowd stepped nearer. They muttered in foreign tongues, their hands touching all over his body. His mind screamed to ward them off.

The noose warned against it.

Kellen closed his eyes as they poked and prodded at him. One pinched his cheeks together, forcing him to open his mouth while they looked inside. Another tugged his head this way and that as if they wanted to judge his resistance.

Kellen endured it all, hate simmering in his heart.

Soon the noose urged him move on again and the hands of those who'd felt him up and down fell away.

Kellen opened his eyes. He saw a row of cages and the faces of those Tieran had previously sorted. *Is this the Block?*

He had little time to think on the idea. The guards led him and his fellow captives to another cage, opposite the block. A gate clanged open and Kellen found himself ushered inside his newest cell.

The noose went lax the moment he entered and pulled free over his head.

Kellen stepped to the back of the cage as his cellmates crowded in behind him. He found them near the water's edge, closer to the stage than the Block captives.

"I'm sorry, Ed." Bryant's shoulders heaved. "God knows I'm sorry. Needed to tell you that ever since they made me put it on."

"It's all right," Edmund replied. "If it helps get you outta this mess, he would've been happy."

"What are you talking about?" Kellen asked. "Who would've been happy?"

"My son," said Edmund. "Bryant's wearing my boy Richie's suit."

Kellen looked on the tannish coat, remembering the youngest marshal who'd taunted him at the jail. Released him from his cell and was cut down by gunfire when he tried warning Kellen not to run. The same marshal the girl, Marisa Bourgeois, had predicted would die that night.

If Bryant's wearing Richie's suit—Kellen touched the hood of his—*whose suit was this?*

Bryant sighed. "You'd think they would've given us the earrings by now."

"No," said Edmund. "No need for it yet. They'll let our new owners buy them."

"Owners?" Marrero asked. "What are you talking about?"

"Look around you, boy," said Edmund. "This is a slave post. And if you're not buying, you're the one being sold. So unless you've got pockets full of anemonies I don't know about…"

Marrero immediately pulled at the neckline of his suit with both hands.

"What are you doing?" Kellen asked.

"I'm getting out of this thing!"

"You can't," said Edmund. "Didn't you hear the seal's voice in your head?"

Marrero stopped.

"I heard it," said Kellen.

Edmund nodded. "Symbiotic. Know what that means?"

Kellen glared at him.

"I thought not," said Edmund. "Means you and the suit need each other to live. From this day to your last day, the seal is part of you."

"I don't believe you." Marrero resumed his efforts.

"There's Salt blood weaved in each and every Selkie suit," said Edmund. "That means only someone with Salt in their veins can remove it. Try any other way, you wind up dead."

Marrero stopped. "H-how can that be?"

"They made these suits to enslave us," said Edmund. "What good are shackles if the prisoners can take them off whenever they want?"

Bryant shook his head. "Even if you find a Salt Child willing to risk their neck—"

"Good luck with that," Edmund cut in.

"It doesn't matter in the end," said Bryant, trembling. "The seal stays a part of you and it always wants to go home. It's enough to drive someone mad…"

"How do you know?" Kellen snarled. "They just put you in one."

"My wife," said Bryant quietly. "It's what happened to her."

Kellen was about to ask more when he saw Tieran approach the pier with a conch shell in hand. Behind him, hooded guards led a line of people. Whenever anyone tugged away, a whip cracked, and Kellen saw the captive fall back in line.

What's going on? Kellen wondered as Tieran put the shell to his lips and blew, its echo reverbing throughout the cavern.

The crowd quieted and settled into the makeshift bleachers built from driftwood. Oscar emerged from their midst, alongside one of the fattest men Kellen had ever seen. Both wore pearl-white suits with black hoods.

"The Crayfish," Edmund muttered as guards carried a regally carved and cushioned couch to the pier for the father and son. "And his little whelp."

Kellen clenched his fists at the sight of Oscar. The fresh scar on his left hand pulled and broke. *Use it,* Kellen thought to himself. *Use the hate.*

"Righ' then," Tieran yelled. "On behalf of his Lord Master August Collins and son, welcome to Crayfish Cavern. Let's get this auction started, shall we?"

Kellen's lip curled at the crowd's applause and cheers as guards led a mother and daughter onto the pier's stage.

"First on the docket is this lovely cow," Tieran began. "Fresh from the mainland, she is, and a fine bet for breeding more fine pups like the one beside her, I'll warrant. Opening bid for the cow by her lonesome is a hundred anemonies."

Kellen stepped back as some in the crowd immediately raised white shells, large as dinner plates, with black painted numbers on them. *This is insane.* Kellen shook as Tieran's voice spouted at rapid-fire, calling out numbers to drive the price up. Standing amongst the crowd, guards yelled to call Tieran's attention whenever a potential buyer raised their shell.

Tieran's voice slowed when the crowd ceased raising their shells.

"Goin' once…twice…" Tieran clapped his hands and pointed to a male buyer dressed in a yellowed shawl of seagrass. "I sold her to buyer number four for two hundred anemonies. Will you have her wee pup, sir, for another twenty-five?"

The buyer shook his head. The little girl screamed as guards tore her mother away and dragged her kicking and screaming down the opposite steps.

Marrero clung to the bars beside Kellen. "What is this place?"

"What'd I tell you, Pinocchio," said Bryant. "Some Pleasure Island, huh?"

Kellen found himself unable to form the words as Tieran sold the little girl next.

One by one, the line of people were led onto the stage and sold like cattle until the last of them had walked off the opposite end.

"All righ', enough with the dregs." Tieran yelled. "Who's ready for some games, eh? Let's see how they fare in a match of Selkie polo—"

"*Polo?*" A bare-chested man in the crowd scoffed. Scars and tattoos littered his body and he grinned as he looked on those in the cages. "This is an outpost, isn't it? Give us some real games."

"M-Master Ishmael," said Tieran. "You ask the Lord Master to lose perfectly good—"

"I ask nothing," said Ishmael. "I *demand* it. You lured me here with the promise of fighters, Tieran. Show me some, and I'll line your master's pockets. Show me not, and I'll find sport enough on my own."

The crowd roared in approval. "Fight," they cried. "Fight. Fight!"

Kellen saw Tieran look to Oscar and his father. Watched them hesitate, then nod.

"Righ' then, a real game it is." Tieran waved at the guards near Kellen's cage.

They opened the cage door.

Kellen backed away into the corner as a guard entered and took the nearest captive.

"Fight them, Bryant," Edmund called. "You can do it."

The guard walked Bryant into the water. Others raised a net

between the piers to keep him from escaping. One dropped a harpoon in front of Bryant.

"Man versus beast, how 'bout it?" Tieran yelled to another cry of approval.

He has to fight a seal? Kellen wondered as a taskmaster led the animal into the water.

The trapped Selkie slipped beneath the surface and disappeared.

"Keep to the shallows, Bryant," Edmund shouted. "Don't let it pull you in!"

Kellen stared wide-eyed as Bryant stood waist deep in water, both hands clutching the harpoon, its tip poised above the surface.

"Fight. Fight. Fight!" The crowd urged.

"Come on, Bryant." Edmund whispered beside Kellen. "You can do this."

Kellen's heart leapt as Bryant plunged the harpoon and called it back as quick. Then he yelped and disappeared below, the water thrashing white.

Fight! Kellen put his face between the bars. *Come on!*

The crowd shouted in approval as the water dyed red.

Bryant's head popped above the surface. Gasping for air, he raised the bloodied harpoon victoriously over his head to a new wave of applause and whistles.

The guards wrenched the harpoon away from Bryant and led him limping up the stony shore onto the stage. Kellen winced at the teeth marks that had torn into Bryant's calf.

"A fine start to his lordship's games," said Tieran. "Who'll have this fighter, then? Let's open him at five hundred."

The raising of shells began anew with Tieran's voice in accompaniment. The bidding reached eight hundred before the sold verdict rang out. The buyer had only one eye, the other covered with a seashell patch.

"Let's have more then, shall we?" Tieran cried as the guards led Bryant off the stage. "Beast versus beast this time, I think."

The guards led two seals into the water next. Looking on the few remaining animals in the seal cage and then on the faces of his cellmates, Kellen knew it would be only a matter of time before he, too, would be led out and forced to fight.

Kellen glared at the crayfish emblem on the back of his hand, clenched his fists, and knew one more thing with utter certainty... he would win.

CHIDI

WHY DID YOU MENTION DECLAN? CHIDI SCOLDED herself for the thousandth time. Yet even now, she simmered at her abandonment. *He left me.*

She glanced at Marisa's empty cage. *They both did. Left me here for Henry.*

You left Allambee, her conscience argued.

"I saved him."

The lie tasted sour on her tongue. Or was it only the air? Parched, Chidi tried to call some little saliva to swallow as she fought the memory of Zymon Gorski. How quick he had been to abandon her and Wotjek. She lifted her knees to her chest then laid her head against them and cried.

Be strong, Chidi. She recalled Marisa's final words. *The waiting time is almost ended.*

Chidi screamed into the void, her echo continuing long after the scream died in her throat.

I want the end, she sobbed in silent prayer. *Not the waiting time. Not strength. Just give me the end.*

Chidi cursed herself for crying, all her strength sapped. She laid her head back against the bars, basked in their coolness. "Ancients, hear my voice," she whispered hoarsely to the dark. "However I wronged you, surely I've paid for it in full. Hear my prayer...bring me my end. Let the waiting time be over...I-I have no strength left to hold to."

Chidi opened her eyes as shadows crept their way up the tunnel toward her.

Henry...

The shadows came too slow for Henry's quick gait, however, and Chidi wondered who it might be. She stepped to the furthest reach of her cage when seeing the aged Selkie who finally appeared. *Fenton?*

The Crayfish's head overseer barely glanced at Marisa's empty cage as he trod toward Chidi. His shoulders slumped and she saw dark circles under his eyes. He stopped shy of her cage and raised his torch higher to look her full in the face.

"You're to come with me, child." Fenton tossed a pair of manacles through the bars.

Chidi winced at the sound of them striking the cavern floor.

"Put them on," said Fenton.

"H-Henry. Did he send you?"

"No."

This isn't right. Chidi hesitated. *Henry would never send someone to fetch me.*

"I may look old to young eyes, but my grip is strong as ever. You don't want me coming in there," said Fenton. "Put them on."

Chidi shuddered. "H-Henry wouldn't want this. Wouldn't allow it."

"What Henry wants doesn't matter anymore." Fenton unlocked the door and stepped in the entry. He loosed the whip at his side with a free hand. Gave it enough of a twitch for Chidi to see its end dance. "Put them on."

Chidi knelt and fumbled at the manacles. No sooner had she clasped them around her wrists than Fenton grabbed the middle chain and tugged her out in front of him.

"Move." Fenton nudged her in the back with the butt of his whip.

Chidi kept her silence as they walked the winding tunnel and into the main shack. Fenton passed her at the last and pushed the wooden door open.

A crowd of voices swelled in the distance. *The auction...*

"Master Collins wanted to buy you." Fenton shook his head as he made for the door. "Thought you'd make a good investment with all those languages Henry said you knew."

"Henry would never sell me," said Chidi. "Not for anything."

"For a slave, you don't listen very well." Fenton looked Chidi in the eyes, his grey eyes tired and stern. "What Henry wants doesn't matter anymore. Not in Crayfish Cavern anyway."

Fenton finished locking the door then took her by the arm.

"I warned Master August against hiring the pair of you," he continued as they walked toward the docks. "Told him I don't know much, but I do know slaves, and a slave with something to live for doesn't stay put long."

"Henry—"

"Not talking about him, girl. It's you I wanted nothing to do with from the start."

"Wh-why?"

"Cause you're a runner." Fenton secured his grip. "Knew it the first time you set foot in this cavern. Now it's cost me two good slaves to Fiddler's Green, two more to the whipping masts, and a captain to the gallows soon because of you. Ancients know I'll rest easier once you're gone."

The crowd roared approval and Tieran's rapid-fire voice continued as they neared the dock.

Chidi saw faces now, all of them casting their gaze toward the water and the stage.

Fenton stepped in front of her to lead the way through those standing in the crowd.

They stopped opposite the holding cages, one with the teens from the boat and the gas station attendant locked inside. She heard Tieran begin anew, auctioning off the winner of a bout as taskmasters dragged a dead Selkie from the water onto the stony shore.

Chidi looked away as they stripped the man of his seal coat. She saw August and Oscar Collins both seated upon the dais to oversee the event. A host of entrees and desserts loomed before the master of Crayfish Cavern. He seemed to have sampled them all, if Chidi rightly judged the number of crumbs and stains upon his coat.

"Sold him for five hundred to buyer number twelve." Tieran glanced at her and waved.

What's he—

Fenton tugged Chidi forward.

When she instinctually resisted, he sneered and jerked her onto the stage.

"Oh, gents, ol' Tieran's got a pretty face for you to buy, he does." Tieran crowed as he skipped over to Chidi. "Now's the time to dig deep in them pockets, lads, for those of you what got 'em! You'll not find a better looker this side of the Atlantic, I'll warrant."

Chidi shrunk beneath the crowd's ogling.

"And look at that lovely coat she has too," said Tieran. "A fine lil' Ribbon Seal suit for a fine lil' lady."

Chidi winced as Tieran stopped behind her and placed his arm about her shoulders.

"What's say we find out what she's hiding underneath, eh lads?"

"*Stop*! Ze girl eez mine."

Though Chidi didn't see him, she recognized Henry's voice.

A moment later, he shoved to the front and leapt onto the stage, his expression daring anyone try and stop him from reclaiming his property.

Tieran melted away as Henry strode toward them.

Fenton did not. "Take him," he said softly.

Chidi scarcely had time to wonder if she'd heard Fenton correctly before several of his underlings restrained Henry.

"Let go of me, fools." Henry snarled. "Crayfeesh! Call your dogs off."

"And why should I do that?" August Collins dabbed his rosy cheeks with a napkin, then waved his Selkie attendants to move the great table aside. His chair groaned beneath his weight as he leaned heavily on the arms to stand.

"She belongs to me," said Henry. "By the laws of New Pearlaya, I own 'er."

"Ah, yes," said August. "By those same laws, you owe me a debt."

"Liar."

"Not actually, no. I hired you to protect my son. A duty which you woefully neglected when you chose to abandon him to the charge of slaves, all of whom might've decided to kill him and take freedom for themselves if they weren't loyal to me."

Henry's face darkened as all listened to August continue.

"You killed one of my slaves without compensating me, had

my auctioneer purchase suits that rightfully belonged to me under the details of our agreement, oh, and let us not forget the uh… larger…issue you helped my son capture." August's great belly heaved. "You bring danger to my doorstep and have the audacity to claim it is I who owe you something?"

August shook his head. "No. I'm merely taking what's owed me. Be grateful, sir, I only take your precious Chidi from you. I could easily have your coat and your life, both, should I will it." August faced the crowd. "But I am a gracious host, am I not?"

The crowd's cheers and whistles made Chidi's ears hurt.

August's flabby arms jiggled as he clapped. "You're all too kind, really." He beamed before turning back to Henry. "Guards, see him out directly."

Henry shrugged free of his captors and bowed low before August Collins.

Chidi's conscience reminded her to breathe.

"My 'umble thanks for your mercy, Crayfeesh."

What?

"Go," said August. "Before I change my mind."

Henry straightened. His eyes found Chidi. Lingered. Then he leapt from the stage and vanished amidst the crowd.

"Guards," said August quietly. "Follow him out."

It won't be enough. Chidi thought as several hastened to carry out their master's command. *He'll kill them before they even know they're dead.*

"Tieran," said August. "As you will."

"Righ', sir. So how much will this pretty lass fetch, eh? Let's start her at four—"

"A thousand…"

The crowd whispered and parted as the would-be buyer stepped to the stage.

Chidi trembled. *Ishmael...*

"What's wrong, Tieran? Aren't you going to ask for more?" Ishmael asked. He glared at the crowd. "Are any of you so foolish to stand between me and what I desire?"

Laughter arose from the opposite side of the stage.

Chidi searched for one could be so foolish and saw Quill nimbly leap onto the stage while his brother, Watawa, waited near the bleachers with a Selkie slave in his charge. Chidi gasped. *They bought the Silkstealer?*

"I have an offer." Quill smiled broadly.

"*You?*" said Ishmael. "Didn't think you would ever lower yourself to own slaves."

"Perhaps I've never found one so pretty as she."

"And what of him?" Ishmael nodded at the Silkstealer. "You find him pretty too?"

Quill smirked. "I have my tastes. My brother has his."

Ishmael chuckled. The sound alone made Chidi's blood run cold.

"No." Ishmael's brow furrowed. "There must be another reason. What would you have from her?"

"Far nobler things than you, old friend." Quill replied, shifting his attention to August. "Will you hear my offer, Crayfish?"

"A-aye, yes, of course."

"Excellent," said Quill. "I offer you nothing."

Chidi heard whispers in the crowd, their sound drowned only by Ishmael's scoff.

"*Nothing?*" August's voice peaked.

"Aye," said Quill. "I propose you give this girl to me as a gift, a pact of friendship between yourself and the Unwanted. It's known throughout the Salt you give nothing freely. To offer such a fine specimen as this," Quill draped his arm about Chidi's shoulders. "Would honor my tribe and our chieftain."

"More like make him look weak and afraid," Ishmael put in. "My offer stands, Crayfish. A thousand anemonies for the girl."

Chidi shivered at the chill running through her as Watawa's lone eye squinted in her direction. It vanished the moment he looked away and again mumbled to his brother.

"What will it be, Crayfish?" Quill asked.

August Collins had repurposed his napkin as a sweat rag. He looked betwixt the two Nomads vying for her, no doubt weighing the options of his decisions.

"Take her then..." he said, "as a gift."

Quill took Chidi by the arm as soon as the Crayfish finished his command.

"No..." Ishmael stopped them from leaving the stage. "She belongs to me. I made the fairer offer."

"And yet I hold the prize," said Quill. He abandoned Chidi, stepped closer to Ishmael. "Unless you'd rather the Ancients decide who has the better claim. I hear you are Salt champion of the pits thrice over now."

Chidi saw Quill rest his palm upon the coral sword handle at his hip.

"Should we put your skills to the test...old friend?"

Ishmael sneered. "Take her then."

Quill nodded in reply, then he had Chidi by the arm once more, his gait rapid as he led her off the stage to join his brother.

"Put these on."

Chidi found a pair of communicator earrings thrust into her palm. She quickly pressed them against her ears, sighing at the familiar clinging as they bound to her lobes.

Watawa mumbled as he and the Silkstealer fell in beside her.

They're coming. Chidi translated his words.

Quill pulled her along faster, near to the point of jogging.

Chidi constantly glanced over her shoulder, expecting Henry to surprise them and take her for his own again. She thought on her new company and realized even Henry would not be so foolish to take on two Nomads and the Silkstealer.

They reached the oldest dock within minutes, but Quill showed no signs of slowing. "Change," he said, before pulling her off the edge and into the water.

Chidi kicked to the surface. The Silkstealer sputtered for air nearby as he donned his hood. Fear reared inside her at the sight of the man she'd once run from and heard horror stories about most of her life.

Watawa's mumbling called her back to the matter at hand.

They're nearly here, brother. She translated his words. *We must hurry.*

"Who is coming?" Chidi asked.

"You speak our language?" Quill asked in his native tongue.

"A-a little," said Chidi. "I meant no offense."

"I told you, brother," said Watawa. "She is the one you sought."

"Aye," said Quill. "Now let us keep her alive. Come."

Chidi watched him dive, his Mako tail flicking above the surface before he was gone. "Wh-what did he mean? Who is coming?"

"Death descends on Crayfish Cavern," said Watawa. "And we must be long gone from here else it claim us too."

LENNY

IT'S ALL MY FAULT. LENNY RESTED HIS FOREHEAD on the stock board. *Racer and his pop dead...Paulie and Ellie beat.* He glanced up at the Collins mansion. The last place he'd seen Garrett Weaver taken. Lenny sighed. *Him too.*

All morning, Lenny had pondered what made Declan run with Marisa Bourgeois. He briefly considered Paulo might have lied, only to recall with great clarity the anger in his former crewmate as he relayed the news.

Pop knows I'm gonna die anyway. Nothin' left to hold him here if I'm gone. Lenny next convinced himself, recognizing it for a lie the moment he had the thought. *Pop neva left nobody. Why would he leave me? It don't make any sense.*

He looked on the empty stock opposite him and knew in his heart he was not as brave as Ansel. That despite the love he bore his father, Lenny valued his own life all the more, especially now armed with the knowledge his fate would soon swiftly fall.

They'll neva catch, Pop. Lenny had never been surer of anything in his life.

Lenny perked, hearing the crowd cheer in the distance. He had listened to them throughout the morning, as well as Tieran's voice echoing over the guesthouses' thatched rooftops.

Lenny winced as he attempted to stretch. His back popped and a groan escaped his lips.

The lone Selkie guard left to keep watch didn't seem to notice. Meandering around the perimeter all morning—*probably to keep from fallin' asleep,* Lenny thought—the guard suddenly straightened. "Halt! Who goes there?"

"Mercy, mercy, friend…I am only a poor, 'umble Lepa."

Lenny recognized the voice and his wrists pulled against their wooden bindings as the lean and long-legged slave owner strode into plain sight. *Henry…*

Two hooded guards tailed Henry, though he paid little attention to them.

"Leper or no," said the guard. "You're not allowed down here, friend. Boss Fenton's orders."

"Ah, *oui,*" said Henry. "But I bring a message from ze Crayfeesh…"

The guard gasped as Henry pulled him close, then tossed him aside to writhe in the throes of death. The other two guards raced up and were both laid low in a matter of seconds.

Lenny swallowed hard as the Frenchman kneeled, cleaning his blade with one of the dead guard's Selkie hoods.

"Help!" Lenny shouted. "Somebody help."

Henry lifted a finger to his ear as the crowd cheered anew. "No one can 'ear you now."

A cruel smile teased the corners of Henry's lips as he stood, blade in one hand and the guard's keys in the other. "And I 'eard your father eez gone. Run off with Marisa Bourgeois." Henry clucked his tongue as he approached. "No one left to protect you now, nipperkin."

Lenny fought to control his breathing and quiet it rather than give Henry further satisfaction.

Henry stopped in front of the stock and placed his hands upon the board.

"Ya come to kill me?" Lenny asked, his voice quivering.

Henry's eyes narrowed in reply.

Lenny glared back. "Then get on with it. Ratha swim in Fiddla's—"

"You were right, Lenny," said Henry softly, his gaze dropping to the edge of his blade.

"Huh?"

"Say what you weel of me, but I am no liar. Ze Crayfeesh…'e deed not pay me, threatened my life…I might've forgave all had 'e not promised me." Henry grimaced. "Or sold my Chidi."

"Cheeds is gone?"

"*Oui*. Sold to Nomads I cannot defeat alone," said Henry. "Will you 'elp me, Lenny?"

"Wha'?" Lenny choked. "It sounded like ya just asked me to help ya…"

"*Oui*." Henry's voice shook. "I weel see your master's cavern brought to ruin. Take all 'e 'olds dear as eet was taken from me. Weel you 'elp me, Lenny? 'Elp me crayfeesh ze Crayfeesh?"

"Ya talkin' about killin' an owna."

"I am an owner too with my property stolen from me. My claim is just."

"They hang slaves for this kinda talk," said Lenny.

Henry glanced at the stocks. "You weel 'ang anyway, no? For your father's crimes?"

"Dolan's don't run."

"Your father deed. You should too." Henry lifted his blade. "Or would you 'ave me keel you now? Quick and painless."

Pop's gone. Paulie hates me. Nothin' left for me here but to die. Lenny licked his dry lips with his even dryer tongue. "I'm not killin' nobody."

"No." Henry put the guard's key to the lock, popped it, and lifted the board from Lenny's wrists and legs. "Leave that to me."

Lenny pulled his limbs from the stocks. Struggled to stand and shrunk when Henry helped him. "W-whattaya need me to do?"

Henry's grin broadened.

KELLEN

WE'RE UP NEXT. KELLEN WATCHED THE FINAL bout of those in the seal cage. Each battle had been to the death and as Kellen glanced behind him, he thought it little coincidence he and three other captives remained. *Even numbers for two more fights.* Kellen studied their faces as he listened to Tieran auction off the last Selkie winner. *Who will it be?*

His companions seemed to have reached the same conclusion, though each handled their fate in different ways. Marrero wore the same dogged expression Kellen saw him don countless times before wrestling matches. His knuckles whitening against the bars, Marrero's lips moved in murmured whisper as he psyched himself for the inevitable match.

Will it be you, Marrero? Kellen wondered. *You or me?*

A part of Kellen suggested his best odds would be against Edmund. Yet when the two of them locked eyes, the competitor in him recognized Edmund as the toughest match of all. Where Marrero had the nervous energy of youth, Kellen looked on Edmund seated with his arms folded across his chest. Indeed, the old Selkie appeared the most relaxed of all in the cage. He gave Kellen a slight nod, acknowledgement to a fellow competitor.

Kellen shivered as he looked on the last of them. He thought it odd he did not know the beefy man's name, viewing him only as some nameless trucker. Then he realized he preferred it that way and hoped they drew each other to war against.

The gate unlocked and the door creaked open.

Use your fear. Kellen glared at the guard studying each of them. *Use it to make you stronger.*

"You." The guard pointed at the beefy man.

Don't look away. Kellen fought the flutter in his chest as he listened to the beefy man struggle against the guards.

The guard's eyes passed over him, stopping on Marrero. "You."

To his credit, Marrero strode from the cage with little hesitation. Then he ran toward the shoreline.

The crowd roared approval.

"Your friend is a true fighter," said Edmund, standing to join Kellen.

He's not better than me, Kellen sneered. "He's a three-time state champion in freestyle."

"Mmm-hmm." Edmund squinted. "But this isn't wrestling."

Kellen shifted his attention back to the shoreline. Guards had again restrained the beefy man with a wire noose as they led him toward the water.

Marrero stood in it up to his knees, bouncing back and forth.

"All righ' then," Tieran called from the stage. "Selkies, don your hoods. Let's—"

"Enough with the seal fights already."

Kellen searched the crowd for the speaker and found the same broad-shouldered man who had previously bid on the black girl and lost. He lingered on the scars littering the man's body. A shudder ran through him.

"I'm sick to death of them," the man said. "This new pup looks Salt worthy. Why not give us a battle we can see?"

Kellen saw Tieran shrug, turn toward the dais where Oscar sat with the obese man.

"Ooh, yes, Father," said Oscar.

August Collins nodded. "The Crayfish is ever accommodating of his guests' wants, Master Ishmael. Make it so, Tieran."

"You heard the Lord Master," Tieran said to the guards. "Get 'em up here, on the double."

The crowd cheered as both competitors were led to the dais.

"All righ', lads," said Tieran. "Neither of you quits till the other stops breathing! On your ready…"

Come on, Marrero. Kellen gripped the bars tighter as the guards loosed the beefy man.

"Fight!"

The beefy man lunged.

Marrero dodged, crouched in a wrestling stance. Always moving, circling.

Don't let him get his hands on you. Kellen thought as the beefy man bull rushed Marrero.

Marrero again dodged him at the last.

"Wearing him down," said Edmund. "Smart."

Kellen looked on his friend with new hope, noting Edmund was right in his assessment. Already, the overweight and out-of-shape beefy man seemed slower, less eager to lash out.

And all the while, Marrero circled.

Come on. Do it. Kellen willed his friend as Marrero feinted forward and back, testing the beefy man's reflexes. At one point, he thought Marrero caught, only to see him duck low and drive his weight into the beefy man's knees.

The crowd erupted as the beefy man grunted and fell.

Kill him, Marrero. End him. Adrenaline raced through Kellen as Marrero scampered up his opponent's body and wrapped the beefy man in a headlock.

"Don't let him on top," Edmund whispered.

Kellen saw his fears confirmed when the beefy man rolled to his side with Marrero still holding tight around the neck.

"Kill…kill…kill," the crowd chanted as one.

Be a man, Kellen willed Marrero. *End him.*

The beefy man crawled to his knees and hands.

Marrero raised his foot and horse-kicked his opponent's leg out from under him.

The beefy man rolled to the flat of his back as he fell, his weight crushing the younger opponent. The crowd groaned as the larger man reached to his throat to unclasp Marrero.

Still, Kellen saw life left in his friend.

Marrero wrapped his legs around the beefy man's and rocked while keeping his death grip around his foe's neck. The beefy man's mouth opened and closed, his face purple as Marrero siphoned his life and fight away.

The crowd cheered moments later.

"He did well," said Edmund as guards dragged the beefy man's body off the stage.

"Well, well, well," Tieran shouted. "Quite the fighter, eh? Wish I'd owned him instead of that fat lot he bested. How much will this strong pup fetch? I'll open him at five hundred."

Kellen saw the bidding for Marrero fiercer than any who went before him.

"A thousand," said Ishmael finally. "Unless any would care to drive the price up again?"

None did.

Kellen watched his friend traded over to the scarred buyer. Then the cage gate swung open.

"All right, you lot. You're up."

"Whatever happens…" Edmund clapped Kellen on the shoulder, "no hard feelings, pup."

No worries. You're the one who's going to die, old man. Kellen followed Edmund out of the cage.

"A fitting final match, this," Tieran addressed the crowd. "Youth versus experience, which will win out? Should they fight with their hands, or might we spice it up a lil' bit?"

"Swords!" Oscar cheered. "Give them swords, Tieran. I should love to see them hack each other to bits."

Kellen's heart hammered as he stepped to the center of the ring. He saw Edmund placed opposite him, but the old Selkie had no love for him.

Why is he staring at Oscar?

"Swords bore me," said August Collins before sampling a cake. "A dagger bout, however. Much more interesting. Makes them draw in closer for the kill."

"Daggers it is, then."

Guards slid a blade across the stage to either combatant.

Kellen focused on Edmund. *Time to die, old man.*

"All righ', lads," said Tieran. "On your—"

"You killed my boy," Edmund glared at Oscar. "You killed my Richie."

Kellen recalled the jail. Remembered the young marshal cry out to warn him and the way his body bounced as Oscar's bullets tore through him.

"Aye," said Oscar. "And I'd kill him again if he were here now. Might be I'd even make the two of you fight it out."

Kellen thought back to the last time he'd seen Oscar. He knelt to pick up his dagger. Remembered the last thing Oscar had said. *I'll ask you one last time. You should be happy with your decision after all. Are you certain in your wish to come with us?*

Kellen clasped his fingers around the dagger hilt. Rising, he sneered at Oscar Collins. *I wouldn't be here if it wasn't for him.*

"Slave," Tieran addressed Edmund. "Pick up your blade."

Edmund did not. "He killed my boy."

Kellen glanced back to Marrero in the crowd. Focused on the noose around his friend's neck and pictured Bryant and the other captives led away by owners.

I'm not going out like that. Kellen clenched the dagger's hilt. *No one's taking me again.*

"*Slave,*" Tieran shouted. "Pick up your blade. Now!"

Edmund shook his head. "He killed my Richie."

A host of guards moved to take Edmund at Tieran's whistle. *Now!*

Kellen rushed the dais, knocked Tieran off balance.

Several in the crowd cried alarm. A whip cracked behind him.

Missed. Kellen witnessed panic in both Collins's faces as he ran at them. Oscar hopped up easily. His father struggled. Kellen kicked him square in the chest.

The Crayfish's fatty arms jiggled as he fell backward off the pier, cannonballing into the water.

"Father!" Oscar cried.

Kellen thought to jump, but hesitated when shapes emerged in the water, swimming to aid their owner. Other seal heads poked above the surface. Growled at him. *Can't go that route.*

"Get him!"

Kellen saw the guards' intent change from Edmund to him.

"How dare you strike my father," Oscar said. "I'll have you—"

Kellen yanked Oscar toward him.

"Get back!" Kellen yelled at the guards, positioning his hostage in front of him with the dagger to Oscar's throat. "I swear to God I'll kill him."

Give me a reason, Kellen thought as the guards looked to one another, each uncertain what to do next. Oscar trembled in his grip. "You brought me here," Kellen whispered. "Now tell them you're taking me home."

Oscar nodded.

"You lil' fool." Tieran rose and unfurled his whip. "I'll have your head on a pike 'fore the day is out."

"Yeah? Make sure you have two." Kellen jerked Oscar's head back. "I'll carve his head off before you get to me."

Someone laughed in the crowd. Applauded.

"You spoke true, Tieran." Ishmael ceased clapping. He tugged on Marrero's collar and led him toward the stage. "This is a rare lot you've brought."

Kellen glanced down at the water. The Crayfish had gone, but Selkie guards still remained to block his exit. *What am I going to do?*

"Boldness, Tieran," said Ishmael. "I like that. How much will you have for this young bull?"

Kellen heard shouting as August Collins walked up the stony

shore, sopping wet and warding away any who tried to help him. He stopped short upon noticing Oscar held hostage.

"You!" August's face reddened. "Unhand my son this instant or—"

"How much, Tieran?" Ishmael asked again.

Tieran's gaze flickered to his master.

"No," said August. "I won't sell this one. Not for any price. I'm going to—"

"Three thousand," said Ishmael. "Will that do?"

Judging August's slack-jawed expression, Kellen gathered it would. August recovered quickly, however, and shook his head. "I-I don't know if—"

Ishmael stepped forward. "Sell him to me, Crayfish."

"I want him dead."

"Oh, he'll die, of course," said Ishmael. "In the fighting pits, it's only a matter of time for a Selkie. I'm willing to risk this one will line my pockets first. Now, will you have me line yours today?"

Oscar shook. "Father...please..."

"Fine," said August. "Take him then. For three thousand."

"Done." Ishmael tossed a leather pouch to Tieran that jingled when he caught it. Ishmael glanced at Kellen. "Best release him now, pup."

No one's buying me. Not going out like that. Kellen shook his head. "I'm going home."

"You'll never see home again, lad," said Ishmael quietly. "But come with me and live another day at least."

Surrounded. Kellen took in the situation. His hand shook at Oscar's neck.

"Let him go," said Ishmael. "Fight for me and it might be I let you buy your freedom one day. You and your friend."

Kellen glanced at Marrero. Saw him nodding. "You won't let them kill me?"

"No." Ishmael stepped closer to the dais. Showed his back to Kellen that he might address the guards. "This lad belongs to me now. Any of you seadogs reach for your whip when he looses the Crayfish's pup...you lose the hand." Ishmael glanced at Kellen. "Now, let him go."

Kellen took the blade away from Oscar's throat and shoved him away to rejoin his father.

Ishmael chuckled. "Bold."

August Collins glared up at him. "Get out of my cavern. And don't ever bring that pup back unless—"

Screams rang from the crowd. Panic erupted as all rushed out of the bleachers, trampling any in their path.

"What in the blue blazes..." August said.

Kellen saw black smoke rising and fire sweeping over the bleachers.

CHIDI

WHERE ARE THEY TAKING ME? CHIDI WONDERED as she followed Quill.

Beside her, the Silkstealer had become a Sea Lion, though he struggled with controlling his new body. His constant weaving back and forth, up and down, made Chidi question whether he wrestled with the seal mind, or marveled at his newfound ability to swim in a way no mere human could ever experience.

Watawa patiently followed him, never once giving the Silkstealer a rebuke.

Chidi caught herself staring at the streamlined Salt bodies of both Nomad brothers. She thought their tails resembled crescent moons, both a blue so dark they almost looked violet.

Neither had fully transformed, but both grew their dorsal and anal fins. Chidi presumed the extra fins helped them slice through the water. She had heard others count Makos among the fastest Nomads in the Salt. She understood why clearly now with Quill frequently needing to slow, and even circle back, to allow her and the Silkstealer to keep up.

"Faster," said Quill. "We should have been gone from here already."

Those are his gills. Chidi enviously studied the five slits on either side of his neck that fluttered whenever he talked. *Wish I could breathe Salt.*

Chidi reeled in his wake as he sped ahead with a sideways swish of his tail. She thanked the Ancients the Nomads did not seem intent on hunting her. The thought of hunting made her glance back the way they'd came. The rocky island had all but disappeared. So, too, had her thoughts of Henry surprising her.

The speed at which Quill flew through the water, his determination at obtaining her from the Crayfish, and Ishmael's sudden reluctance to fight Quill, made Chidi feel strangely safe in the Nomad brothers' company. Even now, Watawa seemed more coaching the Silkstealer rather than shepherding him faster. Indeed, the quieter of the two seemed to notice her watching him. His tail swished and then he sped toward her.

Chidi fought her seal mind to not panic as the predator swam up alongside her.

"Forgive my brother his impatience," said Watawa. "He has waited to find you these many years."

I wonder if he can hear me? Chidi directed the thought to him.

"Yes," said Watawa.

You don't need earrings?

"A Nomad breathes Salt. I have no need for your Maker's gift, or even the mind voice. The Ancients in their wisdom allowed us Salt Children to hear your voices that we might listen and learn."

Chidi nearly snorted. *A Salt Child listen to a Selkie?*

"Aye. There is much and more for all in the Salt to learn from one another if we would only listen. Others name me half-breed. Relegate my kind as Unwanted. My brother and I have more in common with Selkies than you know."

Chidi doubted it. Still, the Nomad seemed willing enough to speak with her, more than Chidi could say of any other she'd crossed paths with. She chanced another point. *You said your brother searched for me…*

"Aye," said Watawa. "He seeks a treasure lost long ago. The Ancients woke me to their calling that I might help him find it. They led me to Crayfish Cavern and sang your face to me."

But I'm only a slave, Chidi said. *I don't know of any treasure.*

"Nor shall you. Each of us swims our own current. It's not for us to know what awaits us on distant shores, or in the darkest of depths. The Ancients give us clues, but never allow us the full sight of their map. They gifted me some few visions, but even I know not where we go. For that, we had need of a guide. A compass."

Me?

"Aye."

But how can I guide you to something I don't know about?

"Does the compass know all its master wishes of it?" Watawa asked. "No. It provides only truth. Direction. When my brother calls, you will know the way to point."

Chidi kept back her true feelings as the Sea Lion swam to join them. She thought he seemed to have a better handle on swimming now, though the Silkstealer still occasionally dipped and spun. Chidi recognized the moves for one new to their coat, a way of allowing himself some little joy in his wakening to a new world. Chidi scarcely recalled her first experiences of changing.

I was just a girl back then, she supposed. *Still crying for mother and father.*

Shielded by his Salt face, Chidi found him not so frightening now. She realized then the pair of them had not said a single word to one another, something Chidi normally preferred. Yet as she looked into the Sea Lion's sad and lonely brown eyes, Chidi felt something stir.

She fought down the urge to reach out, to speak. *Don't go crazy. Remember what he did at the zoo. He hunted Marisa, same as you.*

Ahead, Chidi saw Quill straighten far too suddenly for her liking. He sped away faster than she had yet seen him swim, his blue body helping him disappear in seconds. She sensed Watawa's unease as he left her side and patrolled around the two Selkies.

She shut her mind of thoughts and listened intently for any sign of danger. Chidi swore she heard the faint sound of clicking.

Quill returned nearly a full minute later, his approach so quick and quiet, Chidi near fainted at his sudden appearance from the blue waters around her.

"What is it, brother?" asked Watawa.

"The pod approaches the cavern from the east," said Quill, anger in his voice. "It may be we escaped in time. Still, we would do well to swim faster. Perhaps we'll make the shoreline before their calls reach us and make our presence known."

Who? Chidi asked. *Who approaches from the east?*

Quill sneered. "Orcs."

LENNY

BURN...BURN...BURN. LENNY RAN UNDER THE bleachers, holding a torch over his head.

Heat swelled behind him as the dried wooden boards went up in flames. Buyers screamed as they thundered over one another to not be licked by the flames.

Burn...burn...burn. Lenny grit his teeth, picturing both August and Oscar in his mind. The whippings he had received over the years. The hangings he'd been forced to witness. His keel-raking. *Burn...burn...burn.*

Lenny reached the end of the row and dropped his torch, then sprinted to hide behind the now empty cages. Pillars of black smoke rose from the guest homes, blotting out the stalactite stars. Chaos swirled everywhere he looked, nowhere more so than the dais.

Lenny reveled in it.

Buyers ran for the water, changing as they leapt off the pier. Some abandoned their newly bought property. Others tugged their slaves toward the shoreline. Lenny spied Kellen on the dais and enviously noted the make of the Leper suit. *When did he get Salted?*

The marshal, Edmund, had managed to obtain a dagger and now fought against guards, his struggle emboldening other Selkie slaves. Three other Selkies toppled their Merrow owner and rained fists upon him.

"Stay calm, everyone!" August Collins roared.

Lenny grinned when no one listened.

"Guards," Fenton shouted. "Protect the Lord Master!"

Lenny looked across the way, wondered if he could sprint the open distance without being noticed. He glanced back to the dais.

Guards had swarmed August and Oscar to shield them.

"To the mansion!" Fenton called.

Lenny crouched lower seeing them headed toward him and the path leading up the hill. He slunk around the opposite cage side as they passed. He glanced over his shoulder toward the Block in hopes none of the guards left to defend the Collins's retreat would see him. He found most of them dead or engaged in other fights to quell the mob attacking Tieran for the monies he kept.

Edmund had won his bout and taken up a guard's coral short sword.

Who's he lookin' for? Lenny wondered as Edmund surveyed the area, settling on the party headed up the path. Lenny waited until Edmund passed before sprinting from behind the cage.

"Collins!" Edmund cut down two of the guards before they recognized him as a threat.

Lenny ducked next to a home not yet afire and peered around the edge.

"Take my son away," August commanded.

"Collins!" Edmund yelled as he took on another guard. "You killed my Richie."

Help him. Lenny thought. Years of fighting back inaction against the taskmasters kept him huddled as August waddled up the path after his son and Fenton. Then, time seemed to slow in Lenny's mind as Henry Boucher emerged from a burning shell of a guest home, dagger in one hand and a torch in the other.

What is he...

Lenny burst from his hiding place upon seeing Henry thrust his dagger up into August's back. "Stop!"

Henry did not. "You took my Chidi!" He stabbed August, again and again. "Liar. Thief!"

Lenny halted a few feet away, witnessing life drain from the only owner he'd ever known.

"Father!" Oscar shrugged free of Fenton's grasp and ran back down the path.

Hate reared inside Lenny. He sprinted at Oscar, all the memories of the owner who caused him so much pain careening to the forefront of his mind. Lenny dove, tackling Oscar. Then his mind went blank and his sight went red, a single thought repeating in his head. *Are ya laughin' now?*

The thought didn't cease until someone choked Lenny back by the hood.

A guard stood over him, sword raised high. Heaving, the guard swung.

"No!" A grey shadow leapt in front of the blade, knocking Lenny away.

He rolled to his feet. Saw his savior upon the ground, gasping, with the guard's sword sheathed in his side and lifeblood pooling around him. Fenton reached out to Lenny.

"B-boss," the guard stammered. Then, he ran.

Lenny knelt beside Fenton. "Wh-why did ya do that? Why did ya save me?"

"You're…your father's son…" Fenton choked. "F-follow in his f-footsteps…"

"I don't understand," said Lenny. "Whattaya mean?"

"H-help your people…lead them." Fenton smiled. "Always liked you…L-Lenny…now, go. S-Swim…"

Lenny watched Byron Fenton breathe his last breath, his feelings mixed on whether he cared or not. Still, he reflected on all Declan had said of the old overseer and of how Fenton had given him a chance to live when Oscar urged for execution.

Sorry, boss. Lenny thought as he removed the dead man's earrings and took them for his own. The earrings familiarized to their new owner, gifting him the power of mind-speak. He rose to leave, yet something inside him stirred. Called Lenny to look again on the overseer who had shadowed over him all his life.

Staring into Fenton's unblinking eyes, a single thought plagued Lenny. *Why did ya save me?*

A flood of memories washed over him then, and Lenny realized he did care that Byron Fenton had gone from this world. He remembered the same overseer he feared for so many years had also been the one to stay Declan's hand the time Lenny stole a fish to feed a slave condemned to death. Then, Lenny recalled the number of times the old Selkie had barked at him when catching him out of quarters without leave.

Barked, but never bit. Lenny smiled against the tears in his eyes.

His hands trembling, Lenny draped his fingertips across the dead man's brow and let them drift downward, closing Byron Fenton's eyes forever.

"Go now, brotha," Lenny whispered his father's prayer. "And swim Fiddla's Green. Don't dive below, to the depths unseen."

Oscar groaned behind him. "F-Father…"

Lenny glanced back, his anger toward Oscar now lessened with Fenton's sacrifice. As he looked on his former co-captain, crawling toward his dead father, Lenny felt nothing.

"Father…" Oscar sobbed. "What did he…d-do to you…"

August's bloated body resembled a beached whale, to Lenny's mind. He looked around the area, but Henry had vanished.

"Collins!" Edmund raced up the path, an uncoiled whip in hand. He fell upon Oscar, tying the whip's end around his neck.

"Whattaya doin'?" Lenny stood.

"Stay back, Dolan." Edmund pulled tight on the whip. "He's not yours to kill."

Lenny saw Oscar's face grow purple and his hands reaching out for aid.

Not laughin' now, are ya? Lenny glanced away, surprising himself that he didn't want to watch the end of Oscar Collins.

"I'm sorry, Richie…" said Edmund not long after Oscar uttered his final gasps.

Lenny glanced back.

"Sorry I couldn't save you, boy." Edmund laid Oscar's body over his father's. "But I got him, Richie. Now you can swim in peace."

Lenny sighed as he looked on the destruction of Crayfish Cavern. The screams continued down by the dock. Lenny briefly wondered how long they might go on, then realized he didn't care. *Leave. Swim to shore and swallow the anchor. Live free.*

"So much death," said Edmund. "Never thought I'd live to see so much death again."

Lenny frowned. *Me neither.*

"Then again," Edmund chuckled. "Never thought I'd be escaping with another Dolan either."

Lenny glanced back. "Wha'?"

"Your father, Declan. He never told you about us running together? The part he played in the Selkie Strife?"

Lenny grimaced.

"Doesn't surprise me," said Edmund. "So what's your plan now? You Dolans always have one."

"Swim outta here. Make for the Hard."

"I have a better one," said Edmund. "Where's the Orc?"

"The—"

"Garrett Weaver. Where is he?" Edmund asked. "I know you took him from the jail."

Lenny glanced up the path, toward the Collins mansion. "Whattaya want with him?"

"I told you once I was a releaser." Edmund knelt beside August Collins and pawed at him.

What's he lookin' for? Lenny wondered.

"Garrett Weaver's innocent to the Salt," said Edmund, tugging a set of keys from August's Selkie pocket. "What's say you and I do something good before leaving this place?"

Lenny grinned.

KELLEN

WHAT IS HAPPENING? KELLEN WONDERED AS Ishmael pulled him and Marrero through the crowd. The former buyers teemed around them, some fighting with those they bought. Kellen wondered if he and Marrero shouldn't try double-teaming Ishmael. His gaze fell on the scars and thought it best to wait. *At least he seems to know where he's going.*

Ishmael stopped as they approached the stony shoreline.

Kellen stepped around him.

The buyers who had escaped to the water had now reversed course, turned to swim back for the safety of the shore.

What the…

Tall, black fins rose from the water like submarine periscopes. Their backsides rose and fell, in tandem, and air plumed from their blowholes.

"Orcs…" Ishmael drew the sword at his side. "I hate Orcs."

Kellen stepped back as a Killer Whale exploded from below the water and sent a Selkie flying into the air. Another jumped and landed atop the animal, squealing with what Kellen assumed was glee. Awestruck, Kellen saw buyers dragged from one end of the cavern to the other, fighting for air, the playthings of the beast holding them from below.

"With me, pups," Ishmael retreated from the shore and grabbed both Kellen and Marrero's hoods.

Again, Kellen glanced back in time to see another Killer Whale leap from the water. At first, he thought it meant to crush the pier. Then he saw the animal change into a man, larger than any he had ever seen. His patchwork skin of black and white made Kellen think of Garrett Weaver, though the comparisons stopped there. Barrel-chested and bald, Kellen thought of professional football lineman as five more Killer Whales leapt and morphed behind the first.

"Find me our Orc brother!" the largest of them boomed. "Kill the rest."

Kellen nearly wet himself and kept closer to Ishmael, now running toward the Block.

More of the two-toned men awaited them there. Women fought beside them also, their hair wild and free.

"Fight with me, pups," said Ishmael. "Time to earn your scars."

Both Kellen and Marrero hung back as their owner ran into the midst of Orcs with a feral roar. Ishmael's blade rose and fell, his blood lust insatiable as he hacked down Orc defenders, steadily clearing a path.

"Wh-what do we do?" Marrero asked.

Kellen glanced back and saw more Orcs behind them than in front.

No chance we make it out that way. He knelt beside a dead Selkie guard and picked up his harpoon. Kellen charged into the mix, stabbing an Orc in the back.

The Orc spun to see its attacker and caught Kellen with a backhand that sent him reeling.

Kellen fell to the ground, dizzy.

The Orc dislodged the harpoon from its back as if Kellen's blow had been little more than poking him with a toothpick. "You'll die for that, Selk—"

Kellen shrunk as the Orc's head tumbled off its shoulders, decapitated.

The massive body fell to the wayside.

You scared, Kelly? His father's voice rose to haunt him. *No son of mine would be scared. But you're not a man...are you, Kelly? Get up...*

Kellen blinked and saw Ishmael standing where the Orc had been, his sword bloodied.

"I said get up," Ishmael barked at Kellen then hurled himself back into the fray.

Kellen stood, steadying himself as he followed Ishmael's lead. The throbbing in his head disoriented him. The hate in his heart drove him onward. He honed on the sounds of battle, pictured his father, and lashed out at anything that moved.

He briefly saw Marrero, shadowing Ishmael. Kellen attempted to make his way over. A whip cracked near his ear—Tieran warding off an Orc that meant to skewer him.

The auctioneer called his whip back and forth with one hand and swung a sword in the other, ever moving forward, until he came to join Kellen's side.

"Stay with me, seadog!" Tieran shouted.

Kellen nodded and followed the sounds of the auctioneer's whip, inching closer to Ishmael.

"Tieran," said Ishmael, noticing them. "The Orcs have the Salt. Is there another way out?"

"Aye. On me, you seadogs. Ol' Tieran'll lead you out."

Kellen and Marrero ran after Tieran as Ishmael drifted behind to defend their escape. They abandoned the boardwalk and cut through the salt ponds and fields.

Kellen glanced over his shoulder and saw Ishmael slay another Orc, then run to join them. Kellen winced at the woeful cries that seemed to follow them throughout the cavern.

"Where are you taking us, Selkie?" Ishmael called.

"Out the Gasping Hole." Tieran called. "Too small for Orcs. Lead us to the lighthouse, it will."

"No, you fool," said Ishmael. "It'll swarm with Orcs, waiting to scoop us up."

"What do you mean?" Tieran stopped.

Kellen halted to catch his breath, arms over his head. The throbbing in his head had gone, replaced by addictive adrenaline at surviving his first real battle of life and death.

"Say what you will of them," said Ishmael. "Orcs are no fools. The lot who came into the cavern meant to flush us out. The rest of their pod will be waiting at the exit points."

"There's more of them?" Marrero asked.

"Aye," said Ishmael. "They are the Violovar...led by Malik Blackfin."

"No, no, no. Not him." Tieran trembled. "Can't be. H-his lot patrols the Southern Salt. They can't have got here so soon. I-it's not possible."

"It is," said Ishmael. "He stood on the pier and I know his face well. His pod will be waiting."

"Who cares?" Kellen asked. "We'll fight our way out, like we just did here!"

"Fight our way out?" Tieran said. "We barely got through a couple Orc calves just now and the rest of 'em down there's not just

Orcs. They're the Violovar…rabid seawolves, them. Th-they don't even answer to the Painted Guard."

Ishmael chuckled and clapped Kellen on the shoulder. "I like your spirit, pup, but no. We can't win this fight. Not this time. They are too many. Even for me."

"Okay, so what do we do?"

"What Selkies do best…" Ishmael turned to Tieran. "Hide."

"Righ', I got just the place."

Kellen followed Tieran southward, not stopping again until they reached the shack he'd seen earlier that day. He saw the door locked. "How are you going to get in?"

"Kick it down," said Marrero.

"No, you idiot," said Kellen. "If anyone comes by they'll notice."

"Just you leave it to ol' Tieran, lads. He knows what to do." Tieran shoved Kellen aside and produced a key from his pocket. "The Lord Master told Boss Fenton not to give me a second key, but ol' Tieran knows what's best, he does."

The lock popped open. Tieran pocketed it before plucking the last torch free and leading the way inside. He moved them quickly through the tunnel and veered right when the pathway ended in a Y.

What is this place? Kellen wondered as the walls sloped inward, forcing him turn sideways to fit. The tunnel dead-ended near thirty yards later in a dark pool.

"Another Gasping Hole?" Kellen asked.

"Nah," said Tieran, donning his hood. "This is where the Lord Master hoards his bounty."

Kellen glanced at the black water. "Down there?"

"Sure enough," said Tieran. "Can't expect him to keep it all in his mansion now, can you? Come in handy at a time like this and that's for sure. Righ' lads, get your hoods up. Time to get Salted."

Kellen donned his hood alongside Marrero. He closed his eyes and pictured the Leopard Seal in his mind's eye. The tickle changes moved through him and, when he opened his eyes, the seal mind returned.

Get in the water, it said. *Get in the water where it's safe.*

Kellen obliged, diving into water that was warmer than in the pit. Slimier.

A Sea Lion swam beside him.

Marrero. Kellen reminded the seal. *Not food.*

A Common Seal dove in front of him.

That's Tieran. Kellen gave a flick of his hind flippers and followed. He found the water around twenty feet deep and followed Tieran under a rock ledge, then through a series of tunnels that progressively narrowed. Then, Tieran shot upward unexpectedly.

His seal body reacted accordingly, his former speed tugging his lower half under him as Kellen twisted his snake-like neck and turned his nose up to follow. He thought it crazy how he would have missed the opening had it not been for Tieran.

The waters lightened as he rose to the surface and Kellen gave one last swoosh of his hind flippers to jolt him out of the water. His wet body slid along the cavern floor and he found himself near powerless to stop without hands to grab hold of anything.

He blinked at the dark as another seal careened into him.

Kellen lost control and snapped at the other animal before he regained mastery of his seal mind.

Light flickered in the corner.

Tieran approached in human form, bearing a newly lit torch. "Open your mouth."

Kellen obeyed and felt his seal lip tugged back as the changes reversed. Moments later, he stood on his human legs. "Tieran, how did you do that?"

"Do wha'?"

"Why can you change on your own, but I can't?"

"I'm a free man, aren't I?" Tieran answered as he loosed Marrero of his Salt form. "The pair of you are just a couple slaves. Even Selkie suits know that."

"But how?" Kellen asked. "You act like they can think for themselves."

"Look, pup. I dunno how the suits work. How they know. You figure that out, you let ol' Tieran know. Might be we'd make some monies."

"Whoa…" said Marrero. "Kell, check this place out."

Kellen looked around the room, noticing the natural grandeur of it for the first time. The ceiling domed over them with brilliant emerald geodes that caught the light of Tieran's torch. Silver veins lined the walls like they carried the cavern's lifeblood.

Tieran ventured to the far corner, near stacks of food stores—salted meats, cheeses, and kegs of various ales and wines. Medieval weaponry hung from wooden racks next to a shelf of folded garments.

"Are those Selkie suits?" Kellen asked.

"Aye." Tieran broke off a hunk of cheese and downed it. "The Lord Master likes to collect 'em. Who knows…might be it's time for ol' Tieran to switch this rag of mine out. If I can talk Ishmael into helping me change coats, that is."

As Tieran pilfered more of the food stores, Kellen looked on the weaponry and found himself drawing closer to the killing tools.

We could take him. Kellen touched the hilt of a sword. *Me and Marrero. Double-team Tieran, kill him, and wait out in here until the Orcs leave.*

Water splashed behind him.

He turned to find Ishmael climbing out of the pool.

Kellen released the sword hilt and stepped away as Ishmael's lower half changed from shark tail to human legs. *He won't be as easy to kill.*

Ishmael wandered over to join Tieran. "Nice of the Crayfish to provide while we wait, eh boys?"

As both captors opened a bottle of wine and saluted one another before tipping them back, Kellen stared at the whip dangling at Tieran's side. His gaze dropped to the Crayfish emblem branded across his left hand.

Now's not the time to make your move, Kelly. He flexed his hand and lived in the pain flaring up his forearm. *Not yet.*

"To your boldness"—Ishmael grinned in a way that stoked Kellen's anger anew—"and the monies you'll bring me."

Not yet. Kellen studied the necks of his captors as they drank down their cups. *But soon...*

GARRETT

GARRETT STARED UP AT THE CRAYFISH EMBLEM hung from the tops of his four-post bed. He willed his body to grant him more tears, but it had nothing left to give. He passed the time counting the cheers and applause echoing through his window.

He didn't care what they cheered for, wishing only that it continued so he wouldn't have to see August or Oscar again. It was only when the cheers changed to screams that Garrett rose from the bed and ventured to the window. *What the...*

Heavy, black smoke billowed off the guest homes. From his high vantage point, he saw people run frantically about the dock as taller men and women, all with two-toned skin, emerged from the water.

They look like me... Garrett reeled at the realization. *Orcs. They're the ones who've come to rescue me.*

"I'm up here!"

Garrett's hope died the moment he witnessed the Orcs slaughtered those that ran with no hesitation. He recalled Watawa's mention that Orcs had not kept the peace between the races. Remembered Oscar's words on the yacht. *Orcs are the finest killers in all the Salt.*

Garrett left the window and ran for the door. "Let me out!" He beat his fists against it. "Someone please let me out!"

He put his ear to the door and heard yelling in the hall.

What do I do? Garrett backed away. *Where do I go?*

He surveyed the room and saw he had little chance of escape. The window blocked by bars, a fire raging in the hearth, and all the walls stone.

Garrett returned to the window.

The Orcs were finishing up their bloody business down at the docks. Several ran up the path toward the mansion, giving chase to those with a head start. Others swept through the fields and ponds, rounding up slaves.

"Weava..."

Garrett perked at the faint voice, one with a Boston accent. *Lenny?*

"Weava...where are ya?"

He stepped toward the door. Put his ear against it.

"Garrett Weaver!" yelled a muffled voice. "We're here to take you home!"

Home...

"He's not up here..."

"He's gotta be," said the Boston voice. "*I'm tellin' ya. He's here. Weava!*"

*Don't leave...*Garrett put his palm against the door. *Don't leave me here.*

"We need to go, Dolan. Now."

"Wait!" Garrett attacked the door. "Come back. I'm in here!"

"*Ya hear that? Weava! Where are ya?*"

"In here," Garrett shouted. "Lenny, I'm in here!"

"*This one!*"

Garrett found he still had a few tears left. "Lenny!"

"Yeah, it's me, pal. Listen...get back from the door, all right? We gotta bust it down."

Garrett hurried away. "Okay. Do it."

The door shuddered.

"Again, Eddie," said Lenny from the other side of the door.

*Come on...come on...*Garrett prayed as the door shook on the second blow, but held. Three more times he counted the bangs until the door broke off its hinges.

A familiar face peeked in the door.

"Lenny!" Garrett ran to hug him.

"Hey, getoffame, will ya?" Lenny grumbled.

Garrett let go. Wiped his cheeks with the back of his forearm. He noticed Lenny was not alone. "You...you were one of the marshals at the jail."

"Aye, name's Edmund. We'll catch you up later. Right now, we need to move."

Garrett hesitated, his stomach twisting with August's earlier threat.

"Wha'?" said Lenny. "What's wrong? Come on already."

"A-August...said he'll send a crew to k-kill my mom."

Lenny shook his head. "Not today, pal. Not eva. The Crayfish is dead. Oscar too."

"Are you serious?" Garrett asked. "B-but how...when?"

"Dolan," said Edmund gruffly.

"Right, let's go," Lenny tugged Garrett's hand.

Mom is safe. They can't get her now. Garrett smacked the walls, elated, as he ran down the hallway after Lenny and Edmund and then to the stairs.

They reached the landing and he found the mansion far different than the first time he'd toured it. Doors had been flung open and paintings ripped off the walls. The few candelabras that had not crashed to the floor now swayed loosely from what few strands remained to hold them. Small fires singed the once regal rugs and carpets.

Still, Edmund and Lenny never stopped.

Garrett didn't either. They passed the library and a tall, balding man with a torch lighting everything afire.

"Come on, Weava," Lenny hissed. "Before Henry sees ya."

Garrett obeyed as the mad pyro continued on from piece to piece.

"Keep moving," Edmund cried. "We're almost there."

The heavy oaken doors at the entrance hung open, flames licking up the sides of them. People poured inside the mansion, most of them screaming.

Garrett crowded closer to Lenny and Edmund. "Where are we going?"

"I gotta warn my crew," said Lenny. "Need to tell 'em—"

"Lenny?"

Garrett glanced up and saw more familiar faces in the doorway.

"Elle…" said Lenny. "Paulie…whattaya doin' here?"

"We heard August was dead and decided to escape," said Ellie. "But then we saw Orcs in the cavern. They have the entrances blocked. There's nowhere else to go. We wouldn't have got away if it weren't for—"

"Orcs in the cavern?" Lenny asked.

"Trannies," said Paulo, his tone grim. "The Violovar, Len."

"Th-those are the bad ones, right?" Garrett asked.

Paulo nodded. "They're headed up the path. Killing anyone they come across."

Garrett shuddered. "They're here for me…aren't they?"

"Yeah." Edmund surveyed the area. "Doesn't mean we let them have you. Any of you seadogs know a better way out of here?"

"Sure," said Lenny. "The Crayfish invited us up here all the time for tea and biscuits. Whattaya think we are, Eddie? Honored guests here?"

Garrett fought to breathe. *They're killing everyone to get me.*

"I think you're a dead nipperkin if we don't put our heads together," said Edmund. "Now, think, all of you. How can we get down the path and avoid the Orcs? There has to be a way."

Garrett turned upon feeling a tap on his shoulder. "You…"

"M'lord," said the slave girl who Oscar had offered as a gift. "I-I know a way. A secret way."

"Where?" Garrett asked. "Will you take us there?"

The girl spun on her heel and ran.

"Come on." Garrett waved to the Selkies.

"Who's the broad?" Lenny asked as they followed the girl up the long hall.

"Don't worry about it," said Garrett.

The moment he set foot in the dining hall, he knew where she would lead him. *Of course!* Garrett sprinted past her and leapt to grab the tapestry rope. Hand-over-hand, he yanked it down.

"Wha'…" said Lenny. "How did ya know this was here?"

Does it matter? Garrett wondered as Paulo yanked open the door.

"Awfully dark…" Paulo glanced at the slave girl. "You know where it leads?"

"O-out…M-Master Oscar used it to come and go as he p-pleased."

Paulo frowned. "We have to go. Have to chance it."

"Aye," Edmund yanked a second torch off the wall and handed it to Paulo. "But I'm not fumbling around with no light."

Garrett hung back as Edmund led the charge into the stairwell with Ellie in tow.

"Come on, Weava," said Lenny. "We gotta move."

Garrett looked at the slave girl. "Come with us."

She shook her head.

Screams echoed into the room. "Orcs!"

"Weava…"

"No," said Garrett. "I'm not leaving her."

Soft lips grazed Garrett's cheek.

The slave girl pulled away. "Thank you," she said quietly. "For your kindness."

"*Weava*. It's now or neva."

Garrett allowed Lenny to pull him into the secret stairwell as the slave girl stepped toward the tapestry string.

Goodbye. Garrett thought as Paulo closed the door with a thud. Then he descended into the black pit, following the light of Edmund's torch.

LENNY

THANKS FOR COMING TO WARN US, LEN, SAID Paulo. *I see you're still looking out for number one.*

And ya not? Lenny didn't bother looking back as they followed Garrett down the spiraled cavern stair. He placed his left hand against the cold wall for comfort and peeked over the steep, open drop off to his right.

Edmund's torchlight bobbed a few levels below as the older Selkie led Ellie and Garrett around a turn.

Bet the first thing ya did after hearin' about Orcs was run to the stocks to free me, yeah?

No, said Paulo. *Ellie wanted to release you. My mother and I knew better.*

Hang on. Lenny stopped. *Where is ya ma, Paulie?*

You know where she is. Paulo pushed past him and continued down the stairs.

Lenny followed. *Whattaya talkin' about? Ya sayin' she's dead?*

How else do you think we made it up the hill before the Orcs? Paulo cursed aloud. *Told her it should've been me that stayed behind, but she said my job is to protect Ellie now.*

Lenny paused to catch his breath. *Sorry, Paulie…for everything.*

Paulo snorted and continued on. *I don't want your apologies. I don't want anything from you. Just 'cause we're running together now doesn't change anything.*

Paulie—

You lied to me. Used all of us as part of your plan.

I wanted to help us, said Lenny.

Stop lying! Paulo continued his descent. *You wanted to help your-self. Everything you've done to this point is only one more move to help you get what you want.*

Ya wrong.

The problem is you believe that, said Paulo. *You think the reason you came to the mansion was to free Garrett? I know you better than that, Len. He's still a faceless ticket to freedom for you.*

Lenny huffed for air. *Ya don't know what ya talkin' about, Paulie.*

I do. You heard Orcs were in Crayfish Cavern so you ran to the only one who might get you out alive.

And you're so much betta? Lenny asked. *What'd ya run to the mansion for?*

Even rats know to head for higher ground when a flood comes. Should've known you'd be the first to reach the top.

Lenny recoiled. *Oh yeah? I probably shoulda figured ya'd be the last, then. Makes sense, without me there tellin' ya what to do.*

Maybe, Paulo acknowledged. *But at least I can live with myself tomorrow.*

Whattaya want from me, Paulie? Huh? Spit it out!

We get out of this cavern, I want you to go one way and I'll go the other.

Fine by—

A door slammed against rock high above them.

"Mmm," said a deep voice. "A secret stair, is it?"

"Aye…and I smell Selkie scum…"

*Orcs…*Lenny sped faster. He glanced over the side, swearing he saw a faint glimmer of blue below. The smooth and slippery stairs warned him not lean too far over for a better look.

"Come back, Selkies," said one of the Orcs, his footsteps gaining. "We just wanna play!"

The other laughed in such a way that it gifted Lenny new strength in his legs. He ran faster around the spiraled stairs. His added speed made him slip and he leaned for the safety of the wall as loose rock scattered over the side.

Ya neva gonna be big, Len. He could almost hear his father's voice. *Gotta be fasta or smarta if ya wanna survive.*

Lenny stepped close to the drop off, peered over the side into the abyss.

Below, someone splashed.

Above, the Orcs sounded closer. "The seawolves are coming for you!"

Yeah, Pop. Lenny took a deep breath. *But a lil' crazy neva hurt.*

Lenny leapt off the edge, his stomach fluttering as he prayed for a watery landing. Seconds later, he splashed into the Salt. He kicked to the surface, sucking in air, and found Edmund and Garrett treading nearby, their faces lit in the bluish hue the waters emmitted.

"Lenny…" said Garrett. "Where did you—"

"Why haven't ya changed yet? Where's Ellie?"

"Dove to check out the tunnel," said Edmund.

"We don't have time for that," said Lenny. "Ya gotta change now. Orcs are—"

A wave of water somersaulted Lenny before he finished. Sputtering, he righted himself and reached for his hood the moment he came back up for air.

Paulo surfaced next to him.

Lenny slapped the water. *Whattaya doin', moron? Ya coulda killed me divin' in like that.*

Paulo shrugged. "Ellie said the tunnel's too small for Garrett to fit in Orc form."

"Wha'?" said Lenny. "Ya nearly as big as he is."

"Yeah," said Paulo. "But I don't have a dorsal fin."

Lenny swam to Garrett's side with the crowing from the Orcs ringing in his ears.

"Fine," said Lenny. "Paulie, think ya can pull Weava through before his lungs give out?"

"Aye." Paulo donned his Elephant Seal hood. "I'll make it."

"I'll push from behind," said Edmund.

Lenny nodded. "Listen, Weava—"

"Yeah?"

"Get a good breath in…"

Garrett shook his head. "But Lenny, what if we don't make it? What if I dr—"

"Ya won't," said Lenny. "We'll get ya out and then you'll change. Trust me."

Unless he changes before we get outta the tunnel. Lenny tried not to imagine Garrett as a Killer Whale, stuck in the cavern with nowhere to go. He shook the thought away upon hearing the Orcs footsteps, loud and clear.

"We gotta go," Lenny hissed. "Eddie, why aren't ya Salted yet?"

"You took my earrings back when you kidnapped me, remember? I'm deaf and mute to all of you once we're below."

"Oh, great…"

Edmund pulled on his hood. "Just saying, don't forget to free me on the other side is all."

"Got it. Get goin'."

Lenny looked at Garrett. "Ya wanna go home, right?"

"Y-yeah."

"Good. Get a nice long breath."

Garrett glanced at the water.

"Hey," said Lenny, drawing his attention. "Ya can do this."

The Sea Lion swam in front of Garrett, snorted at Lenny.

All right, Eddie, we're goin'. Lenny donned his hood and saw Garrett grab hold of Edmund's flippers before the darkness took over. He reopened his now seal eyes.

His companions had already gone.

"Selkie!" Two hulking Orcs stood on the shoreline, coral swords in hand.

Lenny dove and followed the churning trail of bubbles.

An echolocation blast followed him.

Lenny swished his flippers faster.

Look at him, an Orc voice pervaded Lenny's mind. *This one's so small he won't make a mouthful.*

Fine by me, said the other. *I could do with a bite to eat.*

Paulie! Lenny caught up. He looked down and saw Garrett's eyes closed, cheeks full of air, as he pinched his nostrils shut. *Gotta swim fasta.*

I'm not a sprinter, Len. You think you can pull him faster? Be my guest.

A Killer Whale shrieked behind them, gaining.

Lenny's pulse quickened at seeing the tunnel narrowed ahead. *Paulie…*

Yeah?

Get Weava home, will ya?

What? Paulo said. *Len, what are you—*

Lenny somersaulted and swam toward the Orcs.

Len, get back here!

Sorry, Paulie. Only doin' what ya asked me to.

Lenny...

*Ya wanted to go one way...*Lenny saw the Orcs clearly now. One full on Killer Whale, his partner in half-human form and wielding both swords. *I'm goin' mine.*

The half-human grinned and raise his sword.

The Orc shrieked, opened its mouth for the meal to come.

Come and get me. Lenny swerved up at the last.

The sword cut through the water behind him in a rush that sent him off kilter.

The Orc screamed at the miss and tried to spin back.

Lenny grinned inwardly. *Ah, Whatsamatta?* He taunted. *Too small in here for ya?*

Lenny rose then dove. *A captain does right by his crew.* He ducked and rolled as his larger hunters found the quarters too cramped to meet his rapid turns.

Stay still! one of the Orcs cursed.

Move, move, move. Lenny willed himself, following another of Declan's mantras. *Always keep movin', son. Ya tread water...ya die.*

Len, said Paulo. *We're almost out. The tunnel gets too small for Orcs. Get out if you can!*

Lenny tucked his nose and flipped, felt a swoosh of water on his hind flippers as the Orc rose behind him. His flippers grazed the rocky ceiling and he gulped a fresh breath before reentering. He found the waters dyed crimson, bloodied, Lenny assumed, from the Orc cracking its beak against the cavern ceiling.

Fasta! Lenny swam back up the tunnel, the Orc's murderous howl trailing him.

A shadow appeared as if from nowhere.

Lenny thanked the Ancients for his seal mind instinctually diving beneath it.

Still, fingertips grappled with his hind flippers. *Gotcha.*

Lenny hacked at the Orc's hand with his claws.

The Killer Whale barreled toward him.

*Gonna smash me...*Lenny curled and bit the Orc then kicked away, narrowly dodging the blow meant to kill him. He flipped and sped toward the narrow opening Paulo mentioned, entering the smaller, safer, zone unreachable by the Orcs. Ascending, Lenny found only the slightest gap between the water and cavern ceiling. He peeked his nostrils to nab fresh air.

Echolocation clicks reverbed up the tunnel behind him.

They can't fit like they are now. Lenny fought the seal mind, reminded it not to panic and to pay the Orcs little mind. *And they'll be slowa than me if they change to human form.*

His seal mind urged the clicks didn't come from behind, however.

*Paulie...*Lenny sent the thought.

He swam for the tunnel's end with new urgency when he received no reply.

Come on, Paulie. Lenny broadcast his thoughts. *Eddie...Elle? Where are ya?*

The tunnel's mouth seemed barely wide enough to fit someone of Paulo's Salt size. Lenny sped through it without thinking to slow and entered a living nightmare.

Black and white giants crisscrossed through the water, hunting seals.

Lenny!

Elle?

He saw her in Elephant Seal form inside a weighted net, dragged by Orcs who retained their upper human forms as they followed their Killer Whale counterparts. *Elle...*

Watch out! Ellie cried, the net dipping as she moved to warn him.

Lenny's seal mind cued to the fear in her voice. It tucked its nose and flipped back into the tunnel as an Orca shot past, shrieking with the glory of the hunt.

He watched from safety as an Orc taskmaster smacked Ellie for weighting the net down.

I've seen this... Lenny knew as Ellie shifted again and cried out.

Paulo, no!

A Southern Elephant Seal barreled up from the depths. Its nose aimed full force at the Orc that slapped Ellie.

Paulie... Lenny drifted out of the tunnel, swam toward his friend. *No. Paulie, stop!*

Bright streams of light streaked in the waters near Paulo, lashing around him. *Jelly whips!*

Paulo's screams echoed in Lenny's mind and he recognized them not meant for his benefit, but broadcast in pain for all the Salt to hear.

I'm comin', Paulie. Lenny kicked his hind flippers again, seeing Paulo struggle to free himself of the jelly bindings.

The Orcs laughed as more and more whips encased Paulo's girth.

Lenny saw Paulo continue his fight to reach the Orc who struck Ellie. Then he heard a dark chuckle and a deep voice's singular command. *Hold him steady.*

Buckets a blood. Lenny swore as death barreled through the water behind Paulo, the size of the Killer Whale bull larger than even its companions. *Paulie...*

The Killer Whale drew closer, echolocated. *Hold him...*

Lenny saw the Orc holders pull tight on their whips, stringing Paulo suspended.

No, no, no! Lenny choked as the Killer Whale plowed into its prey, bursting through the Elephant Seal.

Paulie! Lenny screamed to the tune of Orc laughter.

Got him.

Nice one, Malik, another Orc jeered.

Lenny stopped, his stomach warning he might vomit as he looked on the scattered pieces of Elephant Seal remains. *P-Paulie...* he choked. *N-no...*

Lenny. Ellie shouted in his mind. *Swim!*

His seal instincts keying on her panic, Lenny spun and saw Paulo's killer swimming directly at him. Lenny kicked for his life.

Too slow, said the Orc.

Lenny glanced back. Saw the Killer Whale's teeth and beak bloodied from the fresh kill. Its mouth yawned wide behind him.

Time to die, little Selk—

The animal's jaw jolted sideways. Knocked off balance by a fellow Killer Whale, a smaller one that positioned itself in front of Lenny as it broadcast its heated voice for all to hear.

Stay away from my friend.

Lenny gasped. *Weava.*

GARRETT

KILL HIM. GARRETT'S ORCA MIND WHISPERED. *Show your strength to the pod. Take your place among them.*

The larger Killer Whale's face melted away, transitioning its upper half into human form while keeping the Orca's tail. *That's quite the punch for a seapup.* The Orc-man grinned, working his jaw back and forth. *And you're not one of mine...*

Maybe he should be. Another Orc drifted behind Garrett.

Perhaps. Allow me to introduce myself, o headstrong one. I'm Malik Blackfin. He dipped his chin. *Captain of the Violovar. You're the one we came for, aren't you? The little lost Orc, hauled in by a bunch of Selkie slaves. What's your name?*

Garrett listened to the Orcs clicking around him. His mind translated their messages and warned more left their hunt to surround him.

Lenny, Garrett asked, *what do I say to him? He wants to know who I am.*

Tell him to screw off.

Are you kidding me? This guy's huge.

Ya knocked him a loop, right? The Ringed Seal swam to Garrett's side. *And he hasn't killed ya yet. Pop always said Orcs value strength. Show 'em all ya got more fight left in ya.*

Garrett swallowed hard as he looked at Malik. *S-screw off.*

Catcalls followed his answer and teased another smile from his opponent.

Try again. Malik gave a swish of his tail and circled Garrett. *You have to mean it when you give a threat. We didn't earn the title Killer Whale by being soft, did we? Not like our squealing, giggling, Blowhole cousins, are we, lads?*

The surrounding Orcs laughed harder.

So when I tell you that first punch granted my attention—Malik swam closer—*you know I mean it when I say if you don't answer my question, I'll have my seawolves drag your bloody carcass from here to the Southern Salt. Now again…what's your name?*

Show them, Garrett's Orc mind whispered. *Take your place.*

Garrett closed his eyes and thought of his dad. The changes pulled back from his face and chest like removing socks from feet. He stopped the memory before he lost his tail and reopened his eyes. *Show them…* his Orca mind whispered.

You want to know my name? Garrett asked Malik. *Come beat it out of me.*

Malik howled with laughter. *That's more like it. I still don't believe you, but for a calf who allowed Selkies to capture him.* He shrugged. *It'll suffice until my pod toughens you up. Now, a real test.* Malik's gaze drifted. *Kill the Selkie.*

Garrett glanced at Lenny. *Why?*

Why? Malik's brow furrowed. *Are you a real Killer Whale, or a false one? A Selkie's life is worth no more than krill to our kind.*

He's my friend. Garrett replied.

An Orc has his pod. No one else. Malik circled again. *And if you take offense with killing a Selkie slave, what will you do when I call* upon you to war against our spineless Merrow cousins? Mmm? Would you shrink from ferocious Nomads and abandon your Orc brothers?

I'm not a killer, said Garrett.

Not yet. But most of these around us weren't either. Malik grinned. *I turned them into seawolves.*

Aye, said Malik's fellow. *And we're hungry.*

Garrett watched their leader float in front of him.

I sense a seawolf in you. Malik's grin vanished. *An alpha, perhaps. Let me call it out of you.*

The pod clicked and shrieked around Garrett. His Orc mind swelled to heed their call and add his voice to theirs. Garrett fought it back. *No. I want to go home.*

And where is home? What part of the Salt do you hail from?

Why do you care? Garrett asked.

It's not often one learns my name and doesn't flinch, said Malik. *You'd never heard of me before today.* Malik cocked his head to the side, swished his tail.

I haven't heard of a lot of people, said Garrett. *The world's a big place.*

Is it? Malik chuckled. *I've figured it now. You're one of those refugees who swore to swallow the anchor, aren't you?*

I don't even know what that means, said Garrett.

No? You didn't swear to give up the Salt for life on the Hard?

Coward, said Malik's companion. *An Orc without his pod is noth—*

A conch horn echoed through the waters. Garrett heard shrill whistles and clicks reverb around him. *Charge!* His Orc mind translated.

Buckets a blood, Lenny muttered. *Look at 'em.*

Garrett shifted. *Whoa...*

A super pod of Orcs swam directly at Malik's group. Those that retained their human torsos wore black-plated armor with a blaze of pearl-white across their chests, the symbol shaped like an upside down trident with a spear bisecting the middle.

Garrett's heart leapt as Merrows streaked paths behind their larger companions. Those with hands wielded swords and tridents, shields and harpoons, and those with dolphin tails joined their Killer Whale counterparts who shrieked battle cries as they came.

"Violovar," Malik swam to meet them. "Attack."

The two groups collided, hacking and biting, dying the waters red.

Weava. Lenny yelled as he swam away from the battle. *The nets...*

Garrett guessed where Lenny headed. Malik's group had abandoned their prizes. The Selkies they'd captured remained trapped in the weighted nets, unable to wriggle free.

They're drowning. Garrett kicked his tail and scooped Lenny in his arms as he passed. He kept his focus on the falling net, dodging an Orc attack meant to take off his head. He released Lenny as they reached their goal and found several Selkies still struggling, one larger than the rest.

Elle! Lenny nudged the Elephant Seal's head. *Elle, can ya hear me?*

Garrett saw her seal eyes flutter.

Hang on, Elle, said Lenny. *Weava's gonna get ya to the surface.*

Garrett grabbed hold of the net and groaned as he kicked his powerful tail and began to rise. He glanced down as Lenny smacked a Sea Lion with his flipper.

Eddie, said Lenny. *Eddie, keep fightin'.* The Ringed Seal glanced at Garrett. *Come on, Weava. They're drownin'.*

I'm t-trying. Garrett looked up. His Orc mind told him the surface was less than twelve feet away. *Come on...*

Weava, they're leavin', said Lenny. *The Violovar are leavin'. The other pod ran 'em off.*

Garrett didn't bother looking. His arms hung saggy and weak. He noticed the Sea Lion's mouth opening and closing, swallowing water. Garrett closed his eyes and grunted. *Come on...just a bit further.*

The clicks and whistles drew near. The net lightened.

Garrett opened his eyes and nearly cried.

Merrows had joined him in his cause, their dolphin tails tickling his own as each tread water to hold their place.

Garrett gaped at the two-toned faces of armored Orcs rushing to aid them.

Heave! one of them cried in his mind.

As one, they kicked toward the surface and ascended, reaching the surface in a sudden jolt. The Merrows deftly worked their coral daggers to cut the ropes while the Orcs pulled the Selkies from the bindings.

The Ringed Seal swam up beside Garrett. *Come on, Elle. Ya can make it, Eddie.*

Garrett saw life return to both the Elephant Seal and Sea Lion, their movements slow at first, but finally swimming free of the nets and taking a breath at the surface. He grinned as Lenny swam to join them, clapping them on the backs with his flippers.

Garrett? a familiar voice echoed in his mind. *Is that really you?*

*It can't be...*Garrett choked on water as he gasped. *Sydney?*

Her dolphin tail gently swished to tread water not twenty from him, her long black hair suspended in Salt.

Garrett! Sydney grinned and sped forward, throwing her arms around him, wrapping him in a watery embrace.

*How did you...*Garrett pulled back. *Y-you're a Merrow.*

She nodded. *I came looking for you the second I found out what you were.*

You didn't know?

No, said Sydney. *Mom told me it was our family secret. I couldn't tell anyone.*

Your mom, she's—

*Hey...*said another familiar voice. *Is that Garrett Weaver I see over there?*

Garrett saw Nattie Gao swim toward him, her white torso gleaming the same as Wilda's had back at the Indianapolis Zoo.

Nattie stopped. *Get over here already and give me a hug.*

Garrett's tail refused to work. *I don't understand. H-how did you all know where to find me?*

Word travels fast on the currents. Nattie cast a disapproving look at the seals. *Especially when it's an Orc slaved by Selkies. It's lucky we had already come looking for you.*

The super pod formed ranks around them, helping what Selkies remained out of the nets and carrying others too weak to swim toward the surface.

Who are they? Garrett asked.

They are the Painted Guard, said Nattie. *Protectors of the realm. They uphold the laws of our capital, New Pearlaya.*

Watawa said Orcs didn't keep the peace though. Garrett kept the thought back, not wishing to offend those who saved him. He marveled at their skin and powerful frames. His spirit soared as he thought on Wilda's words to him. *You are a painted beauty, child. Don't never let anyone tell you different.*

I'm one of you. Garrett thought. *I'm an Orc.*

Garrett, honey, said Nattie. *We need to leave. The Violovar don't suffer losses lightly and Malik Blackfin is sure to send his seawolves out, calling for others to join his cause.*

Are you taking me home then? Garrett asked.

Not yet, said Nattie. *Like I said, word of you has traveled fast on the currents. Others will want to hear your story, especially those who sent the Painted Guard to find you.*

They saved us too, said Sydney.

You were in trouble? Garrett asked.

Sydney…

Right, sorry, Mom, Sydney replied. *I'll tell you on the way.*

On the way where? Garrett asked.

New Pearlaya. Sydney grinned. *We're going to the capital!*

CHIDI

WHY ARE WE SWIMMING TOWARD LAND? CHIDI wondered.

She had followed the brothers westward after Quill warned of the approaching Orc pod, but he surprised her by veering north upon hearing the boats in Boston Harbor. Still, she recognized she had little choice in resistance, knowing either Nomad capable of swimming her down with little effort. She glanced back the way they'd swam, the thought of Henry following a constant in her mind.

She felt safer among the brothers anyway, Quill's confidence and Watawa's gentle speech a welcome relief from the back of Henry's hand.

The rocky bottom turned sandy as they closed in on the shoreline.

Quill's shark tail split in two and morphed as he placed his now human legs under him and waded to shore.

"Go to him, child," Watawa said to Chidi.

Hope swelled in her as she swam beside Quill and nudged his hand with her seal nose. She opened her mouth and allowed his fingers take hold of her upper lip, peeling back the changes from seal to her human form.

She stood in Salt up to her chin.

Quill shifted his gaze westward toward the shore and waded in. "Come with me."

Chidi followed.

The beach looked mostly abandoned. Some few cars parked in the distance. Teens threw Frisbees, while families lay on blankets. A few splashed in the Salt, blissfully unaware of the watery world from whence Chidi came.

"Look at them," said Quill. "Would you live as they do, Chidi? Live without fear or real worry?"

Chidi hesitated.

"Of course you would," said Quill. "As would I, if given half a chance. Our world won't allow it yet, but some day...some day we might again live as they do. I often wonder if the Ancients welcomed your kind among us Salt Children as a lesson."

Chidi wished to ask him more, but kept quiet.

Quill faced her. "I am ready to listen and learn, if you will teach me."

"I-I don't know what I could teach." Chidi swallowed. "And I told your brother I know of no treasure."

"That doesn't mean you can't point the way."

"B-but how?" Chidi asked. "How can I if I don't know where you want to go?"

"When I first saw you in Crayfish Cavern, we were in the company of an Orc."

Garrett Weaver, Chidi thought.

Quill studied her. "He mentioned seeing your face once before. Far from the Salt and near his home... You were among the Selkie crew who captured him, weren't you?"

Chidi nodded.

"Good." Quill helped Chidi step from the Salt onto the Hard. "Then you remember where you found him."

"Aye," said Chidi.

Quill grinned. "Take me there."

APPENDIX

SELKIES

AUGUST "CRAYFISH" COLLINS, slave trader and owner, *Harp Seal.*
+ his son:
⌃ OSCAR COLLINS, heir to Crayfish Cavern, *Harp Seal.*
+ his staff:
⌃ BYRON FENTON, head overseer, *Common Seal,*
⌃ TIERAN CHELLY, dockmaster and auctioneer, *Common Seal,*
⌃ SILAS, boat captain, *Common Seal,*
+ his property:
⌃ DECLAN DOLAN, slave catcher captain, *Ringed Seal,*
◆ his son, LENNY DOLAN, slave catcher captain, *Ringed Seal,*
◆ his pet, ENDREES, a *Sea Otter,*
⌃ ELLIE BRICEÑO, slave catcher brute, *Southern Elephant Seal,*
⌃ PAULO VARELA, slave catcher brute, *Southern Elephant Seal,*
⌃ RACER, slave catcher speedster, *California Sea Lion,*
◆ his father, ANSEL, a field slave.

EDMUND CASPAR, also known as DEPUTY SMITH, U.S. Marshal, *California Sea Lion,*
+ his son:
⌃ RICHARD CASPAR, also known as DEPUTY FOSTER, deceased.

HENRY BOUCHER, owner and freelance slave catcher, *Leopard Seal,*
+ his property:
⌃ CHIDI ETIENNE, linguist, *Ribbon Seal.*

MARISA BOURGEOIS, runaway slave, *Cape Fur Seal.*

ZYMON GORSKI, runaway slave, *Common Seal,*
+ his guardian:
⌃ WOTJEK, *Leopard Seal.*

DRYBACKS

KELLEN WINSTEL, high school senior and convict,
+ his friends:
    ⋏ BRYCE TARDIFF, high school senior and swim teammate,
    ⋏ EDDIE BENNETT, high school senior, deceased,
    ⋏ JUAN MARRERO, high school senior and wrestler,
+ his former cellmate:
    ⋏ BOONE MERCHANT, town drunk.

ALLAMBEE OMONDI, Kenyan teenager and one-time ward of MARISA BOURGEOIS.

DAVID BRYANT, U.S. Marshal, rumored SILKSTEALER.

NOMADS

ISHMAEL, also called RED WATER by Nomads, pit fighting champion, *Bull Shark*.

QUILL, emissary of the Unwanted tribe, *Shortfin Mako Shark*
+ his brother:
    ▲ WATAWA, also called OPEN SHELL by Nomads, priest and emissary of the Unwanted tribe, *Shortfin Mako Shark*.

ACKNOWLEDGEMENTS

Malik Blackfin's associate mentioned an Orc is nothing without his pod.

I say an author is nothing without readers. Thank you, dear reader, for breathing life into these characters.

Thanks also to an incredibly talented team—Annetta Ribken, Jennifer Wingard, Valerie Bellamy, and M.S. Corley—for navigating these treacherous waters alongside me. I could not have accomplished this without each of you.

For my crew of Selkie beta readers—Gene, Debbie, Sarah, Whit, and Amber—thank you all for your invaluable insight and your honesty. I appreciate it more than you know.

To my parents, siblings, and the countless family and friends who have followed my crazy antics all this way, my sincerest gratitude for your continued patience and support.

Last, but never least, all my love to Karen and our little Silkie. Thank you both for putting up with me on grumpy Lenny days, gifting me time to write, and believing in me.

ABOUT THE AUTHOR

Aaron Galvin cut his chops writing and performing stand-up comedy routines at age thirteen. His early works paid off years later when he co-wrote and executive produced the award-winning indie feature film, *Wedding Bells & Shotgun Shells*. Aaron has since penned two YA series and a middle grade novel.

He is also an accomplished actor. Aaron has worked in everything from Hollywood blockbusters, (Christopher Nolan's *The Dark Knight*, and Clint Eastwood's *Flags of Our Fathers*), to starring in dozens of indie films and commercials.

Aaron is a native Hoosier and a graduate of Ball State University. He currently lives in Southern California with his family.

For more information, please visit his website:

www.aarongalvin.com

Made in the USA
San Bernardino, CA
23 March 2017